This is an adventure story set in the period of change and conflict following the break up of the Roman Empire. It is also a cautionary tale for those who see their culture being replaced by another or their nation taken over by newcomers.

This novel is set in the early Saxon period at the time when Roman rule in Britain was coming to an end. The events are seen through the eyes of two soldiers who arrived in the British Isles as Anglo Saxon incursions were beginning. Many of the events – battles etc. actually took place, many of the characters were real people and their exploits were recorded by the chroniclers of the time. The men ruling the island are featured – i.e. Ambrosius Aurelianus Dux Britanniarum the last of the Roman rulers, and his unpredictable rival Vortigern the High King of the Celts. Hengist the leader of the Germanic tribes is also a major character. This is the story of the three way fight which took place for mastery of the British Isles.

Circa A.D. 450

Marcus Germanicus, a young Roman from a good family finds himself at a loose end when his legion is disbanded. He has heard reports of Ambrosius Duke of Britain who is trying to save civilisation in the islands, and decides to travel to Britain and offer himself to Ambrosius as a mercenary. Before crossing the channel he meets a traveller named Galarius who offers to go with him and be his guide.

After landing in what is now Dover they travel to the northern coast of Kent. There they meet Hengist the leader of the Saxon tribes and his beautiful daughter Rowena, who is to marry Vortigern the High King of the Celts.

Next they visit London and then travel to East Anglia to return Vortigern's first wife Severa to her family, before joining Ambrosius at his headquarters in Winchester (Venta). The 'Night of the Long Knives' is described. Marcus is involved in the battles of Aylesford and Crayford and goes to North Wales where he recovers the duke's daughter who has been abducted by one of the Celtic chiefs. Eventually he marries the girl, and when she is again taken he recovers her once more. Later he travels to what is now southern Scotland, and while returning south is an uncomfortable witness at the execution of Hengist, which is believed to have taken place in the 490s.

Published by History Faction Books
Hafan Wen · Bettws Ifan · Wales SA38 9QL
Tel: 01239 851092
www.hf-books.com
email: info@hf-books.com

ISBN 0-954-8225-0-1

Printed by Withybush Printers, Haverfordwest Pembrokeshire
Tel: 01437 769181

Last Flight of Eagles

the MAKING of ENGLAND

———— J. Pomfret ————

Published by History Faction Books

last flight of Eagles

CHAPTER I
The Last of the Legionaries
(circa 450AD)

"The island of Britain is shaped like a two headed axe." The old man told the young officer. "To the south it's much like Gaul: fertile and gentle, with prosperous towns, vineyards, and fields of grazing cattle. To the west it's inhabited by barbarians, and to the north - who knows?"

The soldier was curious, and after ordering the serving man to bring two more flagons of wine he pressed his companion further.

"Did our legions not march into Caledonia?" he asked, "did Rome not build roads, forts and a great defensive wall in those northern lands?" And the old man nodded.

"They have taught you well my son!" he said, placing his gnarled hand on the younger man's shoulder." And you are right, the legions did march into Caledonia. They fought battles and built forts as you say. But the wild natives always drove them back, beyond the great wall that Hadrian built."

At this the young man seemed downcast.

"What then remains of Rome among the tribes of the north?" he asked, and his companion shook his head.

"As a young man I trod the ramparts of that great wall and marched into the lands beyond," the little man confided. "But there was little left of Rome even then, and many a comrade we left behind in those bogs and forests. That was all we left of Rome, as the roads were grassing over even then, and we found the drains blocked from lack of maintenance. The Antonine barrier meant nothing, and the tribes scurried over it as they do now, over that other wall to the south."

"Tell me about the south then." The young soldier suggested, leaning forward eagerly. "That's still Roman is it not?" And the old man agreed.

"Aye, there's still civilisation in the south, as the tribes in those regions were never as wild and loved the comforts that Rome brought from the start." For a moment the old man's lined sun-tanned face relaxed in a smile of reminiscence, then he became serious again as he studied his new friend. "But of course you must remember that even in those days the real glory of Rome was long gone. And we were just the remnants who witnessed the death throes of the empire." Then the tired face clouded and the old man looked down to gaze dolefully into the dregs of his wine.

So the young officer in the bright uniform of a centurion waited, and at last his companion went on.

"There are still some among the British who are trying to keep alive the

1

glory and civilisation of Rome, but they are weak and divided," the old man sighed, "and though many have Roman blood their tribal loyalties and divisions will always confound them." Then he shook his head sadly and seemed reluctant to speak further.

As the evening wore on the wine flowed freely for the young man had plenty of gold, and the traveller's tongue loosened as time passed. He told of the island across the water, of its cities and forts and its industry and commerce. He told of the Celtic people with their love of music and beauty. He told of their enthusiasm for warfare and the strange ways they honoured their dead. He told enough to wet the appetite of Marcus Germanicus, for that was the young man's name. And seeing Rome disintegrate, Marcus wondered if he could recapture the past by travelling to Britain. The British wanted to maintain the way of life they'd known for so long, but would they succeed? He asked himself. And the island, visible on a clear day from the shores of Gaul seemed to say that they might as it beckoned to him.

Early next morning Germanicus went down to the harbour.

"Where can I find a ship to take me over the water?" he asked, waiving his arm in the direction of Britain. As he knew there were still ships trading in lead pottery and wine as they had in more peaceful times. Then he turned to see that his drinking companion of the previous evening had joined him.

"What makes you rise so early my friend, do you want to go with me?" he grinned. But though the jest slipped easily from his lips the old man didn't laugh. Instead he stood looking out over the calm misty water nodding silently, and Marcus' brow furrowed.

"Hold on! You told me last night of the danger that awaits a man over there. Were you lying, or do you seek your death in that wild land?" And at this the traveller put his arm around the youth.

"No, I'm like all men and will live as long as the gods allow," he answered. "But I know the good and the bad to be found over yonder as well as the dangers to be faced. And if I come with you I'll be your guide and protector."

Marcus Germanicus, a Roman of nobility, a patrician descended from a long line of soldiers and colonial rulers laughed out loud at this as he stood on the quay his armour and weapons glistening. Then he shook his head in disbelief.

"Very well my friend, we will go together and you will protect me!" he laughed. As he knew that the old man was poor, and as his new friend was familiar with the land across the water they would go well together.

2

The little ship tossed about like a cork though the water was calm, and as Germanicus leant over the side he was determined that the old man shouldn't see his discomfort. After a while he felt better, and when the captain offered them wine from a skin and some bread they ate gratefully, straining their eyes into the distance for their first sight of the opposite coast. It now occurred to Germanicus that the little man wasn't as old as he'd first thought, and though his face was weather beaten and scarred he was probably not much above fifty.

"I don't know your name." The centurion ventured, and slowly the older man answered.

"My name is Galarius, and I was of the Sixth Legion. Ten men I had under me when I was young and handsome as you are now." he grinned.

Though there was a hint of cynicism in the voice it held no malice, and Germanicus smiled too as he looked down at his grand attire.

"No doubt I'll soon be reduced to more humble garb?" he suggested ruefully, but Galarius shook his head.

"By no means sire, as the British love us. They have often begged the legions to return, and some native chief will pay well for a Roman of your standing to lead and train his army."

Tall white cliffs were looming out of the haze. Beyond them the land was green, with red roofed houses and villas in the Roman style dotted among fields of yellow corn. Marcus paid the ship-owner for their passage and they set foot on the 'island of the mighty' as Galarius had called it.

"Who calls it the island of the mighty, and why?" the young man asked, and Galarius scratched his head.

"Whoever conquers these lands proves that he is mighty. Until he in turn is driven out!" he declared ominously.

"Did the Celts we Romans conquered take the land from others before them then?" Marcus enquired, and Galarius nodded.

"So the legends say. They tell of ancestors coming by sea - from Rome itself some say, and long before Great Caesar conquered the islands. There are kings here who claim descent from Brutus the grandson of Aeneaus." he added, and Germanicus smiled.

"Then we can't fault them on their ancestry or their good taste!" he pronounced with mock gravity.

As they left the quay they saw what looked like a scribe coming towards them. The man was wearing a worn toga and leather sandals, while around his waist hung his writing materials.

"Welcome Romans, I am Anthony, secretary to the civil governor of this town." The newcomer announced with a bow, "and if you follow me I will take you to my master."

Germanicus and Galarius agreed and set off after the secretary towards the town, passing through a square with well laid out gardens and fountains playing in front of the public buildings. Half a mile or so further on they came to a villa, its rendered walls shining creamy yellow under a low roof of the usual red tiles. But though Marcus followed Anthony into the inner courtyard, Galarius held back.

A large cool room where several clerks worked led onto a veranda, at the far end of which stood two women and a man engaged in conversation. The man Marcus assumed to be the Governor looked harassed, but seemed relieved when he saw a Roman.

"My friend, we are indeed pleased to see you!" he said as he grasped the young man's hand. "Do you bring news?" And Germanicus was nonplussed.

"I fear not sir, do you expect news?" he replied. And it seemed that the governor shrank a mite in stature as he shook his greying head.

"I am a man of hope young man," he sighed, "but it seems that my hope is but foolishness and I must accept that no one will come to our aid." Then he made an effort to be more cheerful. "Come now, you have travelled from Gaul and must have some news." But Germanicus shook his head.

"I've come because my legion was disbanded!" he murmured.

The women hovering in the background were both handsome, and Marcus could see that the elder of the two had been a beauty in her time. The younger was obviously her daughter, and as the governor turned away preoccupied with his problems his wife took his arm.

"We are failing in our hospitality husband, should we not introduce ourselves to our visitor?" she smiled, and the governor nodded his agreement.

"Forgive me young man, it has been so long since my last letter to Rome that I fear the hope of a reply has affected my reason." Then he motioned Marcus to a couch and taking a goblet of wine from a servant offered it to him. Nodding his thanks Marcus sat down, and taking a seat himself the governor leant forward, concentrating intently on the newcomer's face. Then he coughed nervously.

"My name is Alexander Severus, and I'm a native of these parts," the older man explained. "At least my ancestors have lived here since the conquest, though I fear the Celts wouldn't consider me such!" They all laughed politely at this, then the woman came in.

"And I am Julia Decima," she announced taking her husband's hand,

4

"and I too come from a family long domiciled in these lands." She was watching the eyes of Marcus Germanicus as they strayed across the room to where her daughter stood. "And this," she added holding out her hand to the girl, "is my daughter Alexandra." The girl was smiling faintly Marcus observed. She was pale and thin with whispy hair the colour of sand, and her freckled face wore a far away expression.

"I am pleased to meet you," the girl said hesitantly. "We... we were hoping for news... and perhaps supplies?" she added with a glance at her mother, and Julia laughed.

"Though my little girl knows the gravity of our situation she still dreams about new clothes and hopes for news of the fashions in Rome," the older woman confided with a shrug, and when the girl looked embarrassed her father waved her away impatiently.

"Enough of this foolishness, we men must talk of more serious things!" Alexander snapped as he rose to his feet, and as Julia made to leave followed by her daughter, Marcus had the feeling that the girl always followed her mother like this - like a nervous shadow.

The secretary had told them a little about the town as they walked up from the docks.

"This place is called Dubris (Dover), he'd told them with great solemnity, using a form of Latin that was old fashioned and difficult to follow. "And it has been a major military and administrative centre since the earliest days of empire."

Returning to the present Marcus saw that the governor was pouring more wine.

"When I first saw you my friend, I hoped..." Alexander was saying. Then his voice weakened. "You see... our requests for help have brought no answer, and we need soldiers if we're to garrison the forts along the shore." Then he sat down again heavily, and Marcus felt sorry for him.

"Is it not too late to garrison the forts sir, as I hear the enemy is well advanced into the interior," he observed hesitantly, and Alexander nodded.

"That's true enough, but if reinforcements were to arrive..." Marcus was shaking his head however.

"There will be no reinforcements," the centurion stated flatly, and the governor's head bowed.

"Of course we've known that for some time... but we still hoped. It seemed right to hope somehow... and we've suffered setbacks before. Legions were recalled to fight on the continent but they always returned," the older man added with a hopeful glance at the younger, but Marcus said nothing and eventually Alexander nodded in acceptance of the inevitable.

Germanicus did his best to try and cheer him.

"We must accept that the legions have gone for ever sir.... But there's still a great deal that can be done to maintain civilisation," he suggested, and Alexander lifted his eyebrows as his guest went on. "Rome is in turmoil," Marcus continued, "and I don't know if my family is alive or dead. My legion was ordered this way and that by rival commanders fighting for ascendancy and in the end we were forced to disperse as we'd received no pay for months and the men left to forage where they could."

"I feared as much," Alexander nodded, "as we've had little news and what reached us was bad." Then he changed the subject suddenly. "What will you do in Britain?" he demanded almost aggressively, and Marcus smiled.

"I intend to offer my services as a mercenary sir, as I hear you have a leader who's mustering forces to repel the Saxons?" The younger man answered with a hint of relish, and at once the governor's frown cleared.

"Yes, we have a leader, and he's the finest of men!" Alexander almost crowed. "His name is Ambrosius Aurelianus, and he holds the highest Roman rank in the islands – the title of Dux Britanniarum (Duke of Britain.)"

By the end of the sentence the confidence had evaporated from the governor's voice, and as he could see that Marcus was puzzled by this sudden lack of enthusiasm he set himself to explain.

"You see Ambrosius has his headquarters at Winchester to the west of here, and as Dover is so much closer to the Saxon hoards we're sure to fall first." Alexander's voice had descended to a kind of groan now, and in his despair he rested his head in his hands, knowing that Marcus couldn't disagree with him.

The governor had arranged a meeting between the military and civil leaders in the area. Though the remnants of the military were few, just half a dozen old men who had at one time served in the legions. The civil authorities were better represented however, and included many young men of Roman blood from the families who had farmed the rich lands around the town for centuries. And there were Celts too, from the local tribe – the Atribates, descendants of even earlier immigrants.

Marcus noticed how well the elderly Romans fitted into the great municipal council chamber, blending like the statues into a perfectly organised whole. While by contrast the Celts were ill at ease. They came in what passed for war dress, their costume consisting of polished metal helmets and leather tunics studded with shiny disks. They wore their hair long, and strangest of all their naturally pale skins were tattooed all over with blue swirling patterns, of no significance to a Roman but carrying ancient meanings for their own people.

When Marcus looked up into the balcony he saw Julia, and as he'd expected she was accompanied by her daughter. The girl looked away when he turned his head, but he had the feeling she'd been watching him. It was a strange gathering, and although all the rules of debate were followed by the Romans, who addressed each other formally, kept to the ritualised procedures and generally behaved as Romans did the world over, the Celts were altogether different. Alexander had warned him of course: -

"Marcus my friend, don't be too disturbed by the behaviour of the native chiefs," he'd told him, "as it seems that every act of politeness or precedent is demeaning to them, and they must be forever making a show - of their manhood, their nobility, their prowess in arms, and only the gods know what else!"

Germanicus could see what he meant, as all Alexander's efforts to form an allegiance so that resistance could be offered to the Saxons had floundered hopelessly. They couldn't agree on who should be their leader. Alexander was no soldier, and Marcus had the feeling that he'd accept almost anyone, Roman or Celt. But the Celts had no leader of standing. Their chief was old and deaf, his would-be successors were at odds with each other. And as Marcus knew that organisation and discipline were the lifeblood of any fighting force he doubted that this rabble could ever fight effectively. But Alexander simply shrugged when he voiced his fears.

"They do well enough strange as it may seem, and their methods are not unlike those of the Saxons and Angles."

Marcus walked on the governor's terrace after dinner. He hadn't seen Galarius since they arrived at the villa the previous day, and was wondering sadly if he would ever meet his wrinkled friend again when he sensed movement in the bushes.

'So much for the one who was to protect and serve me!' he sighed, resting one leg on the lower rim of the parapet and letting the leather strips of his kilt divide either side of a sunburned knee. Then suddenly he felt himself watched. From the corner of the villa came a giggle followed by a firm voice issuing instructions, and after a moment Alexandra appeared followed by her more substantial mother.

Julia was pushing the girl forward.

7

"Entertain our guest as I ask you daughter, your father and I have matters to discuss." She hissed, before disappearing with speed leaving Alexandra twisting her hands behind her back. The girl was scowling hard at the ground. Then she looked up and spoke.

"They want me to be nice to you," she whispered, and Marcus smiled encouragingly.

"Is that so hard?" he asked, and shooting him a suspicious glance Alexandra made a point with her toe on the mosaic floor.

"I'm as able to converse with gentlemen as any maid in the land!" she declared defensively, and Marcus experienced a sudden urge to be mischievous.

"You're a maiden then?" he enquired innocently, and the girl gasped and gazed blankly up at him.

"Why yes.... of course!" she protested, and Marcus shrugged.

"You don't seem very sure." She was so delightfully vulnerable and the inexplicable desire to take advantage pricked him on. "Many young women claim to be maids - so I've heard." he observed laconically as he leant against the carved stone balustrade to study a tree on the horizon. Then he looked down at his feet "They say it to snare a husband... So I've heard."

When he looked up again Alexandra had tilted her head.

"It's true that my parents want you to stay and help us defend ourselves," she admitted guiltily. "As they believe that if you were to stay..." Then her voice faltered, and as the finger twisting became more intense Marcus fought the urge to smile and lifting his brows let her struggle on. "But they did not instruct me to tell you that I am a maid!" Alexandra insisted, "and indeed I don't know how we came to be discussing such a subject!"

"A man knows of course – if a girl is truly a maid." Marcus observed wisely, and Alexandra looked at him appealingly.

"How?"

But Germanicus was studying the garden again. Then he turned.

"Do you wish me to show you?" he asked, and Alexandra looked even more uncertain.

"I may," she whispered, and Marcus nodded.

"How old are you?" he asked suddenly, and Alexandra's uncertain expression turned to intense confusion.

"Sixteen." she answered, "how old are you?" And he turned to her grave faced.

"I am twenty three, that's the age when a man can tell!" So she thought for a moment.

"All right you may show me," Alexandra replied. "But I'm already quite certain that I am a maid." So he laughed and put his hands on her shoulders.

"It's done like this." Marcus whispered, bending to place his mouth over hers, which remained completely still and unyielding. So he shook his head.

"That's not right I'm afraid." He told her disapprovingly, and this puzzled her even more.

"Why is it not right?" she demanded, and Marcus shrugged wearily.

"I'll try once more, but only once mind you!"

This time Alexandra lifted her head with lips slightly parted as Marcus pulled her to him a little roughly and kissed her again. And to his surprise she put up her hand after a moment and held his head down on hers. He could feel her sharp little teeth and the exploring point of her tongue. Then with little panting movements she took his hand and put it to her breast.

Pulling away Marcus looked round furtively. Then, after running a hand through his red brown hair he took a gulp of air. Alexandra's face was shining like the face of a mystic who has seen a vision, and after closing his eyes for a moment to shut out the sight of the enraptured girl he took her hand to pull her after him into the villa.

After depositing Alexandra he went back into the garden, where a movement in the bushes made him draw his sword and retreat a few paces. But it was only Galarius who emerged grinning from the shadows, and Germanicus glowered at him.

"Why do you grin fool?" he growled. "And where have you been this last night and day?" But the wanderer just grinned even harder.

"I've been gathering information for the use of my centurion of course!" Galarius declared with a mocking bow, and Germanicus felt a little less aggrieved.

"Where were you just now?" he hissed, but the brown face close to his was now expressionless.

"Just now - when you were on the terrace with the governor's daughter?" the little man asked innocently, and was rewarded with something close to a scream.

"Yes!" Then Germanicus realised he was shouting and repeated the word more quietly. "Yes." And as a deliberately blank look came over Galarius' face he shrugged.

"I must have been making my way into the garden about then... from over there perhaps?" He suggested, pointing a waivering finger towards some distant trees.

he governor's wife was too tired for conversation, so when her daughter appeared at her bedroom door flushed with disappointment and eager to unburden herself, the girl was hustled hurriedly to her own rooms and deposited in the arms of her ever sympathetic nurse. After all, the woman was so much more experienced in these things Julia told herself by way of excuse. And in any case her husband needed her.

Alexander had been moody and despondent ever since the two newcomers arrived the previous day, and Julia felt she should try to discover the cause.

"We need to discuss our future," the governor told her as she settled herself next to him in the deserted atrium. "Are we to stay here and hope for the best? Should we travel north to the wall and make a home with my brother in the garrison? Or should we do what so many Romans are doing, and return to our homeland?"

"Are things really so serious?" Julia asked reaching to touch her husband's arm. And Alexander shrugged.

"I've been deceiving myself for too long my love and we must do something," he confided sadly.

"But Ambrosius... you had such hopes of him," Julia reminded him. And Alexander shrugged again.

"I know my love," he confessed miserably. But the time for putting on a brave face is long past, and though Ambrosius may save much of the islands... for us here in the south-east it`s already too late."

"Too late!" Julia repeated, and Alexander rested his head on her shoulder in a gesture of despair his wife had never seen before.

"The legions have gone, so has our income," the governor admitted. "I can't go on deceiving you any longer my love, and as for deceiving myself? That strategy has become counter productive I fancy."

Julia was shaking her head in confusion as her husband went on.

"You see how exposed we are here?" he murmured. "You see that all the traffic passing through the town seems to be on its way west?" and Julia nodded uncertainly. "Well," the governor continued, "I've decided it's time for us to leave too, though the men of my family have held the post of governor in this place since the conquest four hundred years ago. Do you know that fourteen, yes fourteen generations of my family have lived on this spot?" he asked wonderingly as he pointed down at the mosaic floor, and Julia's mouth fell open as the implications of what was being said bit into her.

"The Celts won't fight. Why should they?" Alexander was saying. "To them the people of this region are as foreign as the Saxons. They hardly understand each other's language, and now Rome no longer rules there's no trade between the different regions. Can you imagine the Celts of the far west travelling here to fight for the Canti, a tribe they've probably never heard of, while at the same time they're fighting invading Celts from over the water in Hibernia (Ireland)?"

"But Vortigern!" Julia interrupted, and her husband made a little grunt.

"To rely on him is like building a house on shifting sand," the governor sighed. "No. Without rule and direction from Rome there is no rule and direction. We are rudderless and must fend for ourselves."

The two Romans were sitting in Germanicus' room studying the map. Galarius had drawn it from memory and was pointing out the major towns and places of interest.

"Along the coast," he explained, indicating the shoreline of Kent, "are forts, here, here, and here." And Marcus nodded.

"I heard Alexander call this the Saxon Shore." he mused, and Galarius nodded.

"The Saxons and other Germanic tribes have been raiding in the east for a hundred years or more," he said, putting his head on one side. "They're a persistent lot!" Then they smiled at each other and Marcus pointed to the Isle of Thanet.

"Is this the land the Saxons hold at present?" he asked, and Galarius nodded.

"Yes, some of it. But if we are to be correct as Roman officers like to be in my experience?" And they exchanged another understanding glance. "Then we must say that the Jutes hold it." Then the little man paused and turned the map round. "This piece of land is cut off from the mainland by rivers," he went on as he traced the course of the waterways with his finger, "and it was given to the people of Hengist in return for their services as treaty troops."

Germanicus knew all about the Roman practice of giving rewards to barbarian tribes in return for military service. And it was not always a successful ploy as far as he could remember, as the mercenaries sometimes took the lands they were meant to protect for themselves. This seemed to be what was happening in Britain now he thought as he scratched his head.

"Who gave them the lands?" he asked, pointing to the spot on the map representing Thanet, and Galarius grinned his gap toothed grin once more.

"The high king of the Celts goes by the name of Vortigern, perhaps you've heard of him?" he asked, and Marcus nodded. "Well, Vortigern invited Hengist to bring a couple of boat loads of his men over," the little man divulged twisting his mouth in distaste. "The idea was that the Saxons fight off the invaders who were giving Vortigern so much trouble - Picts, Scots and the rest." Germanicus understood.

"And now these helpers from abroad are taking more land for themselves?" he whispered, and Galarius nodded.

"Exactly! They've broken out of Thanet and are taking lands belonging to the Canti, the Celtic tribe in the region. You can imagine their reaction, their king is furious!"

"What does king Vortigern think about it?" Germanicus asked, opening his eyes wide, and Galarius wagged a forefinger at him.

"That's a very interesting story my friend," came the reply as Galarius poured himself more wine before offering the jug to his companion. "King Vortigern just sits up in Londinium (London) with his Roman wife and dithers! He's a weak man and afraid to offend Hengist. But they do say..." The little man went on leaning forward conspiratorially. "They say Vortigern plans to put away his middle aged Patrician wife and contract a marriage with the daughter of Hengist the invader!"

Germanicus whistled softly at this.

"It seems the Saxons want the whole land, not merely Kent," he suggested, and Galarius nodded.

"The Germanic people are so strong and fertile they could conquer and populate the entire island in my opinion!" he asserted, but Germanicus just laughed.

"Now you're being fanciful!" he grinned turning back to the map. "Here's Winchester where you say Ambrosius has his headquarters," he muttered tracing a line with his finger from Dover to Winchester. "How lies the land here guide and protector?"

Galarius drew his stool closer, and the two men set about planning their journey to the command post of Ambrosius.

CHAPTER II
INTO the Lions Lair

Relaxing with Galarius the next morning, Marcus tried to put himself in Ambrosius' place. The legions had left, the barracks were empty, and if he were to challenge the Saxons the Duke of Britain would be forced to call on the veterans and their families. He'd seek help from the Celtic nobility and their high king Vortigern too, the centurion guessed. And as the Celts were already losing land to the invaders and the residents of the old cities were desperate to retain their life style perhaps he'd have some success?

But without trade with the empire and the money that came from it, it would be impossible to keep up an army. As no one paid taxes any more the authorities would be unable to pay wages. The break with Rome had brought benefit to no one, the young man had learned. And even the potters making imitations of the red continental ware so popular in the markets would gladly have returned to the old days.

Long years had passed since the legions forsook the shores of Britain, but the economy had collapsed only gradually and the rule of law didn't disappear overnight. With agonising slowness Roman ways had been diluted, but the invasion of the Germanic tribes would speed the process enormously, and if they took over everything of Rome would be swept away.

As he pondered on how he could best help Ambrosius, Marcus' mind turned to the leaders of the Jutes who'd settled in Thanet, and after a moment he turned to Galarius who was lying beside him on the grass.

"I'm minded to go east before we travel to Winchester," he murmured, and Galarius sat up as if stung by an insect.

"But the Saxons are in the east!" the little man protested in surprise, "and you must be addled in your brain even to think of it!"

"Perhaps I am," Marcus admitted lazily, "but what is there to fear when I have you to protect me?"

"I'm beginning to regret making that promise wolf cub!" Galarius grunted as he got to his feet. "Do you know something I don't about these Germans, or is it ignorance that makes you so bold?"

"When I was a child my mother told me that I count Germans among my ancestors," Marcus smiled, ignoring the jibe. "One of my forefathers married a German princess it seems... hence my name!"

Galarius wasn't impressed.

"So you have German blood!" he scoffed, "but I fancy it will flow as freely as any other were we foolish enough to go east."

The young soldier's confidence wasn't dented in the least however, and leaning back in the grass he turned his face into the autumn sun.

"I'm not a novice," he smiled, "I've fought the barbarians before, though brave they're disorganised and a proper battle plan would defeat them."

"But would they follow your battle plan?" Galarius snorted, taking his knife from his saddle bag and beginning to sharpen it feverishly. "The word Saxon means 'people of the axe' " he went on. "It's their favourite weapon and they wield it very well!"

"There's nothing to fear I tell you!" Marcus murmured placing his hands behind his head as he lay in the grass. "I'm familiar with both their tactics and their weapons, as we studied the methods of all the enemies of Rome in training."

"Aye, we soldiers of empire were well schooled in the arts of formal warfare," Galarius admitted grudgingly, "and it's true we can't be bettered when it comes to military engineering and reliable supply lines. We're so organised and so civilised!" he sneered, his expression set in irittation. "But can't you see, that's what makes us so vulnerable? The Saxons don't need supply trains as we do, they live off the land!" he continued angrily. "And they don't need earth works or walls, as they use the features of the land as their defence works. They have only one battle plan!" Galarius hissed as he knelt to look into his master's face. "And it's a simple one: every man is bound to his lord in a fighting band and their loyalty lasts till death! If their lord is killed or injured they're honour bound to fight until dead, and have you any idea how strong this makes them?"

But Germanicus simply yawned as he stood up and stretched.

"I don't intend to fight!" he protested patiently. "I just want to make the acquaintance of the savages and learn their secrets." As he looked down on his friend the expression on the centurion's face was almost appealing, but Galarius remained unconvinced.

"They'll kill us as soon as they see us!" he grunted, but Germanicus shook his head.

"Not if they know we pose no threat!" he concluded determinedly.

Alexander waylaid Germanicus when he returned to the villa that night, and as usual the governor's face was lined with the weight of responsibility.

"I must speak with you," he began, and following the governor into his study Marcus threw himself onto a couch and waited.

"I'm offering you the post of military commander here in Dubris," Alexander confided as he looked down at his visitor. "We'd pay you well and you could recruit men in the surrounding countryside. Though the Saxons are all around us," he admitted, the hope suddenly gone from his eyes. "But there are many loyal men remaining" he went on determinedly after a moment, "the veterans... and surely you'll at least consider my offer...?"

Marcus felt tremendous sympathy for this man as well as gratitude that he was not in his position, but he was shaking his head as he stood up and placed his hand on the governor's arm.

"I only wish I could and that such a strategy would save you," he murmured.

"Then you refuse to help?" Alexander demanded, and Germanicus rubbed his shaven chin..

"Believe me... I'd stay if I thought it would save you, but I'm convinced that only a national effort can succeed," he concluded sadly as he moved to the window.

The townspeople were lighting the lamps in their windows, but how long before the lights of civilisation were extinguished forever? Marcus asked himself. Then he turned back to his host.

"I travel to Winchester as planned!" he stated determinedly, "as I believe our only hope is to join forces with Ambrosius."

As Germanicus let himself out of the tidy room he looked back at the tall figure in the white toga, but Alexander didn't turn to say farewell. The centurion suspected that he and Julia found it hard to remember the days when Rome held sway in Britain, those golden days before the legions left. And though they'd kept everything as much like the old days as possible he couldn't help wonder who paid Alexander's salary. His guess was that the governor was using his own money to pay his staff, and had long since ceased to receive payment for his own efforts.

Galarius and Germanicus left Dover early next morning before the town was awake, the centurion riding his own horse brought with him from Gaul and Galarius going on foot. They found the roads still easy to follow, though beginning to grow over as they fell into disuse.

As there were no fellow travellers going in their direction they travelled alone, and their sense of isolation increased as they left the outskirts of Dover behind and the presence of invaders began to make itself felt. From time to time they passed a deserted farm, the corn still unharvested in the fields. Then about mid-day they met a family travelling in the opposite direction.

Galarius ran forward to hail the man walking with his plough horse at the head of the little procession. Some children and a couple of servants were trailing behind, but when the Romans saw the woman they presumed to be the mother they drew back, as the face of the female riding on the cart piled high with household belongings held a strange far away expression and they were keen not to frighten her.

The children started to cry when they saw the strangers, but when they recognised them as Romans their fear turned to relief.

"Good day my friend!" Germanicus called, addressing the leader of the little group in Latin. And the man understood, coming forward at once with relief.

"Thank God you're Romans!" he answered, "for a moment we feared the devils were coming after us."

"Saxons?" Germanicus asked, lifting the smallest child in his arms, and the man nodded.

"We're Canti, the people of Kent," he explained, and "we're fleeing west as our lands have been taken by the Saxons. They came at night without mercy," he added, gazing sorrowfully up into the tear stained face of the woman on the cart.

Abandoning their journey for the present both parties sat down in the grass, and leaning against the trunk of a tree the Celtic father nursed his youngest child. When he looked up into the branches there were tears in his eyes, and he swallowed hard before speaking.

"You'll know that the Germans were given lands in Thanet by our king - Vortigern?" he whispered, "well it wasn't enough for them and they're taking more."

"We heard that the Jutes had broken out of Thanet," Marcus answered, "and that the brother of their chief leads his war bands into the interior to conquer more land."

"Two brothers came over the water with two boat loads of men," the Celt told them. "And more arrive with every tide. Hengist is their leader, the name means Stallion. It suits him well as he has amazing courage and strength, and though his brother Horsa is younger he's almost as formidable."

Germanicus was intrigued by the Christian symbol hanging round the neck of one of the children and wanted to know more.

"You're Christians?" he asked, and the Celt nodded.

"Aye, and it's Christians they hate most as they say we carry enchantment," he told them, taking a loaf of bread from his wife and breaking it in two. "My name is Paulinus, and this is my wife Veronica," he went on, offering half of the loaf to each of the Romans. "And these are my children," he whispered kissing the little girl in his arms.

Germanicus knew he should feel sympathy, but Christians made him uneasy and he was frowning as he turned to to Galarius.

"Give me the soldier's cult of Mithras any day!" he whispered, "as a god who sacrifices himself disgusts me."

"A man needs a soldier's religion if he's to be truly a man!" Galarius hissed in reply, and the two turned to study the Christians, who were accepting their misfortune in their usual gentle way. "Their god tells them to be meek, how can a man live like that?" Galarius demanded, glancing at his master who's mind was following the same path. Then suddenly his muscular little frame tensed, and jumping to his feet he took a step towards the Celt and bent forward aggressively.

"Why didn't you stay and fight, die on your own land?" he demanded, but the Christian just smiled.

"Because our Lord tells us to love our enemies," he answered softly. And at this Germanicus gulped, swallowing the lump of bread in his mouth all at once and nearly choking as a result.

"Love!" he coughed, "love... those who've taken your land, driven you from home... and..." He was staring at the woman, but the wan smile on the face of the Christian remained fixed.

"That is the teaching of our saviour," he asserted, his voice almost breaking, "and I must not hate them... for the rape of my wife... for anything, as Christ commands us to love our enemies."

"We'll go back with you and drive them from your property!" Germanicus declared jumping to his feet and lifting his sword in the air. But the Christian shook his head and his wife started to sob..

"No, we could not do that," the man answered gently. "We must accept the will of God and travel to the west where we'll find new lands to farm, and peace."

As they set off Germanicus walked alongside trying to encourage them.

"When we've spied out the Saxons we intend to go to Winchester where Ambrosius, Duke of Britain is gathering a force to defend the land. Perhaps we'll meet you there?" he called as he was left behind, and the Celt waved his arm in farewell.

"If it were God's will that we hold this land he'd not have sent the Saxons to dispossess us," he called over his shoulder, "but we've sinned and must accept our punishment. Goodbye my friends, may God go with you and grant you peace."

When he returned to the resting place Marcus found his friend again reclining on the grass.

"Why does he wish me peace when he sees I'm a soldier....?" he demanded wonderingly, and Galarius smiled at his aggrieved expression.

"He wishes what he thinks is good for you," the little man explained, "and it's their practice to wish all men well, even those who steal their land and rape their women."

They travelled on, and at last reached the lands held by the German invaders. They met no more refugees, and all the folk they passed from then on were Saxons. The newcomers were repairing the buildings vacated by the Celts as if they intended to stay. And though one or two approached the Romans laughing and threatening, when Galarius told them they were travelling to the hall of Hengist they were allowed to pass. Marcus was grateful that Galarius spoke their harsh gutteral tongue, and though his guide seemed reluctant to tell how he'd learned the language, he discovered eventually that his little friend had once lived in their continental homeland. Then Galarius had become tight-lipped again, but though Marcus sensed sadness in him he was determined to learn more when the time was right.

The Romans were watched every step of the way now, and it seemed as if a broad blonde warrior stood by every tree. The Saxons wore simple wool tunics held in at the waist by leather or metal belts. Their helmets were worn and dented, and they wrapped their feet in soft leather bound with thongs. Not every man carried a sword, and when one appeared wielding an enormous specimen the centurion assumed that he was some kind of leader.

"They have names for their swords and hand them down through the generations," Galarius explained pointing to the Saxon, "and they rest them in places of honour when not in use."

"Surely a sword of that weight is too heavy for a man to wield effectively?" Marcus suggested, but Galarius shook his head.

"Only men of importance carry the big ones," he whispered, "and as they spend their days swinging them in practice their arms grow strong."

As they drew nearer to the Saxon leader's camp the number of immigrants increased, and it seemed that in these parts the Celts had completely disappeared. The tall blonde men were accompanied by women now, well rounded beautiful women, Germanicus noted with admiration. And there were children too, with hair even fairer than their elders.

The invaders were taking over the dwelling of the Celts, and where there were no existing buildings were erecting wooden huts and crude tents. There was a feeling of purpose about the place. Every adult was engaged in some activity, and even the children worked with their mothers at flaying and grinding the newly gathered corn. As this area was newly colonised the corn must have been planted by the Celts, Germanicus knew. But the natives had left and it was the Saxons who'd eat it.

As they entered the centre of the conquered lands Germanicus noticed the German he's seen earlier following a few paces behind, and with a growl he turned and challenged him.

"Why do you stalk me Saxon?" he demanded, and the broad face of the warrior split into a grin.

"I am Octha the son of Hengist," he announced proudly, and as Marcus thought it best to show deference to one so elevated he bowed.

"We are honoured to meet you." he answered warily, clasping forearms with the man in the Roman fashion before walking on with him.

"I have some Latin and am no savage!" Octha declared, obviously considering this a reason for pride, and Germanicus was quick to congratulate him.

"Your Latin is excellent my friend," he answered, looking the Saxon up and down, noting his fine physique and presuming that Octha spent his hours swinging his great sword as Galarius had described.

They came at last to a Roman fort like the one they'd seen at Dover. This was Reculver they learned, and Hengist had made the great tower his headquarters. Germanicus was sick with disgust as they entered the old fort. As it would be easy to defend a building like this he knew, and even poorly garrisoned it could hold out almost indefinitely. But the Celts had left the shore forts ungarrisoned, and since the departure of the legions the great shell had stood empty.

"Repairing and manning defence works doesn't appeal to the Celtic temperament," Galarius put in, seeming to read his master's thoughts. "And long hours keeping watch and pacing out a measured mile is not their way. Had they wished they could have kept these folk out," the little man went on with a nod at Octha who was climbing the stairs ahead of them. "But the British tribes can't agree amongst themselves and scorn anything that requires patience or discipline. They've not the wit or the imagination to take precautions against an enemy they can't see!" he added wonderingly as they reached the landing. "So they wait till the wolf is at the gate!"

Octha was leading them into a large stone chamber and Marcus supposed they were entering the quarters that would have housed the commander of the garrison. At the end of the room was a long table, and at it's head sat a broad man of about fifty, his hair faded but still very fair. His face was red and heavily scarred, and the uneven healing of a cut crossing the left eye socket and distorting his gaze struck the young Roman hard. The yellow green orbs flecked by constant movement were the eyes of a man accustomed to obedience.

The Saxon chief was in conversation with men Marcus assumed were his generals and advisors, but when he looked up and saw his son he lifted a heavy hand and at once the murmur ceased.

"What brings you to my halls whelp?" Hengist demanded impatiently of Octha, and Germanicus felt the man at his side flinch.

"I bring two Romans to you father, men who've travelled far to speak with you..." Octha stammered, and frowning hard Hengist beckoned them forward.

"Are you Romans or Britons?" he demanded, "if you're Britons you're indeed brave men to enter my lair!" And he laughed, waiving his arm expansively.

The others were smiling obediently Marcus noticed, and lifting his arm in a Roman salute he took a step forward, thinking it best to flatter the Saxon if he could.

"My greetings to you, King of the Jutes!" he announced making a stiff little bow, and it seemed Hengist was impressed as suddenly he smiled and looked the young man up and down almost approvingly.

"You're a fine bird my boy, and your face tells me you have Teutonic blood!" the Saxon leader bellowed. And with gratitude to his long dead German ancestor Marcus bowed his head.

"They tell me that long ago my great-grandfather loved a lady from the Saxon lands," he smiled, "she was a beauty so they say, and from that day on men have called his descendants Germanicus."

"Is that your name stripling?" Hengist demanded as he rose to his feet. And as Marcus who'd always thought of himself as tall was beside Octha, and the son of the chief measured nigh on six feet six, he could understand why Hengist addressed him so.

"I am Marcus Germanicus sire, a centurion of the twentieth legion," the young Roman asserted pulling himself up to his full height, and Hengist lifted his bushy brows,

"And where is your legion now?" he asked, shooting a mocking grin at his advisors, who smiled back as Marcus shrank a mite in stature.

"It's... disbanded... sire." the centurion answered, and Hengist nodded wisely.

"Then why are you here in Britain?" he asked, and the Roman shrugged.

"I've come to rebuild by fortunes," Marcus answered. "I'm a good soldier and will sell my skills..... if there are any who value them." he added nervously as Hengist came round the table to peer down at him.

For a moment the steel grey eyes of the Roman and the yellow green of the Saxon met and held. Then Hengist turned away.

"I like him well enough," he conceded with a nod at Octha. "And is this your servant?" he asked tipping his head at Galarius who was lurking behind his master.

"Galarius is well travelled and speaks many languages," the centurion informed Hengist, "we travel together in search of our fate."

"Ah, we all await our weird my friend!" Hengist replied with a nod of his heavy head. But no man can tell what it will be..." he added with a crooked smile. As Hengist was a pagan like the Romans, and they understood each other.

Octha took them down into the camp, and as they entered one of the wooden huts surrounding the tower Marcus noticed with surprise that it was well furnished, with animal skins and rugs on the floor.

"I was told that these people were savages, and their rude huts covered pits where they dwell in underground misery!" he whispered as they entered the hut, and Galarius laughed quietly.

"Nay, they are civilised enough in their way, though no doubt a pit lies beneath these boards for the storage of grain and goods," he added stamping his foot.

Octha was pointing to some pallets against the wall.

"Your beds my friends, mattresses will be brought!" he grinned showing perfect teeth. "You'll be accustomed to the soft life I vow, and my father would not have you share the earth bed of the soldier!" he concluded, still laughing as he left.

"That man despises us!" Marcus whispered, and Galarius shrugged.

"He despises the Romanised Britons, but he does not have the measure of us yet centurion!" The lined face had hardened, and not for the first time Marcus wondered how the little man would conduct himself in a fight.

As the sun dipped behind a line of trees a Saxon entered the hut. He didn't speak but gestured the Romans to follow him, and in silence they crossed the camp and entered a long low hall. On a dias at the far end sat Hengist in a high carved chair, while a similar chair to his right stood vacant. The Romans were led to the high table, and Marcus was given the seat on the left of the Saxon leader. Galarius squatted on a stool behind in case he was needed as interpreter, and Octha hovered in the background, his hand never far from his sword hilt.

Seeing Germanicus glance at the empty chair Hengist sighed and placed his huge hand on the seat.

"This chair is kept for my brother Horsa," he smiled, "his fame has reached your ears perhaps?" Marcus had to admit that it had, and as he took a lump of bread and dipped it into the communal pot he nodded.

"Where is your brother now sir?" he enquired, and Hengist smiled.

"Oh, somewhere in the Celtic lands," the king of the Jutes confided airily. "His fancy is to reconnoitre, choosing new towns for us to conquer and so on." he added letting out a great roar of laughter, and everyone within earshot joined in. Marcus cast a worried look over his shoulder at Galarius at this point, but the little man just shrugged.

Taking an enormous leg of mutton from his mouth Hengist turned to his guest.

"You'll see a sight worth seeing now Roman!" he grinned, pointing down the hall with the joint. And as Marcus squinted into the darkness surrounding the entrance the gloom was banished by four jarls bearing torches. Standing back they formed a guard of honour, and with every face turned towards them waited.

The woman was silhouetted against the darkening sky for a moment before entering the area of illumination. Then to the surprise of the Romans the entire company with the exception of Octha and Hengist rose to their feet and lifted their flagons. The shout issuing from their lungs made the rafters ring.

"Hail! Rowena daughter of Hengist! Hail! Rowena daughter of Hengist!" they shouted, the salutation repeated over and over until it rose to a hypnotic climax in tune with the drumming of more than a hundred flagons.

Blowing air onto his perspiring forehead Marcus looked at their host, who was smiling benignly at his lovely daughter. As she approached, the king rose and held out his hand, and taking it across the table the fair Rowena came to join him. Horsa's chair had been moved, another, well upholstered in the Roman style took its place at the king's right hand. And after kissing her father the girl looked from him to Marcus, who closed his mouth which had somehow fallen open and swallowed hard.

The woman studying him so confidently was the most beautiful he'd ever seen, though she was far too tall and well built for Roman tastes. A mane of corn coloured hair his countrymen would consider vulgar crowned the vision, and it was a vision of strength and vigor not wilting feminine weakness. Turning his gaze away lest she think him impertinent Marcus fixed his eyes on the smoke blackened rafters. But the green and yellow eyes of the woman, her father's eyes, pulled them back. Lifting an arm heavy with bracelets she threw her sheep skin mantle from her shoulders. And when she spoke, though Marcus found her voice deep for a woman, he knew for the first time how musical a Germanic language can be.

After lowering her eyes Rowena lifted them and sought his.

"Why are you here Roman?" she asked, in Latin as heavily accented as her brother's, and Marcus swallowed again.

"As I told your father... I need to sell my skills as a mercenary," he stuttered.

"Perhaps you're a spy?" Rowena suggested, taking a rabbit joint still dripping from the stewpot. And trying to bring the moisture back to his mouth Marcus frowned and shook his head somewhat unconvincingly.

"A spy... for whom lady?" he enquired, in a highpitched voice totally unlike his own.

"Why, Ambrosius of course." Rowena smiled.

"Ambrosius is my countryman... and I owe him allegiance ..." Marcus faltered trying to sound dispassionate. And as Rowena smiled again showing teeth as perfect as her brother's, Marcus felt his stomach turn over. She was studying him intently, and to his immense delight she seemed to like what she saw.

As they lay side by side on their rough beds Marcus discussed the evening's events with Galarius.

"She's a beauty and no mistake," he hissed, and turning over on his pallet Galarius faced his master across the gap.

"Aye, she has power too, and it's not good for a woman to wield power over men," he yawned.

"You think her beauty would corrupt?" Marcus asked eagerly, and turning onto his back Galarius studied the roof.

"Her beauty can direct and control that's for sure!" he grunted, before turning his face to the wall.

The Romans spent a lot of time with Hengist, riding out with him across the Kent countryside and along the sandy shore. And as they'd been his guests for a week now they were familiar with the pattern of a day's ride. As the sun reached it's highest point Hengist would give the signal to eat, and with the ease of a much younger man would jump from

23

his horse and signal Germanicus to join him on the sward.

"You know Vortigern, Roman?" The yellow eyes demanded truth and taking the food offered Marcus nodded.

"I know of him, he's high king of the Celts and holds court in Londinium (London)."

"Do you know what kind of man he is?" Hengist demanded, tilting his lion head, and Marcus shrugged.

"Men say he's weak." he answered, and Hengist jabbed him in the chest with a stubby forefinger.

"You think the country needs a strong ruler, eh?"

"And you're a strong ruler?" Marcus retorted, and as Hengist laughed out loud at his insolence heads turned towards them.

"I am friend!" the king of the Jutes answered, "and what's more I intend to rule this land." His eyes had narrowed and as he threw his well picked bone at a sparrow his lips were set. "One way or another I'll conquer this place of timid folk!" he told the Roman before taking a noisy gulp of ale and wiping his mouth. "I'll conquer however I can, by might or by cunning." he added placing a thick finger to his temple. "By the way we're to meet Vortigern soon, at a neutral place on the edge of the Saxon lands. And I've decided that you'll come with us."

Marcus was in no position to argue, and next day he and Galarius set off with the Saxons to meet Vortigern. Hengist was taking no chances. Several hundred heavily armed warriors marched in front and behind him. And the Romans, who'd been well guarded during their stay in the Saxon camp were surrounded by mounted troops.

"It seems that Hengist is unwilling to deprive himself of our company!" Marcus grunted. He was feeling the strain of the constant surveillance, but Galarius just shrugged.

"We're as safe here as anywhere else I fancy," he muttered, but Marcus wasn't convinced.

"I think they're only keeping us alive because they have some use for us," the younger man whispered, and Galarius nodded.

"I've always been a useful man to have around, and find it lengthens the life considerably," he grinned, and Marcus allowed himself to be amused.

"All right guide and protector, I'll trust your word... until it proves false that is!"

CHAPTER III
The Oak Grove

They were to meet Vortigern half way between London and Kent where both leaders felt safe. The journey was uneventful and at last the Saxons and their reluctant guests came in sight of the villa where they were to encounter the king of the Celts.

The place was in good order with buildings well maintained. The farm was still functioning and the family of Romanised Celts who'd held the property for as long as anyone could remember was still in residence. Slaves worked in the fields and everything about the place was familiar to Marcus, who wandered round the square with its outbuildings and servants houses as if he'd been transported to a time before he was born.

But the family who'd ruled the surrounding lands for so long was uneasy. They kept out of the way as much as possible and the servants were nervous too. The Saxon soldiers camped in the open, and only Hengist with his body guard his children and the Romans were housed in the villa, which was built on a rectangular plan surrounded by gardens.

Though the landowner sat nervously with his guests for a while he left as soon as he decently could, and Galarius was indignant about this.

"That's the Briton's for you!" he sniffed, "do you see how nervous the master of the house is as he waits to discover his fate?" But Germanicus thought this judgement a little hard.

"Why have they changed?" he murmured, and the brown face of his companion wrinkled in distaste.

"They haven't changed, as they were never capable of independent action!" Galarius grunted. "Britain was a colony, men of talent saw their future in Rome and now the umbilical cord is severed the child will die!"

Marcus was frowning as he took a bunch of grapes from the wall trellis and offered some to his friend.

"But there were rescue attempts, and troops were sent from Rome to drive the invaders back. Why did they fail?" he pondered, and Galarius scowled at him.

"They didn't fail!" the little man retorted. "I was with the third rescue and we did everything we could to teach the natives to fend for themselves." he added firing a succession of pips into the spittoon at his feet. "We taught them how to make weapons and the use of light cavalry," he continued looking hard at Marcus, "and as you served in a cavalry unit you'll know how easy it is break the spirit of a force on foot. We went through the land like a wave!" the little man explained proudly, "the Picts and Scots fell back as we advanced and our losses were minimal."

"You say you taught them the arts of war, but did you teach them the workings of a soldier's mind?" Marcus asked, and Galarius shook his head.

"Was it not enough that we warned them?" he demanded angrily. "The Saxons were raiding the east even then and they were just one of the threats. We identified a dozen different sources of invasion, but though the Britons listened politely we knew they weren't really taking heed. A child who's always looked to others for protection finds independence painful," he went on sadly. "We knew they wouldn't learn till they'd suffered defeat, and by that time it would be too late."

Sitting down on a bench Marcus unsheathed his dagger and ran his finger along the blade.

"What's their strategy if not force of arms?" he asked, and Galarius thought for a moment.

"They don't have one!" the little man answered at last, "some want to fight and others see negotiation as the best way. They tell themselves that the invaders will be reasonable if treated with respect, and when they've won enough land for their needs they'll leave the rest to the natives."

"The Britons have forgotten what it's like to be land hungry," Marcus sighed replacing the ornate dagger in his belt, "they've had peace for so long they think it's the natural state of the world." And Galarius confirmed this assessment as they set off in the direction of their sleeping quarters.

"The chaos these Saxons bring will force them into the real world soon enough!" he growled.

Rowena was sauntering through the Villa marvelling at the luxury, and as she held her finger in the stream flowing from the mouth of a carved lion into an onyx basin Germanicus watched her.

"You'll live like a Roman lady when you're married to Vortigern," he said as he approached, and the Saxon princess turned to face him.

"It's small recompense for the sacrifice I'm making!" she snapped, and picking a blossom from above the fountain Marcus threw it into the water.

"Are you not proud to be marrying a king?" he enquired scornfully, and Rowena almost spat at him.

"Vortigern is an old man... older than my father," she hissed looking up at him through heavy lashes. "He's putting away an old wife to marry me... am I supposed to be grateful for that?"

"You'll be the mother of future high kings of the Britons!" Marcus told her cheerfully, and Rowena's expression grew even more bitter.

"I'm the daughter of a king already, and a better king than Vortigern!" she asserted proudly, "and my father's kingdom will grow while Vortigern's slips away."

For a moment she watched the swirling water disappear through the drain hole, then she laughed and retrieved the blossom.

"And there'll be no children!" she stated determinedly, "as if I bore boys Vortigern's other sons would kill them. So perhaps I should marry one of them instead of their father?" she concluded throwing the blossom aside.

"It occurs to me that you'd rather not marry a Celt at all!" Marcus ventured, and Rowena reached to touch the epaulette on his shoulder.

"Do you think I'd rather couple with a Roman?" she asked, and Marcus took a step back.

"It doesn't concern me lady," he said bowing his stiff bow. And as he left her the feeling of her eyes on him burned his back like summer sun.

Out in the open again Marcus took a gulp of air and began to climb the hill to where he'd left his horse.

"Why can't women be as simple as you Romulus?" he murmured, burying his head in the yellow mane, and the animal seemed to look at him questioningly as he ran his hand along the smooth back. When Romulus nuzzled his tunic Marcus fumbled for a piece of bread, then he saw Rowena climbing the hill towards him followed by three burly body guards.

Smiling her confident smile Rowena put her arm round Romulus' neck.

"I've a mare the colour of milk who'd mate well with you," she whispered into the horse's ear. But Marcus was watching the three men, who'd stopped about twenty yards away.

"A woman who needs such a strong guard should stay at home," he grunted, and immediately Rowena waved them away.

"My father is afraid for my safety, but he'd trust me with you," she simpered, and as her guards disappeared into the trees she took Marcus by the hand. "Will you walk with me?" she smiled beginning to pull him along, "I want to see the oak grove, they tell me there's a holy tree there."

Casting regular glances over his shoulder Marcus allowed himself to be led into the sacred grove where twenty or more gigantic trees stood in a rough circle. In the centre stood another, so old that the trunk had hollowed out.

Resting her back against the broad base of the hollow oak Rowena was smiling even harder at him.

"The servants here accept the religion of their masters and follow Christ," she told him, "but they still remember the old ways and told me about this place." Then her brows lifted in question. "Are you a Christian?" she asked, "they say all Romans are."

Germanicus felt stung and denied the slur at once.

"I'm no Christian! How can a soldier be a Christian?" he demanded, and Rowena put a finger to her lips.

"The old men of our tribe tell of a great battle fought in these islands, they say a bishop came over the water to aid to his fellow Christians," and Germanicus nodded reluctantly. It seemed Rowena knew about the so called 'Alleluia victory' when the Pagans had been defeated by a Roman army years before, and when he replied his tone was cold.

"That Bishop claimed his mitre in old age, as a young man he was a soldier and he used his soldier's mind to win the battle not his faith," he told her. And still smiling Rowena came towards him.

"They say his name was Germanus," she whispered, and Marcus felt acutely embarrassed. How did this woman know that a member of his family had been a Christian and led one of the rescue attempts? he wondered, as he hadn't even told Galarius. Did he know too, and was his friend laughing at him behind his back?

"My kinsman was no disgrace to our family... even after he became a Christian," he answered at last in a low voice. "He drove the invaders from this land, does that not prove his manhood?"

Rowena was sitting under the central tree patting the ground at her side in invitation, but Marcus was trying to locate the men he knew were watching. Even the branches above his head were examined, but eventually he sat down a few feet away from the girl.

He was afraid of a trap, and could it be that Hengist wanted him dead and just as he was beginning to like the man too?

"Your father won't want us to be seen together... alone," he told her, and rising to her feet Rowena rested her hand on the tree.

"My father loves me, but he hates Vortigern," she pouted moving slowly towards Marcus her face infinitely sad. "My father loves me..." she repeated, running her hands over her plump breasts in a tense little gesture.

Then she looked at him and standing very straight launched into what seemed like a prepared speech. She spoke slowly making sure he understood.

"I'm to marry Vortigern, but my father wants to insult him and hopes I'll be no virgin when I go to his bed." She was looking at Marcus to gauge his reaction, and seeing both amazement and amusement in his face she took his hands. "My father has allowed me to chose the man I love!" she whispered urgently. "Don't you understand, I've chosen you!"

Marcus was gripping his short sword, he wore no armour and this was his only weapon. The old man wanted him dead for sure he decided, but though he tried to disengage himself Rowena was holding his neck.

"You're a pagan like me," she whispered, "and if we lie together in the sacred grove the gods will bless us!"

"I'm to be the instrument of your father's trick on Vortigern?" Marcus gulped, and lifting her heavy breasts in her hands Rowena nodded.

"Am I not worthy of your love Marcus Germanicus?" she asked.

He stood with his back to the tree waiting, and sure enough after a few tense minutes two of the Saxons appeared out of the undergrowth. But Rowena seemed surprised and marched forward angrily.

"Leave us alone dogs or my father will know of this!" she screamed, and the leader of the pair made a little bow.

"He knows of it already princess, we're here on his orders," he smiled, and Rowena gave him a push.

"My father knows about my meeting with this Roman," she yelled with a gesture at Marcus, "and he has given us his blessing. Go away, both of you!" she added at the top of her voice giving the man another hearty shove, and he stepped back a pace.

"We have our orders lady," the warrior told Rowena calmly, and when she took hold of his arm he elbowed her aside. For a moment she hesitated not knowing what to do. Then she began to run towards the villa, shouting to Marcus over her shoulder as she went.

"I'll bring my father and he'll stop them!"

Marcus knew that Hengist would do nothing of the kind, but he let her go, watching with narrowed eyes as she stumbled down the hill. The two men were coming forward smiling, and offering a silent prayer to Mithras the Roman moved into the open. The elder Saxon had started to swing his great sword, and under his breath the centurion said to himself:

"This is a fine time for physical jerks!"

He was weighing them up. The younger man was bringing the shaft of his axe down repeatedly into the palm of his hand as he advanced, and Marcus had to decide which man to tackle first. As his his ears were assaulted by the singing of the heavy blade and the slapping of the axe shaft he made his decision, and backing a hunch that the sword would be difficult to wield however strong the biceps he ran at the elder man. As his short sword came in under the Saxon's descending arm the huge sword whistled by harmlessly, and though his thrust had gone astray too he could re-aim his blade more quickly than the Saxon could lift his.

It was done in a moment, this time his aim was true and the blade went in under the heart. For an instant the face of the Saxon still smiled, then showed surprise, and Marcus became aware of the second man's axe descending on his unprotected head. He'd thrown himself desperately to one side, but even so the blade found it's mark cutting a deep channel in his cheek and going on to graze his shoulder. On the ground now and totally exposed he swept his sword in front of him as the Saxon lifted his arm for the next blow, and after striking at the axe shaft he fell back. But his enemy had been forced off balance too, and staggered for an instant. It was enough.

Marcus was on his feet before his adversary was ready to strike again, and still smiling the Saxon retreated a few paces before beginning to swing the axe again with strong even strokes. The Roman judged that they were now equally matched. Of the partnership between Saxon and axe he thought the axe more menacing, but of his union with his blade he knew himself to be the stronger.

The young man in the red tunic waited for what seemed like an age as the broad warrior came in for the kill. But the Saxon knew nothing of cavalry warfare or the speed and agility of light horsemen. And Marcus was thinking how Romulus would respond to this situation, swerving retreating and coming round again.

The cavalry commander had to be be both horse and rider now, and Marcus knew the heavy Saxon couldn't move as swiftly as he could. As the huge axe continued to swing two handed the Roman ran to the right, and obediently the Saxon turned to his left to keep face with his opponent. But the weight of the axe carried him further than he'd intended. The swing was impeded as he tried to bring it back into equilibrium, and in that second Marcus jerked in under the right arm. As the little sword plunged in the Saxon reeled back, his strong arm lost its grip and the axe swung limply on his left side.

Gripping his sword with both hands Marcus lifted it over his head. The Saxon was taller than him and he was about to use his cavalry knowledge again and strike at the neck as he would when mounted. But it was hard from this angle and his enemy was recovering. Changing his grip on the axe the Saxon was holding it half way along the shaft on his un-injured left side as he prepared for the next strike, but before it reached a sufficient height to begin it's descent Marcus' little sword came in on the muscular neck.

The artery severed by the stroke sent a great spume of blood over Germanicus. Its force blinded him and he felt the Saxon falling across

30

him, the weight seeming to force him onto the turf where he lay for long seconds stunned. After a while he tried to rise however, and lifting the corpse from his body made sure the man was dead. But the blood continued to flow, soaking him from head to foot.

Dizziness came over him and he clambered to his feet trying to clear his eyes. For a moment he stood swaying. Then as he bent to retrieve his sword he paused, watching fascinated as the blood of the young Saxon sank into the thirsty earth. Both his adversaries lay still now, and he contented himself that they were really dead. The first lay on his back open mouthed with his heart pierced. The second slumped face down in a pool of blood so well fed that the dry earth couldn't drain it fast enough.

Germanicus fell down and stared at his weapon. For the first time he felt the pain in his face and at the same moment remembered the third Saxon. To his horror as his vision cleared he saw the man a little way away, and beside him Rowena. It seemed she'd stayed to watch his destruction!

Then to his surprise the Saxon turned and started to walk head down towards the villa. But the girl was standing her ground, and Marcus felt the hate rising inside him when he remembered the fine men who'd sacrificed their lives for her.

Sitting on the rim of the little hollow above the sacred grove he allowed himself to fall backwards as if in a faint, then holding the bloody sword over his head he rolled slowly down. Eyes closed he listened to the sound of the girl as she slithered after him. But not till he felt her hand on him did he drop his sword and grip her wrists, and laughter welled inside as he imagined the sight he must present, covered in swiftly congealing blood.

He fancied that Rowena's face showed relief, but the memory of her trickery told him he was wrong and as he held her arms he revelled in the pain he was causing. The third Saxon was probably bringing help at this moment, but Marcus didn't care. And if a Saxon sword severed his head as he ravished the daughter of Hengist he'd die content!

Pulling Rowena to her feet Marcus dragged her down the slope into the grove. And as they entered a nest of young oaks and he looked down at himself he found himself laughing, as never in his life had he felt so elated, so alive! The girl was frightened he could see, and grinning like a loon he smeared her face with the fresh blood. What did he care if she was frightened? He wanted to frighten her!

His face was stinging his head ached and tentatively he touched his wound with his finger. Rowena reached out as if to touch it too, she was crying but he pushed her away. And could her concern be real, he wondered, before thrusting the idea aside and gripping her arms even

31

tighter. Blood was still pouring from his wounds and catching a quantity in his hand he looked calmly into her face before pulling her tunic away and smearing her heavy breasts.

"Here is my blood lady, do the war maidens of your gods not love it?" He was smiling and the smile came from deep inside. "See how my blood mixes with the blood of the men who fought for you!" he grinned gripping her round breasts hard. But Rowena made no sound, and all the while new blood continued to run down his chest.

"See my blood? See the blood of your brethren?" Marcus laughed, bringing his gory face close to hers. "They mix well and they'll mix with the blood of another before long." Lifting his sword he saw terror in her eyes, and he liked that as he wanted her to feel what he'd felt a few short minutes before.

"I swear I knew nothing of their orders!" Rowena was sobbing as she rose to her knees. "My father gave me a choice of men and told me that his only desire was to make a cuckold of Vortigern." Her eyes said it was true, and Marcus could believe it of Hengist. But the pupils wide in their green pools roused no pity in him, on the contrary they made him want to laugh and still laughing he pulled her after him into the nest of saplings.

For a moment he studied her. No sounds of pursuit came through the dark woods and he was beginning to relax.

"Do you think I'd stoop to kill a woman?" he asked, and the condescension in his voice made Rowena wince as calmly he pulled away the remaining strips of her tunic. Then pushing her to the ground he put his weight on her and she gasped and lay still.

"We'll see if you're a virgin princess!" Marcus sighed as if such a thing were impossible," and if you are I'll take your maidenhead as you wished. I'll see your blood mix with mine," he whispered, stroking her tear stained face with his bloody hand.

The white naked body, frightened and stained with blood, seemed to relax into the grass like a corpse. Then she smiled nervously and pulled his head down onto hers. He saw her lips parted and her eyes half closed as he kissed her, then the pool of vicious mirth bubbling inside came to the surface again. It was boiling now, and how could anger mirth and lust mix like this? he wondered.

"Do you think I'll go easy with you if you welcome me?" he murmured lazily, but the anger was still putting up a good fight against his gentler self.

For the present he'd let the anger rule Marcus decided, as the girl needed to have her pride dented. So he pulled her white limbs apart roughly.

"I'll see blood from you madam, and there's no blood without pain!" he declared joyously as he placed his short sword at the entrance to her open body. "Shall I cut the hymen as the barbarians do?" he enquired laconically, and as Rowena felt the cold metal she began to struggle and shout. But he covered her mouth.

For a moment they lay still as Marcus listened for sounds of their recent companion, but nothing stirred among the trees. Perhaps Hengist had planned this too? he speculated, and as the face of the soldier king rose in his mind he began to relax. Of course the old stallion would test him, but he wouldn't deny him the rewards of victory, Marcus concluded at last. And lifting his weight from the girl he threw his sword aside. They were alone.

Rowena had been cold and imperious, and Marcus remembered how intimidated he'd been when they first met. But now he was master, and though she cried out when he entered, her contorted face only served to revive the thrill he'd felt after cheating death. So he rode harder, and when he was spent lay in the softness of her flesh sticky with blood. It seemed to be sealing them together, and though he'd wanted to kill her a few minutes before when she kissed him he responded with gentleness. For a while they lay in the blood, then they made love again, and this time the conquerer wasn't thinking of conquest.

Hengist was standing at the villa gate laughing as they approached.

"You look like a butcher!" he hooted, "have you brought fresh meat from your hunt?" And as the sycophants joined in the laughter Marcus pushed Rowena forward.

"I've brought you back your daughter!" he grunted as he wiped his brow, but his attempt at a sneer sounded sheepish.

As the servants rushed to cover Rowena with a cloak Hengist sensed the resentment and made to take the young man's arm, but Marcus freed himself and set off towards the house.

"I understand your anger friend, but meant no harm," the Saxon king protested as he followed. And holding out a bloody hand Marcus turned on him.

"What's the meaning of this?" he demanded pointing back the way they'd come. "Two of your men lie dead... what's the meaning of it?"

Hengist was shrugging uneasily as the wounded man eased himself onto his bed and Galarius silent as a shadow began to bathe his wounds. But when Marcus looked up he wanted to laugh again, and was the proud and warlike Saxon really apologizing? he asked himself wonderingly.

Waiting in silence Marcus watched as the old warrior sat down and cleared his throat.

"I meant no harm!" Hengist repeated, reaching to slap his ill treated guest on the back and then thinking better of it. "I knew you'd triumph..." he shrugged, and Marcus looked at him doubtfully.

"I wish I'd known that!" the centurion answered, wincing as Galarius touched his face wound. "But I did not, indeed I was sure my death had come!"

"You fought like a lion my boy!" Hengist enthused, relinquishing restraint and slapping Marcus cheerfully on the back. And when his guest winced again he looked aggrieved and moved away a little. "The men you fought both wanted my daughter," he explained as if this made everything all right. "They were two of my best warriors and I'll feel their loss when we next take the field in battle."

Marcus could hardly believe his ears, and was the king of the Jutes trying to elicit his sympathy now? he asked himself as Hengist patted his shoulder gingerly.

"They had a right to challenge you for her!" the older man was saying as if this could not be argued with, and Marcus scowled at him.

"Did I have any rights in the matter?" he grunted, but Hengist just shrugged again and lifted his heavy brows in surprise.

"Of course not!" he answered with a puzzled frown before making to re-commence the back-slapping. But Marcus edged away, and accepting this as the churlish fancy of a wounded man Hengist nodded. "Of course I respect you my friend... now." he explained. And as the sight of Hengist trying to look sympathetic brought back the amusement Marcus relaxed.

"What of Rowena, what did she want?" he asked, and Hengist smiled broadly.

"She wanted you of course!" he bellowed. "As a loving father I couldn't deny her, and surely it wasn't unreasonable to see the best man win?" he finished in an offended tone.

Marcus understood. The Saxon concept of fair play was different to the Roman and he wasn't one to hold a grudge.

CHAPTER IV
aT The couRT oF kiNG voRTiGeRN

A hum of excitement ran round the room as the king of the Celts and his party entered, and rising to his feet Hengist motioned his servants to seat Vortigern in the place of honour at his side. On Vortigern's other side sat Rowena, plaited hair hanging down over her breasts, and as the chatter died away the king rose to speak.

With his nobles at his back Vortigern made an imposing sight, and seemed pleased, even relieved, by the courteous behaviour of his hosts. He was smiling as he looked about him, as if comforting himself with the notion that this wasn't going to be be too bad after all.

The high king of the Celts must be nearing sixty Marcus guessed, but as Vortigern bowed in response to the applause, a toga edged with purple over one arm and a gold circlet on his sparse grey hair, the centurion had to admit that he made an impressive sight.

"My friends," Vortigern began, his cultured voice somehow strangled and reedy, "it gives me great pleasure to welcome you. It's not good for us to fight," he piped, waving his thin arm round the crowded room, "as we're Christians, civilised and educated men."

The Saxons didn't care if these sentiments didn't apply to them as most of them didn't understand Latin anyway, and after a few minutes they began to laugh and chat to their neighbours as they would during any normal meal. Nevertheless Vortigern persisted.

"We've come together friends..." he droned, casting an irritated glance at Hengist who was chewing noisily on a ham bone. "We have come to make peace and welcome our Saxon brothers..." He'd been forced to raise his voice to compensate for the din, but to his credit he didn't give up. "And perhaps more importantly..." he croaked, "to finalise the marriage agreement between myself... and the beautiful Rowena." Vortigern was bending over his betrothed as if expecting some response, a sign of affection perhaps? But Rowena simply went on eating determinedly.

Then when she saw her father scowling at her she rose hurriedly to her feet to acknowledge the compliments of her elderly suitor, and wiping her hand on her gown gave it to Vortigern, who kissed it reverently. The centurion was watching Hengist's body-guards. Armed to the the teeth as usual they'd drawn back into the shadows he noticed, and in spite of his new friendship with Vortigern the Saxon leader was taking no chances it seemed.

The king was offering his hand to Hengist as Marcus turned back to the high table.

"Welcome Hengist... Welcome father in law!" Vortigern declared loftily, but though everyone cheered Hengist looked aggrieved. "You'll soon be one of the chiefs who owe me allegiance." the Celtic king was saying, waiving his arm in the direction of his underlings. But when Marcus tried to catch Hengist's eye the old boy was staring up into the rafters.

How serious and respectful he looked, Marcus thought, and there was no hint of amusement or triumph on his crafty old face. While in contrast Vortigern seemed nervous, constantly shrugging his shoulders and making jerky little movements of his head. Then the two leaders joined hands, and when Hengist put his arm round him Vortigern seemed pleased.

The Celtic nobles weren't so easily fooled however, and standing with arms folded they were watching like hawks. Marcus was particularly aware of Vortigern's two sons, who were wearing expressions of undisguised resentment. There could be no doubt about their opinion of their father's behaviour. Both were handsome he noted, and he could understand Rowena's desire to marry one of them rather than their father.

The Saxon girl had come to the table with eyes lowered, and though Vortigern bowed low she'd given only a curt nod in return. Hengist was primarily concerned with the edible component of the evening as always, and clapped his hands in delight as each dish was brought in. Wine poured, musicians played, and as the company settled down to eating and arguing Vortigern's birdlike eyes flickered round the room.

"You have Romans in your company I see," he murmured to Hengist, "are they Ambrosius' men?" And shaking his head vigorously the Saxon king adopted his affronted expression again.

"No... No... my friend, there are no spies here!" he laughed, "not alive anyway! Ha Ha!" And Vortigern smiled, his sharp little eyes still raking the room.

"They're everywhere I tell you, Ambrosius doesn't trust me!" he whispered. And as Hengist's bushy brows shot up in feigned amazement he placed a hand on Vortigern's shoulder as a sign of sympathy.

"But surely we're all friends here?" the Saxon king gasped in mock horror. "See, here is my beautiful daughter, your future wife." And at once Vortigern's rheumy eyes turned to his bride.

Noting the old man's thralldom Hengist winked at Marcus, and the centurion smiled in response.

"The old fool is enamoured of my little girl isn't he?" the Saxon king whispered mischievously, and when Marcus failed to join in his glee he put on his injured air yet again "Surely you don't reproach me? Hengist asked wonderingly, and when Marcus looked away he took hold of his tunic. "I know you won her in a fair fight," he hissed, "but this marriage is important as we need more land, and what better way to stop the Celts driving us into the sea than this? It's an honest bargain, Rowena in exchange for peace... or more accurately surrender!" he chortled behind his hand. "She's mine, mine to give as I chose," he added more loudly, sensing that Marcus was not impressed. "And I give her to the great and noble king Vortigern!" He'd lifted his stien in salute to his prospective son-in-law, but Marcus saw that Vortigern's smile had faded, and he was looking past his prospective father-in-law... at him!

The meal went on and on and the negotiations too, but after a week Vortigern and his party set out for London.

Germanicus was at the gate when Hengist returned from saying his farewells.

"What's the agreement? I see it pleases you," he muttered sulkily, and the Saxon slapped him on the back.

"The only agreements I make are those that please me!" Hengist boomed, and with a smile Marcus followed him into the house.

"I fancy it won't please Vortigern when he recovers from his infatuation," the centurion suggested, and Hengist swung round.

"She'll be a good wife... for as long as necessary," he stated narrowing his eyes. "And as I understand young love you can be with her till she goes to London. But after that..." he added drawing a thick finger across his throat, "if you try to spoil my plans I'll kill you!"

Germanicus and Galarius were to escort Rowena to London, and as Hengist said his farewells Marcus saw that there were tears in his eyes. Holding Rowena against his barrel chest he stroked her long blonde hair. He was whispering to her, and she smiled, reaching to kiss his grizzled cheek. Did their conversation concern him? Marcus wondered. As the Saxon princess had come to him again the previous night, and though her love had been intense she'd seemed afraid, as if clinging to him for protection.

Feeling a knife turning in his innards Marcus wondered if he could be falling in love with this wild German woman. But he put the idea aside, together with the picture he'd carried for the last few days, as it brought a pain that was almost physical. However, in spite of his efforts the vision rose again in his imagination: - Rowena, standing in a great marble hall with her hair hanging free. She was loosening her gown and letting it slip to the floor, her figure surrounded by unearthly light, while in the corner sat Vortigern clouded in shadows. Older and more bent than the reality he seemed to be sucking the life and beauty from her, so with an enormous effort Marcus screwed his eyes and tried to think of something else.

The city of London with its the huge walls and civic buildings impressed them, but as they sat on the river bank looking out over the docks something was worrying Marcus.

"You were right about this place," he told Galarius as he skimmed a stone across the water, "and though it's as well built and laid out as anything I've seen there's something wrong. And it's not just the dirty water in the baths and the insolence of the slaves either."

"For four hundred years Britain has been part of a great empire," the older man sighed, "and now she's alone descent into barbarism is inevitable."

They walked through the city, where the classical buildings stood as if fixed forever. And though a drain was blocked here and there, fountains no longer played and rubbish was beginning to accumulate, the smell of decay seemed in keeping somehow. Long years would pass before the stonework crumbled and the roofs fell in, but as the skills to carry out repairs were no longer available it would happen eventually. However, if Vortigern was aware of the world collapsing around him he didn't show it, on the contrary he was enjoying his hour of glory to the full.

Rowena was standing at the window looking down into the courtyard where her wedding guests were assembling. Then she turned back into the room and a poorly dressed girl came forward with a polished metal looking glass.

"Who is that woman?" the Saxoness asked suspiciously as she peered at her reflection, "is it an enchantment you put on me?" The girl holding the mirror was smaller than the new queen, more slender. And as she'd been brought up with the comforts of the rich she was disdainful.

"Civilised people don't consider it such!" she sniffed, using her best Latin, but Rowena wasn't overawed.

"Mind your manners girl!" the Saxoness snapped, "my husband tells me you claim to have noble blood, and if your ways don't improve I'll see the colour of it."

Rowena was growing accustomed to her reflection and admiring her hair with obvious pleasure. Then she pursed her lips.

"Are you of the old order Cordelia?" she demanded, and the girl scowled. How could her uncle Vortigern treat her like this? she was wondering. Though she knew the answer very well, as he was enthralled by this Saxon woman and would do anything she asked him to.

"May I go now madam?" the girl muttered, making no effort to hide the scorn in her voice, and Rowena narrowed her cat's eyes.

"You may go," she agreed, "and when you return let me see you in a better temper." Then she smiled as she remembered Vortigern's eagerness to please her. "But remember, my husband will think the worse of you if you anger me!" Making her hands into fists behind her back Cordelia stood defiantly in front of her mistress.

"My aunt Severa was Vortigern's queen until you came!" she told the German girl, but Rowena just shrugged.

"Until I came!" she repeated. "But I have come, and I'm queen now. The lady you speak of is to be sent into exile I understand, and I'll hear no more about her."

When the girl had gone Rowena made an effort to feel the elation her father felt, and spinning round so that the folds of her dress fanned out she told herself that she was a queen. But she couldn't forget Vortigern's two sullen sons. The memory of them made her uneasy, and there was another who stalked her mind too.

The new queen was sitting with her husband at the high table, and before long Vortigern put his hand over hers.

"Is everything to your liking my love?" he asked. But though Rowena smiled she looked away as if afraid to speak, and Vortigern was all concern. "Is something wrong my love?" he demanded, and Rowena shook her head quickly.

"It's only..."

"Something is wrong I can see, won't you tell me what it is?" Vortigern pleaded, and Rowena began to play with the gold torque round her neck.

"It's my maid Cordelia... she's so proud and insolent," the new queen sighed looking helplessly at her husband, and Vortigern laughed.

"Is that all? Then we'll replace her when the festivities are over."

"Why must I wait till then?" Rowena pouted, and Vortigern shook his grey head slowly.

"Because many of my supporters are here my love, they watch me intently and I must not offend them," he whispered, waiving a greeting to one of his guests to illustrate the point.

Rowena was looking hard at him. Should she have one of her sulks, or one of her tantrums perhaps? she wondered. But no, she couldn't be too demanding till she'd found her feet. So after a while she smiled, and Vortigern let out his breath, relieved that her mood had passed.

"Shall we retire my love?" he whispered.

Marcus watched them go with a feeling of dark despair, and on an impulse decided to follow at a distance. As the couple sauntered hand in hand along the corridor leading to the royal apartments he hid behind the pillars keeping out of sight, and at last his chance came when Vortigern was drawn into a side chamber by one of his advisers.

Then the centurion hissed to attract Rowena's attention, and she turned and put a finger to her lips.

"Why are you here? My husband will have you killed if we're discovered!" she whispered as Marcus pulled her behind a pillar. He was listening to Vortigern and the other man across the hall, and making sure they were safe before putting his arms round her.

"You must come away with me, I can't bear to see you with him!" Marcus whispered with a nod in the direction of the nocturnal conference, and with a smile Rowena drew her finger over his lips.

"Don't fret my love, we'll be together before long and I'll come to you tonight if I can."

"You'd leave his bed for mine?" Marcus demanded incredulously, but Rowena just shrugged.

"Why not?" she asked, furrowing her brow, and releasing her from his embrace Marcus removed her hands from his shoulders.

"Either you come with me now or we never lie together again!" he told her. "We'll be married in any way you chose, but I won't share you with another man."

"You're a fool, and I'd not taken you for a fool!" the new queen hissed, starting to move away as she heard her husband approaching.

"See, I've waited for you, and Germanicus has kept me company," she smiled taking Vortigern's hand. And glancing scornfully at Marcus the king of the Celts led her away. 'How can any man be so fortunate?' he was asking himself, 'and can it be that the gods are smiling on me at last?'

Rowena lay in Vortigern's bed with her eyes open and the damp body of her husband against her. He was cold and bony, and closing her eyes she remembered another who was warm and hard and strong. An awful fear gripped her when she remembered the centurion's last words, and could he be serious when he said they'd never be lovers again? she fretted. But no! she decided. She knew men and was aware of her power over them, and soon Marcus would repent of his harshness she was sure.

In the wavering light of smoking torches Rowena looked down at the panting fool with his grey head buried in her bosom and was disgusted. But this was just a means to an end, she told herself. And though she must do her duty and use her influence for the benefit of her people she'd be in the arms of a real man before long.

40

Galarius was watching a unit of Vortigern's troops drilling, and he knew they weren't Celts as Celts wouldn't submit to the discipline the old Roman in front of him was tying to impose. The soldiers were mainly ex-legionaries and boys from Roman families he guessed, and he smiled as the drill sergeant came towards him.

"Good morning friend!" the little man called, jumping down from the wall where he was sitting, and the sergeant wiped his brow.

"And a good morning to you too stranger," he puffed.

"You've got a difficult task there!" Galarius observed with a nod at the men in the square, and the sergeant nodded. He was overweight and sweating in his tight curias, and he sighed as he patted the straining straps.

"I can't abide drilling in armour!" he laughed.

"You're a Roman aren't you?" Galarius grinned, and the man nodded as he brushed the dust from his sleeves.

"I am indeed friend, or I was!" he added, lifting his arms and letting them fall in a gesture of resignation.

"Why are you serving Vortigern?" Galarius enquired, and the man shrugged.

"It's about all the likes of me can do!" he sighed, "as I've a family and a little business mending harnesses ..."

It appeared that the man was only drilling through habit, and the same was true of the others Galarius guessed.

"Life's not too bad really." the sergeant admitted. "And the tribes obey Vortigern as often as not... though it's not often he gives any orders if I'm honest!"

They talked for a while of old campaigns and old heroes, then Galarius pointed to the men, now sprawled on the grass.

"You'll make no headway with them here, so why not join Ambrosius and be among your own kind?" he asked. And as the sergeant stroked his stubbly chin he was nodding.

"I might do that friend, though some might say I'm too old to be a soldier!" he answered. Then they laughed again and Galarius went on his way. But when he looked back the sergeant was watching him, and wearing a thoughtful expression as he stroked his rough chin.

Vortigern had sent for Germanicus. But as the young soldier entered the royal study the king continued to work on his papers, and only when the shadow of the centurion fell across him did he look up.

"You're dressed like a peacock!" Vortigern observed, glancing scornfully at the red tunic and shining armour as Marcus gripped his plumed helmet and stood to attention. "You brought my queen here," Vortigern went on sitting back in his chair, "and now it's time you left us." Then he went back to his papers, and when he looked up again his expression showed annoyance. "What are you waiting for?" he demanded petulantly as Marcus continued to stand to attention.

"I came to these islands to offer my services as a mercenary sir, and as you don't seem to need me I intend to travel to Venta (Winchester) and offer myself to Ambrosius," the Roman muttered.

At this Vortigern began to cough nervously, then he lifted his hands as if to defend himself.

"Now don't be too hasty my boy!" he urged, resting his elbows on the desk and putting his fingers together, "as I've a proposition to put to you."

Marcus lifted his brows at this, as the Celtic king seemed ill at ease and the younger man suspected he was making this offer on the spur of the moment.

"I need a man like you," the Celt went on, "as my army needs to be... how shall I say... brought to readiness?"

Marcus' would have put it differently, what the troops needed was complete re-training and re-equipping. But he listened politely as Vortigern's grey head rocked back and forth and his musical voice droned on.

"I'll pay you... to train my army..." the Celtic king was telling him. Then suddenly the vague tone became firmer. "But first I have another task for you, I want you to escort a lady..."

Marcus heart leapt and as his face flushed Vortigern read his thoughts.

"Oh no, the lady you brought here is not to be your charge!" The thin lips were twisted in malicious enjoyment, and running his snake-like tongue over them Vortigern shrugged. "I'm minded not to trust you with THAT lady again... tut, tut." His eyes were piercing and there was a question in his voice. But Marcus ignored it, and sitting back Vortigern steepled his thin hands again. "There is a lady, two ladies in fact... my, er... the lady who was once my wife, and her niece." He was making circles on the desk with his finger, then suddenly he looked up. "I gave the girl a position in the service of my new wife," he mumbled hurriedly, "but the lady Rowena finds her, er... unsuitable, and she's to return to her family with her aunt."

"Are you saying that your niece was Rowena's servant?" Marcus asked incredulously, and Vortigern shook his head.

"Let us say that she was lady in waiting to my queen, will that suit you?" The last words were hissed across the wide desk, and Marcus was finding it hard to keep a straight face.

"I, I understand sir," he agreed at last, holding his lips tight together. And Vortigern nodded with relief.

"Then you leave tomorrow, take as many men as you need."

"Where am I to take these ladies?" Marcus frowned, and shaking his head impatiently Vortigern waived his hand.

"To the east, to the east, to the land of the Iceni on the east coast. There's an inlet there," he explained wearily as if giving directions was beneath his dignity. "And you won't be travelling for long my boy," he concluded under his breath as the Roman closed the door behind him.

Cordelia was told of her expulsion by one of the slaves, and as she hadn't seen Rowena for days and wasn't sorry about it, she packed her bag. As she looked at the palace where she'd once been so happy the memories of childhood flooded back, memories of the days she'd spent playing with her cousins, Vortigern's sons. Through rooms along corridors in formal gardens and by the river they'd run. But her Aunt Severa had been queen then, and their family had looked down on Vortigern, who'd more Celtic blood in him than Roman. His marriage to the daughter of Magnus Maximus the ruler of most of Britain had been advantageous to the petty Welsh chief. With the help of his father-in-law he'd become the voice of the native population, and eventually Magnus' heir.

When Cordelia's thoughts turned to Rowena her expression became distasteful, but as she'd soon be free of her German mistress her step was light as she approached her escort.

However she drew back before the Romans caught sight of her, as she'd seen this centurion before. He was one of Rowena's admirers she knew, and what possible reason could such a man have for travelling with her? she wondered.

As a cloud of foreboding descended Cordelia moved under the arch at the entrance to the courtyard and waited. Did Rowena have something in store for her? she asked herself. Was she really going back to her family, or did the Saxon girl have another fate in mind?

A few paces and she could make a run for it Cordelia decided, and she was sure that if she headed for the watergate one of the boatmen would help her escape. So, keeping her eyes on the Romans she began to retreat.

Her heart seemed to stop as the arms came round her, but though she knew at once that it was Vortigern and her cry of surprise was hastily stifled, Germanicus and the others had been alerted.

"It's good of you to bid us farewell sire!" Marcus called, bowing his head to the king, and Vortigern drew a hand across his mouth in an embarrassed gesture.

"Just common courtesy!" he laughed, still gripping Cordelia's arm. And was the girl some kind of prisoner? Marcus wondered as he took her bundle. One thing was certain, she'd been trying to get away and Vortigern was uncommon anxious that she didn't.

His charge was well wrapped up for a journey she didn't intend to take, the centurion thought as he strapped the girl's bundle to her horse. And Vortigern's eagerness to see her gone was apparent as he helped her to mount.

"I'm sorry about this Cordelia... but my new queen is a jealous woman." Vortigern sighed with a wink at the Romans. "She wants you gone, and who am I to disobey?" he added, turning sorrowfully to Marcus as if seeking male confirmation of his sentiments.

"We're well supplied sir," the Roman grunted, patting one of the bulging saddle bags. "And well armed too," he added placing his hand on his sword-hilt.

When her uncle reached to kiss her Cordelia bent to meet his lips and he squeezed her hand.

"Give my love to your family," Vortigern whispered, and for a moment Cordelia fancied she saw sadness in his face. But the moment passed, and slapping the horse's rump Vortigern turned away. He didn't stay to watch the little party leave the defences and ride out into the threatening world beyond, and Cordelia found herself wondering why he was in such a hurry to get rid of her. She was still wondering when they passed through the city gates and two more riders joined them.

Bringing his mount alongside Cordelia's Marcus looked her up and down. She'd be pretty if she'd smile more he thought to himself, and her profile, outlined against the autumn sky, reminded him of the girls he'd known in Rome. Their heads were full of lineage and self importance too he remembered, and like this girl they'd held themselves stiff as if they had a bad smell under their noses. He was trying to meet her eyes, were they blue or grey? he wondered. Cordelia was staring straight ahead, but when he took her rein he was rewarded with a resentful almost fearful look, from eyes that were steely blue.

He wanted to reassure her, as she seemed to be afraid of him.

"You're very ill at ease.... aren't you glad to be going home to your family?" he asked at last, and Cordelia narrowed her eyes.

"I'm no fool soldier, don't patronise me!" she snapped, and Marcus sighed.

"I'm no common soldier, and I wouldn't dream of patronising you!" he told her quickening his pace, and they rode on in silence for a while. Then he turned to her again.

"I asked if you're pleased to be going home as I hear your relations with Rowena were somewhat strained," he smiled. Then as those within earshot laughed Cordelia made a sudden attempt to break away, and after bringing her back Marcus halted their progress altogether.

"I think it best if I discover the cause of your ill humour," he sighed, "believe me we won't move from this spot till I do."

For what seemed like an age they waited, outlined against the yellowing trees on the hills. As the stiff wind pulled at their cloaks and the horses stamped with impatience Galarius shrugged his apologies to the others. But he knew his master well enough to say that they'd be enjoying the view from their present perspective till the girl relented.

CHAPTER V
INTO THE UNKNOWN

The others were growing restless as they watched the sun sink lower in the sky, and eventually the guide rode up to Germanicus. He was waving his arm towards the darkening west, and when the centurion continued to sit immobile he turned to Galarius.

"We were to spend the night at a ruined villa near here," he explained looking nervously over his shoulder, "as these regions are dangerous, there are bands of robbers and wolves in the woods..." And as if to confirm his words a long howl echoed down the valley from the forested slopes above.

As an answering howl was heard the girl pulled her cloak tighter. She was near to tears, biting her lip and staring accusingly at Germanicus.

"You're close to the Saxon woman Rowena," she sobbed, "and can it be you've brought me here to kill me?"

"I don't take my orders from Rowena, and why on earth would I want to kill you?" Marcus demanded bad-temperedly, and Cordelia began to feel foolish.

"I'm an embarrassment to my uncle," she explained defensively, and as Germanicus waived the column on he smiled to himself.

"Perhaps you are," he agreed wearily. "You remind him of his first wife, isn't that why he packed you off home?" His tone made it clear what he thought, and sensing his offence at her mistrust Cordelia was silent as they increased speed to make up for lost time.

Before the sun sank completely they arrived at the villa where they were to spend the night. The horses were housed in the old stables, and mangers full of fodder seemed to indicate that they were expected. As Cordelia followed the others into the house she was still wary, but as she settled herself by the fire she began to doubt her initial judgement of Marcus. Her fear that she was about to be murdered seemed silly now, and she found herself wondering how she could have been so self-important. After all she meant nothing to Rowena, she reasoned. And though her uncle had been glad to see the back of her, she knew he wouldn't hurt her.

Cordelia was stiff cold and hungry, and though she'd been determined to spend the night in the open well away from the Romans she was beginning to reconsider. Outside the crumbling villa wolves howled. The cries of night birds sounded like lost souls, and with a shiver she stretched her hands to the fire.

After a while one of the other women came to sit next to her, and when she pulled back her hood recognition dawned on Cordelia.

"Aunt Severa... they didn't tell me you were with us!" the girl gasped. But the drawn face of the older woman was expressionless.

"It wouldn't have been wise to advertise my departure, as I still have friends at court and don't want them to suffer on my behalf. My husband thought it best if I left quietly," the old queen added sadly, and Cordelia jumped to her feet.

"Why didn't you face him and denounce that woman?" she demanded angrily, "the people love you... you're the daughter of a great man!"

But ex-queen Severa simply smiled as she pulled her niece down beside her.

"Don't make a fuss Cordelia," she whispered, "if I hadn't left quietly who knows what would have happened?" She was glancing nervously at the soldiers, and Cordelia was nodding as she stirred her thick porridge, as it seemed her fears had some foundation after all.

"Why did you think I'd want to kill you?" Marcus asked as he sat down beside them, and Cordelia shrugged.

"No reason, perhaps I'm just a silly girl!" she snapped, and sensing the resentment Marcus smiled

"Yes, perhaps you are," he grinned, rising to his feet and making a mock salute.

Cordelia found herself hating him all over again and was certain she couldn't trust him. But she was attracted to him in spite of the fact that she hated him, and she desperately wanted him to like her.

Though Marcus was dead tired sleep evaded him, and as he lay on the kitchen floor his mind went back over the last few weeks. Galarius said that Rowena had the power to rule men, and he was right the centurion realised, as her face was still occupying his mind. As drowsiness overcame him he could still see her, eyes dreamy and half closed as she cupped her breasts in her hands in the oak grove. So muttering a curse under his breath he buried his head in his makeshift pillow and tried to think of something else.

The villa had been important in its day and the decoration was grand. Its situation was idyllic and powerful men had once lived here Marcus suspected as he walked on the terrace and looked out over the surrounding land. He could still see the outlines of fields, now abandoned to birch scrub. The servants' houses now derelict and roofless were of good construction, and though weeds were lifting the mosaic floor of the terrace he could still recognise the Christian chi-rho symbol that formed the centrepiece. At the margins of the circle swam jewel blue fishes, and kneeling on the hard stone Marcus traced the pattern with his finger. Round and round they went in eternal dance, even as the weeds swallowed them.

No one remembered the owners of the place, they'd left long ago Marcus learned, and half a dozen families now occupied the buildings. They'd lit fires on the patterned floors and obliterated the wall paintings with grime and hanging skins, and the centurion wondered what they thought of the decaying grandeur. To his surprise not one of them remembered the days of empire, and they'd never known a better life than the one they had now. Hardly a generation had passed since the last rescue, but already memories of Rome were dim. As the lives of peasants were short Marcus knew, and the unwashed children who pressed round him had never seen an imperial soldier before.

Next day they set off again, and as the little compound faded into the distance their spirits sank. Their guide's pony was small and he had to look up as he came alongside Romulus. His face and hands were tattooed with the familiar blue swirls, he was young and spoke tolerable Latin. He was cheerful and the Romans liked him.

"Some of my people met a group of Saxons in the woods a few days back, and one of our men was killed," he told them.

"How many were seen?" Marcus asked as he studied the woods on either side of the road, and the man shrugged.

"Only a dozen or so... a foraging party, but our folk were sure that their lord was close by with his main force." Marcus understood the strategy, as Saxon lords often led their men out in small bands seeking plunder and he knew that such a force was unlikely to number more than twenty.

Marcus was mildly surprised when Cordelia came to ride at his side.

"Perhaps I've misjudged you Roman," she ventured, and he smiled.

"My name is Marcus Germanicus," he told her, and she nodded nervously.

"The villa reminded me of my home and made me afraid of what we'll find when we reach my father's estates," she confided, and Marcus smiled again.

"Only the gods know that!" he answered sadly.

Cordelia opened up as they rode and it seemed to ease her anxiety to talk about her home. The house stood in an area of flat country she told the Romans, and over the centuries improvements had been made and the land drained.

"There are orchards, vineyards, and fields of corn as far as the eye can see," she told Marcus almost happily, and again he noted how pretty she was. Then suddenly her smile faded and she frowned. "We took it all so much for granted, like people under a spell, and now everything has changed..." Her eyes were appealing to him to contradict, but Marcus rode on without speaking.

Late in the afternoon they stopped by a stream and the women watched nervously as the men investigated the woods. The sense of danger was palpable, and when the snapping of a twig confirmed their fears Marcus placed a finger to his lips and Galarius pointed to a break in the scrub before throwing himself to the ground and crawling towards it. Signalling to two of his men Marcus made to circle behind, but it was too late.

Seeing they were discovered the enemy let out blood curdling war cries as they broke cover. And though the Romans fought desperately, as they were out-numbered ten to one the outcome was inevitable.

There were too many blond men to count and the extras formed themselves into a circle, like spectators at a gladiatorial display. They cheered as one by one the Romans were overcome, and though Marcus reckoned he'd killed at least three Saxons it seemed his force was vanquished.

As the centurion waited for the next man to come at him he glimpsed the emblem on a shield which told him their opponents were Angles. And picking himself up with a sinking heart he saw their leader bearing down on him. The man was as tall as Octha and his smile of anticipation said his love of combat was no less intense. Scars from past fights bent the intimidating mouth awry, but the eyes were straight and even and as the great sword whistled through the air Marcus set his feet apart and gripped his weapon.

He was determined to use all the skill and agility he possessed as he had in the oak grove, and was telling himself that if he could kill two men then he could surely kill one now. But the endless faces around him said no, and even if he disabled the giant a line of fresh men were ready to take his place. And all the while the huge sword continued to swing, its measured strokes suggesting that the Angle wanted to play a while before dispatching his enemy.

When Marcus ran in his weapon was deflected, and when he tried to aim high his opponent's sword came in at knee level forcing him to jump aside. This went on for what seemed like hours till the Roman was nearing the end of his strength, then after a desperate parry he fell to the ground and the giant was on him.

Everything seemed to happen in slow motion from then on, and pulling his opponent to his feet the Angle took the short sword from his hand as if he were a child. Marcus' head rested painfully in the crook of the man's elbow as he was dragged towards what was left of his little group. His feet were dangling six inches off the ground and he was straining for a sight of Cordelia, hoping desperately that she wasn't watching.

The girl was the cause of a dispute between two of the Angles, but Marcus could only watch as they argued over her. The scene was played out, but he had no part to play in it as any minute now the giant would snap his neck and there was nothing he could do about it.

The centurion was impotent, swinging like a felon waiting for his end. He couldn't speak and the others were powerless to help him. An agonising pain in his neck made thinking difficult and he was aware of a growing numbness in his limbs. He felt as if his head was bursting and he winced as the barely healed scar on his face was pulled open.

Then out of the corner of his eye he saw a boy of about twelve picking his way through crowd watching his misery. The urchin was on all fours crawling forward, then suddenly he jumped up and removing a knife from between his teeth spoke to the giant.

"Shall I cut his hamstrings father?" he chirruped, and laughing at his son's enthusiasm the giant turned to face another figure approaching from his right. Marcus, who was nothing more than an appendage moved with him, then to his surprise he heard the voice of Galarius addressing the Angle in his own language.

"Aelwulf! Do you not know me?" the little man grinned, and the giant frowned for a moment. Then as recognition dawned a huge smile spread over his face and he went to greet his long lost friend, at the same time letting go of Marcus, who fell to the ground like a dead man.

His legs had no bones! the centurion noted uneasily. They wouldn't bear his weight, and the sight of the huge Angle hugging Galarius made him wonder if his neck had snapped and he was in the afterworld.

Aelwulf was holding the little man at arms length as Marcus rubbed his neck and tried to sit up.

"Galarius the weasel!" he bawled, hah! We meet again!"

Germanicus could understand enough of what he was saying to follow the meaning, and his efforts to rise were more determined than ever as Galarius took the man by the arm and pulled him to where his master lay.

"I know this warrior!" the little man announced triumphantly as he looked up into the smiling face of their recent enemy, "I lived with his tribe... and..." then he broke off and looked away.

The Angle was still grinning broadly as he slapped Galarius on the back nearly knocking him over.

"I have fought many battles at the side of this weasel," he laughed giving the little man another hefty slap. "He's my kin too, as he married my sister!" But though Aelwulf seemed delighted by all this, Galarius looked embarrassed and turned his head away.

"It's true!" the little man admitted with a shrug, "didn't I tell you I once lived with the German tribes?"

Germanicus was intrigued, and watched without speaking as Galarius patted Aelwulf affectionately.

"We were like brothers then, though he was just a boy," the little man explained tipping his head at the giant. "And we were comrades in arms too, as when I returned to the legion after my wife died Aelwulf enlisted with me. We served together in these very lands," he chortled, and suddenly the giant grabbed Germanicus by the wrists and pulled him to his feet.

The tingling in Marcus' legs made him stagger as he tried to stand up, and Aelwulf, concerned that he'd been the cause of such distress began to brush him down with his hand.

"If you're with the weasel we'll not kill you!" he growled in a matter of fact way, and Germanicus found himself wondering if he should say thank you. However he limited himself to a brief nod as Galarius placed an arm round each of them.

"I'm happy to be here with you both!" the little man declared joyfully. But though the combatants smiled down at him they continued to eye each other warily.

After a while they set about burying the dead, and Marcus, who'd dispatched three of the Angles noticed that one was just a boy. Three soldiers from his unit were dead too, and another badly wounded. They were reduced to less than a dozen men and he was still responsible for the women.

They sat in a disconsolate circle, the old queen and her serving woman, Galarius and Marcus, with Aelwulf towering over them still grinning. It was not till the Angle sat down that Marcus noticed the girl was missing. Then he saw her under a tree a few feet away, tightly held by the boy he'd seen a few minutes before. The child got up when he felt himself watched, and brought his prize to Aelwulf.

"This is a fine wench father, can I have her?" he asked, and Aelwulf laughed.

"What would you do with her wolf cub?" the giant sneered, and the boy scowled.

"Please father!" he begged, "I'd keep her from gossiping and making trouble if I married her!"

"You're a good judge of woman flesh wolf cub, but I have first call!" Aelwulf laughed taking a strand of Cordelia's hair between his thick fingers. And as the girl pulled away Marcus reached for his knife, but it wasn't there. "Is this your woman, Roman?" the giant demanded, but Marcus shook his head.

"We're taking her to her family in the lands of the Iceni," he mumbled.

"Perhaps we should fight for her?" Aelwulf suggested as he pinched Cordelia's thigh, "and though she's a mite bony she'd keep one of us warm tonight!"

Marcus was looking uncertain, then to his relief Galarius stepped in.

"The girl is in our charge... a kinswoman of our master," he said, "and we must deliver her safe to her home as it's a matter of honour." But Aelwulf seemed reluctant to accept this, and was frowning as he stroked the girl's arm.

"We'll see!" he grunted, "but I'm minded to have her..."

The nearer they came to the sea the more Angles they met. Aelwulf seemed to know them all and as he was a man of standing Marcus knew he could take Cordelia if he wished.

It was almost a week since they'd left London, and as Marcus strolled aimlessly round the camp he pulled down a branch and struck the undergrowth with it. They'd taken his weapons. In spite of Aelwulf's affection for Galarius they were not to be returned he gathered, and the soldier in him was screaming with frustration as he plunged into the woods kicking at the fallen leaves.

A bend in the valley brought him to a flood plain where the stream wound into a loop, and using all his strength Marcus threw the branch across the water before lying down on the bank to think. They'd been prisoners for more than a day now, and as he didn't trust Aelwulf he had to do something.

The only emotion Marcus experienced when he saw the girl was irritation. She was sitting a few feet away brushing her hair, and though she must have seen him she'd not acknowledged him. As he wanted to be alone he resented her presence, but he watched her for a while and she went on brushing as if she were still alone.

He was contrasting Cordelia's recent gratitude with her initial hostility towards him. And was this done to confuse him he wondered idly.

Aggression one minute and come hither glances the next, what was he to make of her? But when she stretched out her hand he strolled over and sat down at her side.

"I'm afraid of that man!" Cordelia whispered, meaning Aelwulf. "Will you protect me?" And Marcus threw another stick into the water.

"It would be my duty... were I able," he muttered without taking his eyes off the opposite bank. It was clear that he didn't thank her for reminding him of his match with the Saxon and her eyes were making him uncomfortable, so she tried a little harder.

"I'd be grateful for your protection," Cordelia whispered, placing the brush to one side and rising to her knees. Then taking his face in her hands she kissed him. His surprise made her laugh, and as he hesitated she drew back and smiled. Her dress was tied at the shoulders, and looking first at one little knot then the other she gazed at him.

As she untied one knot with each hand and let the bodice fall away Marcus watched. Then she closed her eyes and inhaled, raising proud little breasts with prominent pink nipples. She was on her knees still, and holding out her arms.

"Am I not worth defending?" she demanded condescendingly, as if she were buying him.

Marcus had never been seduced, and if there was to be any seducing he felt that he should be the one doing it. So with both hands he grasped the round softness of her breasts, eventually letting go a little reluctantly. The blue eyes were half closed and she was moving closer. Her fingers touched his hair, her lips were wet and slightly parted.

Making an effort to clear his mind Marcus pushed her to the ground, and placing himself astride held her hands over her head. Throwing her head back Cordelia arched her spine and took a long breath, and was that triumph he saw in her eyes? Marcus wondered. His head was swimming, his body responding involuntarily as the hypnotic gaze pulled him down. But when she whispered to him hoarsely he didn't hear, as his mind was on other things. It would be so easy and he'd owe her nothing, he was telling himself. And no doubt many women had given themselves in these woods before today, for nothing more than mercy.

Pulling his head up with an effort he got to his feet, and the girl looked surprised, surprised and vulgar he thought.

"What's wrong?" she demanded, and pulling her up Marcus wrapped his cloak round her.

"If there's to be any lovemaking I'll be the one doing it!" he grunted. His amusement annoyed her, and putting her aristocratic nose in the air Cordelia shrugged.

54

"Your chance has passed now soldier, I've changed my mind!" she snapped.

Aelwulf watched them approach suspiciously, and some of the others laughed as Germanicus pushed the girl forward.

"I'd give you this woman were she mine to give," he murmured, and Galarius looked surprised.

"That's generous of you!" Aelwulf hooted, "but as you say she's not yours to give."

"For that I'm thankful!" Marcus sighed, picking up his blanket and starting to make his bed, "but when we reach our destination you can discuss the matter with her father."

Washed free of blood Aelwulf was not so fearsome, in fact he was almost handsome. He had a clean glowing quality. No one could fail to be impressed by his physique, and as the muscles of his arms rippled either side of his sleeveless jerkin the centurion wondered if he devoted much time to sword swinging?

The girl was subdued when they rode on next day. She'd made no attempt to mend her friendship with Marcus, and seemed intent on making him jealous. She was studying him, seeing a young man of above average height for a Roman, taut and muscular and with a calm almost sardonic expression. His hair was thick and wiry and his uniform, even in these conditions impeccable. Every piece of equipment was polished, his stallion moved with self satisfied grace, and no doubt he thought himself every inch the romantic hero! Cordelia thought to herself. But did she hate him or was she falling in love with him? she wondered. She certainly wanted him to fall in love with her, so why had she been so foolish the previous day?

It was easy to conjure a memory of the room in Vortigern's palace where the maids slept. When the lamps were snuffed the talking began Cordelia remembered, and though she'd been a total innocent the other girls were very knowledgeable when it came to matters of love.

She particularly remembered a Saxon slave called Hilda.

"When the Romans came to our village I ran like a hare!" said the guttural voice in Cordelia's imagination. "I was twelve and terrified of men, but I'd not have run so fast if I'd known what was waiting for me!"

"Get to the point, and remember we've heard it all before!" It was Bronwen a girl from the west, and Hilda pretended to take offence.

"You're always the one who begs me to tell the tale!" she snapped, and

Bronwen shrugged.

"All right, but get on with it."

"They were legionaries from Cisalpine Gaul," Hilda giggled and Bronwen let out an appreciative sigh. "They came to our village at night after defeating the men of our tribe as I remember."

"Go on, Go on!" cried little Mary the Christian girl, and Hilda's voice had been warm and very German Cordelia remembered..

"I ran... I ran till I could run no more..."

"How many?" Mary asked, but Hilda couldn't count.

"As many as the leaves on a tree." she'd shrugged. Then Bronwen had come in again with her sing-song Welsh voice.

"As many as the grains of sand on a beach?" she'd suggested in fun, and Hilda hadn't liked that.

"The only men running after you Welsh are chasing you back into your awful country!" she'd snapped, and Cordelia had been fascinated. "They pulled me to my feet and ripped away my garment!" Hilda had whispered to the accompaniment of indrawn breaths, "but they didn't harm me and instead took me to their officer... Ah! He was handsome!"

"Like the one who pays so much attention to Rowena?" Cordelia hadn't meant to speak and they'd all squinted at her through the gloom.

"Yes just like him!" Hilda confirmed, welcoming the comparison, "in fact it might well have been him! He was the first to take me, and though I fought hard it was all in vain."

Everybody had sighed, and Cordelia had been thinking of Germanicus as Hilda's voice flowed on.

"There were others after him, more than I remember, but I'll always remember him."

"Perhaps you'll meet him again one day?" Mary had suggested, and Hilda had smiled.

"If I do I'll not run away, I'll hold his eyes in mine and give him my hand and he'll know that I'm his!"

"But you're old now, all of twenty, and he'd run screaming to his mother!" Bronwen had sniggered, but Mary had been kinder.

"Don't pay any heed to her Hilda, as I'll warrant he'd reject you kindly as befits a gentleman!" she'd suggested innocently. Their laughter had risen Cordelia remembered, then fallen again as the guard passed the door.

When Cordelia brought herself back to the present she knew she'd done it all wrong, as Germanicus had thought her a lady and she'd behaved like a slave girl. Remembering the contempt on his face still made her wince.

But she wanted him all the same, as something had moved inside her last night, something even stronger than the thrill she'd felt when Hilda told her story.

Then her thoughts turned to Aelwulf. He'd not have rejected her she knew, and as he was attractive in his rough way perhaps she'd be nice to him? He'd be less likely to hurt her if he thought she liked him, she reasoned, and if her strategy made Marcus jealous... so be it!

They rode in single file, as the narrow paths through the woods were difficult to negotiate and the men were forced to dismount time and again to clear the way. Cordelia was trying to catch Aelwulf's eye, and when she smiled shyly at him she could see he was flattered. When she looked at him again he was a little nearer, so she slackened her pace and soon they were riding one after the other. When the path widened he came alongside, but Cordelia seemed to have lost her tongue. She spoke only Latin and the language of the Iceni, but Aelwulf knew some Latin from his days in the legion and as he talked Cordelia studied him.

He'd seemed old when he first burst into her life, but looking at him now she realised he couldn't be much above thirty. His hair and beard were thick and creamy, and his eyes, transparent and glassy, reminded her of the empty eyes of a statue. He rode with the ease of a man who spends hours in the saddle and expends no unnecessary energy. He was watching her without blinking and she'd have to speak soon.

"I was frightened, should I be frightened of you?" she whispered at last, and the huge shoulders shrugged.

"It's wise to be afraid of us!" Aelwulf grunted.

"Do all men fear you?" Cordelia enquired, and the Angle narrowed his eyes.

"Some fight and keep their land... for a while," he smiled.

"Do you speak of anyone in particular?" Cordelia asked, and Aelwulf shrugged again.

"At the place we're heading for they've kept everything.... and killed many of our men." He told her.

"Do you know the men at the Villa?"

"We see them when there's fighting, they call their leader Cordelius."

"He's my father!" Cordelia chirruped, but Aelwulf seemed to find this no surprise, and smiled showing good teeth.

"I'm the leader of the Angles in these parts, and as your father leads the Romans and Britons we've crossed swords more than once!" he boasted looking her up and down with approval. "We should make an alliance, as if I married the daughter of Cordelius there'd be no need to fight."

"You'd win the lands you couldn't take by conquest too!" Cordelia suggested, and ignoring the sarcasm Aelwulf took her rein.

"Do you like my proposal Cordelia?" he asked, and when he put his hand over hers the girl felt the same sapping of will she'd experienced the previous night. She'd meant to lure Marcus into desiring her, but when he was near she'd felt confused, as there was something about men that made her weak and powerless.

She was still thinking about this when Aelwulf spoke again.

"You can see that I'm a warrior of worth, and witnessed my triumph over Germanicus?" he muttered. And Cordelia nodded as she remembered her would-be husband hanging on Aelwulf's arm. It made her want to laugh, but she reproved herself instantly, as her love for Marcus was true! she told herself. She'd loved him for almost a week now, and wasn't she being nice to Aelwulf just to make him jealous?

Cordelia was looking at the German, letting her eyes wander over his broad shoulders and massive thighs when suddenly she felt her stomach contract. 'What a warrior! What a lover he'd make!' she thought as something inside her saw the challenge. They rode on in companionable silence, his heavy horse matching the pace of her palfrey till evening, and by then they were firm friends.

The last thing Cordelia remembered before sleep overcame her was the sight of Aelwulf leaning against a tree a few feet away. His figure seemed to shimmer in the firelight, and though there were Romans all around including her own dear Marcus, it was the presence of Aelwulf that made her feel safe.

It took only half the morning to reach Cordelia's childhood home, a low red roofed villa sitting at the landward end of a promontory half a mile or so from the sea. The flat land leading to the shore was divided by narrow channels, and Marcus could see that these drainage ditches had made the land fertile. On the seaward side the ground was protected by earthen dykes strengthened with stone, as the fields and vineyards could be reclaimed by the sea at any time and only constant vigilance had kept them dry for four hundred years.

The villa sat on a platform protected from the tides, and un-drained tidal land began where the cultivated fields ended. Long legged cranes and other waterfowl together with a multitude of wild creatures inhabited these wastes. And the inhabitants of the villa had hunted and enjoyed their recreation here since the conquest. Though there were no hills to speak of all her father's land sloped towards the sea, Cordelia told them when they halted to look down at the villa.

"My family has lived here since the first colonization," she told Marcus, who was on the lookout for danger as usual. But everything seemed normal and there was none of the decay that had disfigured the last villa they'd visited. The corn would be safely in the barns by now, and the fields were empty. Well-tended vines suggested fertility, and the animals grazing round the farmstead added to the feeling of peace.

But the centurion was still wary as he watched the tiny figures moving below them. Though he could see that these were no Saxons, and the dark haired slave with his uniform tunic was as easy to recognise as the Roman lady gathering late flowers by the pool.

It was all so normal, and turning as the Angles came up he pointed to the settlement.

"Do you know this place Aelwulf?" he asked, and the blonde warrior nodded.

"Aye, but as you see we've not overcome it," he grunted. "There are soldiers here who train the slaves and peasants. And though we've fought them more than once the land isn't worth the blood!" he scoffed as he turned his horse.

They were about to part company it appeared, as Aelwulf's family was building a village to the south. Then two Angles rode up and dropping a bundle noisily on the ground scowled at the centurion.

"Your weapons Roman!" one snarled, and as Marcus nodded he noted their chief's last longing look at Cordelia.

Someone below had seen them and the yard round the villa was suddenly alive with figures. The gates defending the compound were secured with beams slotted into heavy cradles, and Marcus could see a tall man who seemed to be giving orders. As they approached the place was silent, and still out of bowshot he helped Cordelia and her aunt to dismount. Then they waited as the girl called out.

But though the defenders must have recognised them the gates didn't open, and instead a slave appeared at a spy hole. Calling them forward he demanded proof of their identity, and to their amusement went to great lengths to satisfy himself that Severa was really who she claimed to be. But eventually the Romans were ordered to retreat leaving the women by the gate.

Half an hour passed before a small door in the gates opened and the tall man came out.

"I am the father of that woman!" he yelled from a distance pointing at Cordelia, "and the other is my sister-in-law. I owe you a debt it seems..."

he added, taking a few wary steps towards them and allowing Marcus to greet him in the Roman fashion.

As they clasped arms Germanicus was smiling, but his face took on a puzzled expression as the tall man stared uncertainly back at him. Then after a bout of nervous foot tapping Cordelia's father nodded vigorously.

"Yes, yes, of course.... I'm grateful to you for bringing her back..." he declared as if he wasn't quite sure which 'her' he was referring to. "But if my humble kinsman Vortigern... kinsman by marriage only you understand... If Vortigern wants me to pay you... or thinks that sending Cordelia back will induce me to..."

Cordelia who'd been admitted first was standing by the little door as the others stepped over the threshold. Her hair was brushed and dressed in coils and she was wearing a gown of fine linen that Marcus hadn't seen before. It hung in limp folds on her boyish body, and he was beginning to wonder if he'd been mistaken in his judgement of her when her father began to speak, as if carrying on where he'd left off.

"Yes... yes, she's every inch the lady isn't she?" Cordelius frowned poking the jewelled band under his daughter's bosom with his finger. "No doubt Vortigern gave her that!" he grunted, "but if he thinks I'm going to pay him for... for it..."

As he watched the flustered father Marcus offered silent thanks to Mithras for his strength in resisting temptation by the river. The memory made him shudder, as he'd come dangerously near to de-flowering the girl. But the regret he'd been feeling (worries about bringing dishonour on himself and his countryman etc.) was replaced now by relief. Relief that he'd avoided an alliance with this strange family. Cordelius would have been within his rights to demand marriage had he acted differently Marcus knew, and he found himself congratulating himself that he'd delivered the girl intact in spite of the difficulties.

At Cordelia's side stood her aunt Severa, still wearing the funereal gown she'd worn throughout the journey.

"I see you've met my father, and you already know my aunt of course," Cordelia smiled, dismissing the subject of the old queen without further ado. And Germanicus realised not only that his charge was back to her old self, but that she wanted no mention of her aunt's former life.

To his relief Marcus discovered that Cordelius was a different character when dealing with his men, and his orders were delivered in an authoritative voice without any of the nervousness he'd exhibited before. He was respected as he'd served in the legions. And his men trusted him, as his less confident side stayed hidden when he was among those he knew.

Once inside the defences the newcomers were taken to an airy veranda where refreshments were laid out for them. The breeze coming from the sea lifted linen cloths covering low tables spread with food. Here and there stood vases of flowers, and suddenly Germanicus remembered his mother's home. It had been so much like this, but would he ever see it again? he wondered.

CHAPTER VI
a rough wooing

The luxury of the villa was welcome, and Galarius who'd spent his life watching others enjoying the comforts of rank could now share the experience. The hypocaust, like everything else in the house was well maintained and the rooms were always warm. Hot water for baths and servants to care for clothes and uniforms, it seemed like a dream. The nights they'd spent under the stars contrasted sharply with the soft beds they now enjoyed, and freedom from fear was a strange bedfellow. But even so Galarius stayed close to his master, sensing that in a world of transitory alliances here was a man he could trust.

But plentiful food and comfort are not all a man needs, and for Marcus the sights and sounds of the villa brought back another world, a world of intelligent conversation, beautiful rooms and clever women. For him the need for adventure was always close to the surface and the inactivity was becoming irksome, as boredom was beyond his experience and he couldn't deal with it.

They were lying on low couches surveying the remains of their evening meal - a roast hog speared earlier in the woods, mushrooms baked in honey and lobster caught not a hundred yards off-shore. The aroma still lingered, but when Cordelius offered them more wine Marcus waved it away.

He was remembering the provisions that had kept them alive on their journeys, and when a picture of Galarius pounding flour to make cakes over the fire entered his mind he jumped to his feet and made to leave the room. Cordelia started to follow him but he shook his head.

"I'm poor company tonight," he told her, but she persisted.

"Shall I walk in the garden with you?" she asked, and taking her hand Marcus kissed it.

"I'm tired Cordelia, and you must forgive me if I retire," he murmured. But though Cordelius waved him away with a smile the girl's eyes followed him as if trying to pull him back.

After throwing himself onto his bed Marcus removed his sandals.

"We must get away Galarius, this place is choking me!" he muttered. And though he'd been expecting surprise and resentment the walnut face of his friend broke into smiles.

"I wondered how long it would be," Galarius grinned, and Marcus scowled at him.

"What do you mean?" he demanded irritably as he watched the thin brown hands already at work gathering clothing and giving the plumed helmet a final polish.

"How long before you tire of this womans world?" the little man laughed, and Marcus allowed his mouth to bend.

"Do you remember the night in Kent when we lay soaking in our blankets listening to the thunder?" he asked, and Galarius chuckled.

"Aye, we were dreaming of a comfortable billet like this, and said we'd never leave if we found it." Then as they laughed together Germanicus drew out his sword, which shone with polish and disuse.

"Tomorrow we make plans to leave," he smiled.

The mistress of the house was indisposed they were told. Though now and then they heard her strident voice berating the servants, and there was no need for Cordelius to tell them that the strain was affecting her reason.

Aunt Severa was better able to cope as she'd had already withdrawn from reality, and her thoughts seemed pleasant albeit far away. Absent and preoccupied she seemed to drift through the place like a well meaning spirit, as the present was too taxing for her and she preferred to live in the past. But her quiet acceptance that Rome was no more struck Germanicus as sensible as well as brave.

"I was married to Vortigern for more years than I care to admit," the old queen told them more than once with a sad smile, and they'd nodded in understanding. "My husband won't fight the invaders you know, he prefers to make treaties with them," she'd say lifting an elegant eyebrow in question, and the Romans would answer with more nods of sympathy.

Cordelius however remained confident that another rescue would bring salvation.

"We must go on hoping for relief..." he'd tell them. "It will come in time believe me. And though Vortigern is no soldier perhaps there's some wisdom in his strategy, as if we avoid all out war we may save something." An embarrassed silence always seemed to come over the Romans at this point, and an irritable shake of the head was Cordelia's only response.

"Oh, father! can't you see?" she'd answer." It's too late for hope, too late for rescue and too late to rebuild, as the Saxons fill the woods and more arrive every day!" She'd be clenching her fists and close to losing her temper by this time. "Even Rome has fallen to the barbarians!" she'd sob. "There are no legions left to come to our rescue, and if you don't accept it I think I'll go mad."

But as Cordelius got up and put his arm round his daughter he'd wink at Marcus.

"I can't accept it child, as Ambrosius is still resisting and as long as he's alive I'll go on hoping."

The elaborately dressed hair of the ex-queen was all grey now, circling a weary face. And Severa's narrow shoulders would make a little shrug as she entered the conversation.

"What will happen to us... here?" she'd ask, and the eyes wide in her thin face reminded Marcus of the eyes of a starving child.

"We'll go on fighting of course, for as long as we can." Cordelius told her on one occasion from his place at the window, and Germanicus came up behind him.

"Is there no chance of making peace?" he whispered, " as Aelwulf isn't an unreasonable man." And Cordelius didn't reject the idea outright.

"We could make efforts to organise a truce... do you think we might succeed?" he whispered in reply, and Marcus shrugged.

"Perhaps..." he conceded doubtfully.

Cordelius believed that the Germanic tribes could be driven out or at least absorbed and civilised, and was still hoping that before he died everything would be back to normal. But Marcus saw only a soldier's optimism ossified into stone.

The aging man found it impossible to accept that everything he'd lived for was gone. He knew only how to be a soldier, running the house like a fort with his men looking up to him as if her were a god. And as their whole future was bound up in him who could blame them for trusting him? Marcus pondered as he stared out over the flat grey sea that brought the English from Germany.

A week of restlessness followed, restlessness tinged with guilt. As though Marcus wanted to stay he wanted to join Ambrosius too. But though sympathy for Cordelius sometimes gained the ascendancy he'd decided that they had to leave, as winter was coming and if they were to get the journey over before bad weather set in their departure could not be long delayed.

He was finding the artificiality of villa life more irritating by the day. The world he'd been so glad to enter was no longer enough, and when he told Cordelius they were leaving his reaction, though sad was not angry.

"I knew you'd leave us one day," the older man sighed, placing his steepled fingers to his lips as he stared out to sea. "But I fancied there might be something to keep you here?" he added, with a smile over his shoulder. Then he shook his head. "We've taken too much or your time already, and of course you must join Ambrosius," he murmured before returning to his thoughts. And Marcus didn't disturb him again, as no doubt the old soldier had his memories.

But at the door he paused, as Cordelius was speaking, half to himself. "I'd come with you... but my duties here must come first," the old man was murmuring as he glanced in the direction of his wife's quarters where the servants could be heard trying to pacify her. "I feel I can't leave you see... even for a day... who knows what would happen...?" And when Marcus nodded he turned back to the window.

A dozen men on horseback set out before it was light and the calm morning welcomed them. Then as they entered the trees Germanicus took one last look at the villa, so untroubled in its isolated self sufficiency.

Romulus was skittish, thrilled be free with a good road in front of him and the men felt the same. Galarius was riding a horse from Cordelius' stables, a stallion almost as lively as Romulus. And as it was years since he'd ridden such a horse it made him feel young again. He was feeling good for other reasons too, as accepting the inevitable long before it dawned on his master had given him cause to congratulate himself, and the fact they were now of the same mind pleased him even more.

As Germanicus watched the leathery hands controlling the spirited animal he was smiling.

"You've known horses before I see... and not just travelling beasts either. You've ridden a horse with life in him!" the centurion laughed as they came to a halt after a trial of speed, and the little man shouted back.

"I've ridden with the cavalry as you have centurion, does that surprise you?" and Germanicus' grin grew even broader.

"Nothing about you surprises me weasel!" he replied using Aelwulf's name for his friend, and received a look of mock resentment for his pains.

Jumping down Marcus pulled the harness off and left Romulus to graze. Then after giving orders to make camp he turned into the woods as Galarius set about lighting a fire.

As his mind went back over his farewell to Cordelia Marcus found himself wondering why he'd been so uncomfortable in her company. Then he shrugged, as no man could be at ease with a woman who'd seen him humiliated he told himself. And as recollections of his combat with Aelwulf made him squirm he put the memory aside and tried to think objectively about the girl.

She'd been walking in the garden by the fountain when he'd arrived to say goodbye, and though he'd taken care with his appearance he'd been sure that nothing would change her opinion of him. She'd laid the flowers she'd gathered aside and sat down on a bench he remembered.

"They're the last of their kind Marcus, a long winter lies ahead and there's no certainty that they'll bloom again," she'd whispered, and he'd taken her hand.

"They'll bloom again come spring Cordelia never fear," he'd told her, "and somewhere they'll find ground that suits them. Perhaps their life will be harder and the weaker ones will die," he'd added touching a lily, obviously an import from warmer climes, "but the strong will survive." And Cordelia had nodded sadly.

"But I'm not strong Marcus Germanicus, I need a protecting wall to shield me from the north wind," she'd whispered lifting her eyes in mute appeal. And was she seeking a declaration of love? he'd wondered. But no, it was more complicated than that he'd decided. She wanted him to tell her what would happen, she wanted him to tell her what her own feelings were too, and how to cope with her conflicting emotions.

"The gods hold us in their hands Cordelia, and they'll speak when the time is right," he'd muttered, and she'd put her hand on his leather kilt close to his sword.

"Must we wait for the gods to speak Marcus?" she'd whispered, and as he looked away he'd nodded.

"There's a certainty that the gods send to guide us," he'd murmured uneasily.

"You don't feel that certainty?" she'd asked, and he'd shaken his head.

"It's not in your mind either, is it?"

"Perhaps I won't feel it till a man shows me that he feels it?" she'd suggested sadly, and he'd nodded and smiled.

"You'll feel it when the gods decree."

As Cordelia watched him leave she'd wanted desperately to remember him as he was now. Even the the gods themselves could not be so perfect she'd told herself, and from the leather straps binding his calves to his glowing hair Marcus Germanicus was the glory of Rome personified. He'd lifted his shining helmet with its bright crest in salute as he bowed his farewell, and face blank she'd clenched her hands and turned away.

By the time Marcus threw himself down under a tree the memory was fading, and the smell of cooking from Galarius's fire made him think of simpler things: of food and sleep and tomorrow's fight.

Nearing its full a heavy yellow moon hung low on a calm sea. And though these shores knew storms and flooding tonight was all glassy stillness. Autumn mists wreathed the base of the woods, and unseasonably warm air clung to the earth.

Inside the villa everything was quiet, as the family had retired and only a few servants moved, snuffing a candle or extinguishing a lamp as they carried out their last duties of the day. The sentry at the main gate was struggling to keep his eyes open, and most of the others whose duty it was to watch along the parapet were huddled in corners, their voices rising now and then in response to the click of falling dice.

Sounds of the night came to them now and then, and if they'd been listening they'd have noticed a change in the nocturnal hum. As a cloud crossed the moon the lookout rubbed his eyes, asking himself if he'd really seen something move in the open ground between camp and trees? Then he'd resumed his measured pace.

He was never to tell the story to his comrades, for as a hand came over his mouth a knife found his heart. Carefully they lowered his body to the boards and no words were spoken as their leader signalled them to follow him. Others were dispatched to deal with the rest of the watch, and waiting for the darkening of the moon and keeping low to the ground more agile blonde men crept across the open land.

Cordelius was the first to wake, his soldier's ear pricking his brain into life as Aelwulf and his kin entered the atrium. Like shadows the Saxons moved among the marble statues, pressing against the walls and letting the gentle gurgling of the fountain cover their breathing. Aelwulf kept his sword sheathed, and when the moon appeared again its gleam was reflected in the blade of his long knife. The rooms leading off the courtyard were quiet, and nothing stirred but water falling into a marble basin.

Cordelius sat up and putting his bare feet to the floor closed his fingers over the hilt of his sword. But he was allowed no time to don his armour, and as he rose to his feet the door opened and two pale warriors came towards him.

Though his weapon flayed the air Cordelius was soon overcome, and pinioning his arms the Angles tied him securely to the bed where he lay gagged and mute. The invaders made no move to leave, and instead took up positions against the wall. Arms folded they stared at their prisoner, and from time to time one peered through the crack in the slightly open door. Sounds of struggle from outside were of no interest to them. And the screams and crashing of furniture left them unmoved, as did the smashing of pottery and the clash of arms.

After directing the two men to the master's quarters Aelwulf had gone in search of Cordelia's room. A servant sleeping at her threshold woke as the giant crept towards him. But though he reached for the pike at his side his fingers failed to close, and stepping over his still form Aelwulf pushed the door open. His men were gathering the servants and women in the inner court, and Cordelia's mother and aunt were shivering with cold and fear as Aelwulf opened the door of the girl's chamber and stood watching her sleep.

He stood for what seemed like an age looking down at her face shining white in the moonlight and her hair flying out across the pillow as if cast in bronze. He waited till the noise outside had died away, then placing one brawny arm under her back and another under her knees he lifted her from the bed.

Making no attempt to silence Cordelia's screams the Angle threw her over his shoulder, and when he passed her father's room no sounds came from there. Across the court he could see the surviving servants and the women, and though congealing blood made the floor sticky it caused no delay in his progress as moving the body of an elderly man aside with his foot he stepped into the moonlight.

Aelwulf's gait was cheerful now, wide and swinging. And it continued for a quarter of a mile to the point where the spiky grasses of the dunes gave way to clean soft sand. Then he put the girl down.

What have you done to my father... my family?" Cordelia demanded, her eyes wide and frightened in her pale face, and Aelwulf shrugged.

"No more were killed than was necessary and your father and mother are both safe," he told her, but when she tried to rise he pushed her back. "You'll remember that I was minded to take you to wife?" His voice was matter of fact, and when he began to gather drift wood for a fire Cordelia took a deep breath and gathered her courage.

"Have you brought me here to kill me?" she gasped, and the Angle shrugged again.

"Surely there's no need for that?" Aelwulf smiled, and Cordelia was puzzled now as well as afraid.

"What do you want? Tell me what you want!" she screamed, and as Aelwulf continued with his efforts to light the wood he shrugged again.

"I've already told you.... I want to make you my wife."

"Without my consent?" Cordelia sobbed, and the giant nodded as he lifted his broad shoulders and let them fall again.

"Yes, if that's is how it must be."

As the flames flickered weakly Aelwulf blew life into them.

"You knew that I wanted you, and you know I want peace with your father and his people?" he asked, and Cordelia nodded unhappily. "So you'll be my wife and your father will be freed. Is that not good?" the giant smiled, and Cordelia's sobs turned immediately to unsteady laughter.

"But you can't take a woman just because you want her... and you can't threaten me with the death of my family!" She was almost choking and Aelwulf looked up from the fire.

"I make no threats!" he protested, "but if you won't accept me willingly..." He was shrugging again, then he pushed her to the sand and there was no time to cry out before his hard mouth stopped her breath.

Then he seemed to soften and after kissing her gently he rolled to one side and pulled her night-gown away.

"There's no cause for alarm Cordelia, as you'll be important among the women of my people. My father wears the earls' belt, and I'll wear it when he travels to Valhalla," he added lazily as he stroked her hair. "I'll be good to you and we'll have many sons."

Cordelia was thinking of Marcus. Where was he now? she wondered, and if he were here... ? Then her mind returned to the present and as Aelwulf kissed her again she began to reconsider her love for Marcus. She was finding his face strangely difficult to recall, and if her parents were safe could she love Aelwulf instead? she wondered. As his caresses became more demanding she began to suspect that she could, and inexplicable as it was she felt as she had beside the river with Marcus. She wanted to be loved... she desperately wanted to be loved now!

Neck arched Cordelia stretched into the sand and looked up into the determined face above her. There was no possibility of escape, and was this what Marcus had meant, was this was how the gods had willed it? Perhaps it was, and perhaps the future would be bearable she told herself.

Though she was proud she couldn't help welcoming him, and as the intensity of his efforts increased Aelwulf seemed to wear away her reservations; as a boat moored to a long disused jetty shells away the barnacles.

Cordelius was walking the walls as the sun came up. The Saxons had gone, three of his men were dead and his daughter was missing. His surprise when he saw her approaching almost outweighed his relief, but the sight of Aelwulf at her side sent his heart plummeting again.

"Cordelia my child... are you safe?" he called down, and the girl looked back at Aelwulf.

"I'm safe father," she replied with a smile, then Aelwulf shouted up to say she'd be returned before long.

"What's your price Saxon?" There was venom in Cordelius' voice as he was not beaten yet, and his unlikely son-in-law stroked his yellow beard.

"My folk want peace as yours do, and if we're honest is there any other way?"

"Perhaps not," the old soldier sighed as he gazed at his daughter, "but if I were younger things would be different. What am I to do?" he asked, lifting his palms, and Cordelia looked away in embarrassment.

"We should make peace father, and if you agree I'll fulfil my part of the bargain."

Aelwulf was smiling the victor's smile as he offered his friendship and gave his promise of marriage, but Cordelius was infinitely sad.

"I'll make peace with you for her sake," he said tilting his head at Cordelia, "and for the sake of the others who look to me for protection." Then after walking away a few paces he turned. "But it grieves me that I should be brought to this, and may the gods grant me an early death to end my shame."

Cordelia was trying to run to the gate but Aelwulf pulled her back.

"When the marriage treaty is drawn up you'll be free to return," he told her as she looked back at her father with brimming eyes. Then she turned to Aelwulf and smiling sadly let him lead her away.

"If only..." Cordelia fretted urging her plodding horse on a little faster. If only she didn't feel so confused. Why did she feel guilt at the price her father was having to pay, and was there anything she could have done to change things? Then she sighed. If only she'd been able to persuade Marcus to stay...

A hundred or more shared the great hut at the Saxon settlement, and as they ate, drank and made love they gave no thought to what Cordelia called privacy. So she tried to explain.

"I was brought up as a lady," she whispered to Aelwulf, and the giant shrugged.

"You're a lady now and no woman outranks you," he told her pushing away a child who was reaching for their food, and Cordelia sighed.

"But I had my own servants... my own rooms," and as the Angle wanted her to be happy he relented a little.

"I'll take you back to the villa," he frowned, "but only when the peace is secured. Does that please you?" And Cordelia smiled, touching his lips with her tongue and placing her hand inside his leather jerkin to stroke his chest.

"I'll take you to my room and we'll make love there. It's better alone," she whispered, and he laughed and pulled her to him.

"You promise it will be better than this?" he grinned, and as his grip made her gasp the melee around them faded.

Women clutched their children and drew them away, but showed no shock, as this happened all the time and it was no novelty to them.

Germanicus and Galarius were as cheerful as the rest. The soldiers Vortigern had sent with them were nearing home, and the prospect of spending winter in the comparative safety of London was nearing reality. Every step brought them closer to civilisation and increased the distance between themselves and the wild Germans. Tension seemed to fade as their journey drew to its end, and their prayers became thankful instead of pleading.

One of the men, a Christian, stood apart holding a holy relic over his head as Germanicus and the others made their obeisance to the setting sun on their last night in the field.

"May the Lord Jesus Christ and his Mother the Blessed Virgin forgive you your blasphemy!" he droned, and Germanicus turned on him.

"Do you presume to instruct me in religion?" he demanded icily, and though the man took a sharp breath he stood his ground.

"My god gives me courage centurion as well as the right to instruct you, as your army is gone and soon the army of God will sweep aside all unbelievers!" His voice had been rising steadily, and by the time he reached the climax he was shouting at the sky. The others were looking uncertain and Germanicus could see they half believed him, so unsheathing his sword he pressed the point to the man's throat.

"I need no army to help me deal with plebeian malice!" he grunted. But the terrified eyes of the Christian remained fixed on the sky and he carried on praying under his breath until Germanicus brought his face up close. "Were I the wretch you think I am I'd kill you now!" the Roman snarled, and the man backed away.

"You may kill me, but the act will bring eternal damnation on you!" he croaked, and though some of the others laughed it was nervous laughter.

Later that night as they lay waiting for sleep Germanicus turned to Galarius.

"Do the Christians really believe this threat of eternal damnation?" he whispered, and sitting up the little man reached for a stick to poke the dying fire.

"Strange to relate but they do, and their belief is so intense... well, it makes you wonder."

"In my experience soldiers will always hedge their bets, and if they think that worshipping this Christ will increase their chances of living for ever they'll happily add another god to their list." Marcus yawned, sitting up and pulling his blanket round his shoulders, but Galarius frowned.

"This god can't be added to any list, as he says that all other gods must be discarded and only he should rule. That's why they call him a jealous god I suppose," he added wearily, and they both lay down again,

"You say the Christians call other men's gods devils?" Marcus muttered as Galarius turned over with the intention of going to sleep. "Then Christianity is just like any other religion in my opinion, as it blackens the name of one god to exalt another!"

As far as Marcus was concerned the subject was closed, but Galarius seemed to have changed his mind about going to sleep.

"The Christians intend to convert everyone to their beliefs... even women. They say that only the shrines of their god should be allowed!" he hissed, and Germanicus sat up again bad temperedly.

"Just what are you saying?" he grunted, "can you imagine Aelwulf and his pagan crew forsaking their Allfather Woden in favour of an executed felon?" But though Galarius saw the ridiculous nature of such a proposition he didn't give up.

"Men will sacrifice a great deal for the promise of living for ever," he whispered across the space, "and as people are so gullible... who knows?" But only the sound of soft breathing came back to him in answer, as his master was asleep.

CHAPTER VII
The centre of resistance

They arrived in a capital city that was still beautiful under threatening clouds. Four hundred years of civilisation were etched on these stones, and Germanicus was acutely aware of their significance. Ghosts of long dead Romans paced the corridors of Vortigern's palace, and the spirits were more in tune with the place than the uneasy king.

Vortigern was preoccupied but seemed relieved to learn that Severa and Cordelia were safely home. The news that Cordelius' garrison was still holding out brought no flicker to his flat grey eyes, and reports of the women's health found him similarly uninterested.

The Romans were wary, and though the Celts treated them with respect Germanicus and Galarius suspected that if they let down their guard they'd fall victim to something unpleasant. Everything about the Celts was intense. They were quick to take offence, and care must be taken not to offend them. Throw away remarks could be taken seriously, and the Romans could find themselves pitted against the family of the man slighted or his whole tribe.

They stayed in London for a week, and on the evening before their departure took their last look at the palace and the river. Marcus' room in the old barracks had been spartan. Vortigern had kept him away from the court as much as possible, and as he watched the pillars and porticoes of the seat of government shrink into the mist he felt no regret.

"I'll be glad to get away from here!" he'd told Galarius. But thoughts of Rowena still haunted him. Not the Rowena who'd smiled weakly at him the previous evening, but another, fresh golden eager Rowena, the perfect woman he'd loved in the oak grove.

"Huh - you can't be more eager to get away than I am!" Galarius answered as he packed their things into the saddle bags, and Marcus nodded miserably.

"How can a woman so pure and perfect change so much in just a few weeks?" he demanded, and Galarius shrugged.

"Didn't you start that change?" he muttered, and Marcus sighed as his mood softened to sentiment.

"But I loved her!" he protested, "I'd have died for her... in fact I nearly did. I'd have betrayed my best friend for her!" But Galarius shook his head.

"I doubt it," he grunted.

Germanicus saw that his weasel wasn't taking this seriously, and in any case there was no point in going over it now he decided, throwing himself onto his bed and pouring himself some wine. But he was determined to enjoy his self pity a little longer.

"She made me her slave!" he moaned, and taking the goblet from his hand Galarius tried to look sympathetic.

"Don't be too hard on her," the little man advised, tilting his head thoughtfully. "As I suspect there's something brewing, something not to her liking perhaps? But if it suits her people she'll go along with it," he added thinking aloud. "What can they be planning, and what occupies her thoughts... something not in your interests perhaps?"

Marcus was shaking his head as he poured himself yet more wine.

"Your imagination is a rich as your store of memories!" he scoffed. But Galarius had suggested an interesting theory, and placing a finger to his lips he frowned. "We know that the Jutes are preparing for war, and we know they want to tighten their grip on the lands they've won. What else could they be planning?" he pondered. But Galarius had no idea.

Marcus decided to present himself to Vortigern again before leaving for Winchester, though the old man had ignored him since his return and the offer of employment seemed to have slipped his mind. But the centurion wasn't entirely sorry about that, as the sooner he and Galarius joined Ambrosius the better.

A servant waylaid him as he made his way to the audience chamber, and directing him into an alcove whispered in his ear.

"My lady would speak with you sir," the man hissed, and Marcus was intrigued.

"Who is your lady?" he asked, but the servant was already hurrying away down the corridor and he was forced to follow at the trot.

When they passed through a room full of young girls sewing Marcus realised with a mixture of elation and suspicion that the man was taking him to Rowena. Then he was ushered into a long room lined with marble figures. The place seemed empty, but as Germanicus sauntered between the statues Rowena's voice came out of nowhere.

"You're an imposing sight centurion!" she observed, emerging from behind an imperial bust, "but you've been neglecting me."

"I've been away... an errand for your husband," Marcus explained hoarsely, as the shock of her appearance had dried his throat. And coming up to him Rowena placed her hands on his epaulettes.

"You're like a god Marcus, a hero like them!" she told him with a nod at the petrified emperors, and Marcus took a step back.

"What do you want?" he grunted. His voice was infinitely tired and with a shrug Rowena turned away.

"We'll not be disturbed as I've given orders," she whispered reaching to stroke his neck. "You know I love you, love me again... I need you to love me." But he pushed her away.

"You're another man's wife and this is his palace," Marcus protested looking furtively over his shoulder, but Rowena still smiled.

"Does that make me less desirable?" she whispered, running her hands over her breasts in that familiar way. And as Marcus watched them rise and fall under her gown the movement roused him. Why not? he asked himself, and why should Vortigern's honour matter more to him here than it had in the oak grove?

Never-the-less he held her away.

"Why are you teasing me?" he demanded tightening his grip on her arms, and she squealed.

"You're hurting me!"

"Am I?" he enquired lazily as he pressed her against the wall.

Her eyes followed his lips as they came down, and though the kiss was without tenderness and his armour was crushing her, Rowena didn't care.

Memories of pleasures he'd taken in the past were flooding Marcus' mind, and with them came the faces of his old comrades in the mess. The girl was struggling, the faceless nameless girl was struggling and breathing hard, so holding her eyes he allowed her to slide to the floor.

There was fear on Rowena's lovely face now and fear in her voice. But Germanicus had lost interest in what she had to say, and throwing his weapon to the floor he listened as the echoes died away. When the noise brought no servants he buried his face in Rowena's neck and allowed his teeth to nip. Her little cry amused him strangely, and why did this particular woman rouse such passion, anger and amusement in him? he asked himself. Why did these strange bed-fellows walk hand in hand with Rowena? he wondered as he knelt at her side, and could it be that she was working some kind of magic?

"I loved you once," he whispered, his lips set in an expression somewhere between sadness and contempt. Then very purposefully he settled himself, and she didn't cry out.

"You summoned me and here I am!" he murmured, his eyes still holding hers, and she wouldn't resist he knew.

But even doting Vortigern would have to respond if his wife were found like this with another man. The chiefs would insist that he send her away and the old fool would have to obey. What little authority he had would be gone and Hengist's influence would be gone too.

"You chose that old fool in preference to me!" Germanicus grunted, grinding his teeth as his injured pride drove him on. And though Rowena tried to call out she had no breath. "Does your old husband love you like this?" Marcus demanded, and gasping and whining the Saxon woman turned her head away.

Tears were forcing their way through her tightly closed eyelids as his breastplate and armbands pressed into her and the rhythm grew faster. And was it jealousy or hate that was driving him? Marcus wondered as he imagined Vortigern's thin body cradled in hers. Was his anger directed at Vortigern, or was he experiencing an excess of love turned to loathing?

Wrenching the braids from her head he twisted them round his hands and pulled her head up for one last vicious kiss. She was crying, and there was nothing in her expression but confusion.

Getting up he straightened his uniform, and retrieving his helmet from the floor placed it on his head. And as he towered over her Rowena stared up dishevelled and humiliated.

"You've haunted me... but I'm free of you now!" Marcus gulped as a tremendous thrill went through him. Suddenly he knew that in future he'd be able to kill Saxons without the vision of this woman rising reproachfully in his mind. And if he remembered her at all the memory would add strength to his arm and venom to his blade.

The sky was leaden, here and there a few persevering leaves clung to the trees and under-foot the discarded canopy groaned. The limited hours of daylight dictated their activity and they rose and went to bed with the sun.

From frozen fields the lapwings rise,
reflected in the azure skies
the stillness of the Earth belies,
the ferment below.

With nothing else on his mind Marcus started to think about the complicated time keeping system followed in Rome, a system clearly impractical in northern regions where a winter's day was no more than five or six hours long. He found himself wondering idly if the rules had ever been strictly followed in Britain even in the high days of empire. As everyone knew the times of day: dawn, morning, afternoon, sunset, lighting up time, depth of night. And dividing the days and nights into hours seemed unnecessary.

The Roman day was twelve hours long throughout the year starting at daybreak, and the night was the same length beginning when the sun set and the day ended. But the system was impractical here, and to alter the length of the hours according to the time of year was just plain silly, he decided. As in these parts a sundial was useless most of the time even in summer, and he hadn't seen a water-clock in working order since he landed.

They travelled for as long as the light lasted stopping when they were hungry, and after making camp and cooking a meal they sat staring into the flames till it was time to sleep. The fire was a comfort and kept the wolves away. They told one another stories and sang songs, then wrapping themselves in their blankets they lay down. If rain threatened they pulled down branches to make a shelter, and with oiled skins capping the fretwork slept dry if not always warm.

Barren fields lay open to the sky, and only the occasional dwelling smoking from it's apex suggested the presence of man. Once a child appeared to stare at them, but a hand from a dark interior soon pulled it back and its curiosity with it. The bark of a dog echoed through the empty woods and they rode on. A woman bending over her washtub sang quietly, her voice carried on the cold air like the notes of a harp in an empty hall. But when she saw them she ran back into her hovel and they heard the bolts sliding noisily into position.

The town of Venta (Winchester) lay in a familiar Roman British landscape, and as there were no Saxons or Angles in these parts everything was as it had been. Slaves carried goods and water through the streets, and as uniformed soldiers stopped to salute a superior officer Germanicus felt his spirits lift.

"This is more like it!" he laughed, "I was starting to wonder if any part of these islands was still civilised."

Galarius was peering into a shop selling pottery and lamps, and when the proprietor came out ready to make a sale he laughed too.

"I'd begun to doubt it myself centurion, perhaps all this is a dream?" he grinned. And Germanicus bowed as two ladies passed, well dressed and at ease. It was clear that in these parts people didn't worry overmuch about invaders, and when Marcus spoke to the sentry at the barracks gate he was confident.

"We've come from London, inform the commander at once!" he told the man, and a messenger was sent to Ambrosius.

Leaving their horses with a groom Marcus and Galarius wandered off in the direction of a familiar little building set into the wall of the fort.

Steps led down into semi-darkness and at the foot they waited for their eyes to grow accustomed to the gloom. Marcus bowed as he entered, and Galarius followed his example, still grasping the bread he'd bought earlier as he stepped nervously into the shrine.

This was the temple of the sun god Helios Mithras. A small vestibule opened into the room where the god dwelt, and on either side stood stone attendants of the deity. After Galarius had laid his bread at the feet of one of these they passed into the inner sanctum. On a dais at the far end of which stood Mithras, a lighted candle shinning from his hollow crown.

Germanicus was warmed to see the temple well cared for and the flame still burning, and as he knelt on one knee a feeling of calm and homecoming flooded over him.

"This cult is part of my life," he whispered, "and I've made my most important decisions in temples like this." Then he took a ring from his finger. "With thanks to Helios Mithras God of the Sun... for his goodness in rising to light my way each day," he murmured.

Galarius who'd already made his gift, knelt too and started muttering as Marcus placed his ring in the receptacle provided for offerings.

"I give thanks for the creed that has been my guide through life, and for the gift of courage." The centurion's voice was strong almost emotional. "I thank you for bringing me safe this far, and ask that when I go out your strength will go with me and I may end my days in honour fighting a just cause."

A noise at the door made them turn. But the temple was dim and the figure in the entrance indistinct, so they waited and watched as the newcomer paid homage. Then he turned to face them, and when he spoke his Latin was perfect.

"I was told that two soldiers wish to speak with me," he smiled glancing questioningly at Galarius, and Marcus smiled too as their host led them out of the shrine into the watery sunshine.

"Have I the honour of addressing the famed Ambrosius?" he enquired bowing low, and moving away a few paces Galarius started to bow repeatedly.

Ambrosius was not much over forty Marcus guessed, and he'd expected him to be older.

"I am Ambrosius Aurelianus, Dux Britanniarum (Duke of Britain) came the answer in a calm confident voice. And unsheathing his sword Marcus held it up flat on his palms.

"We've come to enlist sire," he murmured, and still smiling Ambrosius patted the younger man's arm.

"Come, we'll have some refreshment as you must be tired," the duke said setting off across the square "There'll be time enough for enlisting when you've eaten."

The people they passed made way for the duke, saluting or bowing, and after passing through the administrative building they entered the command centre. The walls were decorated with scenes from Julius Caesar's conquest of Gaul Marcus noted, recognising each panel in turn as Ambrosius watched him

"I see you're familiar with the deeds of our great emperor," the duke observed, and Marcus nodded.

"I lived with pictures like these when I was a child," he smiled, "and Caesar's virtues impressed me even then."

"You follow the cult of Mithras?" Ambrosius enquired approvingly, and Marcus nodded again.

"Yes sir, as he's the soldier's god !" he replied, knowing that this was explanation enough.

Leading his guests to a couch Ambrosius indicated the food and wine on a side table, then he shook his head and laughed quietly.

"You must forgive my amusement, but our soldier's religion is a rare thing these days and I'm surrounded by Christians!"

"Do they support you?" Marcus asked, and Ambrosius put his head on one side.

"I have their support as far as they're capable of giving it," he answered sadly, then he changed the subject. "Come, we don't stand on ceremony here and you must eat," he urged. "Inside these walls there's peace, even if it is the calm at the centre of the whirlpool!"

A little later Ambrosius unrolled a map and drew a circle round Winchester with his finger.

"These lands are safe," he told them, "but here," he went on pointing to a large island to the south, "the Saxons are regular visitors."

Marcus ate with the officers as his family was known to Ambrosius. And as he lay back on his couch he found himself looking into familiar faces. Though he'd never met any of these men before their type could be recognised across the empire, and for centuries soldiers like these had relaxed in surroundings like this. As the wine took effect a strange detachment stole over him and the last three months seemed to melt into a dream. Was the world outside really so threatening he asked himself, or had he imagined it all?

He felt like a man waking up after a nightmare, but made an effort to clear his mind when the man sitting next to him offered his hand.

"I'm Brennus, half Celt and half Roman!" he boomed, then Ambrosius came in.

"When Rome ruled we had regular replacements," the duke explained, "we travelled abroad and others were posted here. But there are no replacements and postings now, and we're a mixture of bloods. Most of us are part Celt and none the worse for it!"

"Some are!" Brennus grunted, and Ambrosius placed his arm round his comrade.

"We must not judge till we know for sure Brennus..." he warned.

Marcus was lost for a moment, then he remembered Vortigern.

"Do you suspect the king of the Celts of treachery?" he asked sitting up suddenly. His voice had been louder than he'd intended and Ambrosius made a quietening gesture with his hand.

"We'll discuss that later my friend," he murmured, and Marcus knew he'd spoken out of turn.

As the night wore on however, he became increasingly certain that Ambrosius had doubts about the situation in London.

"When the time is right I'll make my decision about Vortigern, but for now he's our ally," the duke said as he stood up to leave, "and tomorrow you must familiarise yourself with the garrison." Marcus knew that he was not yet a trusted member of staff, and he'd have to wait to find out how Ambrosius and Vortigern interacted as joint rulers of the island.

They were about to celebrate the feast of Saturnalia, the winter solstice. This was the high point of the year, a day, a night and sometimes another day of eating drinking and pleasure. The women put on their best clothes, some dressed as Venus the goddess of love, and others as Andromeda, as all the immortals came to life for the festival. Feasts were held, slaves were waited on by their masters, and colourfully wrapped gifts were distributed all round.

Every house in the town was full of people, singing dancing and making love. The men polished their armour and one would play Bacchus the god of wine, as he was especially important at this time of year. On this night it was customary to ape the orgies of lust and gluttony that once enlivened the palaces of Rome, and food was consumed in great quantities. Wine was drunk as if they were down to the last amphora, and women were loved as if their sex would be extinct when the sun came up.

One particularly pretty woman stood in a corner of the banqueting hall dressed as Brigantia, goddess of the northern tribe the Brigantes. But the Romans had transformed the Celtic image to fit their own ideas, and a gilded helmet crowned the figure holding the trident staff of Neptune. At her side rested the shield of the endless legions, and for Marcus the symbol had deep emotional meaning. How long before the inhabitants of the islands destroyed this virility? he wondered, and how many years would pass before Britannia's vigorous symbolism was lost in barbarism?

Leaving the great hall of the duke's palace behind Marcus went out into the freezing night. His head was swimming, and the food he'd eaten was complaining audibly as he lent against the veranda rail. Dizziness clawed at his consciousness. The contents of his stomach were continuing to make their intentions known, and feeling himself slipping he tried to fight the nausea and retain his balance.

As the sound of singing and fighting died away he gazed up at the night sky and concentrated hard. The moon was not yet full but shone with unusual vigour, and as the clouds scudded over her face in the westerly wind they became transparent and insubstantial. The moon seemed to shine even brighter behind her veil, and circled by a halo of yellow and blue her features appeared crystal clear, her place in the sky more prominent. As Marcus squinted at the haloed orb in his confused vision it reminded him of a great eye, the yellow centre was laughing he fancied, and the misty gold iris was winking inside its blue circle.

Dragging his eyes from the light he saw the hunter Orion emerging from another patch of cloud. Then he saw Mars the red one. As the clouds raced east the war god seemed to be galloping west at the head of a squadron of Pleiades, as if leading them to some distant battle beyond the sea.

Bringing himself back to earth Marcus tried to focus on the other side of the courtyard where the living quarters of the higher ranking women were situated. He was attempting to identify something familiar - a door or a statue, and concentrating even harder he closed his eyes for a moment before trying again.

When he opened them the scene had changed, and as he shook his head in an effort to clear it he saw shadowy figures moving along the illuminated path flowing from one of the noisy rooms. They were leaving the created light and moving into the silver glow of the moon, there were two of them and they were walking slowly towards the women's quarters.

Struggling to stand upright Marcus tried to plan his next move. He'd eaten, and drunk, and he'd told the story of his life to.... he couldn't quite remember who. And now it was time for love he told himself. But for some reason his body disagreed, and his stomach still felt as if he'd dined on live snakes. They were threatening to retreat up his gullet at any minute he sensed, but he was a man, and he must ignore them!

Love, yes love, should follow wine and music! he decided, trying to ignore the signals from just above his belt and concentrate on the more relevant parts of his anatomy. His legs were there sure enough he confirmed, they were separating his head from the beckoning slabs of stone under his feet. The feet, yes the feet would be a good place to start, he'd begin there and follow his legs up till he came to something else.

He began by tensing his knees, satisfying himself that there were still two of them. Then he moved to the thighs... and how strangely unsteady they were he thought, furrowing his brow in annoyance. But the numbness didn't end there. It continued up till it met the complaining nest of worms under his chest, and stamping with frustration the young soldier decided to investigate and make sure that everything of importance was still intact. But the messages from his fingers brought no comfort. Unaccountably his addled brain was producing pictures from his childhood, and what on earth could be making him think of the small boy he'd once been? he wondered.

There was some good news however, his eyes were working again and he could see the two women more clearly now. The elder was swaying slightly but perfectly clear, and she was pointing at him and shaking her head. Then the other one turned into the light... and he saw a vision!

The bent back of the old woman was turned away now, but the girl was looking straight at him. The moonlight was like day, he could see her face in exquisite clarity, and it was the face of a goddess! But the expression was contemptuous, and why was that? he wondered.

The arms supporting Marcus fed his dream for a while, but when he looked down he saw that they couldn't be the soft arms of the nymph, as they were hairy! However, in spite of the shock he lent back against what appeared to be Galarius and allowed himself to be dragged away. His bed was soft, and as sleep overcame him he slid between the limbs of the delicious girl he'd seen across the court.

At the first sign of spring they set out for the west. Ambrosius spent most of his life on horseback travelling between the various Celtic kingdoms. And his aim was not only to assess the loyalty of the chiefs, but to make sure they knew who was in charge.

They travelled at the head of about two hundred troops, and the duke's body guard resplendent in Roman cavalry uniform led the way. Behind them came contingents of Celts dressed in leather breeches bound with thongs and thick woollen tunics down to the knee. Coats of ringed mail of the same length provided protection, and the whole figure was wrapped in a heavy cloak.

After a good many tests and questions Ambrosius had complemented Marcus by making him his A.D.C. with the rank of acting Praetor, and the young soldier felt his importance rising.

They were heading for the flat lands that Galarius had told him about, vast areas of marsh with here and there a fortification rising on a hill. Some of the hills were man-made the little man said, and long before the Roman conquest the natives had built and fortified them. Marcus didn't know what to believe, as the memories of old men had a life of their own he knew. And as the years passed the women in their stories became more beautiful, the mountains higher and the seas wider.

"You must understand my relations with the Celts," Ambrosius remarked as he brought his chestnut mare alongside Romulus. "Vortigern is one of their own, the chiefs trust him and some of them are more than glad to be free of Roman domination. But a few are wise enough to see that their protection has gone too," he added, and they rode in silence for a while over the frost hard ground. "Basically it's a question of loyalty," the duke continued eventually, "should they follow Vortigern or throw in their lot with a Roman who happens to be to be a better general?" He was smiling in self congratulation but Marcus was confused.

"The Celts supporting Vortigern... they're not our enemies and surely we'll all fight together to expel the Saxons?" he suggested, but Ambrosius shook his head.

"Is that the impression you gained in London?" he asked, "or is it possible that Vortigern will ally himself with the enemy?"

"You mean his marriage to Rowena?" Marcus retorted sulkily, and Ambrosius nodded.

"Yes, his marriage to the daughter of Hengist, the most cunning Saxon of them all."

Marcus could see his point.

"But Vortigern wouldn't conspire with Hengist behind your back!" he insisted, and a thread of anger stretched the duke's voice.

"Do you imagine that I was consulted about this marriage to the Saxon girl?" he demanded, and though Marcus thought not he felt a twinge of irritation at the way the duke spoke of Rowena.

"She's a princess and very beautiful!" he grunted, and his sulky tone made Ambrosius smile.

"No doubt she is!" he conceded. "She's obviously skilled at addling the senses of weak men and boys," he added mischievously, and Marcus swallowed hard.

"I've seen battle sir, I'm well blooded!" he sniffed, and Ambrosius put a hand on his arm.

"I meant no slight on your abilities as a soldier Marcus, but as a lover... are you blooded there too?"

The duke was making fun of his young companion, but as Marcus remembered the oak grove he found he could think about it now without pain. So he sat up a little straighter.

"Perhaps I'm not as wise to the ways of women as you are sir," he admitted, and Ambrosius nodded sadly.

"They make fools of the best of us!" he laughed, "but a commander has to be above such weakness."

"And Vortigern isn't?" Marcus suggested, and the duke's fine features stiffened suddenly.

"Clearly not! Has he not married the daughter of our enemy?"

"But dynastic marriages are often made with subject peoples... it helps to subdue them if they see their blood running in the veins of the ruling class." The younger man replied by way of explanation, and Ambrosius sighed.

"This is not a dynastic marriage Marcus! And the Saxons are not a subject people!"

Germanicus sensed a rebuke, but went on with his argument anyway.

"Vortigern hopes that the Saxons will settle the lands they've taken and melt into the population," he reasoned. But the look on Ambrosius' face left no doubt about his view of such naivety.

An area of land enclosed by a loop in the river housed a village. A few immature trees straggled among the round huts, in the middle stood a long hall, and everything was huddled together inside a wooden palisade.

When they dismounted their horses were taken away and the whole party crowded into the chief's hall. A continuous fire burning along a central channel filled the place with smoke and the rafters above their heads were stained black as a result. Marcus fell into a coughing fit as they jostled for a place at the table, and as Ambrosius drew off his gauntlets the chief who'd led them in began to serve food to them with his own hands.

What think you of Vortigern, Mermier?" the duke asked, and the chief spat into the fire.

"May his god curse him for his treachery!" he snorted.

But Marcus was nothing if not stubborn.

"The Celtic chiefs in London don't see it that way!" he told their host, and Ambrosius lent forward.

"Would you say they're content with their leader and their new queen?"

he enquired wearily.

"No, but when Vortigern's plans for peace come to fruition..."

"They won't!" Ambrosius retorted impatiently, "as Hengist's brother Horsa is already gathering troops along the River Medway which marks the boundary between Saxon territory and the lands they've yet to conquer."

This was news to Marcus and his eyebrows shot up.

"Does Vortigern know about this?" he asked, and the duke turned down the corners of his mouth.

"No doubt his spies have told him... but perhaps he chooses to ignore them?"

"Will there be battle?" the younger man demanded eagerly, and Ambrosius nodded.

"There will indeed!" he smiled. "There'll be war, and I'll make it if Vortigern doesn't!"

"Will Vortigern support you?" was the next question, and the duke stroked his chin.

"Perhaps not," he admitted, "but his sons will. The eldest is a good soldier and he'll bring some of the chiefs with him."

As they lay waiting for sleep Marcus recounted his conversation with the duke to Galarius.

"How can Vortigern fight the Saxons with Rowena waiting for him at home?" he whispered, and a tired voice came back to him from the darkness.

"Beckoning him to her bed?" Galarius enquired scornfully. It was too dark to glare at the weasel, and anyway this wasn't a sensitive spot any more Marcus had discovered.

Next day they entered the marshes, reining their horses on a spur jutting out into the bog before descending. There was nothing but coarse grass and pools of stagnant water as far as the eye could see, no road and no clear water for a boat.

Then a dirty little man with blackened teeth arrived at the head of the column and Ambrosius waived him in between them.

"This is Callidus, a man much valued by the chief whose hospitality we enjoyed last night," he explained. And Marcus, who hadn't enjoyed the hospitality one bit rubbed his smarting eyes.

The newcomer was scratching himself vigorously and grinning.

"I'm one of the few men with knowledge of the ways!" he boasted.

"What ways?" Marcus grunted as he peered across the marshes, and

Ambrosius smiled.

"There are ways here I assure you," he confided. "I've travelled them myself many times." And Marcus nodded unhappily as they set off. But Romulus was uneasy and tried to pull back.

As they moved into single file Ambrosius leant back in the saddle and spoke over his shoulder.

"There are causeways through these marshes built by the folk who lived here before the conquest." he explained. "They sited their villages on platforms of wood and reeds, and as the waters rose they threw on more staves. The villages were abandoned long ago," he added, "but the paths remain."

"Where exactly are we heading?" Marcus asked uneasily, and behind him Galarius chuckled. No doubt he'd been this way before too, his master suspected, and the duke seemed amused too.

"Never fear, we'll arrive before darkness," he assured them.

"Arrive where? Marcus muttered to himself, hoping fervently that his superior was right as he tried to smile at their infested guide.

Romulus whinnied and shied when they came to the slatted wooden road, but tucked in behind Ambrosius' mare things were better. He kept his head down from then on and there were no more displays of temperament.

Here and there the wooden slats had rotted and the causeway was threatening to sink under the slime. The rushes hemming them in were peeping between the boards, and moss had made the surface treacherous. They could hear the frogs croaking in the reeds, and now and then a water fowl rose in alarm before sweeping away across the bullrushes.

As a side avenue led off into hazel scrub Marcus saw how important Callidus was to them, as taking a disused route would be disastrous. They'd have no room to turn, and there was no possibility of hauling a frightened horse out of the sucking mire. The morass on either side lay thick black and frightening, but Callidus took every fork in the path in his stride.

"Many of these tracks are disused and sunk, to take the wrong one would be fatal and I alone know the ways!" he called back to them in his sing song voice, and Marcus heard Ambrosius grunt as they plodded on. Another causeway went off to the right, rotten with age it disappeared into the bog before it had gone a dozen feet.

Ambrosius grew more talkative as the afternoon wore on, but though he liked Marcus he couldn't trust him till he knew him better.

"Why did you go to the camp of Hengist?" he asked, turning in the saddle to look back, and Marcus shrugged.

"We were uncertain of what to do next, and I wanted to learn more about the Saxons before coming to Winchester."

"The intelligence you gathered was welcome, but it was foolish of you to venture so close to the invaders and you might have been killed."

"Galarius did warn me," the younger man admitted sheepishly, "but we went anyway." He was shrugging uncomfortably and Ambrosius laughed.

"Youth is ever foolish, and one day the memory of your impetuosity will make you sweat!"

"I can already see how risky it was," Marcus conceded as the duke pointed ahead.

"To the south lies the port where I'm building my fleet!" he announced proudly, and Marcus' mouth fell open.

"Why on earth do you need a fleet?" he demanded, "surely you have enough to do fighting the Saxons?" But Ambrosius shook his head.

"It doesn't matter how many times we drive them back as they'll keep coming!" he called. "And before we go any further perhaps I should tell you a little about the Celts my friend, as you don't seem to have the measure of them yet. They're not an easy people to understand," the duke continued. "Most of the nobles are nominally Christian, and the ones who stick to the teachings can't drive out the invaders as that would mean killing them, not just in battle but in their villages, women and children too. And as for the Celts in the far west, they don't care what happens elsewhere as they're convinced that the Saxons will never threaten their lands. Yes...the natives are a mixed bunch," the duke reflected quietly. Then turning again in the saddle he looked questioningly at the man following. "You'll have read Ceasar's 'Conquest of Gaul' I expect?"

This was a rhetorical question Marcus knew, as Ambrosius was referring to the most important treatise ever written on military matters, and all Roman officers were required to read it.

"I see that you have!" the duke laughed, noting Marcus' affronted expression. "And you'll know about the so called 'Alleluia victory?'"

"An ancestor of mine was involved I believe," Marcus answered sheepishly. "They say he led one of the rescue attempts, and won a great victory... through good generalship!"

"How could it be otherwise?" Ambrosius laughed, turning again in the saddle, "but the story of the battle has been distorted by legend hasn't it?"

"What does the legend say?" Marcus muttered, though he knew the answer already, and Ambrosius' mouth twisted in distaste.

"This illustrates the Celtic character as well as anything!" he asserted almost angrily, "as when the bards tell the story they exaggerate as they do in all their tales. They tell their uneducated listeners that all the Christians had to do was shout 'Alleluia' and at once the enemy fled! Perhaps they did shout," he added cynically, "but as the Saxons are pagan, Christian exhortations mean nothing to them." Then he looked back again. "Do you understand?"

"Yes, you're telling me that they've erased the real battle from their minds and pretend it was a miracle performed by their god," Marcus nodded.

"Exactly," Ambrosius replied knitting his brows. "The Christian religion has a concept they call sin, and as it's a sin to disbelieve anything the missionaries tell them, and failure to believe denies them the gift of life everlasting... well you can guess what happens... The converts strain their credibility to breaking point... and they're willing to believe the impossible if necessary."

Both men were having to raise their voices, as the moaning of the rushes had risen to a roar following the arrival of a strong wind and the duke was becoming hoarse.

"Dedicated Christians can't be effective soldiers as they're told that killing is evil, and though your kinsman Germanus won the battle by the usual means they've made his victory into a miracle to excuse him."

"But the Celts fight among themselves all the time!" Marcus shouted back, and Ambrosius agreed.

"Julius Ceasar met the Celts and described them in his writings."

The wind seemed to be dying as they left the marshes and with relief Ambrosius lowered his voice.

"In his records our greatest soldier described the Celts as having a society strictly stratified under a ruling aristocracy," he explained. "The chiefs have always used religion to intimidate their inferiors, and now they've got Christian teachings on their side it will be even easier."

Then the duke's grey eyes narrowed.

"That's why I'm building ships, as the only way to save these islands is to restore the rule of Rome."

"Surely that's not possible?" Marcus ventured, but the duke shook his head.

"Anything is possible, and I intend to take my army to Gaul and fight for a strong emperor."

"Will that please Vortigern?" Marcus asked, and Ambrosius shrugged.

"Perhaps not, but when the Saxons attack again he'll see that I'm right."

They rode in silence for a while as Marcus tried to digest this confusing information, then as the sun began to set they saw the silhouette of hillfort against the horizon.

"Our destination!" Ambrosius called pointing to the rocky outcrop.

The hill was well fortified and Marcus could see a tower and other buildings on the top. Stone strengthened defence works towered above their heads as they climbed, and bulwarks twenty feet high confined their narrow path. Wooden bridges crossed ditches between the ramparts, which were arranged in a spiral pattern. And every gate was guarded till they reached the plateau, where an area of about three acres had been laid out with round houses a long hall and a small church.

"What do you think?" Ambrosius called as he dismounted. "The place has been abandoned since the conquest but we're repairing the defences," he added with a wave at the scaffolding and platforms.

"These defences will enable you to repel the Saxons? Marcus enquired doubtfully, and his commander nodded.

"They'll keep them at bay for a while," the duke replied, and Marcus sensed suppressed resignation.

"You'll succeed where others have failed?" the younger man demanded, but the duke just laughed.

"I intend to succeed, and believe the gods will smile on my efforts!" he stated flatly. And though Marcus found himself wondering about Ambrosius' optimism he badly wanted to share it.

"Do the Christians support you, knowing you're a pagan?" he asked, and Ambrosius smiled.

"They know nothing of the sort!" he laughed, "as I'm a Roman and it's my nature to have more than one god."

"So you're a Christian after all?" Marcus felt betrayed, but Ambrosius shook his head.

"I don't mind attending their churches now and then, and my daughter has lessons from the monks as they have learning and good Latin," he smiled. "But what goes on here," he murmured holding his hand over his heart, "is none of their business!"

CHAPTER VIII
The Night of the Long Knives

After inspecting the hill forts they travelled to Portus Adurni where Ambrosius was building his navy, and Marcus saw several completed galleys as well as others lying half finished in cradles. But their journey was cut short when a rider from Winchester arrived with news that Horsa was moving his army west. The campaign was about to begin in earnest it seemed.

Preparations for war were well advanced when Marcus saw the girl again. He was watching a century drilling in the barrack square when Ambrosius entered the compound. Behind him trailed a number of scribes and the usual presenters of petitions, but no one paid any attention to them.

Then at the great man's side he saw her. Her extreme youth and almost transparent beauty held his eye. He was so enthralled that he failed to give the command to turn, and as the ordered ranks descended into confusion and the men grinned at his embarrassment a decurian came up to him.

"You've not seen the lady Helena before?" the man enquired, and scowling hard Germanicus started shouting at the men.

Galarius would know who she was he was sure, but the little man just shrugged his narrow shoulders.

"It's hard to say exactly who she is," he muttered. "Some say she's a relative of the duke, but others say something else entirely!" And Germanicus could guess what the men were saying, they were assuming she was Ambrosius' mistress.

Next day Marcus saw her again. She was tall for a woman and carried herself like a Patrician. Slim and long legged, her dress pinched in above the waist emphasised surprisingly full breasts. A sliver of transparent veil hung over one shoulder, and he glimpsed the tips of silver slippers under her hem.

A prickling sensation starting at the back of his neck progressed down his spine to climax in an involuntary shudder, and his eyes followed the girl with wilful independence. Then he swallowed and turning away wet his lips. It seemed he'd been holding his breath, and a cough of embarrassment accompanied his glance at Galarius who was still staring fixedly at the girl.

Marcus turned back to the window just as she looked up. She was speaking to the old woman at her side, and after a moment the crone looked up too and nodded. He couldn't see very well from this distance, but he fancied the girl's eyes were a wonderful cornflower blue. Then she turned away and he watched fascinated as she disappeared, her pale red hair moving gently as she walked.

"She's one to remember... but not one to covet I think!" Galarius advised, and taking a deep breath Marcus swallowed again.

"She's a beauty... did you find out who she is?" he whispered, and Galarius chuckled.

"Aye..." The weasel eyes had narrowed and the little man was extending the pause for an unreasonably long time Marcus thought.

"Get on with it!" he snapped, and Galarius shrugged.

"That, centurion, is the daughter of Ambrosius!" he chortled.

"How old is she?" Marcus asked whistling softly, and Galarius turned down the corners of his mouth.

"No more than fifteen... still a child and her father dotes on her."

Marcus felt somehow cheated.

"It will be years before she's ready for marriage!" he groaned, and placing a finger to the side of his nose Galarius moved closer.

"You haven't heard everything yet!" he hissed, and with his mouth half open Marcus waited. "They say she's promised already, to a Celt by the name of Pendragon." the weasel informed his master lifting disbelieving brows. "She has Celtic blood it seems, as according to the rumours the duke became enamoured of the daughter of a petty king and stole her from a nunnery! So they say!"

"How much of this comes from your tavern friends?" Marcus demanded contemptuously, and Galarius nodded.

"All of it!" he grinned, and Marcus thumped the table.

"Do they say that Ambrosius ravished a... a... nun?" he asked more quietly, but Galarius shook his head vigorously.

"No, they say he fell in love with her and somehow smuggled her out of her convent."

Germanicus was holding his breath again as the story unfolded.

"The duke took her to his fort at Dinas Emrys in the north west," Galarius whispered across the table, "and she was never seen again! Some say she died in childbirth, some say an enchantment took her, and others say the nuns had her murdered for breaking her vows!" Then the little man returned to his usual matter of fact tone. " Oh, and Ambrosius kept the child."

The duke had sent for Germanicus, and as he entered his commander's office Marcus saw maps and lists of requisitions littering the tables. Quartermasters finalising arrangements for the baggage trains rubbed shoulders with armourers and horse traders. And Celtic warriors loitered suspiciously, tipping their heads to look up at the wall paintings and whispering to each other. The scenes so familiar to Marcus were strange magic to them, and now and then one reached up to touch and make sure the military giants couldn't come to life and challenge them.

As Germanicus pushed through the crowd he paused to watch the demonstration of a new cavalry lance. Then Ambrosius looked up, and though his face was tired the excitement in his eyes made him seem like a boy again.

"The lack of organisation is a mirage I assure you, and every man knows exactly what he's doing!" he laughed, and Germanicus was happy to take his word.

"You sent for me sir," the younger man smiled, and Ambrosius nodded.

"I have a special task for you," he confided, and Marcus lent over the map.

The country was unfamiliar, but the rivers, hills and woods were clear enough and he knew that this was the battle plan.

"What part will the cavalry play sir?" he asked excitedly, feasting his eyes on the map as he estimated just where his unit could be put to best use. But Ambrosius was talking over his shoulder to a fat merchant, and the man had increased the price of the rations he was contracted to supply it seemed.

But at last the duke turned back to the table.

"You won't be involved," he frowned without looking up, and Marcus' jaw dropped. "I have something more important for you to do than leading cavalry into battle," Ambrosius went on as he lifted his head, "and though I don't expect you to be pleased, I expect you to obey!" Marcus bent his head, and when Ambrosius threw the list of provisions aside the fat man grabbed it and hurried away.

Marcus followed the duke to his private apartments, and after closing the doors Ambrosius motioned him to sit.

"Your mission is not just dangerous, as it requires the skill of a diplomat as well as courage," his commander told him. But this information failed to lift the gloom and as Marcus stared at his hands Ambrosius patted his shoulder.

"Of course I can choose someone else if the challenge is too much for you..." he sighed, and Marcus looked up suddenly.

95

"Someone else?" he repeated.

"Yes, another ambassador to travel to London."

"But I've only just come from London!" Marcus protested with boyish disappointment, and Ambrosius smiled.

"Then the road will be familiar and you'll travel it all the faster!"

The elder man had seated himself by the window to watch his battalions drilling.

"I want you to go to London because Vortigern is conspiring with his father-in-law Hengist," he grunted, and at this Marcus cheered up a mite.

"Does Vortigern know your plans?" he asked, and the duke shrugged.

"There are always spies in a place like this and no doubt he's aware of my intentions."

"You think he's passing the information to Hengist?" Marcus whistled, and the duke smiled sadly.

"I don't share your faith in human nature Marcus, as life has taught me hard lessons and I trust no one." Then he frowned. "And as young men don't know everything they must accept the advice of their elders!" he added lifting his brows in question.

"I ask your pardon sire,..." Marcus stuttered, and Ambrosius nodded.

"You're disappointed and can't be blamed for that, but this mission will involve more danger and cunning than leading cavalry. And in any case we don't know when the battle will take place, and you could be back in the lines by then," he added encouragingly.

An aid was lurking in the background and Ambrosius beckoned him forward.

"Make sure this officer is briefed and has everything he needs," the duke told the man, then his attention returned to Marcus. "I want you to take your own men with you... ten should be enough. And though I want Vortigern to treat you with respect, he mustn't feel intimidated as we don't want him to hide his doings."

They covered the ground between Winchester and London quickly, but Vortigern seemed suspicious that they'd returned so soon and immediately summoned Germanicus to present himself before the high council.

The huge room was dark, and as Marcus waited by the door for his eyes to become accustomed to the gloom he assessed the scene. Either side of the long table sat the Celtic chiefs, and at the far end he saw Vortigern. The old man seemed lost in thought, but eventually he rose.

"Come forward Roman, I hear we welcome you this time as an envoy of Ambrosius?" he croaked, and Germanicus bowed stiffly.

"The duke has given me that honour sir," he replied, advancing to stand by the king's chair as the others glowered at him. And when Vortigern sat back Marcus noticed that he'd grown even thinner.

"You were a wandering mercenary when we last met," the king murmured, steepling his fingers, and Marcus nodded.

"That is so sir," he agreed.

"And now you've pledged your sword to Ambrosius?"

"I've pledged it to the cause sir."

"This cause... is it my cause?" Vortigern demanded with a grin at his nobles. "Is it our cause?" And as the chiefs glowered even harder Marcus took a deep breath.

"Is driving out the invaders not your cause sir?" he asked, and Vortigern nodded unhappily.

"Mmmm Yes... I suppose it is." he mumbled looking expectantly along the table, and one of the chiefs stood up.

"We don't trust Ambrosius, as he seeks the return of Roman rule!" the man asserted, and as murmurs of agreement ran along the lines Marcus shrugged.

"The duke may wish to re-establish the order of Rome... so would any sensible man were it in his power. But Rome is gone for ever, and the only domination we need fear is Saxon."

"You exaggerate surely?" Vortigern protested with a little laugh, but Germanicus shook his head.

"I don't exaggerate sir!" he replied hardening his voice, "and if your forces are not allied with the duke's all will be lost."

To his amazement laughter rippled through the company at this point, then the chief who'd spoken before stood up again.

"That's what Ambrosius wants us to think!" he grunted as he fingered his dagger, and waiving for an extra chair Vortigern directed Marcus to sit.

"You know my dear wife do you not young man?" he enquired soothingly, and Marcus nodded as a steel fist gripped his innards. "Her coming has been a great blessing..." the king murmured affectionately, "and she has been the bringer of peace."

"Yes sir," Marcus grunted trying to sound convinced, and Vortigern nodded wisely.

"My marriage to the daughter of Hengist has been a blessing to me, and it will be a blessing to my people," he intoned like a priest, and Marcus tried to stop his lips curling.

"Are peace plans afoot sir?" the Roman asked, and Vortigern leant forward confidentially, as they were discussing something to his liking now and he could relax.

"My wife's father and uncle will be arriving soon to sign a treaty of peace!" he smiled, "what do you think of that?"

"I'm most happy....." Marcus lied trying to summon the appropriate expression, and Vortigern patted his arm.

"Ah, but will Ambrosius be happy?" he sighed.

"I can't speak for him sir," came the answer, and the king looked away uneasily.

"Then perhaps you'd better discover his plans... as I don't want them to interfere with mine." With a waive of the arm Marcus was dismissed, and as the door closed behind him he could hear them arguing.

Galarius left for Winchester before dawn with the news of Hengist and Horsa's imminent arrival in London, as this would change everything. The Saxons were pressing against their boundaries in Kent, and if Ambrosius was to drive them back he needed the help of the Celtic nobles and the royal faction. But if Vortigern made peace with the invaders the duke would find himself at war with both Saxons and Celts.

Rowena had been keeping to her rooms, but she appeared to welcome her father and paused as she passed Marcus at table.

"How fare you Roman?" she smiled, and Marcus scowled at her.

"Well enough madam!" he grunted.

"When tonight is over we may be together again," she whispered leaning over him. And this was a statement not a question, Marcus knew.

As he watched her walk towards the high table the Saxon princess seemed more beautiful than ever, as her time in London had smoothed the rough edges. She'd improved her way of dressing, taken on a little of the culture of the place and was more at ease.

In the cause of good relations Vortigern had mingled the two camps, and Saxons found themselves sitting between Celts, Celts between Saxons.

Marcus watched with fascination as Hengist took his seat, and Horsa was here too he noticed. The likeness was striking, though Horsa was younger and a little shorter. But their heavy heads of yellow hair and green eyes marked them out as brothers.

"My Love!" As Vortigern started his speech he was bending over Rowena. "It is indeed an honour to welcome your father and your kin to my... to our court." And everyone cheered except Vortigern's two sons, and of course Marcus, who was watching Hengist intently. The old war horse seemed so harmless, and could he really be here to make peace? the Roman asked himself as Vortigern continued his welcome oration.

"This land stretches far on all sides, and as there's enough for us all why should we fight?" Then his tone changed and his face became sad. "But there are some," he sighed turning his eyes reproachfully on Marcus, "who wish to continue the war that has taken so many of our comrades from us." He was glancing nervously at his sons, and they were both staring defiantly back.

Nevertheless, after a bout of coughing Vortigern gathered himself.

"Ambrosius would carry on this war and re-establish the power of Rome," he continued wearily. And as cries of "No!" and "Never!" came from the hall he lifted a hand heavy with rings. "But I'll not allow it friends!" he assured them. And again everyone cheered except Marcus and the king's sons.

Germanicus was watching the faces around him, and something was wrong he sensed. Shifting in his seat he tilted his head back as if scenting the tension in the air, and it was then he noticed how the Saxons were eying each other. Taught as bow strings they were waiting for something he suspected, and rising to his feet he walked slowly to the door.

When he looked back the impression was even stronger, and though the Celts were drinking deeply and had started to eat, not so the Saxons. They were sipping from their goblets now and then he observed, but their eyes were moving constantly, flitting first to the face of their leader then back to their comrades. It was as if Vortigern wasn't there, and the Saxons seemed to be ignoring him.

As the tired voice droned on Marcus gripped the hilt of his sword and checked his dagger. Then he looked again at the Celts, noting that of the two hundred or so present most were unarmed. Vortigern had asked him not to bear arms 'as a sign of respect to the Saxons' he recalled. But the Saxons were armed to the teeth, and every blonde man in the hall seemed to be resting his hand on his weapon he observed as he tested the straps securing breastplate to backplate and Vortigern came to the end of his speech.

The British were lolling in their seats as the wine took effect, and as Vortigern sat down they joined him in a toast to Hengist. The Saxon king had risen to his feet still laughing at Vortigern's parting wit, and Marcus watched transfixed as he lifted his sword.

"To your weapons!" Hengist roared. That was all.

Suddenly in every part of the hall Saxons were on there feet long knives in their hands, and as the face of Vortigern froze in horror Rowena was ushered away.

She was showing no surprise, and for what seemed like an age the Celts sat staring in disbelief at their drinking companions of a few minutes before. Many were not to rise again as they were skewered where they sat, the surprise permanently etched on their faces.

Germanicus set off down the hall, and as the smoke from the torches swirled round him stumbled over bodies and struggling men. When he passed the seat he'd occupied a few minutes before he saw the man he'd been exchanging pleasantries with sprawled back in his chair. Mouth hanging open his eyes still held the amazement that had entered them an instant before he died. His tunic was pulled apart and a deep valley traced the path of a knife down his body. The abdomen stood open spilling its snake-like contents, but Germanicus pressed on, pushing the Saxons aside and stopping to fight only when forced to do so.

When he saw Rowena almost at the opposite door the old question entered his mind. Did he want to kill her or protect her? And as she didn't need his protection why was he fighting his way towards her? He didn't know, he just wanted to shake her that was all he knew.

Jumping onto the dais he kicked a chair away and looking up saw Horsa smiling down at him. But when he tried to push the Saxon with his shoulder to give himself more room his efforts had no effect, as his opponent was built like an oak tree. Horsa's green eyes lacked the humour Marcus had seen in Hengist's. They were hard and intense, and for a moment the two men glared at each other, each waiting for the other to make the first move.

Horsa struck first, a wide sweeping lunge with his knife, and jumping back in time Marcus ran in with his short sword. They were well matched, and as they eyed each other the din from the hall seemed to recede. Then one of the British chiefs fell on Horsa knocking him sideways. He fell with his right arm against a heavy table, and as a muffled grunt issued from between his clenched teeth the weapon fell from his hand.

The Celt had fallen to the floor dead and Marcus stepped over him, but though Horsa was recovering fast the Roman was distracted by the scene unfolding behind his enemy.

He'd recognised the Celt who'd spoken up at the meeting of the council, and though the man had looked on Ambrosius as his enemy then he'd die knowing the truth. Following his opponent's eyes Horsa saw his warriors holding the chief against the wall, and as torches cast their shifting glow on the scene it seemed to merge with the mural behind it.

Great Caesar stood in the centre with the bodies of Gauls all around, and in a circle about him lounged armoured Romans in poses of victorious self satisfaction. But Marcus saw the picture for only half a second before his attention was drawn back to the execution of the Celt.

Rising above the noise from below his screams tore the air. He wore no armour, had no knife, and as laughing Saxons pinned him to the wall they pulled his tunic away. Then a particularly huge warrior bellowed to the crowd and all heads turned.

"See us draw the eagle comrades!"

"The eagle, the eagle..." came the screaming reply, repeated over and over by the Saxon warriors in the hall.

The British below were silent either through death or terror, and as the Saxons chanted the phrase Marcus remembered the first time he'd seen Rowena. The chants of her father's men as she entered the hall at Reculver seemed to merge with their chanting now as the huge Saxon put the point of his blade to the back of his victim's neck. The noise, the memory, the smoke and confusion were making Marcus' head spin. The rhythm was increasing, then the din stopped suddenly and there followed a moment of absolute silence. When the knife went in the head fell forward, and with mechanical deliberateness the huge Saxon dragged his blade down the spine.

Marcus had heard about the practice of 'drawing the eagle' and the horror fascinated him as one by one the ribs sprang out from the backbone. The noise they made came as a surprise, and if he'd expected anything it was different to this. The sound was like a heavy bow string flexing in practice. "Thrum!" it seemed to say, again and again till the cage was fully open. Then to Marcus' horror he saw that the heart was still beating, purposeful and unaware as it went on with its life's work.

The jab to the neck hadn't killed him, the battle hardened Roman realised, feeling the gall rising in his throat. Amazingly the lungs still filled and emptied, and could it really be possible that the man was still breathing? Then the Saxon plunged his knife into the obedient heart and the hypnotic spell was broken. They let the Celt fall and the spectacle was over.

As the noise in the hall reverted to its former level Marcus turned to look for Horsa, and saw him heading for the rear door with Hengist. Between them hung the limp figure of Vortigern, and when Marcus made to follow Hengist turned.

His smile of recognition could not have been warmer.

"Marcus my friend, it's good to see you. You still live, and I'm pleased to see it!" he boomed. Horsa was looking blank, and Marcus felt his jaw fall open as taking his arm Hengist pushed him through the door after Vortigern.

The corridor was darker than the banqueting hall, and though torches hung along the walls at intervals long patches of gloom stretched between them. Horsa was pushing him now, and it was then he saw that Vortigern was not only alive but uninjured.

Hengist was speaking again, this time angrily.

"Get out of my sight Roman or I'll be forced to kill you!" he barked," and Marcus backed away, keeping his sword in front of him. "For the sake of my daughter's fancy I'd rather not!" the Saxon king added almost appealingly, holding up a thick finger as if lecturing a naughty child. Then Horsa lunged forward suddenly with his long knife before retreating again laughing.

They could so easily have killed him, and as the thought of Ambrosius, heading this way even now for all he knew, flashed across Marcus' mind he turned and ran. Behind him Hengist's laughter echoed along the corridor and the Roman fancied he could still hear it as he approached the walls of Winchester.

All his men had escaped as they'd not been present at the feast. But when the noise alerted them they'd saddled the horses and were waiting when he emerged. No one followed them, and could it be that Hengist wanted Ambrosius to know about the massacre? Marcus wondered.

They were hurried to Ambrosius' quarters and the duke came straight from his bed wrapped in a robe. He was followed by the girl, and at once Marcus' suspicions returned. Why was she here? he wondered as his tired eyes fixed on the grey green wrap that enveloped her. Like the fingers of moss that cloak ancient trees it seemed to cover her completely, and all he could see was a pale face with eager parted lips. She was watching as if they were unaware of her, and could it be that a mere woman understood the urgency of his visit? Marcus wondered, trying hard not to stare.

Her eyes were large and heavy lidded, her lips full, her chin receding her nose straight. And her father seemed happy for her to stay as sweating and mud smeared Marcus told his story.

"I thought as much... but perhaps it's for the best," Ambrosius frowned when he'd finished, "at least the Celts know now who their enemy is." And Marcus looked away, knowing that he'd been wrong and the duke had been right.

Weeks passed before they set out for the east, as the duke was waiting for better weather. Before leaving he called Marcus to his study, and as they'd grown close over the last weeks the younger man no longer felt any conflict of loyalty.

"There's something I want to tell you," Ambrosius began, smoothing the folds of his toga over his arm very deliberately before easing himself onto a couch. Then passing a hand across his mouth he rubbed his shaven chin. "I've no family other than my daughter," he confided looking up, "but the folk at my fortress in the north west owe me allegiance. They're my mother's people," he explained, shifting uneasily. "There's a king whose fortress is close to mine, they call him Maelgwyn..." the duke went on thoughtfully. And Marcus frowned wondering what was to come.

After sitting with his head in his hands for several minutes Ambrosius got up and sitting down at the table filled his goblet.

"This king... Maelgwyn... has a son," the duke went on as if searching for words.

"Yes sir, the king has a son?" Marcus nodded.

"He has a son, and I've promised my daughter to him!" The words rushed out in a flood and the duke lent back as if relieved they were said. Then he shrugged. "I've seen your eyes on her Marcus... but it cannot be."

"What do you mean... it cannot be?" Marcus stuttered, and Ambrosius, who was clearly embarrassed lifted his palms appealingly.

"I'm sorry my boy... obviously I'd rather she married you, and I know Helena would prefer it..."

As the duke's voice trailed away a little spring of joy spurted in Marcus' heart. Helena would prefer him? Had the duke really said that? he asked himself. The fact that she was betrothed to another man meant nothing now, nothing compared to what he'd just heard. And could it possibly be that the lovely Helena loved him?

As Marcus would kill a whole tribe of Celts to win Helena he wasn't inclined to worry about one, and in spite of himself he found himself laughing in the duke's face.

"I'll kill any man who tries to take her from me!" he declared joyously as the confidence flooded over him, and Ambrosius lifted his hand.

"Hold on now.... as she's not yours how can any man take her from you?" The duke seemed amused but Marcus was agitated.

"Then give her to me, am I not worthy of your daughter... worthy to be your successor?" His voice had slowed, and by the end of the sentence had turned to a whisper. His confidence had deserted him, and at that moment the young soldier would have given anything to take back those last words.

But his commanding officer wasn't offended it seemed, on the contrary the duke was nodding as he passed his hand across his eyes.

"That's not the issue Marcus, don't you understand.... I've given my word! I need Maelgwyn to defend my lands... and my fortress at Dinas Emrys will be lost if I offend him."

"I'll be loyal to you sir, but I'm determined to marry Helena!" Marcus was surprised at how strong his voice sounded, and it was strange how his resolve had come together all at once when he thought he might lose something that he had now decided he wanted more than anything. "But she is very young..." he murmured still frowning hard, "and I didn't think she'd be ready for marriage yet awhile..."

"She was promised as a baby," Ambrosius sighed. "I needed allies – Maelgwyn seemed ideal, and if the arrangement proved unsatisfactory or another man appeared... then I assumed he'd take her, as I took... Not that I gave the long term implications much thought," he concluded vaguely.

Then as if to change the topic he grasped the map.

"Shall we agree to resolve this matter when we've dealt with our other problems?" he smiled, and Marcus nodded.

"Ah, the Saxons!" he murmured. The two men clasped arms, the matter of Helena would be decided another day, and first the Saxon threat must be dealt with.

As they skirted the south of London they encountered a band of Celts from the north west, and it was here that Marcus met Helena's betrothed. His rival was several years older than him the Roman noted, and very proud. His dark intense face bore no tattoos, and Marcus thought him a little on the short side. But the lack of height was more than made up by the splendour of Pendragon's dress and armour, and the usual mail coat was replaced by an embossed cuirass of the Roman kind.

Still unaware that he had a rival Pendragon nevertheless paid close attention to Marcus as they ate in Ambrosius' tent, and he watched Helena too. She was to go north the next day with a party of her would-be husband's men from Gwynedd, and her father would follow after the battle if the gods allowed.

As Marcus watched the lover at his wooing he was trying to predict the events about to unfold. And on the basis of what he'd do were he Ambrosius' prospective son-in-law, he decided that Pendragon would leave the field as soon as possible and hurry north to make Helena his wife. So he tried to think of a way to keep her in the south.

That night Marcus walked with her among the trees, while high above in the ink black sky the seven points of Ursa Major rode the clouds. Pulling her cloak close Helena was looking up at him as if waiting for something, and it had to be now he knew. So drawing her into a corner out of the wind he pulled her to him and whispered into her hair."

"I hadn't intended to speak so soon..." then he paused as he didn't know what to say next.

"Tell me what's on your mind Marcus," Helena urged as if reading his thoughts. As he looked down at her in the darkness her young eager face seemed to be appealing to him, so he pulled her closer and kissed her gently on the lips. They tasted of apples. Then he remembered her father.

"If your father finds us here...?" but Helena shook her head.

"Perhaps he's happy for you to be here with me?" she suggested, "and perhaps he wishes...." She'd buried her face in Marcus' chest and the words came up muffled. "My father made a promise and he won't break it, but I believe he'd not be sorry if you broke it for him." She was gazing up at him, her wide blue eyes waiting for his answer as if it were the solution to an intriguing party puzzle. But Marcus' mind was spinning... if could only he get her away... he was thinking.

Bending to kiss her again he marvelled at her warmth, and as she leant on him her hands pressed into his waist.

"I've never kissed a man before... except my father," she told him closing her eyes and lifting her lips for a repeat. And Marcus obliged, pressing his mouth onto hers more forcefully this time. Then he held her away and took her face in his hands.

"Do you love me Helena?" he whispered, and her eyes met his.

"Yes I love you Marcus, do you love me?" and he smiled.

"Yes, I think I do."

Late that night when the camp was asleep Galarius rode out with a party of horsemen. He carried a pillion and was heading for Winchester.

CHAPTER IX
the first Battle

Hengist and Horsa made for the Medway at Aylesford, and on the eastern bank ranged their army. Many of their warriors had taken part in the slaughter in London, and they were joined by others from every part of the conquered lands. After fighting their way across the the river they intended to spread out in all directions, eventually joining Aelwulf and his comrades who were carving out the land they called Anglia in the east.

Ambrosius sat quietly while Pendragon raged, as this was serious and the Celt was threatening to take his soldiers home. As the canvass walls flapped in the stiff wind and smoke from the brazier surged this way and that, the duke just shrugged. He was refusing to take responsibility for his daughter's disappearance, and his expression suggested injured innocence as he gazed up at his would-be son-in-law.

"I'm her father, no one values her safety more than me!" he protested throwing another log into the glowing mass, "and as I share your concern Pendragon, we must pray she's unharmed."

But the dark young man wouldn't accept that Helena might be in danger.

"Don't try to fool me!" he scoffed, "I believe you wanted to break your promise to my father."

How can you say that?" Ambrosius demanded opening his grey eyes wide, "do you really believe that I'd place my own child in danger?" He was waiving his arm somewhat unconvincingly, and Pendragon continued to glare as he loomed over the table.

"I'll bring her back lord duke, never fear!" the Celt vowed swinging his heavy cloak arrogantly behind him as he turned to leave, but Ambrosius called him back.

"Is it possible that brave Pendragon fears the coming battle and is looking for an excuse to go home?" the duke demanded, his voice suddenly hard and mocking. And the prince of Gwynedd sprang back eyes flashing. For a moment he stood staring at his commander, then he left the tent motioning his men to follow.

The duke's strategy had worked like a charm, as he was familiar with the sensitive egoes of Celtic nobles. Any suggestion of cowardice was guaranteed to meet with a display of bravado, and what better stage for such a display than the coming battle? he reasoned. After the battle the suitors could fight for the girl, but for now he needed them both.

Horsa strung out his troops at the ford where the river ran wide and shallow, but the duke refused to accept the site and moved his men to a narrower part where no ford straddled the stream and the water was deeper. Nevertheless Ambrosius began to move his cavalry across, and skirmishing started as soon as the first horse and rider made to struggle up the opposite bank.

The fighting continued as a stream of Saxons from the main body ran along the marshy bank to join in. But the cavalry under Marcus Germanicus was surprisingly manoeuverable, and dancing back and forth in the shallows inflicted a good deal of damage on the land hugging welcoming party. Soon enough were ashore to separate the Saxons from their reinforcements, and the British infantry was crossing now to relieve the cavalry.

Pendragon was still on the western bank as Germanicus led a charge to scatter one of the Saxon warbands, and as the Germans liked to fight in family groups this made the Romans work easier. Like dogs herding sheep their horsemen hived off one section of the Saxon army after another. Then the foot soldiers moved in, steadily reaping along the enemy line as the cavalry used their lances to rob the opposition of their shields. But Marcus soon reverted to his favourite weapon, the short sword, or gladius as it was known.

Wheeling and turning Romulus ran rings round the English. The division between his flanks and the legs of his rider seemed to melt as Pendragon watched, and as animal and man merged into one fighting unit he turned away, impatient to lead his men across and join the battle.

Vortimer, Prince of Britain, the grandson of Magnus Maximus, was met by Horsa as he came out of the water, and jumping from his horse he unsheathed his sword and bared his teeth. As they fought in the shallows each man gained advantage in turn, then Vortimer fell badly and for a moment the huge Saxon towered over him. But Horsa was still vulnerable, and summoning all his strength the Briton forced his sword up into his opponent's groin.

Struggling to his feet as the Saxon fell to his knees Vortimer drove his blade through chainmail and leather into his opponent's abdomen, and Horsa fell back, his bloodstained hands grasping at his wound. When the sword was pulled free he rolled face down in the churning water, and as his livid crimson blood dissolved away, Vortimer who'd lived in awe of him felt a surge of elation.

This was just the beginning! Vortigern's elder son told himself, and if he could kill Horsa he could kill anybody. Then his thoughts turned to his mother Severa, the daughter of the great Magnus Maximus who had wanted to rule the whole Roman world. She'd been replaced and dishonoured by this man's niece Rowena, Vortimer remembered bitterly, and dragging his eyes from Horsa's gently bobbing body he threw his head back and screamed with joy. To his right he sensed movement, but it was too late. The great sword of Octha sliced his head cleanly from his shoulders, Vortimer was dead before Horsa and never saw his killer.

Ambrosius was leading his cavalry away from the water in an attempt to start a Saxon retreat, as when foot soldiers start running battles can turn into routs. But the wild men were brave, and though they'd little experience of cavalry they were learning fast. Stubbornly almost stupidly they were holding their ground, repeatedly swinging their swords and axes at men and horses till the rider was on the ground and the odds were even.

Ambrosius hit the ground hard as his horse fell into a hollow, and blinded for a moment rolled away from the axe threatening him. Then he scrambled to his feet, jabbing with his sword and still holding his spear in his left hand as he faced his opponent. He was matching the man move for move and was unaware of the spear whistling in from the rear.

Ignoring the pain he struck again bringing his opponent to the ground, and when the man was dead he fought on as more Saxons recognised him and tried to win glory by killing him.

The duke could remember only three of the men he'd fought. One who's arm he'd severed, one he'd killed with a blow to the throat, and another who'd broken off to aid a comrade. It was then he realised for the first time that he was growing older. In addition to the pain in his back his sword arm ached abominably and his legs were numb and weak. The next man to challenge him was fresh, his young face wore a calm smile of anticipation and Ambrosius summoned the dregs of his strength.

They sparred for long minutes with little to show on either side, then the Saxon struck lucky with his axe and coming in at the shoulder broke the duke's collar bone. Ambrosius' sword fell useless to the ground and he lay helpless as his enemy came in for the kill.

Then suddenly a horse was above him, and reaching down Germanicus somehow hooked his arm under his commander's limp body. With back-breaking effort he hung on as Romulus dragged the wounded man away, then finding a place of comparative quiet he pulled Ambrosius over his saddle.

After signalling to one of his men the duke was hauled from one horse to the other, and Marcus watched them disappear towards the British lines. Then he set off after the retreating enemy, urging his men to harry their rear as they fled. There was no way of counting the dead and injured on the Saxon side, but after a while the shouting diminished and only the groans of the wounded rose from the place of slaughter.

Taking Romulus to a rise above the marsh Marcus loosed the reins and the horse began to crop grass as if nothing untoward had happened. When the Romans looked out over the plain they could see hundreds of Saxons retreating at a steady run, and behind them came others pulling or carrying the wounded. The few enemy horsemen were now far in the distance, and Marcus could see a man sitting motionless on a great black stallion. Hengist rode a horse like that.... but he couldn't be sure.

Marcus had been been unaware of his wounded thigh till he saw the blood running down Romulus' flank. But as he set off towards the tented camp across the river he sighed with contentment, as he was pleased with himself he had to admit.

Ambrosius knew all about his daughter's disappearance now, and the cold grey eyes had threatened a reckoning after the business of battle was over. But even so the young soldier's mood remained buoyant, and his freckled face had settled into a grin of self satisfaction well before he reached his tent.

Galarius had ridden away from the British camp with some misgivings, as he respected Ambrosius and knew his judgement was superior to that of his master. But he had to follow orders, and the girl seemed willing enough he told himself.

She was terrified of marrying Pendragon that was clear, and though patches of late snow still lay in the hollows and a freezing wind pinched their faces she didn't seem to care.

"Take her to Winchester!" Germanicus had said, "and wait for me there," Galarius recalled as he scanned the surrounding hills. But he'd no way of knowing what lay in the wooded ravines closer to hand, and when a cluster of trees hid his view of the road ahead he became uneasy. His master assumed that Pendragon was as consumed by the prospect of battle as he was, but Galarius knew better.

Suddenly a group of about a dozen horsemen broke cover in front of them, and lifting his hand Galarius signalled his party to stop as they were outnumbered three to one. And though his hand hovered over the hilt of his sword for a moment, the leader of the war band blocking their path shook his head.

"We'll not harm you old man if you hand over the girl!" he called, and Helena, who'd pulled her hood over her face threw it back.

"Do you know who I am?" she demanded, and the leading Celt nodded.

110

"We do indeed madam, you're the betrothed of Pendragon the son of our king, Maelgwyn," he answered, and Galarius recognised the lisping accent of Gwynedd."

"King Maelgwyn has a fortress not far from my father's castle at Dinas Emrys, and he's our ally," Helena put in. Then the leader of the Celts removed his hood and they recognised Pendragon's second in command.

"Where will you take me?" the girl demanded in a confident superior voice, and the man bowed his head.

"To our stronghold lady, where else? And when our master returns we'll celebrate his marriage with him!" he grinned as the others laughed.

"As Germanicus is not here I'm in command!" Helena whispered to Galarius over his shoulder. And though the little man opened his mouth to protest he stopped himself, as the Celt was already pulling at his reins and when he felt a push from behind he allowed himself to slide from the animal without protest.

"No blood must be shed on my account, my father's alliance with Maelgwyn is too important," Helena called as she was led away. "Go back and report to my father, I'll come to no harm," she shouted to their escort. And when Galarius looked to the Celtic leader for confirmation the man flashed him a self satisfied smile.

"We'll guard her with our lives, as our master wouldn't want her damaged!" the Celt laughed as he rode away. And had he made the right decision in not fighting? Galarius asked himself. The resentful stares of his men made him wonder.

Germanicus lay on a couch as his wounds were dressed, while at his feet sat a Celtic slave girl. She was bathing his injured leg with water sprinkled with petals and smiling at him.

"What's your name?" he asked, and though the girl didn't understand she took his hand and kissed it. The gesture was warming, and Marcus was reaching out with the intention of running her dark hair through his fingers when one of Ambrosius' officers entered the tent.

"Is the girl caring for you well?" the man smiled, and Marcus nodded.

"Who is she?" he asked, and the officer shrugged.

"No one rightly knows, but she came over of her own free will, as the Saxons had taken her from her home and made a slave of her. One of the prisoners we took says she was Horsa's woman," he added with a wink, and Germanicus lay back.

"Then she'll need employment till we return her to her family?" he suggested. But his comrade was shaking his head as he lifted the tent flap.

"I know you like to live close to the sword's edge Marcus, but take care,

Ambrosius knows everything that goes on in this camp."

The girl was stroking his brow. How delightful it was to be the wounded hero Marcus thought as she rested her head against his arm. And as sleep overcame him he fancied himself in heaven.

Galarius entered the duke's tent with a good deal of apprehension, to find Ambrosius on his day bed with his arm and neck heavily bandaged. His eyes were closed his face bloodless, but when the guard coughed he opened one eye.

"Well?" he grunted. And the prisoner shuffled his feet.

"I bring bad news sir." Galarius' voice was cracked and when Ambrosius didn't answer he went on. "We were... I was.. I was ordered to take the lady... your daughter, to safety in Winchester."

"Who gave that order?" the duke demanded sitting up suddenly to glare at the old legionary. And Galarius opened his mouth then closed it again without speaking. "I give the orders concerning my daughter, and how could another issue such instructions?" Ambrosius growled, and Galarius hung his head.

"I must obey my master sir..."

"Against the wishes of your commander and his?"

The duke was shaking his head as he struggled painfully to his feet, then he waived his good arm.

"I know your predicament soldier, but you've enough experience to know that my wishes are paramount!" And Galarius nodded shamefaced. "Take him away!" Ambrosius yelled waiving his arm again, and a guard stepped forward.

"No one disobeys my orders!" Galarius heard the duke's parting words as he was pushed none too gently out of the tent.

"What does he mean?" he muttered, and lifting the little man almost off the ground by his hair the guard feigned to decapitate him with the side of his hand.

After struggling into uniform Ambrosius sat down as Germanicus limped in. But though he knew the injured leg was painful the duke left the recently promoted praetor standing.

"I had such hopes for you..." The duke was signing papers, not looking up, and Marcus wondered if one of them was his death warrant.

"Sir I..." But the duke signalled him to be quiet.

"Your man has been taken away for beheading!" Ambrosius grunted, and Germanicus fell to one knee, trying to stifle a cry of pain as he went down.

"Sir... I'm to blame... Galarius was simply obeying my orders."

"What were your orders?" Ambrosius sighed, and Germanicus kept his head down.

"I told him to take Helena..." then Ambrosius looked up and Marcus corrected himself. "The lady... your daughter to...to Winchester for safety."

"Only I have responsibility for my daughter, and I believe she's safer with me, but you question my judgement I gather?"

Marcus wanted to cry, the pain in his leg was contorting his thinking and shaking his head wretchedly he stared at the ground. Minutes went by and eventually Ambrosius came to stand over him.

"I suspected that Pendragon would try to abduct her and she was well guarded," the duke sighed. And Marcus screwed his face in horror as he watched the sandals of his commander circle his complaining body. "You! I did not suspect!" the voice over his head went on icily, "and your servant was able to take her from under the noses of her guards because YOU were trusted! Now Pendragon will demand my agreement to the marriage or I'll lose the support of his people," Ambrosius snorted using his good arm to pull Germanicus to his feet. "It will do your man good to lie under the shadow of death for a while, and I'm resolved to let you suffer too...."

The truth in the words was humiliating, but though the pain still clawed Marcus allowed some hope to creep in.

"Let me go after her sire..." he pleaded.

"In that condition?" As he looked his inferior up and down the duke's expression showed nothing but contempt, and Marcus, who'd been trying to kneel again stopped half way.

"I must sir... I've been a fool and you must let me put things right." But Ambrosius hardened his mouth.

"Only death awaits you if you come back without her!" he grunted, and Marcus nodded. The sweat had gone cold on his face, and as he staggered unaided towards the door dizziness clutched at his consciousness.

Ambrosius was writing again he noticed.

"Send the Celtic slave girl to me," he was telling the guard, "I'll comfort her till she returns to her people."

Marcus couldn't wait for morning before setting out in case the duke changed his mind, so horses were saddled and men chosen. As the wounded man leant painfully against Romulus' flank the seven stars of the plough seemed to wink at him in amusement, and resting his chin on the saddle he traced the path to the pole.

Hearing a sound at his back he began to turn stiffly, and when another rider joined them he saw it was Galarius. The little man's face showed real fear, but Marcus experienced only relief. There'd be no recriminations from him as they were free for the present, and without speaking they set off towards the north west.

It would take at least a week to reach Dinas Emrys, and the more Marcus thought about it the happier he felt. They were heading for the duke's stronghold far from Saxon influence, and to take his mind off the pain he began to make plans. First he'd rescue Helena and marry her of course, and as this was only a dream he was determined not to let worries about Ambrosius spoil his enjoyment. After marrying Helena? Then he'd become commander of the north and lead an army into Caledonia to re-conquer that!

But Galarius was looking reproachfully at him as if reading his thoughts.

"You'd be wise to respect the duke's wishes in future centurion, that's if you want to enjoy another summer let alone the charms of his daughter." The weasel's tone was almost lecturing, but Marcus was too ill to care and resting his head on Romulus' neck he went on dreaming till Galarius gave the order to stop. Ambrosius' camp was some miles behind them now, and they'd be safe till morning at least.

Several hundred Saxon prisoners had been taken at Aylesford. About a hundred were fighting men and the rest were women and children from the pitiful stream of camp followers. No wounded were taken, and if their comrades hadn't got them away they'd been sliced across the throat by the British as they searched the corpses for valuables.

Galarius woke his master as soon as the sun was up, the equinox had passed and the days were growing longer he noted with satisfaction. The hawthorns had been bursting into green as they left the south, but as they were travelling faster than the spring they were soon met by trees still in bud. Marcus was refusing to ride in a litter and his pain was slowing them down. But eventually he was persuaded, and Romulus trailed happily behind remembering the days when his master owned a travelling horse as well as himself!

When they came to a major road they found it grassed over, with the guard posts empty or converted into dwellings. It took several days to reach the midlands, where the land became heavily wooded and the only open ground surrounded the familiar clusters of native huts.

114

Now and then they passed a villa pointing its empty windows to the sky, and the natives still viewed these ruins with awe Marcus was told. When Rome ruled they'd kept clear of the conquerors unless necessity demanded a visit. But though lurid tales were still told about the villas to frighten the children, people were beginning to forget.

A week had passed and Galarius was still bathing his master's wound every day and trying to pull the edges together. The flesh was livid, and as his master suffered more and more the little man searched for leaves to pack the wound and make potions.

Then they turned west into a gentler landscape of hills and meres, and after a poor days progress camped by a stream. Galarius took to his bed with a heavy heart, and waking before the others went out into the spring sunshine, where the sky shone blue with white clouds flying east with the wind. The sun, aiming for its summer zenith was climbing daily higher in the sky. And as everything seemed so well set, surely his master would improve soon he prayed.

Going down to the stream the little man stripped off with the men, and naked and brawny they splashed in the ice cold water and swam in a pool behind a dam they'd built. The others were hugely amused by the weasel's rutted rib cage, and one ran his finger over the ridges.

"The little man has a chest like a harp! Do you hear the tinkling of his ribs as I pluck them?" he hooted, and the others laughed as Galarius emptied his bucket over the man's head.

They emerged feeling like new men, and sitting on the pool's edge one pointed to the north west, where they caught their first glimpse a great massive capped with snow. The peaks they'd journeyed towards for so long were glistening against the sky and Galarius had heard about this place. It had been a refuge for the natives in Roman times, and in his opinion would be again when the Saxons had overrun the lowlands.

After tying the thongs of his sandles Galarius stood up still rubbing himself with the rough towel. Here and there wildflowers were turning their modest faces to the sun, and summer couldn't be far away he told himself as he pulled back the tent flap and threw himself inside.

Resting on his elbows he leant over his comrade. The freckled face was wet with sweat. Though the eyes were open they didn't see him, and placing his cold fingers on Marcus' throat Galarius felt the frenzied pulsing of the neck veins. Then he fetched the bucket and bathed the swollen face till the heat receded.

As Germanicus turned to the light he was trying to get up.

"Who are you?" he whispered fumbling for his sword, and Galarius gripped his hand.

"Don't you know me?" the little man asked as he stared into the fevered eyes with their vast pupils. Then the chestnut head fell back again.

They stayed in that spot for seven days. They practiced swordplay and cavalry manoeuvres, they bathed and swam. They hunted, and cooked the wild fowl they caught. No natives appeared to threaten them, and though Galarius saw faces in the woods from time to time, be they men or boys girls or women they'd been visible only for an instant.

The men weren't impatient as they liked and respected Germanicus and were happy to wait for him to die. And when he did, they'd bury him and carry on with their journey.

The gaping wound was still seeping sticky yellow fluid, and the red line to the groin pulsed as if the poison was trying to break out. Searching for more leaves and herbs Galarius went on with his ministering, and eyes wide with confusion Marcus fought as they poured foul smelling liquid down his throat.

"They're poisoning me... give me my sword! Father, they're poisoning me. Mother where are you? Help, they're killing me!"

He'd fall back exhausted at the end of these sessions. But more often than not some of the physic made its way down his throat, the rest hanging about to soak the combatants and offend their noses..

Outside the tent an owl hooted against the sound of the stream, and lying back Galarius studied a particularly bright star through a slit in the canvass. Germanicus was quiet, for the first time his sleep wasn't broken by dreams sweating fits or convulsions, and pulling his blanket up Galarius went to sleep too.

Light broke through the thin covering over their heads bringing another day to the place where they'd struggled and fought, suffered and dreamed, for so many days and nights. And sitting up Galarius looked at his companion. To his surprise the face was calm and peaceful in sleep, then the eyes opened and Marcus sat up too.

"Where are we?" he demanded. The crisis had passed, the fever had abated, and with a sigh of relief Galarius picked up his bucket and went off whistling to the stream.

CHAPTER X
The Land of Gwynedd

The countryside was pleasant, with rolling hills and wooded valleys sending vigorous streams into wide rivers. The trees were impenetrable where no path cut into their stillness, and even when a meandering track did intrude it made little difference. As unlike Roman roads which stand out from the landscape like measuring rods, the ways of tinkers and drovers are circumspect.

Germanicus had mounted unsteadily, and though the height made him dizzy he'd rested his arms on Romulus' neck and hung on. Seeing how thin his master had grown Galarius was searching his mind for something diverting to say as he brought his horse alongside. Then he remembered his service in Caledonia, and the wisewoman who'd taught him the secrets of healing.

"We've reason to be grateful centurion, grateful to a dirty old woman I once met in Strathclyde," he began, and Marcus smiled weakly.

"It's good to hear you voice... a voice from the land of the living," he whispered, and reaching to steady his friend Galarius went on.

"She had knowledge of the old religion, and the healing properties of plants and such..."

"You used these methods to cure me?" Marcus interrupted, and Galarius shrugged.

"A man cures himself, it's all up here," he said tapping his temple with his finger, and to his surprise Germanicus smiled again.

"Then your vile potions served no purpose...?"

"The plants come from the Earth and go back to her as we do, so it makes sense to treat our ills with the stuff we're made of," Galarius grunted, and Marcus smiled yet again.

"I've reason to thank you," he whispered unsteadily, and the little man was suddenly embarrassed.

"Perhaps...?" he conceded, "but you should be thanking that old woman." Then he frowned as he pondered on how he could make his tale more interesting.

"The Christians want to destroy the ancient knowledge," Galarius continued after a while, as he knew that any talk of Christians would irritate his master and he needed to keep him awake.

"Why would they do that?" Marcus sighed, as he was feeling far too tired for idle conversation. And Galarius tried to remember.

"They believe that everything not ordained by their god is controlled by a creature they call the devil" he pronounced knitting his brows. And sensing that his companion was trying to help, Marcus made an effort to keep his eyes open.

"Who's he?" he asked, laughing for the first time, and Galarius looked puzzled, as he wasn't quite sure.

"The Christians say he's half goat and half man... with cloven hooves and a tail!" he replied determinedly. "Oh, and they believe that everything bad comes from him."

Marcus was laughing openly now, and when he spoke the humour was back in his voice.

"He sounds like the god Pan, and surely the Christians know that there's good and bad in everything?"

"On the contrary," Galarius replied with a knowing shake of his head, "they think their creed is the only good one and all the others are evil."

"That's very ungenerous of them!" Marcus retorted, turning down the corners of his mouth, and Galarius lifted a finger.

"Ah...! it's worse than that, as they say that all the other gods are devils!"

"How can they claim that?" Marcus demanded incredulously. And hearing the familiar scorn back in his master's voice Galarius warmed to his tale, sensing correctly that he was succeeding in keeping the sick man's mind off his pain.

"Consider Oden the god of the Saxons," the little man continued more cheerfully, "the Christians say he's a devil. They call him Grim, and the simple folk believe everything they say."

"How do they view the Celtic habit of worshipping oak trees? Marcus grinned, as he didn't want to be churlish and after all Galarius was going to all this trouble for his sake he supposed.

"The Christians see mother nature and all her works as evil, and try to subdue the natural world whenever they can. They cut down the holy trees and even view the body of man as evil because it's a product of nature."

"And the body of woman?" Marcus was laughing again, and for the first time since his fever he remembered the Celtic girl with the languorous eyes.

Galarius felt he could congratulate himself, as his master was recovering faster than he'd expected.

"They're even worse, as they tempt men to do things the Christians think are evil." He replied.

"Evil? but they're human... and even the monks must have desires?"

"They do, but their holy book says they must be conquered."

118

"How do they do that?" Marcus enquired knowing such a thing to be impossible, and Galarius frowned again as he searched his memory.

"The monks flagellate themselves with whips and starve themselves to suppress their true nature, and of course they keep to the company of other men," he added with another shake of his head.

"They try to kill thoughts of carnal pleasure....but do they succeed?" Marcus smiled, and Galarius shrugged helplessly as he searched his mind for the answer.

"I'm told their methods work for a while...but they have to keep repeating them... I think."

"These monks, are they different from ordinary Christians?"

"Oh yes, most folk mix the old and new religions together, but the monks condemn them for it."

"Do they condemn all natural men?"

"They say we have to reject nature if we want to reach heaven when we die," Galarius continued wearily with a glance at the sick man, as his voice was breaking and in his opinion there'd been enough storytelling for one day.

But as his master seemed so interested he'd no choice but to go on.

"They even condemn Ambrosius for trying to save their wretched skins," he croaked, "as they believe that only their holy book can save a man... and not necessarily in this world at that!"

"And they condemn Ambrosius for fighting their enemies.....?"

"And for his love of wine and women!"

Germanicus was feeling ill again, and perhaps the duke was right he told himself, and such people had no hope of defeating the Saxons. But when he rested his head on Romulus' neck assuming the lecture was over Galarius started again..

"This is the strangest thing," he was saying, "as though their book tells them that fighting is wrong, they think its all right if they're converting others to their ways."

"I suppose that's why they think so highly of my ancestor Germanicus the Bishop," Marcus replied wearily, "they tell themselves he was fighting for his religion not for Rome." And Galarius congratulated himself again, as not only had he kept his master in the sadddle he'd taught him something too!

Forty or so miles further on they came to a hill fort destroyed at the time of the conquest. The enclosure circled several acres and formed a platform guarded by huge earthen ramparts. To the west the land continued gentle and undulating to the horizon, and Galarius was pointing.

"Two more days of travel and we'll reach Dinas Emrys." he announced proudly, and Marcus felt a surge of relief.

They discovered the remains of a Roman signal station at the highest point, and the shelter was welcome after so many nights under canvass. Mouldy straw still littered the floor of the old stables, and the door still swung noisily on rusty hinges. After making a fire they searched for signs of the last occupants. Galarius found a leather bucket and some usable pots, and soon the cauldron was over the flames and a smell of cooking filled the place. They discovered an underground storeroom too, and a cistern still gathering water under a carpet of weed.

The old building creaked as the fire warmed the timbers, and a sense of longing came over Germanicus.

"Is there really any chance of driving the Saxons out?" he muttered, and the brown face of Galarius turned back from the fire.

"Who knows?" he grinned, "but either way somebody will be happy. If Ambrosius wins he'll be happy as the Celts will be under his thumb, and if he fails the dolts won't need need to inflict pain on themselves as the Saxons will do it for them!"

When they'd spread their thin mattresses on the earth floor one of the soldiers came to sit next to Germanicus.

"If you're interested in Ambrosius you'll know what they say about him?" he winked, but Marcus shook his head.

"What do they say?"

"They say that though he's Vortigern's rival they're alike in some ways."

The others were stifling laughter and as Marcus wondered what was so funny the man went on.

"They say they're both sons of Constantine the Third our one time emperor!" he whispered, and after waiting for this to sink in he shrugged. "They had different mothers it seems... Vortigern was the child of a Celtic princess and Ambrosius was the product of another liaison ... so they say. The duke's lands in Gwynedd and his fort at Dinas Emrys came to him from his mother... according to rumour."

As they settled into their blankets round the dying fire Marcus found himself pondering on the implications of this news. Then inexplicably his mind turned to Christianity again. How can a man worship a god and not want to fight for him? he wondered. And the Christians couldn't have it both ways, as if they wanted to make their creed dominant they'd have to ignore it's teachings about peace and humility!

The weather stayed fine and on the second day after leaving the hill fort they had their first sight of Ambrosius' stronghold. High on a jagged outcrop crowned by a ring defence Dinas Emrys lay brooding under banks of cloud rolling in from the west. The entrance was on the south side, leading up through three sets of gates to the plateau. And the place was circled at it's base by round huts, with smoking fires and dirty faced women who stared suspiciously at them. This rock was both defence and domination it seemed.

At the highest point stood a wooden platform, and here the central buildings were sited to provide good views in every direction. The strongest ramparts were on the western side of the hill. And Galarius said they were to discourage raiders from Hibernia the island to the west, as in these parts they were more feared than Saxons.

The garrison troops were Roman in their ways as Marcus had expected, and welcoming the newcomers without fuss they listened with fascination to reports of the battle at Aylesford. But they knew nothing about Helena's abduction.

"Our spies reported a band of Maelgwyn's men heading for Deganwy a few days back, but that means nothing as they come and go all the time," the garrison commander told them with shake of his head.

As Germanicus was still weak he'd have to rest before attacking Maelgwyn's stronghold. But at least he could sleep easy, as Pendragon was still in the south it appeared and with luck Ambrosius would make sure he stayed there.

The campaigning season was in full swing now, and as more movements of men and supplies were reported from the area round Deganwy Marcus deduced that Maelgwyn was preparing for a siege.

"I wouldn't like to be holed up in that place for long!" the garrison commander muttered as he threw a stick over the wall and watched it bounce down the slope, and leaning against the old stonework Marcus allowed the sun to warm his face.

"Surely it can't be worse than any other fort under siege?" he suggested, but his companion shook his head.

"Maelgwyn was almost a prisoner there last summer, as the Irish were raiding and burned some of his villages. But Ambrosius told us to sit tight as he wanted a guarantee of the old fool's loyalty before sending us to help him."

"What happened?" Marcus asked, and the soldier beetled his brows.

"The Irish didn't break in if that's what you mean, and there were enough supplies at Deganwy to keep them well fed till winter if need be."

"Then what went wrong?"

"Nothing went wrong exactly, and you could say that things turned out well for us as they put Ambrosius in a better position to negotiate." The commander was rubbing his lips with his finger as he went on. "The truth is plague got in," he shrugged, "and half Maelgwyn's men died of it!"

"What kind of plague?"

"Nobody knows, and you can be sure we didn't go in to find out. But there were tales... swellings that burst spilling puss and stale blood... you know the sort of thing."

"And Maelgwyn?"

"He survived more's the pity. He visits us now and then to claim that Ambrosius owes him rent!"

"Will the plague come again with summer?" Marcus wanted to know, and the face at his side showed no emotion.

"Who knows? Do you still intend to attack?"

"I do, we must find the girl before the the next bout of sickness."

Next day they set out, and as only a few miles separated Dinas Emrys from Maelgwn's fortress they covered the ground in a day. Germanicus took as many men as could be spared and nearly a hundred troops rode behind him. They weren't hoping for surprise as the Celts had spies too, and in any case they'd be visible some way off.

Sure enough a mile or so before reaching their destination they were confronted by a party of Celts led by Maelgwyn himself. Marcus was surprised by the king's shabby appearance and the poor quality of his horse, but while the horse was heavy the rider was just a bag of bones. Hung with skins and heavily tattooed Maelgwyn was eyeing them suspiciously, and the Romans began to appreciate Ambrosius' problem.

The old king sat between two of his nobles as his horse pawed the ground fretfully.

"What's your business?" he demanded in halting Latin, and Marcus offered his hand.

"I'm an emissary from Ambrosius your ally," came the answer, and the leading Celts exchanged suspicious glances.

"Why has he sent you?" one of them grunted, and Marcus experienced a twinge of impatience at the pretence.

"I believe it's because you have his daughter imprisoned in your fortress?"

Maelgwyn seemed confused at this, and when he looked to the others for support they turned away.

"Why do you say that?" the old man asked at last, and Marcus sighed.

"I was told the girl came north with one of your war bands."

"Why would they bring her here?" Maelgwyn snapped turning his rheumy eyes first left then right. "And you'd best go away as there's plague in my stronghold." Then he swayed dramatically in the saddle and one of his aids reached to steady him.

"Do you have the plague?" Marcus demanded trying to meet the old man's eye. But as the king began to turn his horse he shook his head vigorously, and there was still some strength in his cracked voice as he rode away.

"I warn you... you approach Deganwy at your peril!"

The Celts were making off and a quick decision had to be made.

"If they close the gates against us we'll spend all summer laying siege to the place!" Marcus shouted as he urged Romulus to overtake. "Surround them!"

It was soon done, and as the Romans took control of King Maelgwyn he held up his hands in appeal.

"Ambrosius needs me.... I'm his friend!" he wailed. But Germanicus was unmoved.

"Then give me his daughter," he shrieked.

Maelgwyn's parchment face was turning this way and that as if searching for a way out, and taking his bridle one of the sergeants began to lead him away from the others. Meanwhile, Marcus had un-sheathed his sword and was beginning to circle the group when out of the corner of his eye he saw movement. One of the Celtic nobles had drawn his weapon. His wild blue face was set in determination as he charged, and as Marcus knew that these people were brave and would fight to the death, he signalled again to the sergeant who let go of Maelgwyn's rein and slapped the rump of his old horse. The king's face showed surprise for a moment, then he saw his chance and galloped off. He was bouncing up and down as he clung to his mount, and the animal seemed in complete agreement about where they should be making for.

Seeing their leader taking flight the other Celts broke off to follow, but Marcus intercepted two before they'd gone half a dozen yards and with swift strokes cut their reins. First one and then the other lunged forward trying to regain control, and after more strokes from the short sword two riderless horses headed off towards Deganwy.

At the base of their fortified hill the Celts stopped to look back at the Romans who seemed to be keeping their distance. But any satisfaction was premature, as when the first gate opened to admit the shaking king Marcus led his best riders out in front. They reached the entrance at the same time as Maelgwyn, and the faces of the gatekeepers froze in confusion, as how could they close the gate against their master? An instants delay was enough, and Marcus was inside with his sergeant after him.

Some of the Romans turned on the Celts still climbing the hill and those inside set about the defenders. But though the next set of gates stayed closed for long minutes, the sight of Maelgwyn sharing a horse with a man holding a knife to his throat seemed to dent the defensive zeal of the gatekeepers, and the gates opened immediately when the king spoke.

"Open up you fools or this devil will kill me!"

Though he'd spoken in his own lisping language the words were soon translated by one of the men from Dinas Emrys, and the Romans went through at a walk. Then Marcus brought Romulus to a stop and looked around.

"Where's the girl?" he yelled, but the faces staring back at him were blank. He could see arrows, poised to fly but hovering nervously. And in an effort to confuse the aim he turned Romulus first this way then that.

As he pressed his knife to Maelgwyn's throat Marcus felt the curve of a hard swelling under the king's right ear, and suddenly his desire to get the job done became more urgent. So, lifting his sword he yelled at the top of his voice.

"Bring her here!" he screamed, then sensing Maelgwyn was trying to speak he pulled his scrawny head back to give him air.

"Fetch the girl... she's in the keep!" the old man croaked, and though some of the servants looked uncertain their king's pleadings soon sent them on their way.

The wooden tower at the centre of the camp was devoid of windows. But a flight of steps led to a door in the second storey, and urged on by the old man's screams his folk began to beat against it. At first there was no response, but after Maelgwyn had exercised his larynx again it opened a fraction. After pushing their way into the dark interior the Celts reappeared seconds later with a figure wrapped in a cloak, but the face was hidden and Germanicus was losing his temper.

"Show me the face!" he yelled, and when they pulled back the cloth he saw Helena. Though dirty and frightened it was undoubtedly her, and as Maelgwyn's servants stumbled down the steps pulling her after them the king started wailing as Germanicus squeezed his neck. When they let

Helena fall at at his feet Marcus nodded to the sergeant who scooped her onto his horse, then he young praetor wheeled to face the Celts.

"You'll have your king back when we're safely away," he told them.

The sergeant and the girl went first and Marcus peered into the dark interior of every hut they passed. His men had formed a protective circle, their arrows covering every angle. And no one opposed them, as Maelgwyn obligingly kept up a stream of commands not to attack.

Ambrosius' men had done their job well, and still holding the king against his breastplate Marcus felt pleased with himself. As they passed through the outer gates he began to breathe more easily, but they weren't safe yet as there were men behind every rock and noises in the undergrowth said they were watched.

Maelgwyn slumped to the ground when Marcus let go of him, and when the sergeant pointed to a standing stone a little way away two soldiers took an arm each to half carry the frail king to the makeshift stake.

"Tie him well!" Marcus called as the old man was secured to the post. Then they fell back slowly, keeping their arrows pointing at Maelgwyn all the while.

Then the signal was given to set off at the gallop, and looking back Marcus saw Celts emerging from cover. They were shouting and waving their weapons, but it was too late. Soon their enemies were out of sight and they returned dispirited to the stone where Maelgwyn hung tethered, his head lolling drunkenly to one side.

It was then they saw the swelling under his ear, and as they stepped back one motioned to an Irish slave he'd captured the previous year.

"Here Donnel, serve your master," the Celt laughed, "you're to have the honour of taking your king home." And the others laughed too as the unfortunate Gael set about his task.

"At least we've done some good today!" one of the Celtic elders shouted to his men as they rode home. "As the accursed Roman who held our king will soon share his sickness I vow!"

They reached Dinas Emrys just as it was growing dark and Helena was taken to the best room to wait for her rescuer. The garrison commander's wife was laying the brush she'd used to disentangle Helena's hair aside as he entered, and after bowing she left the room, closing the door behind her.

The fire cast a shifting glow on Helena, who seemed to have lost none of her self confidence.

"You saved me Germanicus, I thank you for it and no doubt my father will reward you well," she sniffed and Marcus smiled.

"But will you reward me maiden?" he asked softly.

Helena was refusing to look at him and twisting the corner of her shawl round her fingers.

"It's not in my power to reward or punish," she replied primly, and coming forward Marcus touched the tips of her unbraided hair.

The action seemed to frighten her.

"Lay a hand on me and my father will know of it!" Helena gasped. And Marcus nodded, staring at her for a moment before abruptly turning to leave.

Ambrosius' daughter was recovering from her ordeal it seemed, but though her air of superiority was only slightly dented Marcus had seen her frightened and vulnerable, and the uncertainty was still there he sensed.

Next day he saw her walking on the hilltop, looking out over the surrounding land.

"Good morning princess," he said with a bow, but she didn't turn.

"Good morning centurion," she replied stiffly without looking at him, and he corrected her.

"You do me an injustice lady, you should address me as praetor now, as your father has given me command of one of his legions."

Making only a little nod Helena started to walk away, and Marcus followed her.

"You seem ill at ease princess, can it be you're missing your betrothed perhaps?" And when she turned he saw distaste in her eyes.

"I'll never marry Pendragon!"

"There are some who say you will."

"My father won't allow it!"

"Your father, who after all arranged the match, is not here."

"But you are!" she told him imperiously, and bowing stiffly Marcus left her to her thoughts.

"When do we set out for the south?" They were eating in the hall at the fort and Germanicus looked up in surprise. It was clear that the girl had been plucking up courage to speak, and after a while he moved to sit next to her.

"When I've seen enough of these lands," he answered lazily, and Helena scowled at him.

"When will that be?" she demanded petulantly, and when Marcus shrugged some of the men laughed behind their hands.

"When I've had my fill of the pleasures of this place," he told her.

"Maelgwyn is dead and they say Pendragon has arrived at Deganwy," Helena whispered urgently, and Marcus nodded.

"They also say that he's camped at the foot of the hill and won't enter because of the plague," he replied, staring pointedly at her hands as she clasped and unclasped them.

"But he's near enough to attack us..." and Marcus nodded again as he got to his feet.

"That can't be denied princess!"

As he returned to his place at table Helena followed him with her eyes, and without looking at her he resumed his conversation with the garrison commander.

It was late when the knock came, and after motioning Galarius to the door Marcus took hold of his sword. But he relaxed when he saw it was Helena and sent his servant away.

"I am honoured by this visit princess," he smiled, but though the girl entered she stayed close to the door.

"What do you want?" she asked. But Marcus just shrugged as he offered her a chair, and she shook her head.

"Why are you delaying our departure?"

"Have I not told you?"

"I... I didn't understand... tell me again."

So he brought her in and closed the door.

"I'm a soldier, and we'll leave when I have the information I need." Then he paused, "and there's something else I want too."

"And what is that?" Helena sighed, keeping her eyes averted.

"You."

She was trying to move away but he detained her, then bending very slowly he kissed her neck. When she tried to pull away his response took her by surprise, and bending to place his arm under her knees he lifted her off the floor and stood holding her.

"Do you hate me?" Marcus asked with a smile.

"No..." Helena demured staring at the floor, "but I don't trust you either." And replacing her slippered feet on the ground Marcus spoke very softly.

"Don't be afraid of me Helena....." he whispered, then his tone changed suddenly, "and don't fight me as it won't help you."

She was looking round as if searching for a way out.

"My father will decide whom I marry, and I can't make the decision for him."

"But I can!" Marcus murmured, bending to kiss her first on the brow then the lips. "You seemed sure enough of your feelings before the battle at Aylesford," he reminded her, and she nodded still refusing to look at him. "Your father is a diplomat and perhaps he used you to tempt me because he needed me?" Marcus suggested. "But I believe he needs an alliance with the Celts more," he added before turning to stare into the fire. Then he sighed heavily.

"I suspect that your father intends to give you to Pendragon," he told her with resignation.

Helena was staring at him in horror now, and her expression left Marcus in no doubt that she had no love for Pendragon. But why was she behaving so coldly towards him? he wondered, could it possibly be that she found him unattractive?

"What's your choice?" he asked, lifting his arms and letting them fall. "I need to know.....now."

At this Helena seemed to melt a little, and when she put her hand on his chest it felt naked without the armour.

"Take me back to Winchester and my father will grant my wish as he'd not make me unhappy," she suggested. But Germanicus shook his head.

"Your father is a soldier and he can't allow the feelings of a woman.... any woman, to override his judgement." She was trying to pull away again but he held her. "But if you give yourself to me now he'll have to bestow his blessing when we return."

The passion in his words had taken Helena by surprise it appeared, and she started to struggle again.

"He'd kill you!" she wailed. But Germanicus just smiled.

"Would that distress you?"

"Yes!" Helena gulped, "but it would distress me more to return home carrying your child!"

Marcus was shaking his head and sighing with the sadness of it all as he walked away.

"Do you love me Helena?" he asked as if he knew the answer would be negative, and foolishly she allowed herself to look into his eyes.

"You're nearer to my heart than Pendragon... and if I love any man it's you," she admitted somewhat reluctantly. But Marcus just laughed.

"You flatter me princess!" he told her before kissing her again as if this were to be his parting gesture. Then to his satisfaction he felt her weaken against him.

"Will you love me?" he asked.

When she didn't answer he kissed her again harder, and pulling away her robe touched the tip of one round breast. To his surprise he felt her

128

respond, and could it be that she was his? he asked himself.

Lowering her gently to the floor and encountering no resistance he sensed that she was. But even so he lay still, watching her face till she touched him.

Then he closed his eyes and drew her to him, as having her like this, willing and gentle,was a bonus he hadn't dared expect.

When it was over she looked at him.

"Are you not afraid of my father?" she asked, and Germanicus shook his head.

"No," he told her as he kissed the tips of her hair, " your father would not have me dead now I think."

"Will I be with child when we reach Winchester?" Helena whispered, and Marcus shrugged.

"If that were so we could be sure the gods approve of our union at least!" he laughed.

CHAPTER XI
The siege

Pendragon's men were surrounding the hill. Dinas Emrys was under siege and presently the new lord of Deganwy appeared from the ranks.

"I've no quarrel with you Germanicus!" Pendragon shouted, "we're both Ambrosius' men and he'd not want us to be enemies."

"How right you are!" Marcus called back from the ramparts, "as we've no quarrel you're free to go on your way." And after glaring at those behind him who seemed to find this funny, Pendragon returned his attention to his rival.

"Only one thing divides us Roman!" he called, "and if you give me the girl I'll return her to her father as pure as they day she left his house." But Germanicus shook his head.

"Somehow I don't think you can keep that promise," he replied, and Pendragon shrugged.

"What must I do to satisfy you?" he asked almost pleadingly, and Marcus smiled.

"All I ask is that you relinquish your claim on Helena and take your men home. You have till dawn tomorrow!" he added turning away without waiting for an answer, as he already knew what it would be.

Since their return from Deganwy Germanicus had lived like a man cursed. Would the plague strike him? he wondered. Were his shivering fits just remnants of his recent illness? Were they brought on by memories of Maelgwyn's diseased body? Or were they the heralds of death?

Perhaps Helena would be first to develop the swellings? he feared. But this was a prospect he couldn't bring himself to face, and when everyone was still healthy after two weeks he began to relax. With a full heart he gave thanks to Mithras at the little shrine, as it seemed his god had granted a reprieve and saved him for a more honourable soldier's death.

The sun was above the horizon the light improving by the minute, and the foot soldiers dispatched down the northern slope under cover of darkness lay motionless, their eyes fixed on the place where Pendragon's line was thinnest. Soon the gates would open they knew, and Germanicus would ride out followed by his best mounted troops. With luck their diversion would come as a surprise to the Celts, and if their prayers to the sun god were heeded the intervention would make all the difference.

The Celts disliked fighting on horseback, preferring to dismount before getting to grips with the enemy. But though the break-out seemed to take Pendragon by surprise, he rallied well enough and was soon galloping about shouting orders.

Germanicus' first priority was to get Pendragon away from his men, but halting the show of bravado was easier said than done and several minutes passed before the king of Gwynedd was distracted from hectoring his troops.

As the two men circled each other a few sword strokes were exchanged, but to the puzzlement of the Romans watching from the fort their leader kept to the defensive and seemed reluctant to to get down to the serious business of killing.

Germanicus' reluctance was well founded, as he knew how much Ambrosius needed an ally in these parts and his commander's reaction would be decidedly negative if he killed Pendragon. But Romulus was eager to start his familiar manoeuvres and after dispatching their current opponent move on to the next.

Though Germanicus was fighting shy Pendragon was in earnest, as in addition to the girl he wanted unchallenged authority over his new kingdom. His expression was implacable as lips pressed together he fixed his eyes on his enemy, and after a period of infuriating pretence luck seemed to smile on him.

There were gasps as his sword swung towards the throat of his adversary, but Romulus swerved away and the blade passed by harmlessly. However the closeness of the stroke forced Marcus to alter his tactics, as he knew he'd no choice but to dispatch or disable Pendragon if he wanted to save himself. It took no great effort, and as Romulus began his oft drilled dance round their enemy he let out a loud whinny, as if to congratulate his master on getting himself together.

Pendragon had no time to react as the short sword came in above his knee then again on the right arm, and as Germanicus broke away he saw the Celt leaning drunkenly on his aimlessly circling horse. Heading back to the others Marcus found one of his men on the ground under the hooves of a frightened horse, and scooping him up he deposited him at the edge of the fray before engaging another mounted Celt.

The foot soldiers were easier to scatter. Soon the ground at the base of the mound was clear of living enemies, and when the diversionary force slithered off the northern slope the Celts waiting to meet them were easily dealt with.

The pounding of hooves made the earth shake as the Celts made off towards Deganwy. But no Romans followed, and instead they watched as the Celtic wounded were led or carried away.

When Germanicus returned to where he'd left Pendragon he found that the new king had fallen from his horse and a minion was trying to get him up again. The Celt was in pain he could see, but the humiliation was more terrible and hate burned in his black eyes as Romulus circled him.

"I could have killed you, you owe me your life!" Marcus shouted to the bloodstained warrior who was almost in tears. But Pendragon's eyes held no gratitude, and as he bit his moustache he was glaring at his enemy.

"You'd have been wise to kill me Roman!" the king of Gwynedd replied with something between a snarl and a sob, "as one day I'll kill you, and what's more I'll destroy your reputation!" Then a choking sound issued from his throat. "In days to come mothers will tell their children about the greatness of Pendragon!" he yelled, and as Germanicus rode away he screamed after him. "I'll live in legend as it's my people who write the legends, but you'll be forgotten in the annals of these lands!"

Pendragon was still screaming the same message five minutes later. His voice could be heard from inside the fort, and the exhausted Roman was cynical enough to believe that he was probably right.

As his master unbuckled his cuirass and threw it onto the bed Galarius watched him, then he searched his body for wounds.

"You've been blessed by the fates again centurion!" the little man murmured as his face crinkled in pleasure. "Your god is good to you, and I think he'll have my sole allegiance in future!"

Marcus was smiling, then he saw Helena at the half open door.

"You're unhurt?" she whispered coming to touch him timidly, and when he nodded she moved closer.

"I hadn't realised how... how I..." So he pulled her to him and kissed her mischievously.

"Do you now?" he asked, and she nodded and smiled.

"I think I do... as when I watched you with Pendragon it wasn't just fear of life with him that made me pray for you."

Marcus was tilting her chin but she turned her head away.

"I gave you my allegiance Marcus... and you'll always have it... ," she whispered moving to look out through an arrow slit. "And as I watched you I knew that even if my father turns against you I never will." Then he pulled her onto the narrow bed and they hugged each other like children.

"Deganwy must be reduced and its inhabitants scattered before I leave," Germanicus told the garrison commander as they walked the ramparts of Dinas Emrys. "The peasants will disperse without much fuss and the buildings will be burned to discourage their return."

The fire would destroy any vestige of the plague too, and few would be sorry to see it at work. Pendragon hadn't shown his face since they fought and Germanicus wasn't sorry about that either. But as soon as they made a move against his stronghold the new king would come out of hiding for sure.

Once more a Roman column left Dinas Emrys for Deganwy, and again Germanicus took as many men as could be spared. But the following events could not have been more different to those of their previous visit, as no welcoming party met them this time and no ailing king appeared to threaten them.

As they approached the two hills the area was strangely silent. No one worked in the fields, no children played at the doors of the round huts, and the commander of Dinas Emrys coughed nervously.

"Is it wise to go any further sir?" he asked as Romulus began to climb the main hill, and Marcus shrugged.

"We need to know what's happened... it could be a bluff?"

"Oh yes! it could be a bluff!" the garrison commander sniffed sending Marcus a disbelieving look. And of course he was right, as the desolation was too real to have been arranged for their benefit.

They were coming on bodies now or what was left of them, as it seemed the people had fled without pausing to bury their dead. Marcus twisted his face in distaste when the smell hit him, suspecting that most of these unfortunates had been alive when the place was evacuated. But though the dogs had stayed to devour the unaccustomed glut of meat, no human moved among the frail dwellings. Maelgwyn's tribe had taken to the hills it appeared. They were putting as much distance between themselves and their fellow men as possible, and the suspicion would last till autumn.

On the summit the Romans saw that care had been taken to secure the buildings, but when a sergeant lifted the beam and put his shoulder to the heavy door of the keep it opened surprisingly easily. After climbing the winding stair to the top they entered the last chamber, where they were met by Maelgwyn's corpse. It was sitting upright in the king's carved chair of state and seemed to be looking out over the estuary with sightless eyes. They'd left him here after securing the doors, and their purpose had been simple - to keep the dogs away from the body of their king.

If the Irish came raiding they'd not venture this far, and when Marcus gave the nod his men went to work with their torches. The wooden buildings burned enthusiastically, and turning to look back as they rode away they saw great plumes of smoke rising from the two hills.

Even after dark when the Romans had bathed in the warm bath house, told the latest jokes and scraped each other clean with unusual vigour, the fires still burned. They'd come out into the warm night still laughing and talking, but their voices lowered to whispers as they watched the red glow.

Eventually a new garrison took up residence on the hills of Deganwy, keeping watch over the estuary as Maelgwyn had. Ambrosius had a station on the coast where he kept a small fleet of galleys, Germanicus had taken men from this to make up the compliment and the place was denied to Pendragon for the present.

It was high summer when they set out, and as warm breezes blew from the south the earth bloomed. Helena was golden again, she'd put on weight and the memory of her captivity was fading.

"Did you not know that I'd come for you?" Marcus asked as they rode, but she shook her head.

"I didn't even know if you were alive."

"Did you hear about the battle at Aylesford?"

"No, the guards gave me no news and were locked in as securely as I was. They didn't speak much, and when they did their language was unintelligible."

"You were very brave." Marcus said taking her hand, but Helena shook her head again.

"No I wasn't..... I even hoped Pendragon would come for me... I think I'd have married him just to see the sun again. And Marcus smiled, as even if Pendragon never forgave him for stealing his bride he didn't care.

Germanicus decided to head for Deva (Chester), as 'the City of the Legion' was famous across the empire and he wanted to see it before returning south.

Leaving Dinas Emrys they travelled north-east, and after camping under the stars for two nights came to the River Dee. Looking across they saw a city even better preserved than London, and Germanicus suspected that little had changed here since the legions left more than fifty years before.

Constantine the third had kept a garrison here but could never build up a complete legion. Nevertheless the soldiers drilled, kept the place in good repair and the Celts out. But now the barracks were empty, and halls that once echoed to the toasts of feasting men and squares where the shouts of drill sergeants once resounded stood silent.

Ambrosius still kept a garrison here of course, as Chester was second only to Winchester in his scale of importance. But Germanicus guessed that there were no more than a couple of thousand men to guard it.

As they rode along the southern bank of the river viewing the imposing walls of the fortress a fanfare of trumpets announced the arrival of the military governor on the bridge. It seemed that news of their approach had reached him and he'd come out to meet them with his guard of rather flashy young officers. They were staring suspiciously at Germanicus, a man of their own age but far superior rank, and they eyed the girl too.

Marcus suspected that Helena was enjoying their admiration, and at first she seemed to preen with pleasure. Then she remembered herself and lowered her eyes. Using the fine stone bridge they crossed the river, and escorted by the governor and his imposing entourage entered the city.

Columns of soldiers passed them in the streets and townsfolk jostled by, some hawking or buying, others driving animals. Street calls familiar across the empire were still delivered in Latin to attract the military customers, but the military had changed.

Men of Roman blood still followed the eagles, but there were no longer any German mercenaries with the device of their tribe emblazoned on their shields. There was little evidence of elite units either, though the governor's guard brought back an echo. But there were few recruits of the required standard to replenish even that small band. They saw a few auxiliaries from the local tribe the Brigantes, and one or two from the wilder areas to the west. But the overall impression was of emptiness, of a place too grand and too big for the people who now occupied it.

There weren't enough people to fill the place or soldiers to defend it. Not enough women to bring the population to its proper level and not enough youths to learn to be soldiers. No ordered ranks of schoolboys chanted their Latin verbs as they passed in procession, and it seemed for all the world as if the guiding force had disappeared and the city was manned by a skeleton crew.

As they sat on the balcony overlooking the river, Gallus Anthonius who'd been governor for nearly twenty years admitted that they'd been years of decline. The thick set man of about sixty offered no solutions, and as he pivoted his heavy head on his thick neck he appeared sad and puzzled.

"They say the gods decreed the end of empire!" he sighed, "but I'm a practical man and look for other causes."

"Do you find them?" Marcus asked leaning forward, and Gallus grunted like a man who's been cheated at dice.

"Perhaps the gods did decree the loss of our colonies, and in obedience to their wishes the colonies destroyed themselves?" he suggested bitterly. Then he took a handful of dried fruit from the bowl and began to study it as if the answer to the puzzle could be found there.

"When Maximus took the last legion across the channel, what happened here?" Marcus asked, and Gallus shrugged.

"Nothing much, as everyone expected Maximus to return in triumph with spoils from the lands he'd conquered... or send replacements for the men we'd lost at any rate." Then after another sigh the governor threw the fruit into his mouth.

"But the years passed and no reinforcements came?" It was Helena who spoke, and though Germanicus looked surprised Gallus just smiled. Then he passed her some fruit in a blue glass bowl and taking an apple she began to polish it.

"The lady is right!" Gallus conceded lifting his cup and taking a succession of gulps, "months went by, then years, and at first news from the continent was good. Maximus had won several victories, and entered Rome itself they said. Then he was killed and we were forgotten!" the governor added, shaking his head as if the conundrum was beyond him.

"These islands were indeed forgotten," it was Helena again, "and for years we've hung on and hoped."

They sat in glum silence for a few minutes as if overcome by the awfulness of it all, but Germanicus was more puzzled than defeated.

"The legions have gone but the people are still here, and why has the process of regeneration not taken effect? Why were the gaps in our defences not mended and filled with strong new blood?" he asked.

But Gallus simply moved his head slowly from side to side.

"It's as if our life blood dried up when the cord with Rome was broken," he sighed, "and as these islands were colonies for four hundred years the natives forgot how to defend themselves. I think they're more helpless now than they were when we conquered them!" he added, and taking a date from the bowl Germanicus stared at it aggressively.

"They were a wild independent bunch in the early years!" he grunted, and the governor nodded vigorously.

"Aye, we all know about the rebellions and the blood they spilt." Then he smiled wickedly, "as well as the revenge we took!"

Rising to her feet Helena had moved to the fountain tinkling in a pond of goldfish and was swirling her hand in the water.

"It's as if the colony had been castrated!" she suggested. And though

137

Germanicus was impressed by her perception he was shocked too, and she'd spent too much time with her father and his generals he suspected.

Then Gallus leant forward to point with his knife.

"That's it exactly, your lady has a way with words!" he grinned allowing his eyes to move down from Helena's face. "It's as if the land was suddenly drained of vigour, and the people have relied on Rome for so long... been forbidden to fight for so long..."

"What do you know about Christianity?" Marcus asked, and assuming his guest wanted a change of subject Gallus got up and threw his date stones out of the window.

"If it were just another cult I'd like it well enough," he answered, "as a man should be free to chose his own gods. But now it's so strong it's trying to destroy the other beliefs."

Gallus was shaking his head as if this too was beyond him, then suddenly he was in full flow again.

"According to the records they've all done some persecuting, and they say the Christians had the worst of it for a while. But since Emperor Constantine made Christianity the official religion of the empire it's been unwise to follow your own gods if you want to get on in the world!"

"It's persecution that worries me..." Marcus pondered aloud, "and in my opinion persecution comes from belief in one supreme god. On the other hand... if all religions were acceptable as they were before Constantine stuck his nose in... and everyone was free to worship as he chose?"

"Then we'd all live together happily?" Gallus chortled as he sat down again.

They'd been given rooms at the river's edge where a veranda stood out over the sucking water, and closing his door Germanicus lay down. Galarius had gone into the town to meet others of his kind, and it was strangely quiet without him.

Going to the window the one-time centurion looked across at the fires on the opposite bank, then he watched an illuminated galley pass by in mid-stream. He could hear them calling the strokes, then the wash hit the wall under his window and the sleek craft slid off into the night.

Moving quietly along the passage Marcus hesitated outside Helena's room before knocking, and after opening the door she pulled him to the window.

"Did you see the galley?" she whispered pointing down stream. "They say the river leads to the western sea... and I was wondering if we could travel along the coast till we found an estuary to take us home?"

"I've planned our voyage a little more precisely than that!" Marcus told her. And Helena ran her finger over his lips, her eyes full of childish anticipation.

Germanicus was wondering at his luck, and why did he have this effect on women? he asked himself. But as it was unwise to question the gods, he decided to just take what they offered and be thankful!

The girl was still tracing the line of his mouth and following the movement of her finger with her eyes, so after watching her for a moment he loosed the cord at her waist.

Then he lay on the bed and studied her figure outlined in the shimmering water reflected light. She was naked now, graceful as a willow branch, and when he held out his hand she knelt at his side and buried her face in the red furze of his chest.

He'd taken her gently the first time he remembered, as she'd been like a flower he might crush under his weight. But she'd changed, and now her heavy eyes demanded more than soft caresses. So he pulled her onto him, guiding her hands over his body as he watched her face in the dancing reflections.

Then they were on the floor with the hard tiles under them. As he came down she stiffened, then his mouth closed over hers and she relaxed. Breaking off for breath he buried his face in her neck and she stretched into him eagerly.

When it was calm again he lifted her onto the bed, soon she was asleep and he found himself looking at an innocent child again.

A fine gilded galley lay at anchor under the castle walls, and fifty broad men rested at the oars.

"My ship is ready sir, she can make good speed in a fight and the accommodation is fit for any lady!" the captain told them proudly, sweeping into a low bow and offering his hand to Helena as they boarded.

Hangings of rich velvet screened the sleeping quarters, but Germanicus saw from the two rows of oars that this was no lady's pleasure barge. On the contrary the ship must have been built for an important man he suspected as he ran his hand along the polished rail and gazed up at the empty mast.

"She was built for Ambrosius himself, to his own specification. And he's building more of the same design," the captain explained still glowing with pride, and Marcus nodded uncomfortably.

So this was his commander's own galley... but why was it here and could it be that Ambrosius had sent it for a purpose?

"I visited the dockyard with the duke not six months ago," he replied eventually, and Gallus was interested.

"Are there others... like this?" he demanded, and Marcus answered thoughtfully.

"I suppose there were about fifty in various stages of construction..."

"Then it's true... the duke intends to make war beyond these shores!" Gallus was obviously enthusiastic, and was running up and down the deck peering into every hole like a schoolboy. But the expression on Marcus' face was grim.

"Ambrosius intends to take his navy to Gaul and fight for the man he thinks will make the best emperor," he grunted with a worried glance at Helena, "as he wants to revive the power of Rome in these islands." But in spite of this downbeat assessment Gallus' face was still shining.

"This way he just might succeed!" he beamed.

Germanicus gripped the governor's arm as they parted.

"Ambrosius will be reminded of you my friend, I think you're the kind of man he likes to have about him."

"Perhaps he'll send for me?" Gallus called hopefully as the distance between them increased, and as the current took them in tow Marcus shouted back.

"Perhaps he will!"

As the outline of the sand warm city faded into the distance the craft made good speed with the current towards the open sea. At the mouth of the estuary they turned south along the coast, and passing through narrow straights skirted the eastern flank of an island. Then a peninsula jutted out with signal stations along the cliff top at regular intervals.

The stations continued along the coast of a large bay, and Germanicus wondered if they were all busy sending information about his amorous doings to Ambrosius.

But when questioned the captain shook his head.

"Some are ours yes, but the Celts control others as Maelgwyn liked to know what was going on." And as they lay at anchor with the glow of the signal fires lighting the night sky Marcus wanted to know what was going on too - just what were they saying, he wondered... and to whom?

Here in this western bay Ambrosius kept his northern fleet, and pointing to the flat top of an old hillfort the captain explained that this was its main base. Behind the hillfort stretched a valley leading to a good Roman road he informed them.

As Germanicus ran his eyes over the rising ground now red with Hawthorn berries it began to rain, and as the sun was still shining the valley shone too. It looked like wet blood he fancied, and he wondered if it could be some kind of omen?

From the base under the hillfort they sailed south again, along the jagged coast and round another peninsula. Then they headed east towards the estuary that would lead them inland. And all along the coast and into the mouth of the Severn the signal fires burned on their platforms.

Helena was disappointed when they reached Gloucester and her father wasn't there to meet them, but Ambrosius hadn't left Winchester and was waiting there with growing impatience.

Summoning the errants to his command centre he stayed behind his desk without looking up as they entered, and Marcus felt the gall rising in his throat as he faced the enormity of his crimes.

"A curse on those infernal spies!" Helena whispered as they were jostled into the room, "did you know he'd find out?" And Germanicus, who'd taken on the aspect of a stubborn red faced youth, shrugged.

"He'd be a poor general if he didn't know the doings of his officers," he grunted.

"But I told you what his reaction would be and you said I was being silly, you told me... you said..."

"Of course I knew he wouldn't be pleased!" Marcus hissed turning to glare at her, "but I had other things on my mind at the time if you remember!" And deciding to forgive him Helena squeezed his hand.

"I expected him to ride out to meet us.... after all I am his daughter!" Her voice was confident and a little aggrieved. But even so she was beginning to wonder if Marcus' wonderful bravado had been misplaced, and in spite of her faith in him she felt a deep well of uncertainty growing inside.

After a while the duke stood up offering his hand to Helena. And she ran to take it, a little too eagerly in Marcus' opinion.

"It warms my heart to see you again," Ambrosius whispered, and the break in his voice gave Marcus cause for optimism.

"Oh father I've missed you!" Helena sobbed resting her head on the duke's chest as he held her against him. "I'm so glad to be home....." she went on starting to weep profusely, and Germanicus felt resentful.

Why was she crying? he wondered, and had she been deceiving him all this time? He was confused and his confusion increased as Ambrosius stroked his daughter's hair.

"Don't cry my darling, you're not to blame for all this," he crooned, at the same time shooting shafts of venom over Helena's head at Marcus. And the young man felt he ought to say something.

"I've rescued your daughter as you ordered sir..." he ventured coming as near to a stammer as he hoped he ever would. But the duke continued to glare at him.

"As I ordered?"

"Yes sir... as you ordered."

When the older man still failed to beckon him forward Marcus started to change feet nervously. He was beginning to wonder if he should make a run for it, but Ambrosius seemed to read his mind.

"It's the custom here to lay down your sword when you enter," he growled. And with a nod of resignation Germanicus allowed one of the guards to take his cherished weapon.

Helena seemed to have forgotten him.

"My poor darling," the duke was murmuring as he comforted her. Then he looked at Marcus. "Do you have something to tell me?" he demanded, and the young man tried to sound confident.

"There's a great deal I have to tell you sire."

"Something concerning my family perhaps?"

As the sarcasm in Ambrosius' voice bit into the young soldier the silence lengthened, then Helena lifted her head.

"Don't blame him father, it was my fault too..."

"How could it possibly be your fault?" the duke demanded turning his frown on his daughter, and she burst into tears again.

Germanicus was trying to make his lips move and at the same time clear his throat.

"I... that is we..." Then he coughed and began again. "I'm the only one to blame sir, and if you want revenge it's against me that you should take it."

"Where's Pendragon?"

"I believe he's still in the north sir."

"Have you killed him?" And at this Helena ran to Marcus, taking up a position very like the one she'd just relinquished with her father.

"Oh no father!" she protested, "Marcus was so brave and could have killed Pendragon more than once. But he didn't.." she sobbed, " and though he risked his life giving advantage to his rival, in the end he had to do something or Pendragon would have killed him....." Her voice had petered out, and Ambrosius nodded and waited.

"I wounded him sir, in the arm..." Marcus whispered, then Helena came in again.

"And the leg!" she added admiringly.

"Have you any idea how much I need an ally in the north? Ambrosius sighed, and the miscreants nodded repentantly. "Now Maelgwyn is dead his son has the allegiance of...only the gods know how many petty chiefs!" Ambrosius went on as he sat down and put his his head in his hands. And when Helena ran to him he pulled her onto his lap. "But that centurion, is the least of my worries!" he added threateningly.

The barb struck home, and as Germanicus lowered his eyes a vision from his childhood crept into his mind. He was standing at the school-room door, the master was bringing his rod down repeatedly into the palm of his hand, and all these years later Marcus could hear it distinctly!

"My love for my daughter overrides even my diplomatic wisdom, does that surprise you?" Ambrosius was asking wearily, and Germanicus had to admit that at this moment it did.

"There was a need for quick thinking sir... Pendragon was at the gates and if he'd taken Helena...." But the sentence was cut short when the duke jumped to his feet.

"If he'd taken Helena he'd no doubt have done exactly what you did!"

Germanicus had never seen his commander so angry and red faced before, and the heads of several well armed guards had turned in his direction. They were smirking, obviously expecting the order to arrest him to be given at any moment. So he waited as Ambrosius shuffled his papers and tried to master his temper.

"I'm told that my daughter was held prisoner for a considerable time before you recovered her?"

"Yes sir."

"How was she treated?" But though Marcus opened his mouth Helena jumped in and answered for him.

"I was kept in an awful tower... it was dark... the smell was terrible and I had no privacy at all!"

"Did they harm you?"

"Harm me...? No, but I was very frightened."

Throwing himself onto a couch and folding his arms Ambrosius was looking very directly at his daughter.

"You know what I'm asking don't you Helena?" he murmured. "I want to know if they... if you..." But Helena shook her head vigorously.

"No... I wasn't... touched."

The duke had risen to his feet, he was closing in on the despoiler of his daughter, and seeing the ornate knife hanging from his belt Marcus started to look round for a weapon. But the danger passed when Helena ran to throw herself at her father's feet, and gripping his knees buried her head in his tunic.

"Please father... I couldn't bear it if..." she sobbed, looking up at Marcus.

"My goods are tarnished are they not centurion?" The words were shouted over the girl's head and Marcus took a step back..

"Don't refer to my wife as tarnished sir! You can take my life but she's innocent."

"Wife you say?"

"We made our vows.... pledged before the setting sun," Marcus offered by way of excuse, but Ambrosius was only a little placated.

"That wouldn't carry much weight with my Christian supporters!" he sniffed before turning sadly to his daughter. "And in any case Pendragon wouldn't want you now I fancy... were I to offer you to him that is."

Then he beckoned to an old man in a long toga standing nervously in the shadows, and as one of the guards took Germanicus by the arm Helena was likewise brought forward.

"You'll marry my daughter here and now!" Ambrosius scowled, "and I'll make what excuses I can if anyone objects."

The old man was mumbling incoherently and waving a branch of some aromatic shrub over their heads. But at last he came to a halt and it seemed they were man and wife.

Marcus wasn't surprised when Helena threw her arms round her father, but when she spoke her words came as a shock.

"You won't kill him now will you?" she wailed, and Germanicus, who'd begun to feel safe was suddenly uncertain again.

"Why not?" Ambrosius frowned, " after all you're a respectable married woman now my love, and we don't need HIM any more!"

CHAPTER XII
PENDRAGON'S REVENGE

Fortunately a look of grudging respect (and could it be affection?) had accompanied Ambrosius' last remark. He'd held out his hand in pax and the two soldiers had clasped arms, holding eyes for long questioning seconds.

Germanicus was the first to turn away.

"I'm sorry I betrayed your trust sir... it won't happen again," he murmured, and Ambrosius put a hand on his shoulder.

"I believe you Marcus..." he sighed, his tone indicating the exact opposite. "And in any case, what better way to secure a man's loyalty than to make him your kin?

I've a villa on the south coast near my dockyard at Portus Adurni," the duke went on after a moment, "you'll like it," he whispered to Helena, "and you leave tomorrow." Marcus was in no position to argue, and in any case he wanted to see the ships again.

The docks were sited on the landward side of a sheltered inlet, and to the south lay straights separating the mainland from a large island. Marcus was looking forward to the experience. He'd go out with the fleet, circle the island and assess the place, he told himself. And he was hoping to take part in the coming campaign too.

The long low roof of the villa crouched under a fold in the land. Cream and red the house had a southern warmth that reminded Marcus of his Mediterranean home, and as he looked out over the water Helena noticed that he hadn't spoken for a while.

What are you thinking about?" she asked, and he sighed.

"About my home, about Rome where I first took up soldiering... about... oh, about everything!"

"It's strange to see you in civilian dress," Helena told him resting her head on his shoulder. And lifting the folds of his toga Marcus let them fall disconsolately.

"It feels strange to be wearing it.... strange and wrong somehow."

"My father's trying to civilise you because he wants me to have a reliable husband," Helena smiled, "but he half doubts the wisdom of it."

Lifting the embroidered hem Marcus started to gather the folds of his cumbersome garment, and after disengaging himself he stood over it in his tunic and sandals.

"Your father never wears a toga, he's always in uniform!" he grunted, and Helena giggled.

"He wears one when he wants to impress the Celts!" she whispered, and Marcus put his arm round her.

"I can't stay here... waiting for the Saxons to make their next move," he muttered, and though Helena nodded she avoided his eyes.

"When will you go?" she whispered, and at once Marcus relaxed, realising that she'd anticipated this.

"I'll go down to the port tomorrow as there's a voyage planned," he told her with barely suppressed excitement.

As she ran her fingers through his hair Helena remembered the news she'd been meaning to give him. But it could wait she decided, and they watched together as the sun disappeared. But when the afterglow set the sky aflame Helena turned away, knowing that soon the horizon would swallow Germanicus too.

Ambrosius was pacing the jetty impatiently, while beneath him twenty long galleys bobbed at anchor. Their crews were aboard, provisions were stowed, and a low hum came from below decks where rows of men rested on their oars. Now and then the hum swelled into a song before dying away again. Deep wave born music it was, interspersed with the rousing rhythms they saved for times of special effort, when the drum of the oar master beat fast and every muscle was straining for extra knots.

As the admiral of the southern fleet waited he rested his foot on a capstan and studied his toes.

"We must be under way soon if we're to catch the tide," he advised, and screwing his eyes Ambrosius peered along the quay. Sure enough the late-comer was in sight, and with a waive of his hand the duke made the introductions.

"My... er, my son-in-law, Marcus Germanicus," he told the admiral, who bowed and looked the younger man up and down. "I've decided to make Germanicus the Count of the Saxon Shore and my second-in-command." Ambrosius concluded most proudly.

"Forgive my lateness..." Germanicus was panting, "but we've had reports of a war band in the area."

"Never a week goes by without reports of landings or incursions from the conquered lands!" Ambrosius grunted over his shoulder as they embarked, and the admiral nodded.

"Aye, and when we've boarded ships making for these shores we've found them full of Celts driven from their homes by the Saxons."

"We don't know who our friends are," Ambrosius muttered running his hand over his smooth jaw, "and only when there's a strong emperor again will we have order and peace!"

As the waves lapped the side of the ship Marcus watched the coast of Britain fade as the coast of Gaul had faded a year before. But though Galarius was still with him everything else had changed. A year ago he'd landed on the islands not knowing what the future held, he remembered, and now he was one of Ambrosius' senior officers.

As he leant over the side peering into the green depths the reflection of the mighty sun god seemed to wink at him. Cloud reflections floated by too, and with the clouds came faces, faces he'd come to know over the last year.

Hengist was there, laughing and snarling alternately. Alexander and his daughter.... And Rowena, eyes half closed and lips parted in invitation. A dark patch drifted by and he saw Vortigern in it. Then came Cordelia the pretty coquette, and Aelwulf, smiling as he came in for the kill. Closing his eyes Marcus opened them again to see the procession still passing. Pendragon dark and vengeful, Maelgwyn rheumy eyed and sick. And last of all the dead face of Vortimer, brought up the from the river like a boy asleep.

Helena was sitting in front of her looking glass as her maid dressed her hair, then she squealed as the comb hit a knot.

"Be careful Gwyneth!" she snapped, and the Celtic girl lowered her eyes.

"Did you tell him madam?" she asked, and Helena shrugged.

"No... there's time yet."

Placing the brush aside the maid moved to the window where a movement in the bushes caught her eye. If Helena had been there at that moment she'd have noticed that the soldier who normally paced the terrace was no longer there, and if she'd gone to the door she'd have found it unguarded. When she called for her maid there was no answer, and on the terrace the only sound was the rustling of mediterranean shrubs in the breeze. The villa was unusually quiet. When Helena heard a sound she began to turn. But a hand came over her mouth before she could cry out, and as brawny arms lifted her off her feet she wondered where everyone was.

The hefty man carrying her smelt of tar and wood smoke, and though he put her down when they entered an adjoining room he kept her mouth covered. Another man was standing with his back to her, and when he turned Helena recognised Pendragon. The King of Gwynedd came forward slowly, reproaching her with the mock hurt in his eyes. And as his hand stroked her cheek the gold torque on his arm pressed cold against her neck.

His voice was gentle.

"Don't be afraid my dove," he whispered, "all is well." And though Helena couldn't speak her eyes widened in horror. But if this was a sign that his advances were unwelcome Pendragon ignored it, and taking the man's hand he removed it from her lips. To the Celt's surprise she didn't cry out, and when his lips moved towards hers she did nothing, not even turn her head away.

"Oh, you're a wise one!" the soft Celtic voice caressed, "you're a beauty cariad and who'd want to change that?"

The threat was real, the question in the soothing Welsh voice rhetorical, and Helena followed him with her eyes as he strutted round her, examining every detail with obvious pleasure.

"You're mine now sweeting," Pendragon crooned. Then the parade stopped suddenly as he sensed the hint of a shake of his beloved's head. "Do you not feel pleasure that your true husband has come for you at last?" he asked.

This time there could be no doubt that Helena's head was shaking, and Pendragon's face took on a puzzled expression.

"Surely you're not disagreeing with me sweeting? Tell me I did not see it," he crooned.

This was too much, and as Helena's head began to shake in frightened obedience she struggled to produce a weak smile.

"That's better," Pendragon nodded, running his finger over her parted lips, "as we're to travel west... to be married." And though Helena tried to speak he forestalled her. "We'll be married in the only true way, in a Christian church by Christian monks" he told her, "as in the eyes of the church you're unmarried still and there's no hindrance to our union."

Then Pendragon's second in command came forward and whispered to him.

"Ambrosius is strong in those parts, and when he discovers..." but Pendragon pushed him away.

"Pah, do you think I intend to linger in his lands?" the new king of Gwynedd murmured with a mischievous glance over his shoulder at Helena. "I know the ideal place never fear, Ambrosius will be away for weeks and when he returns we'll be long gone."

They rode at night towards the south west, and held tight against the Celt who's horse she shared Helena felt his grip constricting her lungs.

148

She could see nothing as there was no moon, and even the stars stayed hidden behind banks of cloud.

When the sun came up they rested in a peasants hut, and the terrified occupants unceremoniously thrown out at sword point, disappeared into the forest dragging their children and animals after them.

Pendragon was congratulating himself as he threw his cloak over one arm and leant expansively against the supporting pole of the little hut.

"We're safe now, and I could take what's rightfully mine if I chose!" He seemed to be waiting for a reaction from the others who were laying out the bedding, and when he coughed they looked up to nod obediently. "But the brothers know that I'm a good Christian and would expect me to deny myself," the king of Gwynedd continued piously. And this time the others started nodding even before their master looked at them.

Helena lay down on one of the trestle beds against the wall, and after a while Pendragon brought her some food.

"Eat some of this Helena," he told her, then he paused. "You have a Roman name... I don't like that, when we're married you'll have a new one," and Helena thought it best to humour him.

"Helena is a Christian name, the name of the Emperor Constantine's mother who was a saint!" she informed her suitor. But after considering this for a moment Pendragon shook his head.

"It's true that the name has been common amongst the Romans since early times... but it's not from the scriptures," he said, taking a bite of the bread he'd been offering to her as he gazed up at the smoke blackened roof. "Perhaps I'll call you Mary in honour of the Holy Virgin, or perhaps Ygern would be better... a noble Celtic name for a noble Celtic Queen!"

Helena had turned her face away, but Pendragon pulled it back, and when he spoke his voice was almost pleading.

"My name will live in history Helena. Men will remember me as the father of their nation, and you could be a part of it my love." Then his tone changed suddenly. "You will be a part of it!" he vowed. And when Helena's only response was to turn away again Pendragon threw the half eaten loaf across the hut before storming out. Next day they pressed further into the far west.

Ambrosius' galleys had landed in Gaul and the duke was preparing to set off and discover what progress had been made concerning the attack on Rome. The latest contender for the Emperor's throne was camped on the edge of the Germanic forest he'd been told, and he intended to go and find him.

But only hours after they landed another ship came alongside the quay, and Germanicus recognised it as one he'd seen at Portus Adurni.

"Is something wrong?" he called as the captain jumped ashore, and the man nodded.

"Bad news I'm afraid," he answered hesitantly, "Pendragon was seen near the villa not long after you sailed."

"Helena?" Ambrosius enquired, and the captain nodded. "She's gone sir... Somehow the guards were overpowered," he added taking a step back, but Ambrosius was already walking away.

"You must go back," he called to Marcus over his shoulder, "take my flagship it's the fastest."

The duke was running now, giving orders to almost everyone in sight. Then he waved as the sleek ship slid away and the distance between them increased.

"I must find the pretender to the throne before he changes his mind!" he laughed. And though the humour was forced Germanicus smiled in return, as he knew how much the man on the shore wanted to go with him. But as always with Ambrosius, duty must come first.

The villa seemed deceptively normal in its hillside niche. Lamps burned in the windows and Marcus could hear the shouts of sentries as he approached. They stood back nervously when they saw him, fearing the worst. And their distraught sergeant tried to explain. Going down on one knee he bent his head, and Marcus heard a woman sobbing somewhere out of sight

"If you value your life tell me what happened!" Germanicus demanded wafting his sword over the man's bent head, and the sergeant shivered.

"They came at the first hour of the night sire, and somehow overpowered the guards... and they took the lady." Then he looked up. "They seemed to know our movements sir..."

"Where did they take her?" Marcus sighed, and lifting his ashen face again the sergeant clasped shaking hands.

" We don't know... but the maid who served your wife... we think she was in league with them."

"Then bring her to me!" Germanicus snapped.

The shout could be heard across the square and only moments later a girl was pushed towards him, her face bruised her clothing torn.

"I see they've used you for their pleasure," Marcus observed wearily, "but have they drawn the necessary information from you I wonder? Where have they taken my wife?" he bawled, and the man holding the shivering girl started stuttering.

"We know she was in league with Pendragon's men as she was seen talking to them, but she refuses to tell us where they've taken her mistress."

Sheer frustration calmed Marcus' anger as he signalled them to bring the girl closer, and arms pinioned she was forced to kneel at his feet .

"Who attacked the villa?" he growled trying to meet the girl's eyes as she turned her head desperately from side to side. And when the guard twisted her arm she started to cry.

"It was Prince Pendragon, Lord Count... he came for his bride."

She cried out again as the guard reacted to her insolence, but Marcus simply felt tired.

"Where have they taken her?" he asked quietly, and the girl cast round as if expecting help. But there was none.

"They didn't tell me sir... I swear they didn't tell me!"

"Why did you betray your mistress?" Marcus asked, and the girl shook her head vigorously.

"Oh no sir, it wasn't betrayal... as Pendragon will be high king one day and the Lady Helena will be his queen. Then as they dragged her away she shouted over her shoulder. "The blood of the great duke must be mixed with that of the Celts if we are to unite under one leader and become a mighty nation again!"

"And the leader of that nation is to be Pendragon eh?" Germanicus muttered under his breath.

As they removed the girl his eye was drawn to a movement in the bushes and he saw an old woman crawling towards him.

"I overheard Pendragon's men talking sir," she croaked as she dragged herself forward, "they spoke of a monastery.... where the sea beats relentlessly against rocks that are crowned by a chapel."

"Do you know of such a place?" Marcus asked, and screwing her eyes the crone tried to focus on his face.

"I've heard the bards tell of it... but I doubt if it's real."

"Where do they say it lies?"

"Far to the southwest sir.. close to the land that sank into the sea."

Germanicus was walking the boundaries with Galarius.

"Have you heard of this monastery?" Marcus asked, and his companion shrugged.

"The Celts mix legend with truth so thoroughly that it's hard to know what's real and what's fantasy," Galarius grinned. Then they paused at a field gate and he pulled a stalk of dead corn. "But the bards tell of a place called Lyonesse, a legendary land that supposedly sank into the sea. They say an earthquake destroyed it in one night!" he went on. "And it disappeared so fast that one man escaped by spurring his horse as the ground slipped away beneath him." Then they leant on the gate and Germanicus rubbed his chin.

"At least we know they went west!" he grunted.

Next day they set out, calling first at Winchester to gather a force of mounted troops. As with luck they'd overtake Pendragon and Marcus wanted to be sure they weren't outnumbered.

Then they were on the road, and the guards in the watchtowers followed with their eyes till the dust of the column merged with the landscape.

At first there were plenty of reports about a party of Celts passing by, but Pendragon was travelling at night and the inhabitants of the farmsteads knew only that fifty or more horsemen had ridden past in the hours before dawn. Then the information dried up completely. The people were suspicious now. Speaking their own Celtic language they felt no allegiance to Rome, and if Celtic men had passed by in the dark they'd not give them away.

When a wide moor rose in front of them they'd no choice but to cross it. On the windswept heights where wild cotton bobbed and moor-fowl croaked in tune with the frogs in the acid pools the Romans were cut off from other men. And though heather clung here and there the black bog was always present under the surface.

Then at last they saw the sea.

"We'll follow the coast as far as it goes... and at least we've found forage for the horses," Germanicus grunted throwing a coin to one of the sullen locals and watching him disappear with it. Then throwing down their blankets they lay down, as no animal could be left unattended hereabouts and a guard kept watch all night.

Next morning they rode on, and occasionally saw a face peering round a barn or heard a twig snap as a watcher ran away. The coast was growing wilder the cliffs steeper. Seabirds wheeled over their heads as they trod the soft vetches. While a hundred feet below the sea threw itself into narrow inlets, drawn into the funnels only to be cast out again like the breath of a winter horse. Here and there a settlement nestled round a church, and the people seemed less afraid here as the threat of invasion hadn't touched them.

When the Romans dismounted in a hamlet the horses bent their heads to crop grass with the grazing cattle. Chickens and hogs wandered freely, and Marcus remembered places like this from his youth. All this place needed to turn it into a replica of the Roman and Gaulish villages he'd known then was a priest, and he laughed to himself when he saw a black robed monk coming towards them.

The man wore a heavy wooden cross round his neck, he walked on bare feet and spoke in old fashioned Latin.

"Good day my sons," he called, making the sign of the cross. And one or two of the soldiers went forward to receive his blessing.

"Good day," Marcus muttered, standing well back as if the priest was the carrier of some infection.

A huge stone oven stood by the road and the soldiers were helping themselves to bread hastily shovelled out by the baker.

"I hope you'll be paying for this my sons, as the folk here are poor while you..." The priest was looking pointedly at the shining armour and gilt handled swords of the officers, but when one of his men started to apologize Germanicus interrupted.

"We take what we need old man!" he growled, throwing down a coin. "And we're searching for a woman taken against her will."

Then suddenly he felt a stab of doubt. Had Helena really been taken against her will? he wondered, or had she gone with Pendragon willingly? The ways of women were a mystery, every man knew that. But though it took some effort he rejected the idea and returned his attention to the priest.

The monk was shaking his head after picking up the coin and placing it in the leather pouch hanging from his belt.

"We don't take sides my son, as we're all children of God." he told them, drawing the sign of the cross again and making to go on his way. But when Germanicus tilted his head his sergeant stepped forward and blocked the path.

"What's this?" the monk sounded aggrieved, "would you detain God's messenger?"

"No brother priest," Marcus replied trying to sound worthy of the old man's trust, "we only ask for directions to take us on our way."

As the friar looked nervously from one soldier to the next the silence lengthened. Then a child ran past in pursuit of a duckling and Marcus nodded to his shield bearer who caught it up laughing.

The priest was worried now they could see. Several villagers had gathered round the baker and a hum of dissatisfaction was coming from their direction as Germanicus took the child. Stretching out its small hand it was reaching for the plume on his helmet, and Marcus started to move towards the monk as if to hand the child to him.

"I'm a normal man brother, and have no wish to hurt any of you," he said with a glance at the crowd, "but my time is precious...." Then his eyes turned to his men and every hand went immediately to sword or dagger. "Tell me where they've taken my wife or I'll pierce your heart and slit this child's throat before your body hits the ground!" he told the priest. "And as for them," he continued with a nod at the villagers, "they'll follow you to paradise."

The priest was holding out his arms for the baby. But the child was happy where it was it seemed, and as it touched Marcus' shaven chin he took its little hand.

"He thinks I'm a woman, do you want him to discover his mistake?" he asked. And throwing his hood back to reveal the beads of sweat on his brow the friar fell to one knee.

"What do you want to know?" he gasped, and Germanicus smiled.

"Did a party of Celts ride though here?" he asked, and the priest nodded and touched his wooden cross.

"May God forgive me......" he whispered.

"Where were they heading?"

"To the sea, to the monastery," the friar chattered frantically.

"How far?"

"Not more than a mile....."

"Is the place defended?" Marcus demanded. And at this the priest laughed dryly.

"Oh no my son, it's a place of worship.... a chapel on a headland," and Germanicus nodded.

"Where the sea beats relentlessly against the rocks?" he suggested, winking at the others as he placed the child on the ground.

They were hungry as it was late afternoon now, and only after finishing their meal with gulps of water from the fountain in the churchyard wall did they mount and set off again behind the standard.

The lands edge (some said it was the end of the world) was jagged with sharp headlands jutting into the swell, and dismounting they stared down at a spur protruding from the base of the cliff.

The promontory rose gently as it stretched away from the shore. And where it flattened into a plateau on the seaward side stood a little church, its bell tolling solemnly in its wooden tower. Though there seemed to be no stone buildings the cliff edge had been ringed by a wall. Sheep grazed on the slopes and they could see a small square of cultivated land inside the retaining barrier. Then a black robed figure came out of the chapel, and approaching a group of buildings entered what they assumed were the monks' living quarters.

Leading their horses they began the steep descent to the point where the headland joined the cliff. Here they found a rough wooden shelter crammed into a cave mouth, and here too they discovered about fifty tethered horses.

"Why would the gentle brothers need so many horses?" Galarius demanded as he stroked one sweating flank, and Marcus smiled.

"Not long arrived I think," he observed as he gathered some fresh hay for Romulus. "The chapel seems undefended and though the approach is open there are no watchtowers."

"What are you planning?" Galarius asked giving him an odd look, but Germanicus just shrugged. "If you give me a dozen men we'll creep round the bottom of the cliff and climb up under cover of darkness!" the little man proposed excitedly, but Marcus shook his head.

"We can't do that, or have you forgotten 'The sea that pounds relentlessly?' And as the water's so deep, waiting for low tide won't make any difference."

"What then?" Galarius demanded in disappointment, but Germanicus was already lying down in the fresh hay.

"We're tired, so are the horses, we need to rest a while."

Inside the little monastery a strange scene was being enacted. The monks were disturbed that a woman had found her way into their sanctuary and the abbot was wringing his hands. He was staring suspiciously at Pendragon's men, who were lounging irreverently against the refectory walls, eating and drinking noisily.

"Don't you see?" Pendragon's voice was testy, "I've contracted a marriage with Ambrosius' daughter!" Then he glowered into his wine cup and finding it empty called for a refill. "She was stolen by the Romans, but I've recovered her..... saved her from a life of sin father!" he added as a monk padded forward clutching the wine jug.

He was waiting for the abbot's reaction and at last the cleric sighed.

"We're men of peace here Lord Pendragon, and we can't take sides over a difference of opinion," he ventured hesitantly.

"Difference of opinion!" Pendragon bellowed, and the monk with the jug shrank back. "Will you marry me to the girl or not?"

"Is the lady amenable to your wishes?" the abbott asked, and the king of Gwynedd thought for a minute.

"You know the ways of women father!" he winked, regretting it immediately as the abbot crossed himself and raised his eyes to the ceiling.

"No, I do not know the ways of women lord king!" The tone was patient and condescending. "Nor do I wish to know them!"

When the abbot entered the cell where Helena was incarcerated the man guarding her went outside, and the abbott sat down on the narrow bench circling the walls.

"You've been brought here by Pendragon the son of Maelgwyn?" he enquired gently. And Helena nodded, as she understood his scholastic Latin very well. "Lord Pendragon says you're betrothed to him... is that correct?" the abbot went on, but Helena shook her head.

"No... No father!" And the abbot sighed.

"But do you wish to marry him?"

"No father, I'm married already!" The abbot was looking very uncomfortable indeed now.

"Married already?" he repeated.

"Yes, to Marcus Germanicus one of my father's officers."

The holy father was looking up as if the answer to his dilemma could be found carved on the ceiling, but at last he seemed to find the words he wanted.

"And where is he now... your husband?" he asked. But the fifteen year old just shrugged and began to cry.

"I don't know?" she wailed, "all I know is that he left for Gaul with my father."

"Oh dear..." the abbot sighed, returning his eyes to the roof. Then he jumped as Pendragon appeared at the door.

"Is everything to your satisfaction father?" the Celt asked with a deferential bow, and the abbot started wringing his hands again.

"No it is not!" he retorted. "I cannot marry the girl against her will, and I certainly can't marry her if she's already married!"

Nodding as if he agreed wholeheartedly Pendragon sat down beside the girl.

"Let's be married Helena, as our marriage would unite the country and without it there'll be war." And when she affected not to hear, the spurned lover turned his attention to the abbot. "I'm a Christian father, and as one of the greatest lords in these islands I can bless the brothers with land." But the abbot was still looking uncertain and Pendragon tried harder.

"This woman is Ambrosius' daughter father, and if she marries a pagan...?"

The Celts had finished their food, and the monks silent as shadows had begun to clear the tables. One by one they left the room, and as the great door closed behind them one of Pendragon's men stood up.

"This is madness!" he asserted loudly, "here we are making war on the Dux Brittaniarum himself, and all for the sake of a woman!" Murmurs of agreement greeted his words, and when he'd finished they sat for a while discussing their predicament. Then one man jumped to his feet.

"Smoke, I smell smoke!"

They were all heading for the door at the same time, but it was locked and when they tried the tiny windows they found them shuttered and bolted. Someone had taken the trouble to seal them in! But after a moment of blind panic they agreed to work together and use one of the heavy tables as a battering ram.

The great oak door shook, the walls shook too, and the noise they made could be heard in the cell where Helena sat between Pendragon and the abbot. The abbot just shook his head, while out in the cloister hooded monks continued to parade as if this kind of thing was normal. Then one stopped at the door of the little cell, and as his shadow fell across the floor Pendragon looked up.

"What do you want?" the king of Gwynedd snapped, and when the point of a sword appeared from under the black habit he jumped to his feet.

"I'm unarmed brother, why do you threaten me?" he gasped, and as the newcomer threw back his hood Pendragon took a deep lungful of air.

"You!" he gasped.

The girl and the abbot were shrinking in a corner and Pendragon was holding up his hands.

"I am unarmed... you can't kill me in cold blood!"

"I can kill you any way I choose." The voice was matter of fact, and as Germanicus stood back to let them pass into the cloister he nodded to Galarius who was holding Pendragon's sword. Lifting his brow a fraction the little man threw the weapon to its owner, and as hope dawned the Celt twitched his moustache in anticipation.

They circled for what seemed like an age, then Pendragon came in with a swipe to the legs and jumping clear Marcus began to circle again. The Celt's next thrust missed by an inch. The weight of his sword carried him on a few paces, and waiting till he turned Germanicus feigned a strike to the head before running in with a plunge to his enemy's left side.

As the short sword pierced his heart Pendragon's face took on an expression of surprised horror, and he stood swaying for a moment before slumping slowly to the ground. The mouth opened as if to speak, then the head fell back, the eyes rolled up, and hardly a second later the short sword severed the head completely.

The monks cowered against the cloister walls as Germanicus turned the object on the ground with his foot, and as the head rolled over, eyes staring as if in expectation, he grasped it by the long hair and showed it to his men.

Even when their cheers had died away Marcus continued to display his trophy.

"The Celts keep these grizzly reminders to show to their children, and to give them strength for battles yet to come," he panted, "and I'll keep this... as my talisman!"

At the top of the winding path the horses were led into order and the riders mounted. Helena was riding a white palfry lent to her by the abbot.

"Goodbye father," she called, and the abbott nodded, before turning away as quickly as he could with the brothers following his example.

The village was deserted as they passed except for the priest. Standing by the fountain he crossed himself as Germanicus rode by looking straight ahead, but Helena turned her head as her palfrey trailed behind Romulus on a leading rein.

"The priest is afraid of you Marcus!" she ventured in a loud whisper. "See how he invokes his god as you pass!" And immediately the freckled face of the Count of the Saxon Shore broke into a broad grin.

"That's because my god is stronger than his!" he laughed. And everyone within earshot looked up at the autumn sun, which was beating down with unseasonable ferocity as if to confirm his words. Then Helena reached to touch her husband's arm.

"If they're so afraid of your god, might they not set out to destroy him?" she whispered, and taking her hand Marcus kissed it.

"They'll do all they can to destroy every god but their own, and perhaps they'll succeed in the short term. But even if their god rules for a thousand years, nay two thousand... the day will come when he falls from their minds." Then he lifted his face to the warm light. "The inventions of men are always abandoned in time," he murmured, "but as long as the sun climbs daily in the sky they can't forget him. He'll be there till the end of time, and when he no longer shines there'll be no men left to worship anything!"

Marcus had sent messengers to all the tribes in the land summoning the chiefs to meet him at Winchester. But when few turned up and those who did spent their time arguing, he lost patience and set off for Portas Adurni leaving them to it.

The villa still squatted under the hill, and they sat in the evening sun as they had only a month before to look out to sea.

"There's something I must tell you," Helena whispered, and Marcus pulled her against him. "In the spring I'll have a child... so they tell me."

"They've told me the same thing so it must be true!" Marcus answered as he stroked her hair. "He'll be a great soldier, remembered through history as a king who was more than a man.... and we'll call him Arturious!" (Arthur).

CHAPTER XIII
holding the fort

Ambrosius hadn't returned. He'd been last seen in the Teutoborge forest where the general aspiring to the emperor's throne was said to be recruiting, and as autumn turned to winter Germanicus grew increasingly uneasy. Constantly straining his eyes across the water he wondered what could be delaying his father-in-law's return, as if the duke was still alive he'd be aware that the Saxons were now threatening the heartland of Britain.

Many Romans found this idea laughable he knew, and as a circle of faces formed in his minds eye Marcus recalled the inhabitants of comfortable cities like Gloucester and Bath.

They were shaking their heads as he remembered them.

"Really dear boy, surely you exaggerate?" Then the plump countenance of his wine loving friend Vinarius was replaced by the granite features of the governor of Gloucester.

"Huh! A fine opinion you must have of us Germanicus, and do you really think we'd allow a pack of barbarians to overrun our lands?" The genteel company had laughed Marcus recalled, though some of the ladies had glanced sympathetically at him.

It seemed that Hengist didn't want to fight till he was nearer London, and running his fingers through his hair Marcus furrowed his brow and thought hard. The experience at Aylesford hadn't been wasted on the Saxons he knew, and though they were seeping out of Kent like water from a skin they'd avoid another pitched battle he believed.

Instead they were using their war bands to intimidate, and as the native population was forced west were taking over whole areas. They were advancing relentlessly, and Marcus doubted if anyone had the will to stop them.

The Saxons were advancing on several fronts, and not only in geographical terms. Of course they were using the age old methods of conquest such as killing the males and ensuring that many of the children born and raised in Celtic communities would in future have Saxon blood. But they were using more subtle methods too, albeit without giving them much thought. They were using the sense of guilt taught by Christianity along with the dislike of killing that came with it to their advantage. And another difference in the characters of the contenders for ownership of the islands struck Marcus too. This was the

161

passion and pride in the Saxon sense of being that was totally foreign to the Celts. 'Blood and Soil!' was a favourite Saxon warcry. And at times it seemed that the two were indistinguishable. In contrast there wasn't even a word in the Celtic language to indicate that an object, person, animal, or piece of land belonged to them. In short they had no word for 'MY.' The Saxons would give their lives for their bit of land, as to them the man the tribe and the land that sustained them were one. However the Celts preferred to move on, and believed that there would always be more land, land that could be bought without blood.

As they moved west they forgot about their former countrymen in the east. And the idea that men from the west should help tribes such as the Canti in the east to defend their land would have seemed strange and perverse to them. The priorities of the two groups could not have been more different. And though Celtic bards often sang about great war heroes of the past, it seemed to Germanicus that the events described were used to serve the song rather than the other way round.

"There's no need for great battles!" the king of the Jutes observed as he rummaged through the remains of their meal with his huge hand, and Octha yawned. They were alone, the others had drifted off in ones and twos and the long hall on the edge of the marshes was empty but for the dogs scavenging under the tables and a servant sweeping the floor.

"It does seem foolish to face an army when we can encourage the dolts to move on in other ways," the younger man agreed, and Hengist rocked his great head back and forth.

"Not that I'm averse to a battle now and then you understand!" he grinned, "in fact I'm sure it will come to that before we take London."

"You want to take London?" Octha gulped sitting up suddenly, the indolent manner that so often irritated his father shocked out of him, and Hengist savoured the moment.

"Why not?" he asked, "if we're to move north we'll need to conquer the capital."

"Couldn't we go round it?" Octha muttered suspiciously, and his father shrugged.

"Aye... we're not city people it's true," the old Saxon drawled beginning to pick his teeth with his dagger and examine the products, "and I can't understand what the Romans see in city life. But it's not the city I want!" he winked, "though they say it's full of treasure... No! it's important because it's Vortigern's capital, and we'll have to take it sooner or later."

But though Octha could follow the reasoning he was still doubtful.

"You'll be setting yourself up as king of the Britons next... wearing a crown and sitting on Vortigern's throne!" he laughed, and Hengist's face clouded.

"That's not my way as you know, I'm a soldier and don't intend to die in my bed!"

"What's your plan then?"

"After London falls?" and Octha nodded. "We press north of course, they say there are fertile lands in that part of the world and it's not all moors and mountains."

"I've heard about the north and the great wall that keeps out the Picts of Caledonia," Octha mused. "They say the Romans up there are rich, and as the tradesmen pay their taxes the towns are prosperous."

"Perhaps they'll be paying their taxes to us soon!" Hengist laughed slappping his son's broad back as he struggled to his feet. And still chortling they drained their jugs and set off down the hall arm in arm.

The serving man leaning on his broom smiled as he watched them weave towards the door, and bowing as they passed continued to observe as they disappeared into the night.

Guthrum had been a landless labourer in the old country, and things hadn't been too bad at harvest time and sowing he remembered, as they'd had enough to eat then. But as all the good land was held by powerful men there'd been no hope of bettering himself, no hope for his kinder or his frau, and no future for the small body growing in her belly.

Guthrum's new life was undoubtedly better, and though he was still a thrall his work in the chief's hall brought him into contact with the great ones and he was optimistic. In time they'd come to look on him with approval he hoped, and perhaps a few acres of the conquered lands would come to him?

He was sweeping faster now as his mind turned to Brunhild waiting in their tiny hut, and though the children would be asleep when he arrived home he'd spend long minutes looking down at them before making for his bed. After watching her husband affectionately and studying every detail of his worn face Brunhild would take his arm.

"Come husband, you must rise early, so take some rest while you can," she'd say. And the red face of the German peasant would break into a smile as he took one last look at his son and wondered what great deeds he'd live to see.

"We're so lucky to have all this!" Guthrum would tell his wife, waving his arm at the rabbit hanging from a beam and the iron cauldron next to the row of wooden spoons on the hearth, "and we owe it all to Lord Hengist! Soon we'll have our own land, and when the boy grows up who knows?"

He'd go on dreaming as his wife pulled him to her under the covers, and how could any man be so lucky? he'd ask himself as he stared up at the Odal Rune he'd carved lovingly from ash wood and nailed to the wall above their heads.

"Thanks be to Odin the Allfather" he'd murmur, "and to Hengist the father of our people."

The mid-winter festival had been celebrated with as much fervour as ever at Portus Adurni, and the solstice was now passed. When the junketing was over the people began to look forward to spring and life settled into it's familiar pattern. But there was no respite for Germanicus.

The great walls of the fort bled emanations as if trying to communicate. Their every strength exuded endurance, and as the centuries passed and nations disappeared Marcus knew they'd stand firm as an enduring memorial to Rome. Gazing up at the cliff-steep heights he wondered if he was more sensitive than other men, as he often fancied he saw figures moving along the battlements. Some were from the past he guessed, but others lacked even the substance of dead souls and inhabited the future world these walls would one day see.

Marcus and Helena spent most of the winter on the coast, but though they'd expected Ambrosius before the end of the year he was still absent.

A cold spell stretching back to November was bringing itself to a climax, and clouds that had threatened for weeks gave up their burden. The snow fell thick and silent, soon the ground was covered to a depth of several inches and travel on land was impossible. But from the highest tower Marcus saw that the sea was still an open highway. No storms threatened, and he knew he could be across in a few hours.

Helena greeted his plan with resignation, as he was taut with boredom and his presence could be irritating. Servants and soldiers often had their feathers ruffled when they tamped against their master's abrasive forcefulness, and no one would try to dissuade Marcus Germanicus from his adventure.

Gallus Anthonius had come south from Chester, ostensibly to update his knowledge of naval warfare. But his interests were in no way limited and he'd plunged into the good life with a relish that made Marcus envious.

Others may wilt or fall asleep, but the thick face of Anthonius remained impassive as one by one the goblets of continental wine were put away. They caused no change in his demeanour, and on more than one occasion

Marcus had held his head in his hands, unsteadily pondering the reasons. Perhaps the slow speech of his friend became a little slurred after a few flagons his fuzzy brain suggested. And could it be that Gallus' customary glazed expression smoothed out a bit more? But the young count doubted even that, and was forced to accept that even after enough wine to flatten a legion his friend remained unaffected.

Gallus' companions would have to be very observant as well as stone cold sober to register any change in him at all, and Germanicus felt aggrieved at this talent for avoiding the effects of good wine. Before meeting Gallus he'd prided himself on his ability to hold his own in any drinking session, and it was easy with the Saxons, as their watery ale made abstinence a pleasure. The thin brown liquid left the body almost as soon as it entered, he remembered. It held no romantic connotations and couldn't be compared to the luscious red liquid in which he was now trying to match Gallus flagon for flagon. So he sighed and gave in, as if he imbibed at the rate his pride demanded he'd need the stomach of a hog!

The drinking match seemed to lose its relevance when Gallus started to recount his news from the north. Something of a power struggle had developed in Gwynedd he told them, as Pendragon had several male relatives as well as one or two natural sons. But though various alliances had been formed they'd soon dissolved as the claimants conspired to take his place as king. And this was not all!

Helena was sitting at their feet gazing at Gallus as if he were a professional story teller, and when the governor of Chester stroked her cheek Marcus coughed uncomfortably.

"There are many claimants to Maelgwyn's inheritance!" Anthonius was telling them, "and the chiefs are looking at Gwynedd with avaricious eyes. Even the lord of the Brigantes has visited Deganwy I hear... looking for signs of weakness perhaps?"

Germanicus was wondering if he should go north, but Gallus shook his head.

"The journey would be dangerous at this time of year and there's nothing you could do!" he frowned, and Marcus had to agree. If the Celts were weakened by their divisions it would do Ambrosius no harm, he told himself. In the past the duke's policy had been to let them get on with it, and he'd do the same.

Helena was collecting things for her baby. She'd arranged her dolls in a circle under her window and as Marcus watched he saw again what a child she was. Though she could discuss strategy like a seasoned campaigner and even swear when the mood took her, she allowed her old nurse to order her about as if she was still a little girl. And she was looking forward to the birth as if it was a festival with presents and parties. So he sighed, telling himself that the old woman would provide enlightenment when the time came.

He felt useless as he absentmindedly rearranged the little pile of toys and clothes, and found himself wondering if Helena had any idea of the ordeal she was facing. The old woman sent him a reproachful glare whenever she saw him, and when he watched his child bride playing with her dogs he suspected that the crone might be right to resent his affrontary.

Helena had a double edged personality, and where the old woman saw only one side her husband saw both. All vestige of the child disappeared when they were alone, and the big eyes lost their innocence immediately she wrapped herself round him. Her curves were more pronounced now, and the vigour of motherhood seemed to have increased her need of him. Her unfailing welcome never failed to surprise, and her passion was growing more heated as the months passed.

As they ran in the snow like children the old woman clasped her hands in horror.

"What if my lady hurts herself... what would the master say?" And Germanicus suspected that Ambrosius would say what he'd said a few minutes earlier.

"You should take more care and think of the child Helena!" But the duke knew as well as he did that as soon as his back was turned his daughter would have her way in spite of him.

Sweeping down the hill on her little sledge Helena came to rest with a bump, and killing his laughter Marcus decided to put a stop to her foolishness. He'd take her back to the house whether she agreed or not, he decided. And predictably her face turned to petulance as he pulled her to her feet.

"I don't want to go back! Don't treat me like a child!" she protested, but Germanicus shook his head.

"Do you want to lose the child?" he demanded angrily, and Helena sulked at him. "Alright, think of yourself... how would you feel if it were lost?" Marcus growled. "You'd have nothing to look forward to...." he added his voice suddenly soft and weedling, but Helena just rolled her tongue and made a little hole in her lips to put it through.

Even so he could see that the message had gone home.

"Don't put your tongue out at me!" he told her sternly, "what would you do?"

"I'd do what I'm going to do now..." "I'd take you to my bed and you'd give me another one!"

She was laughing as she ran off, and throwing snowballs at him.

"If you won't let me to enjoy myself out here," she laughed, "you can take me inside and please me." But Marcus was shaking his head as he pulled her after him into the house, as his role seemed to hover somewhere between lover and nursemaid now, and the latter made him uncomfortable.

A fire burned in his bedchamber, and warming himself in front of it Marcus removed his wet clothes. Then he watched Helena, knowing that she'd wait till he was naked before coming to him. He knew her passions so well, and she'd not hesitate long before creeping over.

Her breasts were heavy and when he pressed his face into them she'd ruffle his hair. When her eyes rolled up she'd clutch him and lie still, then he'd watch her, till sleep weighed her eyelids and the mask of the child came down again.

The governor of Chester was admiring the line of ships tied up along the quay. He'd spent the morning walking the dockyards and was suitably impressed. But as Marcus approached them Galarius saw a shadow cross his companion's face.

"He's a lucky fellow," Anthonius whispered with a nod at the younger man, "but perhaps we should get him away while there's still some vigour left in him?"

"You'd have an ally in the old woman, she'd like to see him gone too!" Galarius whispered back, and Anthonius acknowledged the little man's reading of the situation with a hardly discernible nod.

"Women in her condition have unnatural desires and the child won't makes its appearance for months!" he muttered, and Galarius was all agreement.

"How right you are my friend, the lady should be resting in preparation for her ordeal!" he declared.

Germanicus was watching the weather. Another heavy fall of snow made it hard to believe that in little more than a month the blossoms should be opening, and he feared that spring would be late this year. A dark pall had been hanging overhead since autumn. The sky didn't brighten even when the snow clouds had released their burden, and for some reason the sun god was hiding his face.

Marcus was remembering the previous year when they'd moored under the hill fort, and suddenly a picture of the red glen rising behind the

167

crannog entered his mind. It seemed as if the hawthorn berries, congealed now to lifeless brown, were flowing towards him. And in his imagination the valley appeared to take on the shape of a corpse, which reared up threateningly. Then the dark mass fell back as if in exhaustion. And would spring come this year? Marcus found himself wondering. Or had his god deserted him?

Marcus spent the next morning sauntering aimlessly round the villa, knowing that as the duke's detached manner cloaked a deep affection for his daughter he was unlikely to be delaying his return deliberately.

Then he remembered Helena's mother and suddenly his mind was made up, as it was inconceivable that the duke was delaying on purpose. Helena's face was often clouded with apprehension now he'd noticed. Was she thinking about her confinement, or was she afraid that something was wrong over the water?

The sea was calm, dark and brooding, the sky a perfect reflection of it. And they made good progress as the banks of oars dipped regularly into the metallic water.

No peaks loomed threateningly over their heads, and Gallus Anthonius was enjoying himself as he stood on the prow shouting at the empty sea. But Galarius, small and insignificant at his side, was quiet as he strained his eyes for a sight of the opposite coast.

They came ashore at Boulogne as the light of the invisible sun faded, and Germanicus ran up the hill to the fortress. He was followed by the others, and here where Rome still held a foothold they were welcomed to the fire with flagons of wine. But the garrison commander shook his head when they enquired about the duke.

"We've had no news since he left in September," he told them as he ruffled through a pile of papers. "But the weather's been atrocious and as the roads are impassable we're cut off from the interior."

"How long would it have taken them to reach the forest?" Marcus asked, and the commander shrugged.

"If they took the direct route not more than a couple of days... but I understood their intention was to search for the would-be emperor?" There was humour in his voice and Marcus raised an eyebrow.

"You don't have much faith in our prospective ruler then?" he grunted, and his companion shrugged.

"We've seen enough of them come and go to guess what's to come. They engage a few ex-legionaries, conquer a couple of towns and then disappear!"

"Is this one any different?"

"I doubt it....he'll run out of money or luck or both, and we'll hear no more about him."

The stern soldier's face was impassive as he rose to refill their cups.

"Whether we like it or not the empire has gone," he sighed.

"Civilisation has gone too if I'm any judge, and it's every man for himself now. The duke seemed like a good man....." the garrison commander went on sadly, "but he should concentrate on his own patch instead of plunging into politics!"

Germanicus found himself nodding, but Anthonius was shaking his head vigorously as he patted their host on the back.

"Come now friend, that's defeatist talk. I believe that Ambrosius will find the man he's looking for and we'll have a strong emperor before long. A couple of battles..." the governor of Chester added, taking his sword from its scabbard and holding it up to the light, "and everything will be back to normal!" The others were looking sceptical but no one spoke.

They couldn't leave the fort as the roads were still blocked, but the black pall hanging over Britain hadn't reached their side of the channel Marcus noticed. It seemed to be hovering half way across as if unwilling to leave the islands, and was this another omen he wondered?

There was no choice but to wait for the thaw. February came to an end and March too, then spring was on them and suddenly the earth melted. Pushing up with impudent haste as if to make up for lost time the grass began to grow. Lambs where gambling and winter was forgotten, on this side of the water at least.

But their long planned journey into the interior was of short duration, and instead of entering the dark oak forests they found themselves back on the coast. Setting out in a north easterly direction the rescue party travelled only a day before meeting Ambrosius coming the other way. And this was fortunate, as if they'd gone a little further to the point where the road forked they'd have passed like ships in the night.

His father-in-law's efforts to ally himself with the fledgling emperor had failed Marcus gathered, and he was unusually reticent.

"All in good time and I'll explain everything but for now I'm impatient to see my homeland.... and my daughter."

This was the first time Germanicus had heard his father-in-law refer to Britain as his homeland and he was intrigued. Had the duke really failed in his mission? he wondered, as he seemed happy enough and purposeful in a way they hadn't seen before. What had happened in the Teutoborge forest, and what brought about this change? Marcus asked himself. But though patience wasn't one of his more obvious characteristics, he was powerless to induce the duke to unburden his soul. He'd speak, Ambrosius said, in his own time.

"What's been happening in my absence?" The duke's voice was humming with high spirits as he bounded down the slope to the ship, but Marcus just shrugged.

"Nothing that need concern you sir."

The younger man was feeling resentful. How could Ambrosius behave like this? he was asking himself, not only leaving him out of the action but refusing to say why he'd stayed away so long. It was unforgivable, and surely he had a right to an explanation?

"How so?" Ambrosius had stopped suddenly, his voice was a little less jovial and Marcus tried to remember what he'd said last. Then he smiled to himself, as he'd succeeded in injecting a hint of concern into his commander's voice at least.

"Oh... I meant nothing important has happened." Then he paused deliberately. "Except that Hengist and Horsa have set up new headquarters.... near London."

"Where?" There was real concern in the duke's voice now and Marcus tried to look serious.

"Oh, somewhere on the Thames estuary.... on the edge of the marshes."

As they set off again Germanicus was smiling. 'That would teach Ambrosius to go off adventuring' he told himself, 'leaving him to manage a lot of bloodthirsty natives and repel an invasion, not to mention playing nursemaid to a pregnant schoolgirl!' He'd had all the responsibilities and none of the powers! the young man sniffed, glorying in self righteous indignation and seething away under the surface as he ran to keep up.

"What do you think they'll do?" Ambrosius was asking his advice? Marcus allowed himself a sly smirk.

"I'm only a young man sir.... and a foreigner at that!"

"Who said that?"

"You did sir, you said Britain is your homeland, and I'm a Roman!"

"Anybody else?" Ambrosius sighed stopping in his tracks again.

"The chiefs."

"You called a meeting?"

"I had no choice as we didn't know if... when you were coming back!"

Ambrosius coughed and seemed to take the point.

"What was decided?" he enquired.

"Nothing! I summoned the chiefs I thought we could trust to meet at Winchester in October."

"You knew then, about Hengist?" And Germanicus nodded, deliberately grave faced.

"Yes... the spies say he's built himself a new hall, though he intends to move on again in the spring....and take London."

Ambrosius was rubbing his chin and Marcus could see he was worried.

"I hadn't expected that, I thought he'd avoid the capital and press north."

"Oh!"

"What did the chiefs have to say?" Ambrosius asked earnestly.

"As I said, I invited the ones I thought were loyal...."

"Yes?" The duke snapped.

"You'll know that Vortigern held a meeting of the high council last summer?"

"Yes... did you discover what they talked about?"

"Well, Vortigern seems to have put more effort into encouraging the chiefs to attend than in previous years...."

The duke was staring at him sullenly, wondering what could have prompted this fit of tight lipped reserve, and eventually Marcus went on, albeit reluctantly.

"They say he tried to wean them away from their allegiance to you."

"Ah, I should have expected that!"

Disappointment coloured the duke's voice now and in his present mood Marcus could do nothing but despise him for it.

"It seems I put too much store on Vortigern's reaction to the murder of his people last year," Ambrosius sighed setting off again slowly. "I was so sure it would teach him a lesson and convince him to join forces with us."

"On the contrary!" Marcus grunted, "he thinks he made a fool of himself, and if he has any desire to rise in your estimation it's by making a better job of his peacemaking next time."

"By all the gods!" Ambrosius was speechless, and Marcus wondered if he was going to be sick he looked so miserable as he leant over the rail of the galley. "So the chiefs weren't amenable to your suggestions at Winchester?"

"They were even more indecisive than usual," Marcus replied wearily. "Your absence made the whole thing impossible and they refused to take any action till you returned!"

CHAPTER XIV
The Battle of Crayford

Hengist and Germanicus viewed the black cloud hanging over Britain very differently, and any apprehension Hengist might have felt was dispelled when a longship from the Norselands appeared in the estuary. The Vikings came ashore, and as they were the people of Odin were entertained like long lost brothers. Their stories were almost unbelievable, and when their chieftain began to describe his voyage to the north of Caledonia the previous year the hall fell silent.

"There's an island there that we adventurers call Iceland," he explained.

"Some believe it's the home of the gods, and though I doubted it at one time I now know it to be true."

Every eye in the place was fixed on the chief's face, and after a gulp of ale he went on.

"There's no doubt of it!" he told them, his green eyes glinting, "as when we drew near a great roar met our ears. This must be the nest of Thor! I thought to myself, as one of the mountains had opened up to spew fire into the air. The black cloud we'd sailed under for so many days was coming from there, and it was throwing great lumps of rock into the sea too. 'Thor is displeased with us!' one of the men shouted when one hit the water not a mile away and the wave nearly submerged us."

"Then what?" Hengist spluttered, and throwing back his matt of red hair the Viking wiped his fingers on his beard.

"We turned back of course," he shrugged, "as Thor was angry and went on throwing bolts at us as we rowed away."

'So the black cloud was the work of the north gods!' Hengist thought to himself, 'and as his folk worshiped Odin who was the father of Thor, this must be his way of helping them!'

The duke took a deep lungful of air as he stepped ashore.

"I'm glad to be home Marcus, you've no idea how glad," he declared happily. And the younger man smiled.

"It's always good to be home sir."

"But it's different this time..." Ambrosius confided, "and somehow I feel that this will be the last time they welcome me home."

The implication was disturbing, but Ambrosius laughed their doubts away.

"Never fear, I'll be with you for a good many years yet, and it wasn't death I saw when I looked into the future. My journey to Gaul has changed me," he added as he bounded up the steps from the quay, "changed my opinions, opinions I've held since I was a boy, opinions that were passed down the generations like heirlooms."

Marcus was wondering if his father-in-law had undergone some kind of religious conversion, but the duke's voice was as firm as ever.

"I saw that my place is here, and if history remembers me at all it will be because of what I do here!" He concluded firmly.

Was Ambrosius committing himself single-mindedly to the defence of the islands? Marcus wondered, and were his dreams of helping to choose a new emperor fading? He hadn't admitted it even to himself, but he'd always had his doubts about the expedition to Gaul. And though a show of relief would be out of place the duke's change of mind was welcome, as it confirmed his opinion that they had to concentrate on driving back the Saxons.

Taking his son-in-law by the arm as they approached the villa Ambrosius led him to a seat on the veranda. Then taking another deep breath as if savouring the pleasures of home he waved his leather bound forearm across the water and went on with his story.

"I always believed in Rome Marcus, it was the bedrock of my life and without it there was nothing. I was brought up to believe in the everlasting quality of the eternal city, and my loyalty was to that ideal."

Then a slave padded up with wine, and taking a goblet the duke cupped it in his hands and squinted over the rim towards the invisible coast of Gaul.

"The only rescue I could believe in was a rescue from Rome, my only civilisation was Roman and my only master the emperor," he sighed. And rising to his feet Marcus leant on the parapet.

"Do I understand you correctly...?" he asked, and the suppressed pleasure in his voice amused the duke.

"Don't you see? It's all so simple... so very simple," the older man laughed. "As however much we want the return of Rome it will be denied us. It's gone, and no amount of wishing will bring it back!" he added pressing the heel of his hand to his brow. "But why has it taken me so long to understand?"

"It's like that with all of us," Marcus conceded, "We just refuse to understand. When I first landed here the governor of Dover thought I'd brought news of a rescue, and I'll always remember his words: 'It seemed right to hope somehow,' he said."

"That's it exactly!" Ambrosius agreed avidly, "it was our duty to restore the old order. But something happened as I watched them preparing to attack Rome yet again. I remembered Magnus Maximus," he went on eagerly, "a man who ruled a land that could so easily have become a nation... but it wasn't enough for him."

The duke had rested his elbows on his knees and was staring at the floor between his feet.

"It wasn't enough ... and in the end Magnus' quest for glory destroyed him as it destroyed others before him. The tragedy is that it's taken us... taken me, so long to learn the lesson.... the lesson that a good leader pays heed to his own defences and has no right to take sides in other men's quarrels."

Then, smiling sidelong at his son-in-law Ambrosius changed the subject.

"I've heard more reports of your exploits!" he whispered. And as his commander slapped him on the back Marcus felt suddenly guilty. "Why the modesty my sensitive friend?" the duke grinned, "they say you acquitted yourself with honour!"

"I did nothing I'm ashamed of..." Marcus heard his own voice full of defensive self-justification, and as the memory of his contest with Aelwulf came back in awful clarity Ambrosius watched his face.

"They say a lady of nobility sought your attentions?" the duke smiled, and Marcus blushed and turned away.

"Cordelia...? She was the daughter of a man I respected and I'd have been proud to be his son-in-law.... but...."

"You couldn't love the girl?" Ambrosius had lifted his fine brows, then he shrugged, as his enquiries were unwelcome he could see. "I'm sorry Marcus, a man has a right to his secrets... especially in matters of love!" he grinned.

Then to the younger man's relief the duke turned his attention to Vortigern.

"I hear there's to be another meeting of the Great Council?" he murmured and Marcus nodded as he drew a rolled map from his belt.

"The meeting is to take place at Camulodunum." (Colchester) he explained pointing to the place on the map.

"Mmmm..." The duke had taken the map but was gazing into the distance.

"Camulodunum north east of London?"

"Is there another?" Marcus asked, and throwing the map aside the duke pointed to the sundial on the lawn beneath them.

"As a matter of fact there is!" he frowned raising his eyes to the dull sky before turning back to the dial. "These things are useless here," he grunted, "as the clouds are so permanent!" Then he seemed to remember himself. "What was I saying? Ah yes Camulodunum, the other place of that name is on the road between Deva (Chester) and Eboracum (York). My father thought it might be a good centre of resistance if things went badly in the south."

Germanicus would like to have known more about the duke's father Ambrosius the elder, who'd been duke of Britain in the early days of Vortigern's reign. But this didn't seem the right time to ask.

"I'll tell you something else," Ambrosius was frowning, "I wish Vortigern would hold his council there as it's safer."

"Surely you don't expect the Saxons to attack Vortigern again... he's their most enthusiastic ally..."

"He was."

"You think the night of the long knives changed his views?"

"On the contrary, fear has made him a better friend to Hengist than ever."

Ambrosius was leaning against the parapet, and as he gripped it with strong well-formed hands his voice was tinged with humour.

"I've noticed your habit of judging others by your own standards Marcus," he smiled as he set off into the house. "But Hengist needs to deal with the Celts whether they're a threat at present or not, and there's nothing we can do about it if Vortigern won't face reality. All we can do is wait and see!"

That evening Germanicus walked along the beach with Galarius, and as he recounted his conversation with the duke it was clear how much he appreciated his father-in-law's change of priorities. But the reaction from his friend was unexpectedly negative.

"So one man has forsaken his love of Rome... will that make a difference in the struggle for Britain?" the little man grunted, and Germanicus stopped dead in his tracks.

"The duke is a powerful man and others will follow his example," he insisted, and Galarius tried not to smile at the doubt in his voice.

"So Ambrosius is powerful," the little man replied turning his lined face up in question, "but it hasn't made things any easier has it?"

Marcus was busy skimming a succession of pebbles across the darkening water, and Galarius watched him for a while before speaking again.

"If anyone can do it the duke can!" he ventured picking up a piece of flint and weighing it thoughtfully in his hand. "But the pride that makes men want to be emperor in Rome, or king of Gwynedd, won't go away. And do the petty kings share the duke's determination to save these islands at all costs?"

If these were words of wisdom they were wasted, as his master was walking briskly up the beach and Galarius had been talking to himself.

The child was born, as his father predicted it was a boy and they called him Arturius.

"Why did you choose that name?" Ambrosius asked, and Marcus smiled as he stroked the small face peering out from the crib..

"Because it means 'The Bear,'" he whispered. "They say a name transmits qualities to its bearer, and Arthur will need the strength of a bear if he's to succeed in his task."

"Marcus is fey father, he sees the future or thinks he does!" Helena interrupted taking her husband's arm. And the guests who'd come to celebrate the birth smiled indulgently.

"Are you a seer Germanicus as well as a soldier?" one asked laughing at his own wit. But Ambrosius understood.

"I'd hoped that when this little one takes over we'd have peace.... are you saying I'm wrong?" And when Marcus answered his voice was strangely subdued.

"I don't think that conquering the Saxons will be as simple as you hope," he murmured, and Ambrosius put an arm round his shoulders.

"Have you no faith in me?" he laughed, and the others laughed too, this time nervously as Germanicus looked his father-in-law in the eye.

"No... if any man can drive them back it's you.. but there'll come a time..."

"When Arturius is master and I'm dead?" The duke's voice was still good humoured and Marcus sighed heavily.

"Yes, when you and I are both dead."

Then Gallus Anthonius came in.

"Come friends, this is a joyful day and there should be no foreboding!" But the governor of Chester received only doubtful stares for his pains, and went away feeling less confident than he was accustomed to do.

As the company set off to parade the gardens in the wake of the nurse who held the child Gallus slid in next to Germanicus.

"Surely you can't doubt our eventual triumph?" he whispered, and his companion shrugged.

"Sometimes I do, and if Arturius.. or any ruler were to control Britain, he'd need not only the strength of a bear but the cunning of a fox !"

Accepted wisdom said that a few determined men equipped with the necessary skills, most importantly the killer instinct, could in time

177

conquer any number of lesser men. And Marcus had never doubted that this was an unalterable truth. But the battle for Britain wasn't simply a contest between brave warriors on the one hand and short-sighted natives on the other. As in addition to bravery and perseverance the Saxons had other weapons in their armoury. Not only were they fighting to win land, they were breeding the folk who'd inhabit those lands. They were breeding at such a rate that in a couple of generations they would outnumber the natives. The ways of the invaders would soon become the norm. The language would be the language of the conquerors and in order to be accepted as equals the natives would adopt it. To deviate from the new norm would become first unpopular, then impractical, and finally illegal. True, if future rulers of the remaining Romans and Celts possessed the necessary strength perseverance and cruelty, the invaders could be overcome and expelled or enslaved. To bring this about the people would need the qualities of self-confidence and ruthlessness that had made Rome great. But now there would be no more guidance from Rome and the Romanised ruling class was disappearing, Marcus knew this would not be the case. Then there was religion. A nation's gods represented the spirit of the people, he knew. And as the Saxons were such a bloodthirsty lot so were their gods. Roman religion had been distorted over the years, and as for the Celts, their religion as well as their self confidence had been destroyed by four hundred years of occupation.

A dull midsummer was on them now and the petty kings were gathering in Colchester for the meeting of the Great Council. Ambrosius and Germanicus travelled as far the river mouth with what Vortigern called their 'army', and several hundred mounted troops as well as foot soldiers followed their standard.

The column passed under the town walls before turning away to make camp on an island in the estuary. And when tents were erected and defences secured the duke and his officers left for more comfortable lodgings in a nearby villa.

They'd not been invited to attend the Great Council and Vortigern made it clear he didn't want them in the town at all, with or without the intimidating soldiery. The high king of the Celts was behaving like a child Marcus thought, a child who wants his father out of the room when he entertains his friends.

The City walls enclosed barracks and houses, but the familiar grid pattern of streets and squares had lost its graceful symmetry and every space was filled with dwellings. Wooden booths crowded among the older

178

buildings, and so great was the press that the public spaces were completely filled. Like a flock of birds at a banquet they jostled the rightful guests for space and air. Every makeshift hut seemed to boast a smoking roof, and discharging slowly into the stillness the smoke hung trapped over the once proud city.

The Romans observed and passed on, content in the knowledge that Vortigern was aware of their strength. And soon they were making themselves at home in the villa of Ambrosius' senior man in the area.

Two days were to pass before Vortigern sent his messenger, but Ambrosius seemed resigned to the delay.

"Vortigern is a proud man, our arrival has put him out of temper and I'd half expected him to ignore us altogether!" the duke sighed as Germanicus sat down next to him among the officers.

"Perhaps he wants something... why else would he acknowledge our presence?" Marcus murmured, and Ambrosius waved the messenger forward.

The Celt seemed very proud for a minion Germanicus thought, and his bow was barely noticeable.

"My master the Lord High King of the Celts sends his greetings!" he began, and though the absence of proper titles made several heads turn Ambrosius ignored the slight.

"How can we serve your master?" he asked.

But the mockery in his voice was lost on the messenger, who continued in the same pompous tone as before.

"King Vortigern summons you to meet him outside the town at noon tomorrow, and will inform you then of his plans for the next year."

Germanicus had started to rise intending to knock the fool down, but the duke waved him back.

"We'll meet your master at the appointed place.... Is there anything else?" And the messenger hesitated, uncertain of their reaction to his final instructions.

"You are to come unarmed and with a only few retainers," he told them hurriedly before making off, and Germanicus found it hard to control his anger.

"How can you take instructions from that upstart Vortigern?" he demanded, but the duke was laughing under his breath.

"I agreed to meet the old fool but made no promise to go unarmed." Then he shook his head impatiently. "I doubt if Vortigern expects us to comply with such a condition in any case, and no doubt it was made for the sake of his pride as appearances are important to the Celts."

Next day as the sun reached its zenith Vortigern and his party arrived at the meeting place. The king had chosen a wooded hollow just off the road, but the Romans watched him edge his mount down the slope as if they'd arranged his undignified arrival on purpose.

The old man was taking his time struggling down the rock strewn bank, and they could hear his nobles cursing above the sound of the stream. But at last the royal party with its priests and its crosses reached even ground, and true to form Vortigern scowled at them.

"I didn't expect this of you Ambrosius, I thought you a man of honour!"

"So I am to all who deal fairly with me," the duke replied. Then Vortigern turned his head and Germanicus saw how weary he looked.

But the thin voice was the same.

"You were hidden from the road and we were surprised by the size of your escort lord duke," he complained.

"But you chose the meeting place yourself lord king!" Ambrosius smiled, and Vortigern sniffed as if he had a bad smell under his nose.

"Why have you come to Colchester?" he snapped. And when he replied the duke's tone was still affable, though he dispensed with the affectation of titles.

"You hold a great council to seek the views of the powerful men of the land do you not?" he answered. And when Vortigern looked blank, shrugging his shoulders and fidgeting, he went on. "Am I not a figure of importance in the game we're playing?" Ambrosius continued, and Vortigern nodded grudgingly.

"I didn't think you'd be interested in our CELTIC deliberations," he grunted, emphasising the word 'Celtic' to underline Ambrosius's status as an outsider. But as the duke wouldn't consider inclusion in the Celtic race a compliment he remained unruffled..

"Some things concern us all," he answered in the same friendly tone, and Vortigern made a face.

"Us?"

"Yes! for the love of the gods Vortigern... us!" Quiet venom stiffened the cultivated voice now and the duke sighed. "We're aboard the same vessel lord king, and if we don't join forces we'll all be lost!"

But Vortigern's thin shoulders simply rose and fell again.

"You Romans are the invaders!" he sneered. And as the petty kings laughed behind their hands even the priests smiled.

Ambrosius was trying desperately to communicate, but Vortigern continued to stare at him unmoved.

"If we're to survive we must unite... for the present at least!" Ambrosius asserted. And the appeal in his voice impressed Marcus, who'd never heard such diplomacy before. But when he looked at Vortigern he saw the thin face set in self congratulation. The king was visibly pleased that the great man was seeking his help it seemed, and enjoyed having the duke play supplicant.

"For the present - and how long will that present extend I wonder?" Vortigern enquired. "Our enslavement to Rome has already lasted for four hundred years."

Marcus sensed that the duke was struggling to keep his temper, but Vortigern took the lack of response as acceptance of his point.

"You live in a world of logistics and strategy lord duke," he intoned condescendingly. "But then you are a humble soldier after all!"

This was too much and filling his lungs Germanicus unsheathed his sword. But the duke lifted a hand to restrain him, and Vortigern paused only to send Marcus a contemptuous glance before continuing."

"And there are other considerations... even more important than your earthly strategies." he sniffed.

The priests were edging their mounts forward Marcus noticed.

"King Vortigern is a wise monarch lord duke!" a bony friar on Vortigern's right asserted with calm confidence. And though Ambrosius sent him a withering look his voice remained controlled.

"And who are you brother?" he sighed.

"I am the king's chaplain and advisor... sent from Rome to be his bishop!"

"I'm honoured to make your acquaintance," Ambrosius muttered, and the priest made a curt nod of acknowledgment before hurrying on.

"The king is right, and heavenly considerations must take precedence over earthly wisdom."

"Earthly wisdom?" Ambrosius repeated, and raising his skeletal face the priest lifted his eyes to heaven.

"The desire to spill blood is as vile in the sight of our Lord as any other sin, my sons," he told them. And when they remained unmoved his voice took on the hardness of impatience. "'Thou shalt not kill!'" he bellowed. "The Saxons are our brothers and our Lord demands that we treat them as such. 'Love thine enemy!' This is the word of God and you deny it at your peril!"

Ambrosius who was resting on his saddle horn just sighed.

"Are you saying we should let the invaders take the land?" he enquired wearily.

"You oversimplify matters my son," the priest replied making the sign of the cross over the duke, presumably in forgiveness of his foolishness. "With the blessing of God the pagans will be brought to the true faith, as the ways of the almighty are mysterious and his wisdom is not like yours. Military might is not the only way to triumph over our enemies," he went on, "and is it not better to win their minds than to kill them?"

The duke's face was tired and his voice reflected his expression.

"We are fortunate indeed to receive your instruction brother and we thank you," he murmured before turning his horse and starting up the hill.

Vortigern hurried after him, catching up as they reached the road.

"You should know that my decision is not yet made lord duke," he whispered glancing furtively over his shoulder, "as I must pray and consult my advisors." And Ambrosius favoured him with a look of contempt.

"We travel to the Thames estuary, and if I'm right we'll find the Saxons gathering there in large numbers ready to march on London. Is it your intention to join us?" he demanded, and fear as well as shock paled Vortigern's lined face.

"You exaggerate surely lord duke?"

Ambrosius didn't answer as he set off in the direction from which they'd come not an hour before. Then after a few yards he turned.

"Be there to fight at our side Vortigern... if you value your city!"

Safe again inside the walls of Colchester Vortigern paused only to shiver at the memory of his ordeal before calling his chiefs together.

"Ambrosius thinks the Saxons mean to take London," he told them, and several laughed nervously. But one, an ally of the duke, spoke up.

"The evidence says he is right!" The tone was direct, and Vortigern who was accustomed to having his truths watered down took exception.

"How can you possibly know that, as your lands are far to the north?" he hissed. And though the man lowered his eyes another came forward, this time one of the king's close companions.

"It's true sir... all our spies agree and we must accept the evidence of our eyes. The Saxons didn't halt their progress after Aylesford but simply became less visible."

"Ha! so they've taken to creeping like beggars!" Vortigern was trying to sound confident but no one failed to notice the fear in his voice. Then the chief from the north spoke again.

"I've attended this council as bidden, but my allegiance to the duke remains firm as his is the only way."

Vortigern was growing exited.

"But he's a Roman!" And there was silence along the table as the king could still intimidate when he chose. "Have the Romans not enslaved us for nigh on four hundred years?" Vortigern squealed. "And do you want to return to that slavery?"

The northern chief had risen from the table, and bowing to Vortigern was making to leave. But at the door he turned.

"It seems we must chose between loyalty to our king and survival.... I wish it had been otherwise."

There was quiet for a while when he'd gone, then another voice came in.

"He may be right... joining forces with Ambrosius could be the only way to drive out the Saxons." It was the king's second son Catigern, but though every eye turned on him Vortigern refused to consider the possibility.

"I tell you it's the Romans who're the real danger, the Saxons are just another tribe. Saxons, Picts, Scots, what does it matter? They don't have the power to conquer us, only Rome can do that!" His mind was closed and it was left to the chiefs to decide which way to jump. Should they stay loyal to their king? What did expediency demand? Opinions were divided even about that.

The northern chief had made his decision and so had Catigern the second son of Vortigern and Severa. He'd watched his father make peace with the Saxons, seen his mother set aside in favour of Rowena, and he'd take no more.

Standing with the chiefs loyal to Ambrosius in the inner court of the duke's headquarters, Catigern gritted his teeth and made his pledge.

"We've made our decision lord duke, though some of us have wavered in the past." He was looking uncertainly at his new commander and saw only understanding in Ambrosius' face. "But we're your men now!" he finished determinedly.

Leading them to a room where food and wine were laid out the duke threw himself onto a couch and looked up into the ring of doubtful faces.

"We must not condemn Vortigern yet," he murmured skimming the line with his eyes. "But Hengist is gathering an army, and if I'm right he intends to take London."

"To what purpose?" Catigern looked embarrassed and some of the others were laughing, but Ambrosius just shrugged.

"Why, to enable his folk to move north of course! The Angles are landing all along the east coast and Hengist wants to join them," the duke went on stroking his chin thoughtfully. "And in my opinion he intends to become leader of all the Germans in the island."

"He could be planning to link up with the Picts too?" Catigern suggested perceptively, "after all they were his allies till my father paid him to fight them."

Germanicus felt sympathy for this prince, a man of his own age but already tainted by his fathers mistakes. Then Ambrosius put his hand on Catigern's shoulder.

"Put that behind you my friend, you're one of us now."

Ambrosius led his army south, crossing the Thames and joining the forces he'd summoned from Winchester. They numbered several thousand men even without the units delayed in the north, but the duke hadn't reckoned on a battle so early. Though it was now high summer he'd hoped to delay a month before engaging the English. But it was clear that there could be no more delay, as if the Saxons weren't held at Crayford they'd take London and the rest of the country would lie open.

The battle was short, the Romano British hopelessly out-numbered. At the last minute detachments of citizens from Londinium had joined them. But they were nothing more than civilian levies, interspersed with a few old soldiers who preferred to meet the Saxons before they reached the streets of their city.

They told a surprising tale: The troops garrisoned in the city had been withdrawn it seemed, and Vortigern had abandoned his capital.

"My father's army has withdrawn to Colchester?" Catigern was distraught. "What can he mean by it.. and what does he hope to gain?" But the others just shrugged and turned away, as they were weary of trying to make sense of Vortigern's strategy.

As Ambrosius forced his lance into the ground he gritted his teeth."

"By all the gods, must I believe Vortigern cares for nothing but his own survival?" and Catigern hung his head.

"He's a Christian... no doubt he wants to follow the advice of his priests?"

The duke had turned on him eyes staring, then he lifted his sword and waved it threateningly..

"I've heard that cowards excuse too often, and if I hear it from any man again I'll split him neck to groin! Do you hear me? I swear it by great Caesar himself!" He was shouting with uncharacteristic excitement and his officers stepped back, shocked by his flushed face and glaring eyes. For long minutes the duke continued to stare, catching his breath at intervals and gripping his sword as if his life depended on it right now.

The murmur in the distance rose to a roar as the huge wave of Saxons on the horizon materialised into men and horses. Their surge had the impetus of a landslide, and the noise of their feet drumming the earth almost drowned the clattering of armour and weapons. Every second the din grew louder, and above it all rose the war cries, full of pagan joy at the prospect of a blood feast to come.

The Battle was joined on a causeway elevating the road, and the Romans made their bid to halt the Saxon hordes streaming towards the city. But the line of defence was doomed from the start, and after half an hour all the Roman and British units had been driven onto the riverbank. Desperately struggling to keep to the shore they'd no hope of turning the enemy back or even diverting them.

At this point Ambrosius withdrew his cavalry. The detachments still holding to the land were islands now in a sea of enemy troops, and Marcus had to fight his way to the spot where his commander's horse rose above the melee.

Tears of anger and despair burned in the young soldier's eyes.

"What are you doing? For the love of great Jupiter and all the gods what have you done?" he yelled as Romulus struggled on the marshy ground below the road.

But the duke continued to sit immobile above him. Impassive as a statue he was gazing at the British fighting in the water. They were going down in hundreds under the weight of enemy numbers, but Marcus went on demanding an answer.

"You ordered a retreat! You called off your Cavalry! Why? for the love of Mithras - why?"

"Can't you see why?" And as Marcus followed the duke's gaze across the river his heart sank. Yes he could see. This had been a mistake, they'd been forced to fight before they were ready and the fates had turned against them.

His leader's voice was almost breaking.

"If Vortigern had brought his army perhaps we could have held them back as we did at Aylesford?" Then with a sigh he turned his horse away from the pitiful sight. "What you see is a massacre...and yes, I ordered the retreat and called off my valuable cavalry. They must be saved to fight another day," he went on almost calmly. Then a hint of the anger they'd seen before the battle returned to colour his final words. "Or would you rather we fight and die here... with no hope of survival let alone eventual victory?"

185

Marcus was shaking his head as Romulus backed away, and taking a last look over the bloody river he started to follow the retreating horsemen and foot soldiers to the road. Would they find their retreat blocked? It seemed not, as the Saxons were surging across the ford towards the city, leaving their enemies to retreat and the bodies to the tides.

Strong stone walls towered above them. Vortigern had received news of of their defeat at Crayford it seemed and had closed the gates of Colchester against them.

"I wonder if he's heard about Catigern?"

Marcus was looking sulkily at the duke, still in full armour and sitting perfectly still on his equally immobile horse, but Ambrosius appeared not to hear.

Then after a while he turned his head.

"I'm sure he knows by now." And Marcus took the hint that this was no time for conversation. The duke had taken the defeat at Crayford badly, and the discovery of Catigern's body had sent him into a long self-questioning silence. The Saxons would be sacking London by now and they were powerless to prevent it. So as Ambrosius ground his teeth in impotent rage Germanicus shared his despair and felt doubt pricking at his optimism. If their unshakable leader could be shaken like this....?

Several days elapsed before the siege engines were in place, but once in position the huge catapults were soon firing boulders at the walls and into the city. Rocking back and forth with monotonous and deadly regularity they were bringing panic and death to Colchester. The engineers heaving missiles from carts alongside laboured like ants under the huge defences. But the defences had been built by Romans and were standing up to the attack remarkably well.

After a night and a day of pounding the duke seemed to lose his tenseness and become his old self. Though the debacle at Crayford had struck deep into his pride he was not a man to let setbacks deflect him from his purpose. And as the sun sank and the summer evening turned to night the order was given to replace the missiles with incendiaries.

The only star in the sky was Venus. Then another almost as bright appeared overhead, and Galarius sniffed the air as he left the stables where he'd been filling mangers and water troughs. It was the hour between day and night when the sky is too bright for stars and time hangs suspended. Held for a moment in awe as the pink sunset faded the little

186

man waited for the spell to break. As soon the blue, pink and grey would slip together into the flat blackness of night.

Then he heard noise in the stables behind him, as others were sniffing the air too and stamping their hooves in anxiety. The smell of smoke was unmistakable and Galarius smiled as he turned back to comfort the animals.

He was still smiling as he went along the rows speaking softly to the horses. 'So the duke has tired of Vortigern's tantrums at last!' he thought to himself. 'Colchester is on fire and the rule of the duke's rival is coming to an end.'

He tried to think about the people trapped in the town, running this way and that even now searching for a way out of the inferno. Well respected men would show themselves cowards, he fancied. They'd be climbing on the backs of others to avoid the flames and trying to bribe the gatekeepers, who'd have no power to help or even save themselves. Others, who'd lived lives of obscurity would die heroes the little man guessed. And sadness slowed his movements as he bent to gather empty feed sacks and water buckets.

The needless defeat at Crayford had exhausted the duke's patience. And though Vortigern sent emissaries to make excuses, claiming his forces had set out but were somehow prevented from reaching the battle. It was evident he'd stayed in Colchester keeping most of his troops with him. Some who'd been billeted in the surrounding countryside made their own decisions and joined Ambrosius. And even those who'd stayed behind defected when they saw the duke laying siege to the city.

The citizens of London faced the Saxons without their king and with a depleted garrison. Their only hope lay in surrender, and it was fortunate for them that Hengist didn't intend to stay in the capital.

Nevertheless he accepted the keys of the city rather sheepishly from the aldermen, and even made a half hearted attempt to restrain his troops. But as he often said: he was not a city man. By early autumn the corridors of Vortigern's palace were deserted once more. Hengist was on the road north and the Saxons from Kent were returning to their homes.

Flaming missiles flew over the walls of Colchester, and landing among the huddled houses turned markets and streets into channels of fire. At first it seemed the place must be deserted as nothing moved among the dancing flames. Then figures began to appear against the light, men and women children and animals. There was no lack of willing shoulders to get the great creaking gates open. But they moved with agonising slowness, allowing first a trickle then a flood of terrified citizens to pass out.

"Vortigern is letting the people go at last!" Marcus frowned as they watched from the platform of a siege engine, "but he's left it too late and many won't make it."

One after another the wooden houses were falling into the pool of fire. And the flames were licking at the stone buildings too as they stretched up from the structures resting against their sides. Leaping across gaps and slithering along the ground they seemed to have a life and will of their own.

Vortigern had demolished the central basilica and built a great palace of timber in its place. But the flames were no respecters of rank, and the king's hall fell into the fire as quickly as the huts of the common folk. The fire was devouring Vortigern's symbols of a new Britain, independent and free of Rome!

Guards waited outside the gates with orders to detain Vortigern as he fled, and shrinking against the heat they strained stinging eyes into the flood of humanity. The column of smoke rising from the palace gave them no clues, and crackling wood and screaming women said nothing of Vortigern's fate.

The siege towers had been withdrawn a safe distance and were used now like stands at the races. From these vantage points the Romans watched the end of their reluctant ally, and like theatre-goers applauded the activities below. Then suddenly the last wall of the new palace collapsed sending clouds of sparks into the illuminated sky.

They watched for a long time before descending to take the road to the villa, and no one doubted the wisdom of this night's action. As if Ambrosius was to succeed, a tragedy like Crayford could not go unavenged.

PART II
several years later

CHAPTER XV
The Boyhood of Arthur

Ambrosius was watching the boy run through the orchard after his wolf hound. The duke's hair was grey at the temples now, and there were lines at the corners of his eyes. But he was still handsome, still a champion at swordplay and deadly accurate when he charged the rings in the practice yard. The lad had a look of him he fancied, though he could see traces of the red haired Germanicus in him and even something of Helena.

Sometimes he saw Marcus' determination in the boy's eyes, and now and then caught him day-dreaming as Helena did. He had his father's reckless bravery as well as his stoicism, which tempered what might otherwise have been too impetuous a character.

As he fell to the ground the boy put his arms round the shaggy animal and pulled it to him.

"One day soon when we race Augustus, I'll be the winner!" he laughed looking up at his grandfather. And Ambrosius smiled.

"That day may not be far off Arturius, as your friend is old in the years of such creatures," the duke replied sadly. And the laughter on the boy's face died immediately.

"Oh, don't say that sir... I've had Augustus for as long as I can remember and I couldn't live without him!"

"There'll be other dogs Arthur, and perhaps you should chose one from the litter in the stables?" the duke suggested, but Arturius looked uncertain.

"I'd like another dog... especially one of Augustus' sons, but he won't replace his father!"

"Of course not," Ambrosius agreed, "the young one will be apprentice to his father and learn his ways."

This seemed to please the child and he ran excitedly to his grandfather.

"Let's go to the stables now sir, as I want to choose the best one before anyone else claims him." And Ambrosius noted the pride in the high pitched voice.

"Of course you must have the pick of the litter Arthur, it wouldn't be right if the best dog went to another!" But the humour was lost on Arturius.

"Yes indeed, it wouldn't be good for my standing with the other boys if someone else had a better dog than me!"

A cloud of foreboding had passed over Ambrosius' face but he pushed the doubts aside as he smiled down.

"When you grow up you'll have to be a better man than all your officers if you're to demand the pick of the spoils. Can you do that little Arthur?" And the use of his pet name made the boy frown.

"Of course I can grandfather, do you doubt me?" Then he threw a stick for Augustus and watched the dog run after it. "But you're right sir...he's slower than he was."

The young face was sad, and when a tear wet the tanned skin under the eyes the duke looked away deliberately.

"Augustus will live a good while yet my boy, he's just older and more stiff than he was that's all." And Arturius laughed, a free bubbling laugh.

"Like you grandfather?" he suggested. And Ambrosius nodded.

"Yes like me Arthur, and like me he'll live long enough to train his successor."

The bitch lay in the corner on a pile of hay. She was ignoring Augustus, who was showing no interest in his multiple offspring as he sniffed about. And this was a wise strategy, as his mate wouldn't tolerate him too near her babies.

Arthur knelt by her side trying to glimpse the squirming forms pawing and kneading her nipples, and when the bitch shifted her position he picked up the runt who hadn't managed to find himself a nipple.

"He's very still sir... why is he so sleepy?" he asked. And taking the small form Ambrosius held it between his hands.

"This one's short life has ended already I'm afraid," he sighed, and Arthur snatched the little body back.

"No.... he's just asleep!" There was panic in the young voice as well as hurt sorrow and disbelief, and the duke tried to comfort him.

"Take another Arthur..... chose another." But the boy jumped to his feet.

"I'll chose another grandfather, I'll come back... maybe tomorrow. But I must lay this one to rest first, that's only right isn't it?" There was no doubt about the tears now, they were flowing unchecked and the duke put his arm round the boy.

"Where will you lay him?" he asked. And Arthur thought for a moment.

"In the cemetery with the soldiers who didn't come back from the last skirmish. He'll be their dog if he can't be mine." The tears were drying now and suddenly the blue eyes fired with hope. "He'll ride out with them in the afterworld. But he must have a name, every dog must have a name like every man."

Arthur set off towards the camp cemetery holding the little body against his chest and stroking it as he went. And when they passed the house he went inside and returned with a piece of silk Ambrosius recognised as one of Helena's shawls.

"I'll wrap him in this." the boy whispered, and his grandfather nodded. The sorrow had eased now, and as resentment at his loss faded Arthur was making plans for the next stage in the existence of the small soul in his hands.

This could be quite a gift Ambrosius pondered. And if the boy had the ability to begin again when all was lost, to put defeat and death out of his mind and make plans for another day, then the gods had indeed blessed him. Somehow the old soldier seemed to sense that his grandson's life would involve many disappointments, and if he were to succeed he'd need this stoic acceptance of the inevitable.

The duke was nodding in approval as he watched the boy lay the little parcel in the shallow trench and fill in the earth. Then the grave edge was carefully outlined with stones and the name was written in the same way.

"Maximus" it said.

"Why do you chose such a grand name for so small a creature?" Ambrosius asked, and Arthur got up and brushed the dust from his tunic.

"Because he's a wolf hound sir, and in the afterlife he'll be a big dog like Augustus." The small face was turned up in expectation and Ambrosius nodded his approval.

It occurred to him that Arthur's Christian teachers would disapprove of the events of the last half hour, and the boy seemed to read his thoughts.

"My tutor brother Paul would say it's wicked to bury an animal as if he were a person, and as dogs don't have souls there's no afterlife for them. But I say he's wrong!" The self possession in the voice had caused the duke's brows to rise, and he waited open mouthed as his grandson went on. "Maximus was alive and will be again, and if there's an after-life why shouldn't he go there like everyone else?"

The duke bowed his head as the boy muttered a few words over the little grave. He didn't hear what they were and didn't ask.

Then they turned towards the living quarters.

"You're very sure of yourself Arturius!" the duke observed, and his voice carried approval as well as question.

"I'll have be be grandfather. And though I'll do what you and father and mother tell me now, when I'm a man no one will rule me and I'll make my own decisions!"

"I think you're right about that Arturius, at any rate that's the rule I've lived by all my life," Ambrosius told him. And waiting only till his grandfather had finished speaking Arthur ran off in the direction of the stables.

They were preparing to leave for the north and Galarius was gathering his master's things from the villa. As he scooped the items needed for the journey into the saddle bags the duke's daughter followed him about. And though she couldn't blame him for the loss of her husband the little man sensed resentment and was glad when he'd finished.

"That's all madam.. I think," he muttered with relief as he left the villa, then he saw the others waiting in the sunshine and relaxed.

"I see we travel light as usual?" Marcus grunted, and Galarius laughed out loud.

"Is it not the only way?" he hooted, glorying in the prospect of the freedom he'd been denied for so long. And Marcus found himself laughing too.

The years had shrunk his little friend even more he noticed, as time takes a heavier toll on the old and Galarius had developed a pronounced stoop. Ambrosius had hardly changed since their first meeting, Marcus reflected, but would he be altered when they returned from the north? And what about Helena? She was still a young woman and though marriage had matured her he was sure she'd stay the same as long as she had good health.

Then he turned and saw her leaning on the door-post. She was wearing the uncertain little girl look that always came when no other emotion animated her features, and he watched her for a moment knowing she'd come to say goodbye eventually.

Helena was waiting till everything was stowed, and Ambrosius was standing by the impatient horse patting his sleek rear.

"This fellow is as healthy and skittish as ever!" he smiled, and Marcus nodded as he took Romulus' rein.

"Do you think he'll be ridden in anger while we're in the north, or will the natives welcome us like brothers?" he asked. And as they laughed together Ambrosius ran his hand along the smooth back.

"You know them as well as I do Marcus... and though a soothsayer might be able to answer your question I can't."

Germanicus was mounted now.

"They say the kingdom of Rheged is prosperous, and Lugovallium (Carlisle) is as Roman as ever." And Ambrosius nodded.

"The town was made a provincial capital hardly a hundred years ago, and as it's younger than the rest perhaps it intends to enjoy its rightful life span?"

"This king of Rheged... Urien, are his threats real?" Marcus asked, and the duke shrugged.

194

"Perhaps...? but it could be just posturing. That's for you to discover, and though I know your courage Marcus, try not to antagonise them!" Then he laughed and raised his hand in farewell. "I have no fears for you as you lost your youthful impetuosity years ago," he called as they set off. "And you can be a good diplomat if you put your mind to it!"

With waves to the comrades who'd come to bid them godspeed and to the few weeping women they left the compound, and five hundred men fell in behind them.

They'd been waiting for Arturius and Helena was still lingering in the doorway twisting her shawl through her fingers as she gazed without blinking at Germanicus. So turning his horse he beckoned her forward and reached down to pull her up.

His words were a caress and only she heard them.

"Goodbye my darling, keep safe till I come back." And as his hand pressed into her waist Helena felt the weakening that always came with his touch. He was holding her tight against his armour, and as a strand of braided hair fell over her shoulder she whispered back.

"Oh Marcus... how will I live without you?"

"You'll be faithful I hope?" Marcus smiled, and the humour in his voice roused resentment,

"You know my love is for you and no one else!" Helena told him, and Marcus experienced a glow of pride, as he knew without doubt that this was true. When he kissed her she shivered, and when he let her down she was sobbing.

Helena's love for him was a need only he could satisfy, and he loved her she knew. But his need could and would be satisfied elsewhere, and when the thought of the women he'd love before she held him again struck into her Helena clenched her hands and turned away.

Three figures met them at the outer gate, Arturius, Augustus, and his son Claudius. The boy had been running, he was was dirty and panting. Ambrosius who'd decided to follow a little way was frowning, and Germanicus could see he was angry.

"Your father is leaving on a dangerous journey, and we're grateful you found the time to bid him farewell!" the duke grunted. But little Arthur was desperately sorry and Germanicus was smiling ready to forgive. However Ambrosius waved him to silence. "You may never see your father again! Do you understand? he hissed, and Arthur shivered."

"Don't be too hard on him... he's only a boy," Marcus whispered. Then he saw the fishing rod clasped in his son's small hand. "Did you catch anything Arthur?" he enquired, and the child's face lit up for a moment before reverting to dismal repentance.

"No father... I wanted to... I wanted to catch a fish for you to take with you. But I stayed too long by the river..." he whispered hanging his head. And Germanicus bent to pull him up before hugging him for long silent minutes.

"Take care of your mother."

"I will."

The boy smelt of grass and dog and river water. But what would he be like when they returned? Marcus wondered. Like Galarius he was at an age of change and was nearing the time when the seedling shoots up towards the sun. He could be a gangling youth when next they met... or a hardening man, who could say?

Then Ambrosius reached up and took the boy from him.

"We'll look after her together Marcus, Helena is in safe hands." The picture of his father-in-law holding the boy imprinted itself on Marcus' retina, and he'd see it often in his memory over the coming months.

The first part of the journey was familiar as Marcus had travelled to Eboracum (York) several times during the last years. Arthur, who had his own pony now, had ridden beside him the last time they travelled and his father missed the shrill voice with its constant stream of questions.

"What bird is that father? Which tribe holds these lands? Are they friendly.... are they to be trusted?" And at night as they sat round the campfire: "What star is that father? And where is the Great Bear that gave me my name?"

Germanicus had pointed out every constellation he could remember, and the little bear had remembered some of them including Orion and Canis Major. Putting his arm round Augustus he'd pointed to the bright star that carried the name of the hunter's chief dog. And the next time they were away he'd confirmed his knowledge as he hugged Claudius the huge bouncing pup.

Germanicus didn't dwell on the time that would pass before this scene could be played out again, as other adventures beckoned. Galarius was with him all the time now, and when he noticed the stiffness in his friend's movements others were detailed to cook. But though he was at pains not to make comparisons, Marcus couldn't help remember the food they'd enjoyed in those days long ago.

"Time dims the memory you once told me," he murmured, and the wrinkled face of Galarius broke into a grin.

196

"The memories of old men you said!" he retorted, and as Germanicus watched his friend lay out the blankets the years seemed to roll back. They were heading north to rescue Helena.... And as a sudden pain in his thigh brought physical confirmation of the sufferings he'd endured on that journey he smiled and lay down. He was a commander of proven worth now, he told himself as sleep overcame him, a soldier with countless deaths to his credit. But he was still glad to have Galarius along.

At last they came in sight of the city, it's fortifications still rising like a ship above the plain. And here again they found a perfect Roman enclave, as like Chester, York had withstood the tests of time.

The garrison was kept up to strength, no decay threatened and no Saxons or treacherous Celts disturbed the calm. They could relax in quarters staffed by skilled slaves, and exercise in the basilica with the men.

How hard and fit they were Germanicus noted proudly. Surely these Romans were as fine and noble as their predecessors, and could such a nation ever lose power, or would the events of the last fifty years be reversed?

They passed from the cold room to the cool then the warm and the hot, and lying on marble slabs were scraped and massaged by respectful slaves.

The hands on Marcus' neck were as gentle as a woman's.

"Is there any other service I can perform for you sir?" The voice was soft and boyish, and turning over Marcus looked into the face above him as sensitive fingers skimmed his chest.

"No, I think not!" he answered, climbing down slowly and stretching like a cat. When he sauntered to the pool Galarius followed, and immersed in the warm water they relaxed even more.

Wrapped in huge towels they mixed with the officers who'd come to satisfy their curiosity.

"Your horses are in good condition, where do you find the breeding stock?" one red faced man enquired as he peered through the steam.

"We have our own stud at Winchester, and though the Celts are letting the breed decline we keep our standards high." Marcus answered, and the the man nodded as he rubbed his neck with a towel.

"That's what we should do, but we rely on local traders and it gets harder every year to find the animals we need."

Germanicus was resting back against the hard stones.

"You must come to Winchester friend and replenish your stock, as if Ambrosius finds out you're letting things slip he'll make trouble for you!"

The man had hitched himself forward and was nodding gratefully for the offer.

"Thank you Lord Count...." Then he hesitated and peered across at a thin ascetic man talking with another group against the far wall. "That's our commander, perhaps you'll speak to him about it?" and Germanicus shrugged.

"First tell me who you are," he smiled, and the red faced man put out his hand.

"My name is Titus Eboracus and I'm in charge of the stables." Then he drew himself up. "I was a cavalry man myself once, but a fall put a stop to that and now I run a little shop in the town to supplement my salary."

"Is he a soldier?" Marcus asked tipping his head at the garrison commander, and Titus laughed quietly.

"By all the gods no! Constantius is an administrator and runs the garrison like an accountant. He tries to avoid demanding too much money in taxes, and the locals reward him in various ways...." he whispered, and Marcus was interested.

"Does he not receive funds from Ambrosius?" he asked.

"Oh yes, and he's remarkably adept at making the money go round," Titus confided. "That's why our stock has deteriorated as we have to scrimp on everything.... feed for the animals, livery, everything!" he added as he brought his head closer. "I was admiring your saddles," Titus whispered, "they have the latest stirrups I see. But we have to make do with old livery and developments have passed us by."

"That won't help when you have to defend yourselves!" Marcus suggested as he stretched his legs, and the stable officer shrugged.

"Constantius is sure that won't happen, and sees no point in spending money on equipment we'll never use."

Next day Germanicus accompanied the garrison commander on his tour of the fort. Constantius had been reluctant at first, and Ambrosius' second in command had been forced to draw attention to his rank.

"I'm here to assess your effectiveness, would you rather I report that it's unsatisfactory from my own observations?" he demanded, and at once Constantius' thin clerk's face changed its expression.

"Forgive me sir.... shall we begin in the counting house? You'll be pleased to see how careful we are with the money the duke sends us I'm sure."

"What about the taxes raised in the town?" Marcus asked, and Constantius looked uncomfortable.

"We avoid taxing the locals too highly, and I'm sure the duke will agree it's a wise strategy." He was looking for some sign of agreement but received none. "After all we don't want to offend the people do we? And

I'm sure that when you've been here a while you'll see the wisdom of our actions," he added with a wink.

Germanicus just scowled at this, and deciding to ignore Ambrosius' advice about diplomacy took the direct approach.

"I've heard rumours about bribes from tradesmen ... and in return they pay no taxes?" Constantius' scrawny neck tensed when he heard this, and when he spoke his thin voice was cracked.

"I... I don't understand you sir!" he protested.

"I think you do!"

Sending Constantius a cold stare Marcus started to move away, but the governor followed him.

"Where do you want to begin the inspection?" he whined, and Marcus turned down the corners of his mouth.

"The stables, we'll begin with your cavalry!" But first he displayed his own livery to his nervous companion.

"See these saddles?" he grunted stroking the fine velvet on his own. "And the stirrups? They're the latest design, no cavalry unit can be effective without them." And Constantius nodded before setting off rather reluctantly after him towards the stables.

The horses were a mixed bunch and some were old and underfed as well as poorly cared for. Then Titus the man they'd encountered in the baths the previous day appeared, and continuing to ignore Ambrosius' advice about diplomacy Marcus voiced his criticism.

"These animals are a disgrace!" he snorted, and when Constantius interrupted with a stream of excuses he shook his head. "How much corn do you receive each month?" he demanded, and when Titus mumbled the figures he gathered it was a very small amount. "Do you think that's enough?" he asked the governor lazily, and Constantius turned on Titus.

"If I'd known it was insufficient..."

"It's your duty to know." Marcus grunted as he stroked a particularly thin neck. Then he gave his instructions to the stable master.

"Order what you need at once, and get these animals outside I want to see your manoeuvers."

Constantius was really ruffled now, and when he started shouting orders at nobody in particular several scruffy lads appeared. Out into the spring sunshine went the shambling grooms leading a hundred or so horses of mixed ancestry, and rather doubtfully they began to parade in a wavering circle. The stable master's complaints had been understated Marcus could see, and and some of the horses had no saddles at all, just cloth covers of the kind favoured by the Celts.

The skills of the cavalrymen were worse than he'd expected too. And leaving Constantius and Titus to blame each other Marcus approached the sergeant he took to be in charge.

Orders about training and exercise were fired in quick succession needed or not, leaving the man in no doubt that he was now answerable to the duke's envoy. And finally the instructions Marcus had given Titus about feed and livery were repeated.

"After watching all this in silence the garrison commander interrupted nervously.

"But how... how will we pay for it all...?"

"You'll pay with your lives when the enemy catches you unprepared!" Germanicus bellowed in a voice loud enough to be heard by sentries on the walls as well as the men involved and the spectators. Then he turned away leaving them to get on with it. "You'll take no more bribes and make tax gathering your priority from now on!" he called over his shoulder to Constantius, "and as the townsfolk owe so much tax you'll have more than enough!"

After making a defeated nod the governor started worrying about how to accomplish this unpleasant task. Then a thought struck him. Yes of course, he'd threaten the people with Germanicus and encourage the rumours already spreading about him. Yes... he'd call him 'the red devil' perhaps? Now there was something to frighten the children! The traders could well afford to pay he knew. And as Germanicus might be right about the threats facing them, a few stories about Crayford and Aylesford would do no harm at all!

Constantius was nothing if not expedient, and when the wind changed he changed with it. He'd enjoyed the perks long enough to make himself rich, and if self-interest now demanded that he discharge his responsibilities honestly he'd accept it.

Germanicus had seen this scenario played out more than once during recent years, and though some outposts stayed in line others had allowed things to drift. With a good man like Gallus Anthonius at the helm the city of Chester had held firm in a changing world. But when such a man disappeared he wasn't easy to replace.

York had always been an important civitas, and in the old days its governors had been chosen from the best men the Duke of Britain had at his disposal. In those days every region had been ruled by a count, and as the counts were well educated and well informed no city governor would have dared to enrich himself by corruption.

But as the blood of Rome ran thinner lesser men had come to

prominence, and now the skills of the money lender or clerk were enough to achieve rank. This was how Constantius had come to be running a city Marcus presumed, but the task needed greater talents than he possessed. Accountants and populists had taken over the garrisons, and freeing the townspeople from their duty to maintain the soldiery had laid them open to attack.

Constantius had made himself popular, and the ability to think beyond ones own lifetime was perhaps uncommon? Marcus reflected. But Ambrosius' efforts would bear fruit in time he was sure, and slowly the duke was rebuilding the army and navy. With luck the Britons would form themselves into a unified nation. But the unity relied on one man, Ambrosius, and his ability to win the respect of all kinds of men from old soldiers like Galarius to young nobles.

After leaving York they travelled to the great wall, finding it as strong as ever in its physical presence but unguarded for much of its length..

"You were right about this place, it has a character all it's own!" Marcus remarked as they looked out over the rolling lands of Caledonia, and Galarius nodded."

"I'm glad I came back before I die... it's a magic place and we used to think it was the end of the world."

"There's more travelling in store for you old friend before you rest in death." Marcus laughed uneasily, and Galarius sighed.

"I know that centurion, but I don't look forward to it as I once did and death seems more acceptable as time passes."

The old man was looking sadly at Marcus, who was standing with head bowed resting his hands on the wall's edge.

"Is it wrong to accept the end of things?" the little man asked, placing his arm round his long-time companion. "It's a path we must all tread... and our thoughts change as we grow older.

"I constantly dwell on what will happen when Ambrosius is gone..... who'll lead the Britons then?" Marcus answered, and Galarius looked sidelong at him.

"Will it not be you centurion?"

"Somehow I think not," Marcus admitted. "I don't have the qualities... the Celts try my patience and I'm too Roman for them."

"So is Ambrosius," Galarius shrugged, "they think he's too Roman and suspect his motives because of it."

"His loyalty was to Rome once, but he's spent his life fighting for the Britons."

"Ah, but do they value him for it?"

201

"I doubt it," Germanicus sighed as a soldier passed them pacing out his measured mile. "And though the monks have the learning to record these turbulent years will they do it?" he demanded, turning suddenly to face his friend.

Marcus had started to walk along the wall but Galarius was hanging back.

"They have their reasons for selecting what they record," he was saying, and Marcus turned and waited. His friend walked slowly now, and had it happened suddenly or had he been too busy with his own affairs to notice? he asked himself. "The Christians have a promise from their god that's constantly repeated by the priests." Galarius continued after several gulps of air, "they say Christ will return for his chosen people."

They'd been forced to halt again and Galarius was leaning on the parapet for support.

"Christ rose from the dead so his followers believe. But he'd told his disciples he'd come back for them soon."

"How soon?" Marcus enquired, and they resumed their slow progress.

"The men he told expected it in their lifetimes, but it's more than four hundred years since the crucifixion... by the reckoning of Constantine the Great that is." The little man was gripping his chest and they stopped again, but Galarius seemed determined to finish his tale. "When Constantine became a Christian he drew up a a new calendar starting from the supposed birth of his god... The second coming is the main pillar of their faith... but what's more interesting..." The words were disjointed the sentences incomplete and Galarius was breathing hard as he leant on the parapet.

"What I'm trying to tell you is... the monks think they'll be called to heaven and avoid the corruption of death. Though they're promised resurrection after their death!" he chuckled.

His wheezing had collapsed into laughter, but the effort seemed too much for him and he fell into a fit of coughing.

"Oh, I know it's all contradictions," he went on after recovering himself. "But here's my point.... why labour over a manuscript that will never be read?

"Because their god has taken them to heaven?"

"Exactly." Galarius puffed with satisfaction.

"Pendragon said the legends of his people will be read a hundred generations from now!" Marcus grunted as they set off again painfully. "But the Celts have a history that goes back to the their beginnings and like the Saxons they know the value of tradition."

"Aye... it's history that makes a nation," Galarius puffed. "Your history makes you different from everyone else, makes you special... and if you lose your history you lose your identity."

"And the Christians?" Marcus asked, seeing his friend was struggling and stopping again.

"Ah yes, the monks take the promise of the second coming literally, it's demanded of them. And it's not just because Ambrosius is a pagan that they won't write about him. As for the ordinary Celts.... you must understand their temperament. They see no problem in serving two masters and wear their Christianity like a cloak for hard weather. But they're still Celts underneath, and that will always be more important than religion. Their chronicles will tell of their own heroes... not Romans.

Later that night when they'd eaten with the soldiers in one of the milecastles the conversation continued along the same lines.

"If a leader were to arise who's acceptable to the Celts... and the Christians...?" Marcus suggested as he warmed his hands at the fire, and Galarius understood.

"I believe Arturius could be such a man..." he asserted with something close to certainty, and Marcus frowned.

"How can you say that... he's just a boy?"

"I see it in him, he's more Celt than Roman."

"I know what you mean... but he's been brought up as a Roman."

"That's why he'll succeed where others fail," Galarius replied, nodding wisely as if he were privy to some secret knowledge. "He has a soldier's mind but it's watered with poetry... and he's not as straightforward as you. It was then the tanned face of the boy under its thatch of dark curls came back to Germanicus. The intense blue eyes were studying him as they had when they'd said goodbye. And though it was foolish to judge so early he'd a feeling Galarius was right. The boy had the qualities of both his Roman and Celtic ancestors. And only time would tell if the vices of these two very different peoples would show themselves in him.

CHAPTER XVI
caledonia

As the sun sank in a pool of red fire Marcus and Galarius bowed their heads and asked his blessing on their journey. No one knew what awaited them north of the wall, and the lands they were about to enter were ravaged by both Picts and Scots.

The garrisoning of the wall had been sporadic for fifty years. Thanks to Ambrosius soldiers paced its walks again, but how long this continued depended on what Germanicus could achieve in the next few weeks. A power greater than man would order their lives from now on, and the fates would decide their future. All they could do was make themselves one with those fates, with the earth, the sun, and the great mechanism of the universe.

Fresh news was coming in very day, and when he heard that one of the chiefs was planning to challenge Ambrosius' authority Germanicus summoned his senior officers.

The man in overall charge of the area was sure of himself, and Marcus was relieved to be dealing with an old soldier rather than one of the new style administrators. The commander of the wall was thin and hard. A little older than Germanicus he was an experienced warrior, and could be recognised as a man who'd come up through the ranks as so many emperors had in the past.

Germanicus remained seated as the man entered, but his inferior's salute showed no humility.

"My name is Gius Aquilla, and I hold the rank of praetor (commander of a legion) under Ambrosius Duke of Britain!" Commitment and confidence rang in the voice, and as Germanicus looked the newcomer up and down he remembered Constantius the father of Constantine the Great. They said he'd come from peasant origins, and Marcus wondered if the parents of this social climber had dreamt of great things for him too.

As Gius stood to attention he pulled down the corners of his hard mouth.

"King Urien of Rheged has been spoiling for a fight for months," he growled. "We had a skirmish with one of his bands not long ago, and he's boasting that this was only the beginning. He says he intends to push his frontiers further south," Gius continued narrowing his eyes. "And it's possible he's in league with the Picts. As Urien gets older he grows more truculent, and seems to have turned his attention from the conquest of women to the conquest of Rome!" the praetor added with a smile. "They say he was something of a lecher in his youth and the country hereabouts is littered with his bastards!"

Germanicus was studying the map.

"Where does Urien hold court?" he asked, and Gius pointed to a village on the estuary at the western end of the wall.

"His halls are here."

"Is this city well garrisoned?" Germanicus asked placing his finger on Carlisle (Luguvallium) to the east of Urien's stronghold. But the praetor shook his head.

"Not as well as I'd like....and though we've made good progress re-manning the wall this leaves the city below complement.

"Are you saying it's harder to recruit here?" Germanicus sounded sceptical and the praetor sighed as he shrugged his broad shoulders.

"Strangely enough it is!" he muttered patiently as if he were instructing a new recruit. "And as we man all the milecastles now and keep the patrols regular it puts a strain on the towns.

He'd placed a slight emphasis on the last words, but though repeating information seemed to try his patience he kept to the same tone. "This area was never ideal in recruiting terms," Gius went on, "and in the past the wall was staffed by legionaries from the continent. Other areas draw on local men," he sighed, "but up here the population is thinner." He was speaking slowly and deliberately as if Marcus knew nothing about the army, and though the senior man was irritated he kept his temper.

"I understood   that the local population still provides men?" he grunted, and Gius answered in the same tone.

"That's partly true... there are some old legionary families in these parts and it's traditional for the sons to join up. But the revenues from the towns are variable you see, and you can't engage soldiers when you don't have the money to pay them."

Marcus decided to ignore the condescending manner, as he liked Gius and could understand why he was taking such pains to make everything abundantly clear. Had he not done the same himself in York? he asked himself, limiting his reaction to a deep sigh as Gius waved his forefinger over the map.

"I travelled here in my younger days," the praetor went on pointing to the lands north of the wall. "The third rescue went this far too, and made sure the natives remembered their visit!"

"What about the inhabitants of this place?" Germanicus asked tracing a circle round Carlisle with his finger, and Gius thought for a moment.

"A good many Romans live in the town, as well as in villas in the surrounding countryside. And the Celts...they're like those in the south I suppose..." Gius was wondering if he'd said enough as he sensed Marcus' irritation and knew that all this must sound like a lecture. But he went on anyway, almost as if he'd been asked to provide the Celts with a character reference. "They're warlike when necessary and not lacking in courage.... they're artistic and the men of Cumbria are well known for their poetry and music," he muttered. "They record their history in ballads which they sing on long winter nights ....." Then he seemed to run out of words and made a little shrug.

"In the high country to the north, in an area criss-crossed by Roman roads and lesser tracks stands the fort of Bremenium." Gius told them next day as they looked out from the wall. "It's not much of a place, but its strategically important as it guards the road south and I believe it's where Urien will strike!"

"Just why have you brought us here?" Marcus grunted when he saw Bremenium. As the fort seemed to be situated in the middle of nowhere and he couldn't see its importance.

"Urien has been seen skulking in these hills with a sizeable band of warriors, more than he'd need were he travelling for his health!" Gius answered with a smile.

"You say there have been skirmishes with your units?" Marcus asked, and Gius nodded.

"Yes, they were attacked without warning from the hills above the road."

"What does the fool want?" Germanicus sighed, and Gius shrugged.

"Who knows? Perhaps he wants Ambrosius to know that the men of Rheged are a force to be reckoned with?"

Then Galarius moved silently in at his master's side.

"It seems strange to us Romans, but the Celts often do things for no more reason than pride," he told them. "If Urien's people think he's putting up a show against the military they'll think more of him. And it doesn't really matter if the engagement has any significance, as long as it raises their spirits and binds them to their king." Germanicus considered this a very odd pattern of behaviour even for Celts. But Gius agreed with Galarius.

"It impresses their rivals no end if they can claim a victory against the empire. And of course there's another angle," he frowned. "As they know the power of Rome is declining and probe to assess our strength."

"That's always the way with subject peoples, and it's our job to keep one step ahead of them." Marcus answered.

Life was comfortable enough in the little fort above the river. Cut off from the world and with the camps surrounding it deserted Bremenium seemed to be enjoying its isolation. And though some of the soldiers seemed a little old, the atmosphere was comradely and the company good.

Three days were to pass before Urien appeared with his war band, and Germanicus guessed it numbered about five hundred men. The king of Rheged was making a show of camping on a rise overlooking the fort, and was behaving as if he intended to stay.

"You never know with these folk, and they could be serious!" Gius was half amused. "But then again it could be a sort of exercise... get the troops out, give then some experience, that sort of thing." And Germanicus felt the return of his irritation.

"Do they hope to hold us down here?" he demanded, and Gius made his familiar shrug.

"If they can.... sometimes they intimidate a captain and get away with it."

"They'll find that I'm not such a man!" Marcus spat out the words before stamping off, determined to teach Urien a lesson.

The Celts were camped on sloping ground overlooking the outpost, and now and then they showed their strength by marching up and down defiantly. But for the most part they behaved in their usual fashion: wandering about the countryside, steeling cattle and frightening the locals. Fires burned all through the short nights in their encampment, and the sound of music drifting up with the smoke seemed strange and alien to their foes. But the Romans listened, and patiently watching from the walls of their fort waited for Urien to make his move.

The tribal emblems of the Celts were not unlike the standards carried at the head of Roman columns, but Urien's standard bearer had a religious function too. Hung about with charms and leaf sprigs he wore the head and skin of a fox over his helmet, and from under this flowed his long dirty hair.

With the exception of the nobles the Celts wore no armour, and some scorned to don even a tunic, preferring to run about in their baggy drawers. Most wore beards, all had long hair, and the Romans despised them as wild and uncivilised.

The wind was warm from the south, balmy with the summer smells of flowering plants and hay. From Urien's camp came the sound of the harp, the silver notes mingling with the voice of the bard as he told his tale to campfire comrades. And though the voice was far away the Romans could hear it rising and falling in line with the highs and lows of the story. Now the bard would shout as the victor of some ancient battle struck his foe. Then he'd wail with the women as they followed the bier of the dead hero into his hall. And in among it all flowed the silver notes of the harp.

They carried no torches as the land between camp and fort had been carefully examined in daylight and they knew every inch of it. The site of every boulder and the angle of every rise and dip had been seared into the memories of the hundred men who followed their leader on that warm summer night. And though they'd be out-numbered there were enough for the task. The night was moonless, but the glow that lingers after sunset in northern regions still persisted, outlining the rims of the eastern fells with the promise of dawn.

"Remember, our aim is to teach them a lesson not slaughter them to a man!" Germanicus gave his instructions in a loud whisper when they were still far enough away not to be heard. And as they moved closer the voice of the bard was enough to cover their approach. Creeping in among the rough tents the Romans melted into the shadows, and well away from the fires disclosing glow drew their swords. The noise of merriment was still masking any sounds they made, and it appeared as if the whole of Urien's force was gathered in this spot to enjoy the entertainment.

Marcus licked his lips when he saw so many unprotected backs, and fanning out in a circle to mirror the ring of warriors round the fire his men crept forward. A wave of the arm and they rose from the ground in unison.

Pandemonium ensued as the Celts nearest the fire were pushed forward by comrades falling on them from behind. Blows fell on unprotected backs and there were screams as men fell into the flames. Others died quickly forced onto dripping steel, and though some were flushed out in a wild scramble to escape they found no exit.

The few who'd already gone to their tents, having no taste for bardic warbling, were soon dealt with. Then from the far side of the fire came more Romans to circle the spreading ashes. Those first joyful blows when normality turned to mayhem brought death to many of Urien's men, and other's were felled as they ran in search of their weapons, thoughtlessly left in tents and saddle bags.

Soon it was over and Urien's force was routed. Some escaped by hiding among the boulders, and those lying with the dead and wounded were torn between the desire to call out and the need to stay silent and let the bloody spears pass them by.

Countless Celts were captured and herded into shivering groups, where they waited, enclosed by a circle of spear wielding Romans eager to strike at any movement.

Germanicus was pointing his bloody sword at the man he took to be Urien. Then stepping forward he placed the gory blade against the king's pulsing throat.

"Tell your men to surrender Lord King or it will be the end for you!" And Urien nodded and held up his hands.

"Lay down your arms!" he called, his voice echoing back from the hills as the music had such a short time before. And one by one the surviving Celts crept forward to lay down their weapons.

Germanicus was grinning broadly as he put his arm round the shivering king.

"We mean you no harm friend, but our spies said you were preparing to attack and I felt we should do something." His voice was calm almost apologetic, as if the whole thing had been some kind of misunderstanding. And the shiver spread from Urien's body to his voice

"Nay... nay Lord Count, we are loyal in Rheged. Why would I turn on the Lord Ambrosius?" he wailed, and Marcus shook his head in mock sympathy.

"My sentiments entirely Lord King, but this officer was convinced that the reports were correct and should be acted upon!" Then he sighed and directed a suitably severe scowl at Gius Aquilla. "You think I should discount his opinions in future perhaps?" he enquired of Urien with a smile. And the sensitive features of the king creased in confusion as he looked from one bloodthirsty face to the other.

Urien's shoulders were rising and falling repeatedly.

"Nay, my commander... how can I think ill of such a man?" He was laughing nervously and Gius allowed his face to relax in feigned forgiveness as Marcus patted the king's bent back.

"You are indeed a wise man my friend."

"You'll be wondering why I came north Lord King?" Marcus suggested, and Urien shivered again as a soldier gripped his arm to lead him into the fort. "This may surprise you, but we've come to make peace!" Germanicus told his shaking prisoner, "and we offer an alliance no sensible man could refuse." He was squeezing the king's arm and Urien uttered a little cry.

"Whatever you say noble Roman, I'm resolved to be your man from this day forward!"

"Good!" Marcus grinned, "do you hear that Gius? The king has seen how he can continue his life a little longer." Then he turned and shouted to the Celts still hugging the edge of their camp.

"Your king will be our guest till you return to Carlisle!" And though there were murmurings and one or two stepped forward, Urien waved them back.

A few days later the captive Celts, still roped together to remind their king of his duty set out for the wall. At the head of the column rode Urien, between Germanicus and Gius.

"We're honoured to be visiting the wise men of Rheged in their halls!" Marcus winked at Aquilla, and the praetor smiled.

"It will be a pleasure, as the women of the tribe are renown for their beauty and with luck we'll enjoy more than music and wine when we taste King Urien's hospitality!"

The king was staring ahead trying not to show any emotion. But as the faces of his laughing daughters appeared in his mind his stomach churned, and he tried to look at his tormenters without turning his head. Right then left his eyes flickered as he attempted to read their expressions without them noticing. What kind of men were they? he was asking himself. Surely not the kind to rape virgins? But his experience over the last days made him wonder.

That night the King of Rheged shared a table with the Romans, and coughing nervously tried to make amends.

"I'm sorry if camping so close to your fort gave rise to.. er.. suspicions of my intentions?" And Germanicus shook his head.

"No, friend Urien, how could I think such a thing? What's your view Gius?" he asked, and the praetor pretended to consider the matter.

"If I were a king of Rheged guilty of insurrection?" Gius pondered steepling his hands and turning his eyes to the ceiling. "Would I sit in my hall waiting for the Romans to visit and give me a dressing down?" Then he shook his head and smiled. "No, I think I'd take the initiative... try to catch them unawares and kill a few of them perhaps. Then when the time came to meet my masters from the south they'd treat me with respect."

Marcus was nodding and studying the blade of his knife.

"That thought had crossed my mind too... can we both be wrong?" A soft whining was coming from the king's throat and though his eyes flitted nervously from one face to the other he couldn't garner any clues about their intentions.

Their interrupted progress along the wall continued. Forts were inspected drills criticised and animals admired, or not as their condition warranted. Then at last they came to the western end of the vallum and the town of Carlisle.

Ambrosius was right Marcus noted, and the place had avoided the decay of other Roman centres. The absence of Saxon threat imparted a confidence that no longer existed further south, and though the inhabitants had the raids of Hibernian Scots to deal with this was a familiar inconvenience. Their defences had been designed to cope with such incursions, and the people simply went on defending themselves as their ancestors had in the days of empire.

Germanicus decided to spend a few days with the garrison but found no sign of corruption or incompetence. Prosperity was evident and as the townsfolk paid their taxes the troops were not only paid but re-equipped when necessary. Manning levels were reasonable, and Germanicus felt confident of Gius Aquilla's ability to deal with any emergency.

It was mid afternoon when they set out to the west, where the land round the wide inlet had been colonised by rough grasses. These pastures were flooded at high tide, and as the waters rose the heavy horned sheep jumped from one tiny island to the next.

Urien's hall sheltered in the ruins of an old fort, and Marcus could still identify the ring defence crowning the earth rampart.

"They call the place Burgh on Sands, and as Burgh is a German word perhaps some Saxon legionary brought it from his own country long ago?" Gius Aquilla was smiling his wry smile, and Marcus could imagine how it had happened.

"A Saxon posted here from Chester perhaps?" he suggested. And Gius nodded.

"The troops along this coast were usually seconded from Chester or York. And though the records are lost they say a whole legion once disappeared in these wastes."

"Ah yes - the Ninth!" Marcus murmured, as he'd heard the story as a boy.

The face of his tutor had risen in his memory, the features shifting in the firelight as they had then. The old man had been trying to add mystery to the tale he recalled:

'They say a legion marched north from the wall...an entire legion you understand? Six thousand men!' And when Marcus closed his eyes the clipped voice was almost audible. 'Eagles held aloft they went, with cavalry riding out to secure the flanks. The men on the wall watched them out of sight, and they say their singing could be heard long after their glinting spears disappeared into the mists!'

Little Marcus had held his breath as the white bearded tutor brought his face close to his.

'That legion was never heard of again! And not a whisper came back from those bogs and forests! No wounded soldiers returned to gasp out their last message to the keepers of the wall. No Picts trading in the garrison markets were heard boasting about a victory over a Roman column. No one saw them pass and no one could guess at their fate!'

Marcus closed his eyes as he had then, the better to hear the sound they made - the voices of the men, and the drum of six thousand pairs of marching feet! And as the music swelled in his mind he was transported back to the wall in those far off days of empire. Above the tramp of sandled feet on hard summer earth he could still hear them singing. Strong marching music it was, floating back from the edge of the barbarian world to the ears of the defenders of empire.

They'd come from different lands the soldiers of that lost legion, from North Africa, Germany, and Gaul. And they'd spoken different languages. But in Marcus' imagination they were all singing in Latin: of girls remembered, battles fought, and comrades lost. Their voices were melting into a haze of sound, rising as a troop topped an incline and fading again as it descended into the next hollow.

Then Marcus returned to the present with a start. Of course the politicians and the military had explained the mystery away, he remembered. And though the subject had been discussed fleetingly at training camps and colleges the officers and tutors had skimmed over the disappearance with what Germanicus thought politic haste. They'd tried to present it as administrative error he recalled:

'A commander in the north led his legion into the wilderness and no one saw them again!' was about all they had to say on the matter. But was it was really just a clerical error? Marcus wondered, as the legion wouldn't have moved north all at once he knew, but would have proceeded in cohorts and centuries over a period of time. That would have been the reality, but Marcus preferred the legend.

As he looked out across the estuary and the long disputed lands at the boundaries of civilisation, he fancied that the ever present mist was there for a purpose:

'Don't draw your straight lines here!' it seemed to say. 'I advance and retreat as the barbarians do, clothing my comings and goings in secrecy. And when all that was Rome is gone and the footsteps of the last soldiers have died away, I'll still be here, to wreath empty barracks and rotting stables.'

King Urien wasn't as old as Marcus first thought, indeed he could be described as an almost handsome man of about sixty. His face could be joyful or sad in response to his line of thought. Moving like potters clay under the influence of his emotions his expression was constantly shifting to confuse the observer. And on leaving his presence a man would wonder if he'd been in the company of several different people, people of different ages and nationalities living in different times.

On the hill at Bremenium they'd met an old man, defeated and elliciting their sympathy. More recently they'd enjoyed the company of a poet, laughed at the wit of a jester, and scorned the hubris of a braggart. And though the king's son Myrddin was more predictable, he could draw on this shifting quality too.

Urien sat in his hall under wooden cricks that disappeared into the smoky roof like trees into the clouds and belched as he wiped the grease from his beard.

"This is my son for what he's worth! I have only one son... alive that is!" The royal face had drooped into mourning for the implied dead sons. And they'd been better sons than this one, the expression seemed to say as Urien waved the young man forward. "Myrddin, meet the Romans who've come to intimidate and control us."

Urien was in self pitying mode, but the prince seemed more direct and easier to read Germanicus thought. But was his very openness just a part played for their benefit? he found himself wondering as Gius lent back in his chair and held the eye of a girl in the hall below.

When Myrddin approached their table the faces behind him seemed to melt into a haze, but putting this down to the wine he'd drunk Marcus went on eating.

"I'm honoured to meet you sirs!" the boy said making a little bow. And the two soldiers nodded in a cursory fashion, as Roman gentlemen don't pay much heed to the sons of questionable chiefs.

The young man's face was eager, his eyes bright and alive.

"Perhaps you've heard of me?" Myrddin was asking. It seemed he expected them to know him, and as Marcus and Gius glanced at each other they raised their brows. But Myrddin was not in the least deflated. "It's possible you've heard of me as I'm a poet!" he told them in a voice gleeful with pride, and Marcus frowned.

"Congratulations!" There was condescension in his voice and he regretted it immediately. But the boy was not discouraged.

"I write Latin sirs, as well as the language of Rheged, and I've devised a way of committing the sounds of music to paper too!" he boasted.

The Romans were laughing, as it seemed impossible that the catarrhal whinings of the Celtic language could be written down, let alone their music. Was the boy about to regale them with a bardic dirge they wondered, and as if to confirm their fears Myrddin pulled his harp from under the table.

"When it pleases you sirs... I will play."

Marcus was happy enough to listen, but was it fitting for a prince to entertain like a common minstrel?" he wondered as Myrddin bowed again.

"I am a bard sirs, I write the history of my people and those who visit our land. But enough of that, what would you like to hear?""

"How old are you?" Gius grunted.

"Twenty summers sir... I think!" Myrddin replied proudly.

"Then you've seen little of history and have nothing to fill your books or enliven your songs!" Marcus laughed. And the others joined in, even Urien who's face had illuminated to the point of extreme delight.

"I record the stories people tell me... of Romans and Hibernians and long dead heroes..." Myrddin trilled starting to pluck the strings.

"You won't understand it!" Gius whispered to Marcus, "as they don't tell a story.. just make vague references to their dead ancestors and the like. They expect the audience to know the old tales so there's no need for details... they just praise.. condemn... or whatever!" And Marcus sighed, convinced that he was about to be subjected to a long dirge similar to the ones he'd endured at the courts of other Celtic kings.

What followed came as a surprise. And when a high strong voice emerged from Myrddin's young throat, half singing half speaking in perfect Latin, the Romans turned to face the figure regaling them as it seemed he deserved to be listened to after all!

"Where would he learn Latin like that?" Marcus whispered as he and Gius put their heads together, and the praetor shrugged.

"In a monastery perhaps? Cumbria is famous for its holy men as well as its poets and bards, and it's considered no disgrace for a king's son to study the arts."

Myrddin was watching them as if to still their conversation, holding the gaze of first one then the other.

"I tell of a great warrior," he began, "a warrior both Celt and Roman."

There followed an intimate description of the said warrior's mother, her beauty, her virtue, her fortune etc. Then his father, an emperor no less! Then his father... and his, and so on into the murky past. "Ambrosius hero of our people...!" Myrddin shrilled in conclusion, and Marcus sat up suddenly. All this was to honour the duke!

As Gius blew a kiss to the girl he'd been eying he whispered to his companion.

"We're not sufficiently important to figure in his lays, and you must wait a while for your immortality Marcus my friend!" Then he winked and pointed down the hall. "Do you see the girl with the gold torque?"

"I do indeed, but I think you saw her first!"

"Perhaps I did," Gius agreed waving to the girl. "She's Urien's daughter by a woman he captured from another tribe.. she's a princess... and yet she's not!"

As they'd been drinking steadily for an hour this made them laugh uproariously, then Marcus became mockingly serious.

"Surely we should ravish the the king's legitimate daughters first if we're to teach him a lesson as we promised?" he suggested. And this brought on another bout of laughter, as the wine was good and neither man had denied himself.

Myrddin had been watching their interest in the girl, and after finishing his performance with a flourish of strings he squeezed in next to Marcus.

"Would you like to meet my fair sister sir?" he whispered, and Marcus looked at Gius.

"Can it be the boy is procuring for his own sister?" he demanded in a loud whisper.

Myrddin jumped to his feet on hearing this, and his father was incensed too it seemed.

"What was that?" Urien bellowed at his son, who's own offence whatever it was had been laid aside for the present it appeared.

"Nothing father, it was only a jest," Myrddin replied, and Urien seemed partly placated.

"Make no jests about your sister!" he grunted sulkily, and Myrddin put his hand under his heart.

"Her honour is my honour father!" he vowed sending the Romans a warning glance as he resumed his seat. And though Gius was not one to apologize, on this occasion it might serve two purposes he thought.

"Your pardon sirs, the wine has loosened the tongue of your powerful guest!" he explained. Thus Myrddin and Urien were reminded of Marcus' importance and the apology was accepted at once.

"You are honoured beyond all men, don't scorn that honour!" Myrddin whispered to Gius. And as Marcus shook his head in confusion the boy stood up and motioned them to follow him. When they passed the place where the girl had been sitting a few minutes earlier Marcus saw that she was gone. Then Myrddin bowed and left them.

As they entered their sleeping quarters Germanicus was rubbing his chin.

"The girl is a beauty Gius, and her brother is aware of your interest I think?" But the praetor just shrugged.

"Myrddin was responsible for our coming together," Gius confided. "But though he likes the benefits that come from my goodwill, occasionally his pride gets the better of him... as he cares for her and who can blame him?"

The two men had to feel their way across the room towards the lamp, and as they fumbled for it Gius called for a servant to bring a light. To Marcus' surprise a torch appeared instantly from behind a curtain. It was carried by the dark haired girl they'd seen earlier, and taking the brand Gius lit the lamp and replaced it on the table

The muscular arm of the senior soldier of the north had encircled the girl's waist without preliminaries, but though Germanicus looked puzzled his friend laughed.

"I told Myrddin that his life would be easier if his father's hospitality were a little more generous!" he winked." Then he buried his face in the girl's neck and she folded into his arms as if nothing else mattered. She was making little whining noises as he touched her, and as they were already unaware of of his presence Marcus turned away.

Then he hardened his mouth, as this was no time for the graces of villa life, he told himself. And the situation had the promise and tension of a bawdy house invaded by men limited to the company of their own sex for too long. He was exited by the swift coupling taking place at his feet, and saw at once that the movements of the girl indicated pleasure at the coming of a recognised and valued lover. They showed arousal too, and a desperate willingness to let her body sing again under those strong hands.

Marcus leant against the wall and watched without embarrassment as they panted like mating animals. The sight of each other, a rush of needing passion and union without delay seemed to be the pattern of their loving. Then he stepped outside and watched the sky. The breeze fanned his face and he could hear sounds of revelry from the hall across the moonlit compound. But he made no attempt to detach himself, and instead listened to the groans and endearments coming from the hut.

He knew the form. It was the way of the barracks, the sharing between comrades so common in the ranks. Gius was paying him a compliment and when he'd made love to the girl he'd pass her on to his superior without rancour. It was an honour, one of the habits of the common soldier Gius thought worthy of preservation. And Marcus felt warm inside, as a bond was forming between himself and Gius and this was to be its ratification.

Galarius had always been the servant however knowledgeable, and such sharing could never have taken place with him. They were close and trusted each other completely, but a gulf was fixed between them and they could never be equals. But with Gius it was different and he was accustomed to looking his betters in the eye.

He was looking Germanicus in the eye now.

'I am your equal, Patrician!' he was saying. 'I'm generous enough to share my mistress with you.... good enough to move in the circle surrounding Ambrosius. And when he's strong enough to re-establish the rule of Notitia Digitatum and fill the empty posts in the hierarchy, I want to be one of those who rule under him!'

Marcus had read the message in Gius' eyes, and knew he was ready to accept the challenge by making his comrade a brother and an equal. By sharing his woman Germanicus was promising to be the patron of Gius Aquilla, to take him back to Winchester, present him to Ambrosius and speak on his behalf.

When Marcus re-entered the hut he saw Gius lying back exhausted on a pile of skins. He was quite naked and as vulnerable as such a man could ever be. The girl was stretched out like a cat. She was holding her finger tips to her lips in invitation, and Gius waved his comrade forward.

But this was no sharing of a whore, as the girl was beautiful and the daughter of the king. Gius would have had to fight for her, or perhaps make some concession or payment to her father. He was giving something of value here, something more concerned with himself than the girl.

Unlike the unions between men that make one the catamite and one the conqueror this was to be an equal commitment. And Germanicus frowned, determined that there should not be too much equality about it! He was smiling as he knelt beside the girl on the pile of skins. And picking up his goblet Gius drank, content to relax and watch.

Germanicus had unstrapped his sword, placing it conveniently close to his friend's hand. And the meaning of this was clear, he was trusting Gius with his life. He was about to offer his naked back to the point of his own sword, and in addition he was trusting Gius to protect him in the camp of their enemy. The girl was still wet from her recent lover and if a child were conceived the two men would consider it further evidence of their

218

union in arms.

Marcus was smiling as he threw his tunic and armour aside, then resting his hands either side of the girl's head he studied her face. She'd closed her eyes, and lips parted lifted herself to meet his kiss.

But the embraces of Marcus Germanicus were harder than Aquilla's had been, as another element had entered the ritual, that of contest. And though Marcus was prepared to make this man his brother, their equality would remain contested both in arms and in love. As Germanicus couldn't allow any man to consider himself an equal of right, but only of favour.

He'd ride the girl harder and longer. He'd please her more evidently and draw more cries from her, just as he'd outperform Gius when they sparred together. When they fought an enemy he'd kill more often and exercise more ruthlessness, and in this way his companion's loyalty would be continually reinforced.

Gius Aquilla had placed his future in the hands of Marcus Germanicus. But for that trust to be worthwhile his leader must constantly prove himself the better man.

The girl was a little frightened and gripping his thick hair she pulled his head up to stare into his face.

'Why are you so hard with me?' her eyes seemed to ask. 'Is the man who agreed so generously to share me with you not here to see everything? Does he not love me? And is your sword not close to his hand? What's the meaning of it?' Her questions were unspoken and so was his reply.

Smiling gently into the wide eyes he drew back only to strike harder.

'No lady I don't fear him as I'm the better man, and were he to kill me here and now he'd go to his death knowing me to have been his master. Your loved one would rather die killing my enemies than killing me. As he's a better man as my second than my enemy, and his view of himself stands or falls just so!'

His silent communication had carried the message and closing her eyes the girl gave herself completely. Not because her master had given her, but because she desired it of her own free will. The ecstasy when it came obliterated her memories of Gius, and when she turned her head to look at him she could see that he recognised it.

Would Gius continue to accept it so calmly she wondered, or would she feel his wrath? As he could kill her for what her face had told him a moment before. Then she turned back to Germanicus as he followed her to the peak.

Gius offered his goblet as Marcus rose and they drank from it together. Then the girl lay down with Aquilla's arm round her and they talked together in whispers. But Marcus rested only minutes before pulling her away to take her again, and when it was over she lay against his chest and kissed him.

Germanicus was looking at Gius, as if there was to be brotherhood between them this was how it would always be. They held each others eyes for long minutes, then Gius looked away. This was how it would be.

CHAPTER XVII
ᴍʏʀᴆᴆiɴ ᴛʜᴇ sᴏʀᴄᴇʀᴇʀ

Wherever they went Myrddin followed them. But his presence wasn't resented, and indeed they were often unaware of him till some need presented itself. Then the boy would appear out of nowhere, ready to solve the problem or satisfy the desire.

"He makes me uneasy," Gius hissed with a nod into the hollow where Myrddin was admiring their horses. Then he rummaged in his saddle bag and brought out a piece of hairy cheese. "He's like his father in some ways," the soldier added uneasily, "but where the old man changes his face, the younger changes himself!"

"I know what you mean," Marcus agreed as he studied the slim figure nuzzling his chin into Romulus' mane. "He has a way with animals, and I was the only one who could handle Romulus till he came along."

"That's it exactly," Gius agreed. "Myrddin sees a quality in you, then uses it for his own purposes."

"Do you think he's a threat?" Marcus whispered, sitting up to view the boy better, and Gius nodded.

"Everything and everybody is a threat," he sighed getting to his feet and starting down the hill. "And we must trust no one if we're to see our cause triumph."

Still lying in the grass Marcus stared into the empty blue sky, then after a moment he called out.

"But the boy's clever, and perhaps we can use him to our advantage?"

The battle at Bremenium and their stay with Urien had delayed them. They wouldn't be going into Caledonia this campaigning season it seemed, as October was well advanced and they'd spend the winter south of the wall. Gius suggested that they divide their time between Carlisle and Urien's camp. And the idea wasn't unwelcome to Marcus, as Urien's daughter was as talented as her brother. The long winter nights would be shorter with her to entertain him, but though the girl was diplomatic Germanicus was conscious of her preference for him over Gius.

The down to earth soldier seemed to take no offence however.

"I'd not follow you had I not thought you worthy of it," he winked. But Marcus was uneasy.

Myrddin made it his business to keep close to them, and as there was a special quality about him Germanicus felt he might be useful. His learning was phenomenal, covering not only the history of his own tribe and the Celts in general, but that of Rome too. He liked to recite the names of the emperors back to Julius Caesar, something Germanicus felt he ought to be able to do. And in addition the boy never tired of entertaining them with stories about the eternal city, from the days of the republic to the present time.

But when Myrddin compared Germanicus to Odysseus, who'd been invited into the bed of a godess no less! Gius thought he was stretching poetic licence too far. And though Marcus was flattered at first, as none of his men had been eaten or snatched away by multi headed monsters as far as he knew, he was forced to agree.

Life was harsher in the north, and Germanicus felt a return of the hardness that had once stiffened his body. He hadn't noticed the effects of life at the court of Ambrosius, or the habit of delegation he'd adopted over the years. But the soft life had made a sybarite of him, and only rarely had he spent a night under the stars.

Now the sinews were taught again and the responses sharpened. He was in touch with reality once more and regretted his slide into lethargy. Thoughts of Helena tempted him to re-live the tenderness of their lovemaking. But though he remembered it with pleasure the prospect of new horizons was more compelling.

Urien's daughter was left to Gius now. The experience had been stimulating but Marcus wasn't one to share anything for long, and though the girl pouted her disappointment Gius seemed grateful.

Soon another of Urien's kin had appeared to warm Marcus' bed, and was this Myrddin at work again? he wondered. As intriguing as her predecessor the girl brought the magic of her people with her.

"You'll live long Roman, and wax great!" she whispered as she told his fortune with the help of a few coins. "But you'll suffer hardship and come close to death more than once." She was looking into his eyes to gauge the reaction, and seeing only amusement her face hardened. "And you'll be the father of a great king!" she added almost reluctantly.

They were walking the autumn woods, and Marcus laughed as he drew her to him.

"I think I've had enough of fortune telling for one day, and your predictions are growing wild," he told her, making to pull her to the ground. But the girl wouldn't be deflected.

"The fates have decreed it Germanicus, don't mock their wisdom!" she admonished, shaking her bronze locks as she struggled free. Then she rested her back against a tree, and the Roman watched the rise and fall of her breasts and waited. "The fates are fickle and only I see their secrets." the girl said at last, and the soldier placed his hand on her middle.

"Which of my sons will be a king?" he laughed, and ignoring the question she put her hand over his.

"I see two strands in the life of this king, one is of victory....battles won and enemies thwarted. But he'll know disappointment too, betrayal in love and the treachery of a trusted comrade."

"The wind grows cold," Marcus grunted, "and we must not tempt the fates by looking too deeply into their secrets. Let young Arthur fight his own battles, as they lie in the future and he'll fight them without my help."

His voice was hard as he strode off towards the camp, and he seemed to have forgotten the girl running after him through the sodden litter of autumns leaves.

Spring arrived late and though the trees were putting out new shoots the young oaks still clung to their old garments, as if they were too wise to believe in the promise of spring.

The eyes of the girl widened as she made to caress him one last time.

"You must love me again before tomorrow," she whispered, but Marcus just laughed.

"Is it in the fates my darling?" he asked, and the girl nodded.

"Sometimes it's better not to question them!" she whispered as she pulled his mouth onto hers. And as his hands gripped her waist he tried again to remember the face of Helena, and wondered why his efforts always failed.

They rode north, along the straight road that cuts the wild lands beyond the wall. Ahead of them lay mountains they were told, higher than anything in Wales and stretching as far as anyone had travelled. Some said that in the far north a man could look out over golden sands to see islands, misty and shimmering across the water. But many years had passed since a traveller ventured so far, and perhaps it was just a legend?

At last they left Rheged behind and passed into unknown country. A Pictish village lay a few miles north of Urien's frontier, and they decided to pay their respects to the chief and let him know they meant him no harm. The presence of five hundred well armed troops would persuade him not to take offence they believed, and they'd talk to the people and discern the mood.

The head of the column came to a halt on the crest of a hill overlooking a village, where the familiar round huts clustered under a stone tower. The tower had no windows but they could see a door set in the wall high above the ground. One of Urien's men had been sent ahead, but even so most of the people had taken refuge in the broch.

The Picts were wary but reasonable. Marcus found it hard to match them with the bloody harriers of the wall he'd heard about, and deduced that they'd arrived at a peaceful time.

Their chief was old he learned, and the young men had enough to occupy them fighting the invading Irish. The kingdom of Rheged on their southern flank was strong, and this wasn't the time for expansion. But when a young man with a need to make a name for himself ruled again, they'd revert to their old habits Marcus guessed. Next day they rode on, and the Romans were warned to look out for the Scots from Hibernia who came raiding every year and were now wintering here.

As Germanicus rode at the head of the long column he tried to remember his home in the south. To bring Helena's face into his mind's eye had become almost an obsession, and somehow he must relate what he was doing here to Ambrosius' plans for the future. He needed to detach himself from the present, but found it hard to picture his home and harder still to feel close to Helena. Though he could recall the slave girl he'd visited now and then well enough, and her face came easily to mind.

Perhaps that was because she was in tune with the wild land he now inhabited? he reflected. And though she'd been born and bred a slave on Ambrosius' estates she'd been very like the people he found himself amongst now. He wanted to remember Helena, but found himself wanting his father-in-law's slave instead.

When they came to a wooded valley with a stream flowing over a cliff Marcus gave orders for food to be cooked, as it was midday and he was hungry. Then carefully he began to lead Romulus down the rock strewn slope. After a while the path disappeared. The birch scrub grew thick and the scree was difficult to cross, but after ten minutes of struggle they reached the foot. Then Marcus glimpsed the stream through the close crowding trees and discovered he wasn't alone.

As the scent of wood smoke pricked his nostrils he halted their noisy progress and listened. The sound of the stream overlay everything, but in the midst of it he heard a voice. Was he dreaming he wondered? Was his mind playing tricks and recalling the singing of the slave girl? But no, the sound was real, and tying Romulus to a birch growing almost horizontally from the rocks he drew his sword.

The song grew louder as he approached, and though the words were unfamiliar it carried with it the strange lilting sadness of the Celts.   A clearing had opened up in front of him, and the steep decent to the valley floor had evened out to form a patch of flat land. The ground was sandy with shards of slate and sharp tufted grasses scattered across the smooth earth. In the middle burned a fire, and tending it was a girl. She sat with her back to him, unaware of his approach and still singing.

A tempting aroma rose from the pot over the fire, and though Marcus was close enough to touch the girl she still didn't sense him. He felt that she should, she should smell him as a doe smells a buck. Then suddenly something unnatural seemed to impinge, an irritant in the air.

He was looking down at her hair, deep brown red like rusted iron and shining like a crow's back. The desire to reach out and touch it was almost irresistible, and how pleasant it would be to grasp the thick waves and run them through his fingers, he thought. The mood was hypnotic, the singing, the circular movement of the stick that stirred the pot, and the sinuous shimmer of streaming hair...

Reaching for more wood to feed the fire the girl turned slightly, and perhaps it was then she saw the sandled foot of the man behind her. Or perhaps his shadow fell across her? But his arms closed before she could cry out and her mouth was stopped.   Holding his short sword in front of her Germanicus tilted it to catch the light, then he turned her to face him.

The face staring up was unusual, and stained with grime from the fire it reminded him for a moment of Arturius. The same tip tilted nose, the same weather browned spaces between the freckles, and the eyes that changed with the light. Long lashes shading shifting depths brushed cheeks that led down to berry reddened lips. She didn't cry out as he turned her. Instead her mouth fell open in silent surprise, and Germanicus felt the onset of arousal.

"Are you alone?" he whispered, his eyes scanning the valley sides where birch trunks shone like snail trails against the rock.

As the urchin shook her head she opened her mouth a little more, but did she understand what he was saying? he wondered.

"Are you alone?" Marcus repeated in the language of of Rheged, and when the girl shook her head again, this time more deliberately, he looked back at the woods and called out.

"Hullo!" The echo of his voice came back and an animal ran through the undergrowth, but nothing else stirred. "Is anyone out there, are you alone?" he demanded of the girl shaking her gently by the shoulders.

At that moment the pot boiled over, hissing steam rose from the fire and as the girl bent to ease the stew away from the heat she looked up at him defiantly. Then she spoke to him in the language he'd used a moment before, the language of Rheged. She spoke with confidence, and seemed to have no fear of him.

"You're not one of the Celts from the Solway.... your speech isn't right... and your clothes are strange."

As the herb scented steam enveloped them the Roman crouched at her side and gripped her wrists.

"You're not one of Urien's people either are you?" he suggested, and shaking her head again the girl looked away. "What is it? Is somebody out there?" Marcus was impatient as he didn't trust her. Was something happening behind him? he wondered, the prickling sensation at the back of his neck said it was.

He studied the girl's face for a few seconds trying to gauge the direction of her gaze. But she was deliberately looking away from the spot his ears told him held the danger, and suddenly he jumped to his feet pulling her after him. Grasping her shoulders he swung her round to face the newcomer, a tall man of about twenty five who came forward from the edge of the clearing before retreating again.

Germanicus was sweeping the air with his short sword and the girl said nothing as the man crept forward. He'd picked up a stout stick but was still holding low to the ground, and Marcus decided to take the initiative. Were these the Scots he'd heard about? he wondered, and were there more in the woods? Letting go of the girl Marcus charged the man, who promptly ran back into the scrub. And when he turned back to the fire the girl had gone.

He decided on pursuit, and as the girl must have left the clearing on the opposite side to the man this was the path he took. The track led to the stream, where he found his quarry watching the churning water. She was calm as he approached allowing herself to be apprehended without a struggle, and after pulling her through the knee high bracken Marcus pressed her against a tree.

"Where are they?" he demanded impatiently, but the girl just smiled.

"I tell you there's no one here!" Her musical voice was scornful and Germanicus snorted..

"I don't believe you!" he grunted, giving in to the temptation he'd suffered for the last quarter of an hour and gripping her rust brown hair.

She didn't cry out as he pulled her head back, just closed her eyes and waited. And when he pressed his face into her neck the smell of lavender reminded him of the garden at Portus Adurni.

Dried and weighed... the women would be filling cushions and little hanging bags with it now.... And for the first time in months he remembered his home with something like clarity.

After listening to the sounds of the water for a while Marcus turned the girl's head and made her looked at him. Then he touched her lips with his finger and kissed them. Softly his words caressed her, but he was still gripping the auburn hair.

"I ask you again... are there others in the woods?" And again the girl shook her head.

"I tell you no!" she laughed. Don't you think they'd have appeared by now? I was here alone with my brother and he's away to fetch the others."

"If they come I'll still have time to kill you," Marcus whispered, his tone belying his words as he pressed her close and felt her body shudder against him.

The girl was wearing a tunic of coarse wool held in at the waist with rope, and Marcus stood back to admire her for a moment before cutting the belt with his knife. Then hooking his blade under the hem he slit the garment to the neck.

The urchin was still meeting his eyes as if daring him to do his worst. But as his sword pressed her throat she closed her eyes, and shrugging her narrow shoulders allowed the tunic to fall to the ground.

When she opened her eyes again they were still holding his, and there was no fear in them. Her nakedness seemed to cause her no embarrassment, indeed she seemed to be daring him on. Her figure was boyish but well proportioned and showed none of the signs he'd have expected in one who scrapes a living from the woods.

"Who are you?" There was impatience in his voice but she simply shrugged again.

"Aren't you going to rape me?" she asked, parting her lips and moistening them with her tongue. So with a shrug Marcus pushed her for her insolence and she allowed herself fall into the dry bracken. But as he knelt over her, her expression still registered contempt, and he gritted his teeth.

"Yes I suppose I am... but not here." he scowled. Gripping her wrists again Marcus pulled the girl to her feet. Then he began to drag her behind him, steadfastly refusing to look back at her.

Presently they re-entered the clearing where they'd met.

"I've a better view from here, and if anyone disturbs us I'm prepared," the Roman grinned, and the girl's sulks told him his plan was a good one. Somewhere out there her comrades were waiting till he was vulnerable.

So he sat with his back to the fire and waited. Nothing stirred, he'd already removed his helmet and now he placed it carefully to one side before unbuckling his scabbard. .

Her body was inviting, firm breasts with sharp nipples reddened with berries like her lips and a flat silky stomach that rose and fell with her breathing. She wore no undergarments other than a plaited strip of herbs round her waist. And though Marcus felt she should resist she lay still, staring at him with wide disdainful eyes.

After a few minutes Marcus got to his feet and pointing to her split tunic indicated that she put it on.

"What's your name?" he sighed, and she smiled.

"My name is Morgana, and I am the daughter of a king." She was revelling in his discomfort and Marcus sighed again.

"Everyone I meet nowadays seems to be the child of a king!" he grunted. "Your Celtic kings must be very promiscuous!" And though Morgana glared at him he just smiled and pulled her to her feet.

"Where are we going?" She was frightened now, searching desperately for a sight of her companions as they started back to where he'd left Romulus.

Marcus said nothing as they climbed through the tangled undergrowth, though whenever a sound disturbed the quiet he stopped to listen before moving on. Romulus was still grazing happily where he'd been left, and soon the girl was riding pillion as they headed back to camp.

Urien shook his head when he saw the girl.

"Why have you brought her here? I have my faults lord count, but I'm a good Christian," he lied. "She's not one of us and her people are barbarians!" the king added tipping his head at Morgana, and the fastidious tone made Marcus smile.

"Are you afraid of her?" he grinned, and Urien nodded avidly, "That I am, and so is every man who eats in my hall." Then he looked round furtively. "They're heathens I tell you, from over the water in Hibernia (Ireland)." The king obviously considered Marcus' calm acceptance of the girl as unhealthy, and added in a loud whisper. "They're heathen I tell you... they have the powers!"

"Do you have the powers?" Marcus asked the girl an hour later as she crouched like a cat in the corner of his hut.

"We're an ancient people and we're taught the old knowledge."

"Urien thinks you're evil," he grinned, and the girl smiled in her boyish way.

"To the ignorant all knowledge is magic," she whispered, reaching to touch the cobwebs that draped the corners of the room. And to Marcus' surprise a small creature transferred itself to her hand from the web. "See how the earth creatures trust me?" Morgana smiled, and Marcus wrinkled his nose as the spider ran up her arm.

"Is that the sum of your magic?" he sighed. He was making fun of her and she shot him a hostile glance before returning the little creature to its home.

"Maybe... I have more." Then she set off round the room examining everything in it. "This is a poor place for one of your rank is it not lord count?" she suggested, and Marcus shrugged.

"To the Celts it's a king's palace!"

Germanicus ate in the long hall as usual, but the girl preferred to stay in his quarters.

"Will you bring me some food when you come back?" she'd asked, but Marcus had shaken his head.

"You'll eat with the the rest in the hall, and as you're my property now I'll see you're safe." Morgana was shaking her head and cowering into the corner, but he just laughed and pulled her to her feet.

"I'm not a servant to bring you your vitals wench, and you'll eat in the hall with everyone else."

As he made his way to the high table Marcus deposited the girl with the other women at the lower end of the room. But Urien was still suspicious.

"She'll put a spell on us I tell you!" he hissed, and the make-do priest at his side nodded gravely.

"A Christian man should not consort with pagans lord count!"

"What makes you think she's a pagan?" It was Myrddin who spoke and Marcus turned to look at him.

"The tattoos of course fool!" he grunted, but though this made Urien angry the boy wasn't subdued.

"Perhaps I could learn something from her?" he suggested, as Myrddin was eager for knowledge as usual.

"No doubt you could, if its only the history of her island and her people," Marcus agreed patting the young man's arm in apology as he rose to leave. Then he headed down the hall to where he'd left Morgana.

Peering through the smoke he saw her cowering between two dirty serving wenches. She'd been right to think herself unsuited to such company Marcus conceded. But she'd spend the rest of the evening in the company of a prince if he knew anything of Myrddin.

The surge of passion he'd felt when he first saw Morgana had abated. Though her refusal to respond to him as other women did hadn't injured his pride and he still intended to make her his mistress. But Urien was right and the strange quality about her made him uneasy.

"This Morgana... is she is another woman who likes to rule men...like Rowena the daughter of Hengist?" Galarius had ventured and Marcus had scowled at him.

"Rowena didn't rule me... and as for Morgana...."

The idea was preposterous Marcus told himself, but though Galarius didn't press the matter the Count of the Saxon shore sensed danger when he saw the girl watching him.

He'd brought her a dress of the kind Celtic women wore. And with her hair brushed and her face scrubbed he could almost believe Morgana was a princess.

"Do you think she has magic powers?" Galarius whispered lifting his brows, and Marcus turned down the corners of his mouth.

"The Celts are strange and magic comes naturally to them... so who knows?" He was feeding the fire in their hut with wood. But it was a draughty arrangement and though the smoke was intended to make its way out through a hole in the roof it preferred to swirl endlessly round the room.

Their faces were blackened by soot and their eyes smarted, but it didn't seem to bother the girl.

"In my homeland we burn peat from the earth, it has a sweeter smell than wood and burns longer." There was that lovely musical lilt in her voice again! Germanicus thought to himself, then he drew back.

If she were a witch.. a wise woman as they said, would she not spin her spells just like this? Making him conscious of her lithe young body and drawing his eyes to her luscious hair?

Hauling him into the depths of her eyes she'd try to rouse desire in him wouldn't she? he asked himself. And as this was never a difficult task where he was concerned he became even more uneasy.

After a deal of agonising Marcus had made up his mind not to ravish her. And determined that she should have no power over him he resolved to keep her at arms length. But that wasn't to say he'd let her go... not yet at least!

The fire had gone out and the air was beginning to clear. Galarius was snoring on his pallet and the girl was asleep against the wall. A night bird called, and as he listened to the familiar sounds of darkness Marcus began to feel more secure and in control.

His efforts to bring Urien to an understanding of the value of co-operation were progressing well. The Picts to the north had been amenable to his offer of peace. He'd soon be going home. And only the problem of Hengist remained!

Sleep had begun to drug his senses, and was he dreaming or did a hand touch his neck? Suddenly he was awake, the girl had crept in beside him under the blanket and for a moment he lay still listening to his own heart beating in his ears. The sounds of the world outside had died away and Galarius might be in another country for all he knew of what was happening so close to him.

But Marcus had made up his mind, Morgana was not for him! Then he felt her lips on his neck, wet and warm as they progressed over his chest and down. Was she a witch? Could she make him love her against his will? he wondered. And what was his will exactly...?

Anyway what harm could come from a pleasant interlude on a summer's night? he asked himself. And he lay still under her caress allowing her to please him. Progressing through their union like a man in a dream he felt, sensed, and was aroused, though not fully awake. Heaven must be like this he thought - devoid of all contest, all effort. And as he allowed his eyes to close he pulled the boyish figure to him, content that he was right in letting one of the earth people so close to him. A nymph of the wildwood lay in his arms and her magic was seeping into him.

CHAPTER XVIII
BITTER SWEET VICTORY

Germanicus woke to find himself at the bottom of a dark pit. Several inches of foul smelling liquid swirled round his aching body, and there were others in the hole with him he sensed. Then something touched his face.

"This one's alive!" The voice was Celtic, and as Marcus struggled to stand up his hands closed on a slimy moving thing. "Who are you?" it asked.

They were at the bottom of a what seemed to be a well, and high above a few stars appeared to wink through a small hole. As his eyes grew accustomed to the darkness Ambrsoius' second in command struggled to identify the shape lying almost underneath him, and after a while he recognised a mouth with two glinting eyes above it. Then the rest of the face appeared, covered in hair!

"I asked who you are?" the voice said again, and Marcus swallowed hard. Was he still asleep he wondered, was this a horrible nightmare?

He was struggling to lift himself out of the icy water, but the walls were slippery and as there were no hand holes he gave up and sank back into the mire.

"Aye, we all try that at first," the voice crackled again, and Marcus discovered that if he screwed his eyes he could see the face more clearly.

It was the face of a man sure enough, but what kind of man? he asked himself. Then the voice came again.

"It does a man no good to lie in this filth, and they all try to get out. But they all fail and most are dead in a week!"

"You're not dead!" Marcus was surprised to hear himself shouting, and as the echoes of his voice died away the crack in the hairy face opened again.

"Can you believe I've been here for a hundred days?" it asked, and Marcus lifted his chin to squint at the tiny point of light above his head. "A hundred times the light had come... and a hundred times it had faded..." his fevered mind repeated several times.

"You look as if you've been here for a hundred years!" the Roman answered at last, and to his surprise the face began to laugh.

"The rest are dead and there's just us three now."

"Three?" Marcus repeated looking round for their silent companion. Then the hairy thing nudged a pile of rags on his other side and it moved and groaned.

"Wake up, they've thrown another one in and this one's alive!" the voice croaked, but the third prisoner was past caring.

Marcus was trying to keep calm.

"What is this place... and why am I here?" he asked.

"You mean you don't know?" the voice in the darkness sneered.

"The last thing I remember I was in my bed... in the camp of King Urien of Rheged...."

"Are you a Roman?" the voice demanded, and Marcus brought his face a little closer to the source of the sound.

"Yes... I'm , I was a guest at Urien's court."

"Guest! Ha! Ha!" That's a new one. And what's your opinion of the hospitality eh?"

"I can't remember..... how long have I been here?"

"Less than an hour I'd say. They must have hit you gently or perhaps you have a hard head?" The shadowy outline was chuckling into its sodden jerkin, then it leant forward. "Are you Urien's enemy?" it asked, and Germanicus felt the pain beating in his head.

"We had a skirmish at the end of last year...." he admitted gripping his head in his hands.

"And you trusted him enough to sleep in his house?"

Germanicus could see he'd been foolish, but somehow he couldn't blame Urien. No... he was convinced that his foolishness lay in letting Morgana share his bed.

At last the morning sun arrived to illuminate their misery, and a face appeared at the top of the shaft. Then another and another, and a voice echoed down to them.

"We intend to keep you there Roman!" It was Urien.

"Why? For love of the gods what's your aim?" Marcus demanded.

"Let's say I'm afraid of Ambrosius' reaction were he to hear about my.... my er....adventure at Bremenium?"

"I told you it would be forgotten... we had an agreement!"

"Aye we had an agreement." The king was dissatisfied with the terms it seemed. "An agreement that puts me under Ambrosius' control and obliges me to fight the Saxons when I might prefer to do business with them."

Then another face appeared at the top of the shaft. The light shining in Marcus' eyes made recognition impossible, but the voice was familiar.

"Count Germanicus, are you alive?" It was Myrddin.

"I won't be for much longer if you don't get me out of here!" Marcus bellowed. Then the faces disappeared and he heard shouting and arguing. But eventually the sky was cut by a snaking rope, and grasping it with a mixture of relief and anger Marcus tied it round the waist of his companion.

"What are you doing?" It was Myrddin again.

"I'm coming up of course!" The Roman wanted to fire obscenities, but decided this could wait till he was safe. Then he began to climb the rope, and when the prisoner of a hundred days saw what was happening he put his strength into holding the end secure.

At last Germanicus appeared pungent and filthy at the top.

"Pull him up!" he screamed, pointing into the darkness as he bawled at the shivering servants.

"But he's one of the Scots, the raiders from over the water... Why save him?"

"Pull him up damn you!" What Marcus had intended as a stern command came out as a frenzied scream. But they scurried to obey and soon the figure of the long survivor was crawling over the rim.

"You say there's only one other alive?" Marcus addressed his question to the scarecrow, who nodded avidly.

"Bring him up!"

When he saw the servants looking to Urien for approval Marcus ignored them, and with icy deliberateness fastened the rope round the waist of the nearest man and pushed him over the edge. Urien's pride was hurt it seemed.

"How dare you give orders to my men?" he whined, and Marcus, covered as he was in excrement from the cesspit turned on him with terrible venom in his eyes.

The king's next words came up to them in the form of a scream as he travelled the twenty or so feet to the bottom of the pit, and though the action of their ill-used guest alarmed Myrddin, Germanicus was unapologetic.

"He'll have a soft landing as the place is full of bodies!" he grunted, and the prince looked unhappily over the edge before raising fearful eyes.

"I'd no idea they were left there... to die. I thought it was just a punishment...."

"You father is a hard man Myrddin, did these men deserve this?" the Roman demanded. But he'd a feeling that no one would answer that question.

Dinner was brought to the high table in Urien's hall, and the king, washed but bruised, glared at Germanicus with uncontained hatred. He wasn't too pleased with his son either it appeared.

"I was a fool to bring you up ... and a bigger fool to let you haul him out of the pit as he's better dead!" he growled still glaring at the Roman and ignoring their host's lack of good manners Marcus turned to Myrddin.

"Was the girl involved in your father's plan to dispose of me?" he asked, lifting his nose away from his own body. As in spite of the scrubbing he'd endured he still smelt awful.

But the boy shook his head.

"She disappeared about the same time you did, but I don't think my father would involve himself with the likes of her." Then he laughed mischievously. "And in any case I understand the lady had a favourable view of you.... a view that's now considerably reinforced."

"How so?"

"You remember the wretches we brought up from the midden?" Myrddin chuckled, "well it seems that one of them is her father!" And Germanicus felt a certain gratification, as instead of making an enemy of the girl as he'd feared, he'd made three friends among the Scots now.

High summer was on them now and the leaves in the oak forest were past their new beginnings. The Romans had spent enough time in Caledonia it seemed, and Ambrosius sent a messenger ordering Germanicus back to Chester before the nights began to lengthen.

Time was short, but the task Germanicus had come north to attempt was incomplete. So they discussed the matter with Myrddin, who was gaining a reputation for good sense. Though the boy had his strange side Marcus had to admit. He was fond of casting bones and coloured stones for the purpose of telling fortunes. He was better educated than any Celt had a right to be, and in the opinion of the Romans he knew more of their history than an alien should!

They were walking through the orchard in Urien's enclosure and Germanicus bent to retrieve a fallen apple from the grass.

"Ambrosius sent me north to make a lasting peace... and I've failed," he sighed. But Myrddin was horrified.

"Because my father tried to kill you?" he frowned, and nodding vaguely Marcus scratched the back of his head.

"Yes that does have something to do with it!" he growled through gritted teeth, and Myrddin put his arm round him before thinking better of it and removing it again.

"You mustn't take his little fit of pique too seriously," the boy advised with a nervous cough. "As he's strange sometimes... passionate and swift to anger if you know what I mean?" And Germanicus said that he did.

The young Celt was strolling ahead, self-confident as ever.

"He'd have had you pulled up sooner or later I'm sure," Myrddin called over his shoulder. "He just wanted to get his own back... you know his education isn't all that good." And Germanicus felt he could accept this too, particularly if Urien were compared to his bookworm son.

"What exactly are you saying?" the Roman sighed, and Myrddin came back to take his arm.

"Just leave my father to me that's all! You came to make peace and form an alliance didn't you?"

"Yes...." Marcus agreed wearily, but in spite of his sneaking admiration for the boy he was still suspicious.

"Perhaps my father wasn't listening when you explained the advantages of an alliance with Ambrosius?" Myrddin winked, "and it could be he didn't understand your Latin."

Germanicus was wondering about hidden motives as the boy continued

236

with easy confidence.

"You can go south with an easy mind Lord Count. I'll bring my father round to our way of thinking!" he beamed. And though Marcus smiled in a noncommittal fashion he couldn't help having faith in his new ally.

"Your enemy Hengist is making trouble again in the south!" Myrddin hissed bringing his mouth close to his companion's ear, and Germanicus stopped dead in his tracks.

"How do you know that?" he asked. But Myrddin wouldn't be drawn.

"I have my ways!" The voice was complacent, but when Marcus turned to reprove the boy for his insolence he'd disappeared. The prince of Rheged really did have some remarkable talents, the count mused, and it was fortunate that Roman officers didn't believe in Celtic magic!

They left Urien's court without regret and entered the forest. The path through the trees was narrow, the undergrowth thick and inpenetrable. There were sounds in the woods, the progress of an animal or the crash of falling branches. And sometimes a small creature came out from the darkness to stand transfixed in their path before scuttling away. Light didn't penetrate here, and the forest floor was wet with leaf mould. It seemed to be aiming its odour of death directly at them, and when they came to a fallen tree lying across the track they were forced to dismount and heave it away.

Straining and cursing in the womb-like gloom the men worked quickly, as diverting to either side was impossible. The lower branches on the trees were leafless, only here and there did the sun break into a clearing, and in these places an amazing variety of wild flowers bloomed. But even here the seeds of darkness could be seen, as vigorous young seedlings were already stretching their arms to the sun, not caring that their presence would one day blot it out.

Still vulnerable the Romans camped in the forest, and the noise seemed to increase as they waited for sleep. In the branches night birds were preparing for the hunt. Squawks hoots and scufflings were their lullaby, and above it all they could hear the breathing of the forest: the constant murmuring of ten thousand trees to one another.

"I'm relieved to be south of the wall again," Galarius remarked taking a deep rasping breath. And the tendons in his neck stood out like the roots of the trees they'd passed. "It's the forest.." the old legionary added looking up into the great brooding presence. "It's like a sleeping beast.... it was here before man and will be here when he's gone."

They stopped to eat their midday meal by a stream. The little dell was full of grazing horses and they were surrounded by reclining men.

"Our fear was justified centurion," Galarius coughed as he handed Marcus some bread, "and to have a body of men strung out like that was foolish. It made my flesh creep," he wheezed, "and I thank the gods we're out of it!"

"Which god do you thank?" Marcus smiled passing the wine flask to his companion, "perhaps it should be the oak god?" And Galarius nodded.

"Jupiter!" the little man laughed taking a deep swig before lifting the flask over his head. "Thanks be to Jupiter... Deus Pater... great father of the oak woods!"

The country was more open now, and though there were wooded areas on either side of the road they were less dense and threatening. The number of cultivated fields was increasing and the clusters of round huts were becoming more common. Prosperous villas waited to welcome them with all the comforts of Rome, and it seemed for all the world as if a hundred years had rolled back.

"We've lived in these islands for nearly ten years now," Galarius remarked letting his tired eyes rest on his friend's face, "and I've seen you grow from a promising youth to a man of strength and power."

Germanicus was moved

"I owe much of my success to you old friend," he smiled, but Galarius waved the compliment away.

"Perhaps....?" he conceded, " but the gods brought you here and perhaps our meeting was ordained too?"

The horses were ambling down to the river, and when Romulus bent to drink the others joined him.

"I've grown old...." Galarius sighed as he gazed at them, and crossing the pebbled bank Marcus began to fill his water bottle. Then he looked up as his companion went on.

"There's little time left... I feel it," Galarius gasped placing a hand on his heart. Then seeing the concern on his master's face he smiled. "Nay, don't be sad for me, I've had a good life and my friends have been the best."

"When we get to Chester I'll find you a physician," Marcus called as he straightened his back. But the old man shook his head.

"Aye you'll find me a physician!" he laughed grasping his friend's hand. "But though a physician can cure ailments sometimes... no one can cure me."

"What ails you, tell me, has Urien poisoned you?" Marcus demanded. But Galarius was looking past him to where Myrddin stood in the shallows.

"No one has poisoned me centurian, though some have the ability were they so minded," he whispered pointing to the boy. And Myrddin smiled.

"The old man's right , I have the power to poison him if I wished, and he's right to say that no physician can cure him too."

"You know the secrets of herbs.. make him a physic!" Marcus demanded half pleading half impatient. But Galarius shook his head again.

238

"I'll tell you what ails me centurian," he sighed as he lowered himself onto the grass. "I'm old and tired, I've lived hard and I'm worn out. The gods have spoken and I'm ready."

Germanicus was looking to Myrddin for contradiction, but the boy with the wisdom of an octogenarian just nodded and turned away.

Ambrosius met them where the road crosses the River Ribble at the fort called Ribchester. To the west lay another estuary and soon they'd press on to Chester.

His father-in-law looked older and thinner Marcus noted.

"How are you sir?" he asked, and the duke smiled.

"Don't worry about me, I'm not ill of the plague if that's what you're thinking! I'm just weary, and for the last two weeks I've been led an exhausting dance by our friend Hengist."

"Then he came north as you predicted!" Marcus whistled.

They were relaxing on the veranda of the garrison commander's villa, below flowed the river between low banks dotted with nibbling sheep.

"He came to meet with the Angles from the east, but I intened to cut him off," the duke explained. And as the older man struggled to his feet Marcus saw how stiff he'd grown.

"I have a theory," Ambrosius went on, sitting down again heavily. "If the Saxons continue to move west the seat of resistance will have to move too, and a future commander will need safe headquarters... well away from the Saxon heartlands but close enough to strike when it suited him."

"Somewhere central?" Marcus suggested, and the duke nodded.

"Between north and south," he agreed.

"Between east and west?" the younger man put in, and rising to his feet again Ambrosius drained his cup.

"Come, we've eaten and drunk and we've earned it, and we've earned a night's rest in the decent beds that await us too!"

Arm in arm the two men left the moonlit veranda and the sound of the licking river and entered the lighted villa.

"I'm an optimist!" Ambrosius was saying, "and though we've lived through telling times we'll soon know if our efforts have been worthwhile."

"Do you mean when we take Hengist?" Marcus asked, and the duke frowned.

"If we take Hengist!" he corrected him."

"But we must!" Marcus blurted, and the eagerness in his voice made the duke smile as they reached the door of his sleeping quarters.

"Yes... we must take Hengist," the older man agreed. But the concern in his voice worried Germanicus and he went to bed with something new to think about.

They rested for a few days amid the pleasant rolling countryside, and as there were too many cavalrymen for the fort to accommodate a tented camp grew up on the river bank.

Marcus invited Myrddin to share their accommodation at the villa but was relieved when the Celt made his excuses.

"The halls of Romans are foreign to me," the boy confessed looking up at the mounted man above him. "I prefer it out here and you mustn't feel guilty on my account."

But Marcus, who'd no intention of feeling guilty was experiencing only relief. As Ambrosius had treated the suggestion that a Celt, however royal, should be housed in such close proximity to them as little short of suicidal!

"You say this lad's father tried to drown you in a cesspit?" he'd demanded in wonder, and Marcus had nodded.

"But it was Myrddin who rescued me..." he'd protested. However the duke was unimpressed, and the look on his face needed no words to embellish it!

They rose early as the nights were drawing in, time was short and intelligence about Hengist's movements was coming in fast.

"The King of the Jutes is moving west sir!" one of the men sent to stalk Hengist told the duke eagerly. "Some peasants we captured say a chief from Ireland has landed on the coast. They say he's camped on the peninsula north of Chester with a thousand men.... so they say sir....."

"Go on!" Ambrosius growled.

"They say Hengist plans to meet the Hibernians," the soldier stuttered, "they say he wants to make peace and form an alliance....."

The duke spent the next half hour huddled over the map with the spy before rejoining the others.

"Our friend Hengist is inordinately fond of making peace and forming alliances," he muttered, "and I suppose it's only a matter of time before he gets round to us! But unfortunately we can't wait that long," he went on, throwing the rolled map onto the table before making for the door. "Come friends let's eat, tomorrow we set out for Chester, the City of the Legion!"

The journey took them along good roads and over scrubby heights where birch hawthorn and alder struggled to plant their roots in the thin soil. Then they emerged on the edge of the high moors that overlook the fort at Mancunium (Manchester).

After spending a day and a night there they entered the flat lands to the south. The wide expanse guarded by fells to the east and north lay exposed on the western side, but as few invaders came that way villa life still flourished as it always had. Salt mined in the prosperous little towns

240

was still transported all over the country. And the income had made the area rich. Safe as yet from invasion and still wearing its Roman identity this was one of the last outposts of empire.

After pausing in Chester for a brief respite they moved on along the bank of the Dee estuary. As it was here, among marshgrass and sandbanks that the spies said Hengist was to meet his Irish ally.

The column numbered close to three thousand men now. By splitting into smaller units they could cover a wide area, and it wasn't long before one of Gius Aquilla's centuries found the scent.

Moving under cover of darkness they approached the place where Hengist and his nobles had been seen last, and when morning arrived their suspicions were confirmed beyond their wildest hopes. Hengist had spent the night in the hall of a reluctant local chief it appeared, and riders were dispatched at once to warn the other units.

When Marcus heard the news he was wary. As Hengist's network of spies was almost as good as theirs, and why was the wily old man exposing himself like this he wondered. The Saxons had always stayed clear of Chester and its outposts in the past. But the Romans in their comfortable towns had a reputation for indolence, and perhaps the Saxon king thought he'd be safe if he kept to the marshes?

Soon the enemy had been surrounded by several units, and cut off on a spur with the tide swirling in the Saxons found themsleves trapped between the sea and a superior force. It seemed they had no option but to surrender.

Germanicus felt a pang of sympathy for his old friend.

"Hengist is such a great man,' he murmured to Gius, and the praetor shrugged.

"Perhaps the years of success and lack of opposition have made him careless?" he suggested.

Marcus was half hoping that the old soldier wouldn't live long enough to regret his mistake. Though the Saxon jarls would fight to the death to defend him he knew, and as the Roman cavalry prepared to charge onto the half drained shore they were taking up their positions round their leader.

Ambrosius' horsemen made foray after foray, returning to firm ground to re-group before attacking the enemy scattered in the shallows again. And each time the number of Saxons still standing was reduced and the number of bodies bobbing in the swell increased.

Marcus was looking for Hengist, and seeing the old man sitting astride his great black stallion on a rise in the dunes, he watched as the jarls laid down their lives for him. The warriors were falling fast, and lifting himself in the saddle Hengist called over their heads.

"Kill me now Marcus Germanicus, as I'm no longer a match for you! Or would you rather I make a show of a fight?" the rich Germanic voice boomed over the noise of battle. And cupping his hands to his mouth the Roman called back.

"Tell your men to surrender and Ambrosius might spare your life!" he urged. And though the stiff westerly breeze seemed determined to carry his words away the old king heard his plea.

"Ha!" Hengist appeared to open his mouth wide, but his voice was lost in the din. The once muscular figure of the Saxon was turning to fat Germanicus noticed, and as he slumped in the saddle Hengist seemed to be shaking his head.

"I've lived my life with honour as a soldier!" the old king shouted proudly, "would you have me end it in dishonour?"

"Your fate is not in my hands!" Germanicus screamed back as he struggled to hold Romulus in check.

Marcus wanted the old man to fight, and it was his duty to kill him he knew. It would be an honour to give Hengist a soldier's death," he told himself miserably. But this was impossible if his opponent refused to defend himself.

"I must take you back with me!" Marcus bellowed over the cries of wheeling seabirds and the clash of arms. "There's no other way old man!"

But when Hengist turned his horse in the required direction Germanicus was disappointed by his lack of spirit.

"If you'd only fight?" he ventured as his enemy came nearer, but Hengist shook his heavy head again.

"I'm old and you're young," the Saxon reflected sadly, "would a trial of strength between us be anything but slaughter?" And Germanicus nodded, forced to admit that there was no honour in killing an enemy who was not only old, but if appearances were correct gravely ill.

They rode in silence, the sounds of battle fading as the distance increased. But the remaining Saxons didn't surrender when they saw their leader captured and instead fought on more determinedly than ever. To them Hengist was already a dead hero, Marcus knew. And he'd go down in their chronicles as dying here, as no less honourable death would suffice. His people didn't need to see him die. It was enough that he'd lived and won a fruitful land for them.

With an escort of several hundred troops they rode towards Chester, and as the city gates came in sight Germanicus glanced back at Galarius. The pitifully thin figure was slumped over his horse's neck, and as the old man clung on desperately Marcus lifted his arm.

"You!" he called to an aid, "make a litter for my friend." And though the men were surprised to hear their commander use the word 'friend' to describe an ex-decurian they all thought of as his servant, as always they were quick to obey.

But Galarius was not destined to ride in the litter. And as the column came to a halt Germanicus knelt on the grass beside him, while above them the figures of Ambrosius and his officers bit into the autumn sky.

"We'll take you into the city," Marcus murmured, "there are physicians there who can cure you." He was trying to sound optimistic, but the break in his voice gave him away.

"You're a fine man and a great leader!" Galarius coughed, lifting a bony hand to touch his commander's freckled face as if he were caressing a child. "You'll remember that I promised to be your guide and protector?" he asked with a weak smile. But Germanicus couldn't speak, and just nodded as his mentor struggled on. "Well I think I've kept that promise... do you not agree centurion?" Galarius whispered, still using the title Marcus had held when they first met. As to him the years hadn't changed anything, and to him his master was still a young man in need of guidance.

"You've kept your promise," Marcus answered, swallowing hard, "and I've been honoured to call you friend." Then Galarius tried to raise himself.

"I have a wife who lies beneath the oaks in the forests of Germany." The voice was cracked and weak. "But I have no children...and if I could have counted you my son..."

As the voice trailed away Marcus took his old friend in his arms.

"I'd have been proud to call you father!" he replied choking back the tears. But there was no more time, and as Germanicus heard the rattle in Galarius' throat he lifted his head and shouted at the sky. "No!" he screamed, as if his command could delay the retreating soul. But it was to no avail. Galarius was dead.

On the smooth green sward between river and castle they'd set up a platform, and though it was an hour to the eagerly awaited event the townspeople were already gathering. Something of a party atmosphere was developing. A pedlar was selling ribbons from a tray, and a baker with a basket round his neck was doing swift business hawking cakes.

As Germanicus stood on the wall-walk high above the crowd his feelings were confused, and he believed as Ambrosius did that this one man had been the driving force behind the migration of his people. It was Hengist who'd gathered them together in their homeland, and Hengist who'd brought them over the water. Though there were many leaders among the Saxons it was the brooding presence of Hengist, whether fighting at their side or watching their colonizing progress from afar, that had made them great. He'd been invincible for nigh on forty years and he'd made his people invincible too. As long as he lived their self confidence would live too, and when he was dead ...?

How often had the Romans discussed this eventuality? Marcus asked himself. And when they'd been talking about something else how many times had Ambrosius turned the subject to Hengist?

'If only we could capture Hengist....' the duke would murmur. Or 'if Hengist were to die...?' They'd been so confident that all their troubles would be over if this one man could be removed. But now he was in their hands Marcus began to wonder. Could the whole tribe be possessed of their leader's wonderful qualities? he fretted. And could it be that the Romans had been deceiving themselves all this time?

Birthrates were high among the Germans he knew, and every year a fresh crop of blood hungry warriors eager to fight for lands of their own reached maturity. The more he thought about it the clearer it became. The very fact that they'd captured Hengist and his calm acceptance of his end pointed to the same conclusion:- That Hengist was but one man, and after his death the English surge would continue, enveloping one town after another till the old Britain sank completely. Marcus was shivering, as the prospect was too horrible to contemplate.

He was fast convincing himself that this was not the great coup they'd envisaged. Then his mind turned to Hengist himself. What of him, he asked himself miserably, the king who'd treated him kindly and laughed as he spared his life? The agony inside was unexpectedly sharp, and when they brought the condemned man out, bent under his chains, Marcus experienced the acute pain of guilt.

Ambrosius had noticed this strange loyalty the previous evening when they'd walked together by the river.

"It's not your decision!" Marcus' father-in-law had told him, "and there's nothing you can do." The lips of the Dux Britanniarum had been smiling, but his grey eyes had been deadly cold. "Unless you want to kill me and take over the leadership?" he'd added with a shrug. And Marcus had turned away, unwilling to meet those piercing eyes and painfully aware that as he didn't understand this affinity with the Saxon, Ambrosius felt no empathy.

The governor of Chester's guard edged the path that Hengist must walk to the scaffold, and at the end waited the executioner with his great axe. Ambrosius was there with Gallus Anthonius and Gius Aquilla, and as they looked up to where Marcus stood all three smiled weakly.

As the drums rolled the crimes of the man about to die were read out in Latin. Then as the scribe came to the end of his recitation Hengist looked up and saw Germanicus. As his stomach lurched Marcus felt the gall rising in his throat, and why did he feel like a traitor? he fretted miserably.

The pale old head was lifted, then an arm heavy with chains.

"Marcus my friend, we meet again!" Hengist laughed, "but it's for the last time I fear!" And again his great laugh rent the silence. "There've been times when I've held your life in my hands!" the old king called, and

244

Marcus' stomach took another lurch. 'Oh no!' he wailed inwardly, was the old man about to demand that he return the favour?

Marcus had turned away sick to his stomach, but Hengist hadn't finished yet.

"But I see that it's not in your power to change my destiny," he smiled up, and the man on the parapet almost retched with relief. "I've accomplished a great deal for one man, don't you agree?" Hengist asked, and Marcus lent over the edge nodding dumbly. "I brought my people to a new land!" the old king anounced proudly, "only the future will tell if they're strong enough to hold it...but somehow I think they will!"

They were leading Hengist to the scaffold now, and Marcus watched transfixed as he climbed the steps.

"Goodbye my friend!" the Saxon king called, turning his head as he knelt. "And you must feel no guilt as the gods have decreed this!" He was smiling. "Feel no regret," he urged, "as tonight I shall dine at Odin's table!" Germanicus felt his eyes close involuntarily and a second later heard the dull wack as the razor sharp blade came down.

> Across the sky blood ribbons trail,
> Wind splits the time-trapped Valkyries wail.
> Into the north they bear his pall,
> To Aisir gods in Aisgard's hall.

Early next morning Germanicus gathered a small party of horsemen, and with Octha and some of the other Saxons set out. The cavalry rode at the head of the little procession followed by the the bier on which the body of Hengist lay. The face was uncovered, it's expression quiet and reposed as if waiting for awakening in Vallhalla. Then came the Saxon jarls who'd survived the battle, and last of all the labourers who'd dig the grave.

The place of burial had been chosen by the Saxons, as they knew the holy sites where the bones of such a man should rest.

Ambrosius had given the order personally.

"Take a party of men and bury him in a way that befits the traditions of his people." Then he'd turned away, reluctant to discuss the matter further.

They travelled east across the flat lands to where the Pennine hills rise, and the site was chosen. On a sweeping patch of ground under a hill above the river it looked out across the valley widening into the distance. They chose a place where the earth was soft but the rock close to the surface. Wild flowers bloomed and Germanicus recognised some he'd seen in his travels through the Alps.

The Saxons set to work with a will. In an hour a huge pile of earth stood to mark their efforts and the Romans withdrew. But as the Saxons, left alone with their leader for the last time handed him over to his gods,

Germanicus felt a strange sense of anticlimax. No joy, no victory, no elation, just an empty feeling of bereavement.

How can the death an enemy you've fought and tried to outwit for so long be a loss? he asked himself. But no answer came and all he knew was that an empty place had opened up inside. Then he remembered the old warrior's words as he died: - 'The gods have decreed it....!' And was the old warhorse telling him that his job was done? Marcus pondered. Was Hengist confirming if confirmation were needed, that the groundwork had been completed?

Then the young Roman made an effort to shake off his maudlin mood, as such thoughts always come with funerals he told himself. Mounting Romulus he signalled his men to follow, but for some reason unaccountable even to himself he left the Saxon prisoners behind. Free men in this wild and now sacred place.

Autumn seemed reluctant to advance further, and though the leaves were turning and the days shortening the sun was still warm. The trees saw no reason to discard their adornment yet a while it seemed. And underfoot the ground was dry as down the Roman road the glittering column went, to the south and home.

By the end of October they'd reached Winchester. Every day on the road seemed to lighten Marcus' heart and as the miles fell away so did his gloom. Hengist was dead! he told himself repeatedly, and if ever an omen boded good this was it.

It was Hengist who'd masterminded the Saxon conquests. But he was gone now and Germanicus knew that his remaining sons didn't possess his genius. Slowly the great weight seemed to lift from his shoulders and he could see only success from now on. Though there were still hard battles to fight and harsh deeds to be done. But the future was theirs now he felt. Roman Britain could be saved and their civilised way of life could continue into the future.

Helena was waiting for him at Portus Adurni. The leaves had fallen now, swirling and circling the house under the hill as if reluctant to lie down for their final rest. She was more mature Marcus noticed. And perhaps it was because he needed to put away the thought of her as a girl that her face had stayed so determinedly out of his memory? She'd changed since he left, but he'd changed more.

Arturius had changed too. His muscles were hardening and his face was losing its girlish charm. What the future held for him Marcus couldn't even guess. But one thing was certain, for the present he could live in this haven of peace and enjoy the pleasures of civilised life.